FIREFROST

A FLAMESKIN CHRONICLES NOVEL

CAMILLE LONGLEY

Copyright © 2020 by Camille Longley

ISBN 978-1-952795-01-5

Edited by Theodora Bryant

Cover Design by Aero Gallerie

Illustrations by Pauliina Hannuniemi

Chapter Headings by Amanda Smith

Map by Daniel Hasenbos

To Grant—
You are the origin of all my love stories.

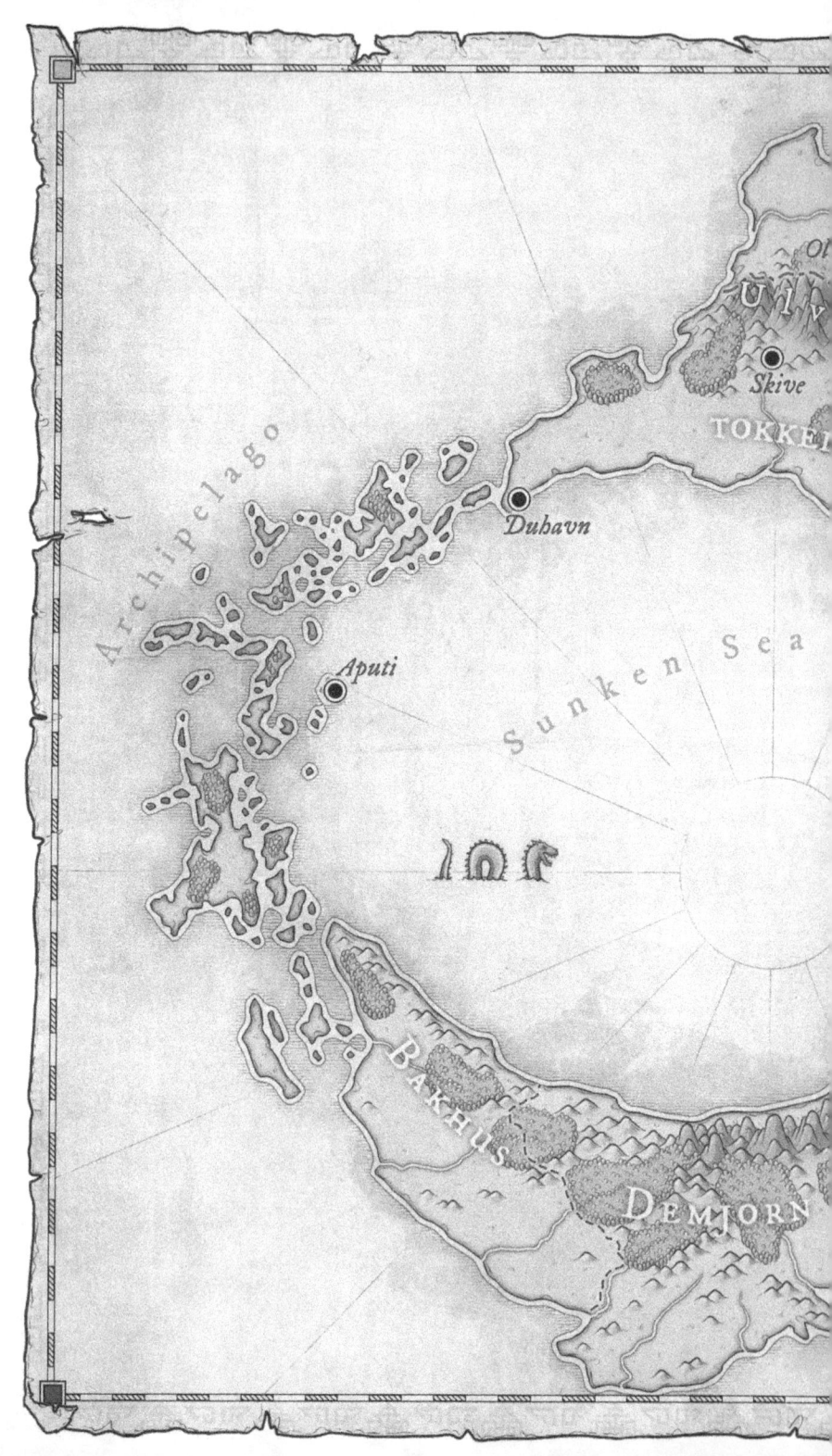

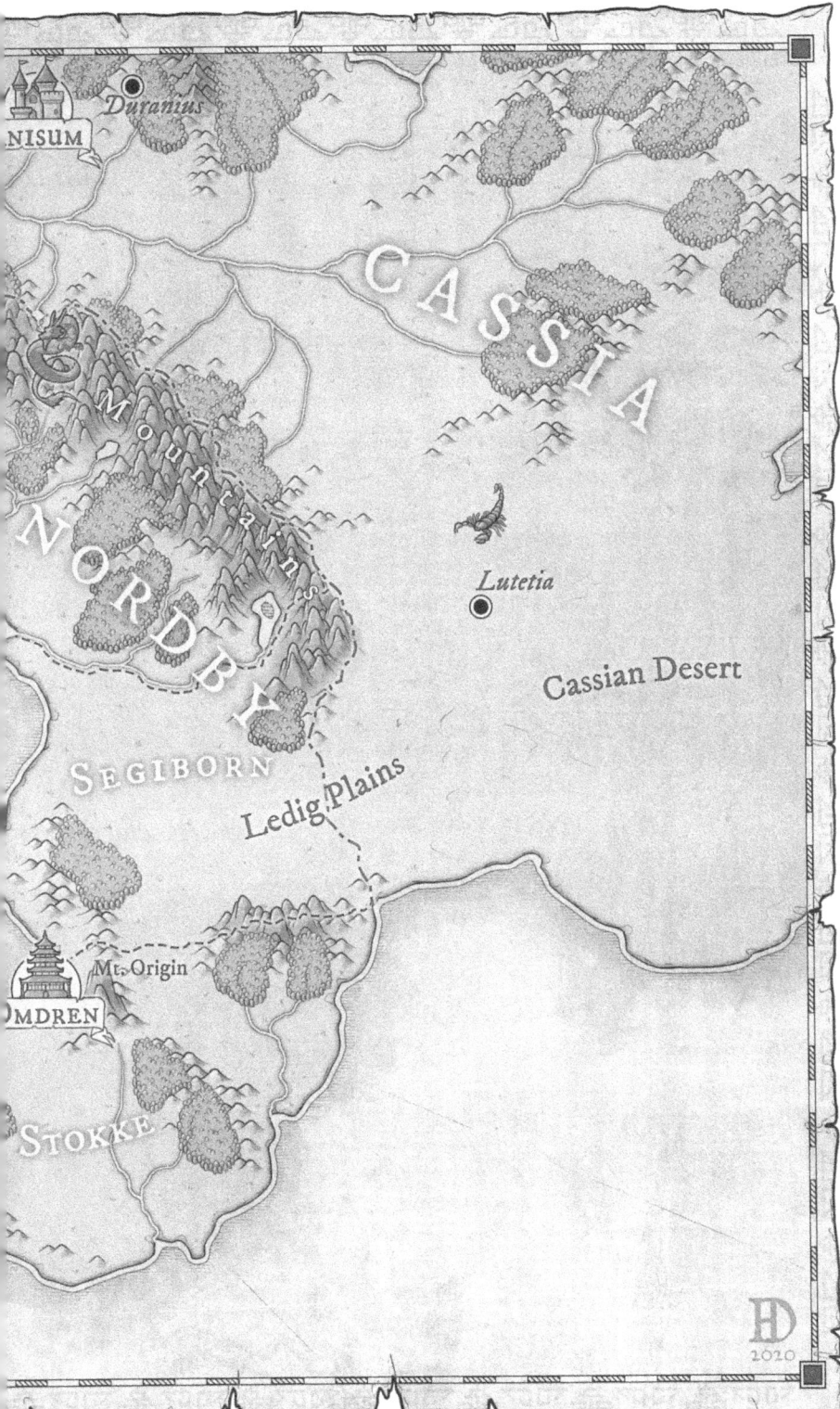

CHAPTER 1
SOL

O nly a fool would bring horses into the pass when there was this much snow, and only a fool would attempt such a journey so late in the season.

You could make it through on foot, with snowshoes; Sol had done it many times with Pa. But with horses? Forget it.

Sol pulled on the horse's lead line. "Come on, girl. Come on."

The horse whinnied and balked as Sol coaxed it through the snowbank. Ice crunched beneath its hooves and lacerated its skin.

"Why are we going so slow?" Lady Isabella asked. She rode sidesaddle on a lovely mare, her elegant skirts draped around her.

"The snow's too deep," Sol said, pitching her voice low.

Isabella's pouting lip was the only thing visible from beneath her mountain of furs.

Officer Poulsen left Isabella's side and stomped his way through snow to help Sol push the horse forward.

"We should turn back," Sol said through gritted teeth. "I told you this would be impossible."

"We have no choice," Poulsen said. "Not unless you want these mountains to burn."

Sol yanked on the lead line. She hated the Tokken uniform

they had forced her to wear. Since when had the Tokken armies done anything for her village? The Tokkens hadn't offered any relief when the Flameskins had burned down their temple, or when they'd torched their fields. Not until they realized they needed a mountain guide did they ever offer aid.

Sol wasn't doing this for the Tokkens and their blasted war, anyway. No, she was doing this for her family, for the food the Tokkens had promised her.

"We'll stop at the bluff ahead for the lady's lunch," she said. "And I'll scout out the easiest trail for us to take down this side of the mountain."

Poulsen nodded and they trudged on.

At the bluff, Isabella's maids quickly arranged a bed of furs on the ground for the lady to rest her weary body and started a fire to heat some food.

Sol scowled at Isabella and her retinue. Two dozen soldiers had volunteered to join the winter caravan to Cassia, and they all hovered around Lady Isabella like a flock of besotted birds. They cooed at her and fawned over her, and she sent them running to fetch sticks for her fire.

Lady Isabella was about Sol's age, eighteen, and they both had the same green Tokken eyes and black hair. But Lady Isabella was a delicate flower who wilted at the first sign of inconvenience, and Sol was a huntress, born in the mountains and raised by its cruel winters and its wild ferocity.

The horses barely moved when Sol brushed a hand over their necks. They were in pretty bad shape. The winter air was too cold, and the snows too thick and deep. She wouldn't be surprised if they froze to death one of these nights. Isabella had forced Sol to lead eight horses up and down the Ulve Mountains. One horse to carry Isabella, and seven others to carry all her silly gowns and the dowry her father had promised her Cassian prince.

Sol sighed as she marched down the slope. She was going to miss the Solstice Festival for this journey, and it felt like a betrayal not to be home with Ma during the holiday. But what choice did she have? If Sol hadn't left, there would've been nothing to eat at Solstice, and that would've shamed Pa's memory more than anything else. He had always made sure they feasted on Solstice. Always.

As Sol descended the slope, the chattering of the ladies disappeared behind her, and the still winter forest enveloped her. This was what she loved about the mountains. The silence, the serenity. The forest was the only temple worthy of the gods. Sol stepped lightly, treading where no mortal had walked before, leaving footprints in the glittering carpet of crystal beneath her feet.

She made quick time on her snowshoes and found one of the trails she and Pa had taken last year. This way was longer, but it wasn't as steep and had been protected from the snow by the cliffs overhead.

Sol kept waiting for Pa to appear on the trail as she walked: *Listen, Sol, a pewter hawk. That's an omen of change.*

She stopped and gazed at the hawk circling above in the blue sky. Pa would've known how to take care of the horses in the snow. He wouldn't have let them suffer from the cold. *Make sure to pick the hooves and keep them dry.* That's what he would've said.

She sighed. It was going to be a lonely Solstice this year.

Something disturbed the sacred silence of the winter. Sol froze midstep, straining her ear to the sound. Deer? The soldiers surely wouldn't complain about fresh venison. They might increase her pay as well.

The *crunch, crunch* of boots without snowshoes alerted her to someone's approach. Had Poulsen come looking for her? She'd been gone longer than usual. Sol turned and saw a flash of red through the trees, and her heart skipped a beat in her chest.

A Flameskin soldier.

She crept forward and hid herself behind a large pine, then peeked around it to watch the soldier. Would it see her tracks? Ashes and cinders, she should've been more careful. Pa wouldn't have been so careless. But there wasn't supposed to be anyone in the pass, not this late in the season; that was the reason they had waited so long to go. Lady Isabella had delayed the trip until the Tokken Army had been sure the Flameskins had retreated for the winter and weren't waiting to ambush them in the pass.

The Flameskin soldier wore a red uniform with brass buttons crossing her chest. She was a true Flameskin and wore no hat and no fur coat despite the bitter cold. The heat of her demon pyra would keep her warm. She slogged through the forest with a hand on the hilt of her sword, taking a curving path through the woods.

Had the Flameskin come to attack their party? Were there more of them?

Sol's heart pounded in her chest. She wanted to run, to tear through the woods and never look back. Flameskins were dangerous, and this one could kill Sol with the flick of her wrist. But if there were more, she needed to know so she could warn the Tokken soldiers.

Sol steadied herself and started forward, sliding her snowshoes slowly and soundlessly through the powdery drifts of snow. It was slow progress, but she was as silent as a dryad in the woods.

The trail the Flameskin's footprints had left was clear, and Sol followed it, watching anxiously for any signs of Flameskin soldiers. She descended the slope and spotted movement in the valley between the trees. Horses. Tents. Red-uniformed soldiers. A Flameskin camp.

Sol covered her mouth with her hand and stifled a gasp. If the Flameskins found her, the blue Tokken uniform beneath her fur coat would be a death sentence.

She started back up the hill at a quick pace. She had to get back and warn Officer Poulsen. Sol silently cursed Isabella under her breath. They should never have come through the Ulves in the middle of winter.

"Hey!" a man shouted.

Sol whirled around. A red-coated soldier stepped out from behind a tree a dozen paces from her. Sol froze in place as he marched toward her. Her hands shook and she tripped over her snowshoes, falling backward into the deep snow.

"What are you doing out here?" he asked, peering down at her.

"I'm—I'm a hunter," she stammered.

"You seen any travelers on the trails? Any Tokken soldiers, or a rich lady?"

She shook her head. Ashes. They *were* waiting to ambush Lady Isabella.

The soldier narrowed his eyes. "You sure?"

Sol stood shakily, and as she rose her fur coat parted, and her blue uniform flashed beneath it. The soldier's eyes went wide, and Sol grabbed her knife.

"Tokke—" His words strangled in his slit throat. Red blood poured from his neck and down his uniform. He dropped lifeless into the snow, spattering it with red.

Sol fell onto her hands and knees, still gripping her bloody knife in one hand. She closed her eyes and swallowed bile. She still remembered the first kill she had ever made, and how she had cried over the rabbit's lifeless body.

This was nothing like that.

A life for a life, Pa had always said. Hunters were guardians of life, and she took life so her village could eat. Huntress, they called her. But she hunted beasts, not men.

No, this creature wasn't a man; he was a demon. This was a mercy killing. *Rabid dogs,* Pa had called the Flameskins. She had freed this soldier from the demonic pyra that had possessed him.

Sol wiped her hands in the snow and took a deep breath. Bury the body. Cover her tracks. Alert the others.

There wasn't time for any other thought.

CHAPTER 2
KELAN

Kelan tore open the letter and scanned the page, then looked up and met his Uncle Haldur's eyes. "What is this?"

"Can't you read? An advancement, Kelan."

A crooked smile lifted Kelan's face. Lieutenant Kelan Birke. It had a nice ring to it.

Osten jumped up from his seat on the floor of the tent. "But, sir! He's barely eighteen."

Kelan covered a smirk. Osten had been passed over for promotion once again.

He's not worthy, Kelan's pyra said.

Its voice hissed inside his mind like a crackling tongue of fire. Kelan winced at the searing burn of its words, and the way his pyra purged his mind of all other thoughts but flames.

Uncle Haldur pulled a brass lieutenant's star from his pocket and pinned it to the lapel of Kelan's red coat. "He can handle the responsibility. He'll be taking over this camp when we leave."

"Taking over?" Kelan asked, gaping at him.

"Yes. I have to return to Cassia and get the reports from our spies."

"I'm not going with you?"

"No. You'll stay here in the pass until Lady Isabella comes. And then you'll kill her."

Kill. Kill. Kill, his pyra chanted.

Kelan winced again. "Lady Isabella can't have left so close to Solstice. She must be waiting until spring."

"Then you'll wait here until she comes."

"But, Uncle—"

"You will call me 'Sir' or 'Commander Birke.'"

"Sir, the war is happening out there." Kelan jabbed his finger toward the tent wall. It fluttered in the icy wind. "I don't want to be stuck in these mountains wasting my time. I want to fight. I want to burn the Tokken Army."

Yes. Burn them, his pyra said.

Kelan mentally shoved it away, trying to block out its commands. Fire seeped into his blood, fueled by his growing frustration. His fingers twitched at his sides, threatening to ignite.

"The army needs you here, Lieutenant Birke," Haldur said. "And I promoted you so you could lead this troop."

"Leave me, instead," Osten said. "We have enough restless Flameskins here already."

"I want to fight," Kelan said. He balled his fists and willed the flames in his blood to retreat, but his anger made it impossible.

"Lieutenant Birke," his uncle snapped, "don't make me regret your promotion. We can't let Lady Isabella slip into Cassia. If she marries Prince Terrulius, this war will get much, much bloodier."

"Osten is fully capable of managing this camp."

"I need Osten to lead me through the pass. And you need the experience of managing a troop if you're going to be any use to me next season."

"But I could gain that experience on the field, fighting. Isn't that what you've taught me to do?"

Haldur eyed Kelan. "Is that Kelan speaking, or his pyra?"

Kelan stiffened and fear coursed through him like ice in his veins. It doused his pyra's fire and weakened the burning voice in his head. "Does it matter?"

"It does, if you haven't yet let it possess you."

Kelan swallowed. Wasn't that what he was asking for anyway? If he returned to the battlefield, he'd lose himself to his pyra's influence. His pyra probed his mind even now, searching for an entry. He had resisted it for six years, but each day his pyra's whispers grew more insistent, and his will to deny it grew weaker.

Was it even his own desire to fight in the war? Or had Kelan confused his own thoughts with his pyra's voice?

Haldur scowled at him. "Why do you resist it? You could be so much more powerful, like Markus."

Kelan gripped the button hanging on a chain around his neck. "I like to be in control, Uncle. I can use my pyra without letting it possess me."

"You're wasting time, Kelan. Embrace your pyra and let it fight for you."

"Sir, has there been any word of Markus' whereabouts?" Osten asked.

Uncle Haldur's face darkened. Kelan went rigid and his breath caught in his throat. No one could ever know what had happened to Markus. Especially not his uncle.

"No word yet," Haldur said. "I fear the worst." He turned toward the tent door. "I'll try to send correspondence during the winter, but I doubt I'll be able to get anything through the pass. You'll remain in this position until you receive word to move."

"Yes, sir," Kelan said, and sighed. If he stayed at least he'd put off possession for the winter. This would be his last season as Kelan, before his pyra took him.

Haldur threw open the tent flap and walked outside. The chill winter air blew in, and Kelan's pyra warmed his blood to compensate for the cold.

Kelan moved to follow his uncle, but Osten grabbed him roughly by the arm. "You Flameskins are all the same. You flare up, burn yourselves out, and die young. The Tokkens will bury your bones in ash, *Lieutenant.*"

Kelan yanked his arm away. "That would be lieutenant, *sir.*"

Osten scowled and shoved him. "The only reason you got that promotion was because your uncle is the commander."

Kelan lifted his hand and the tips of his fingers sparked. Osten's eyes went wide and he stumbled backward, his hand going to the emberstone around his neck.

Yes. Kill him. Watch his body burn, Kelan's pyra whispered.

Kelan clenched his jaw and shook his head, as if that could rid him of his pyra's voice and the fire that raced through his blood. "You don't want to make my pyra angry," Kelan growled. "Watch yourself."

With effort, Kelan retracted the sparks that lit his fingertips and strode out of the tent. Haldur had already mounted his horse, and a second horse waited for Osten. They would be out there fighting, rescuing Flameskins, and gathering intelligence, making a real difference in the world. And Kelan would be stuck at the top of the mountain wasting what precious time he had left.

"I'll see you in the spring, then," Kelan said. His voice had a bitter edge to it.

"And when I see you, you'll bring me Lady Isabella's smoldering body," Uncle Haldur stated. He tucked his emberstone inside his coat and urged his horse forward through the snow toward Cassia.

CHAPTER 3
SOL

S ol tested the tension of her bowstring. A little tighter than
usual, from the cold, but she could pull any bow. She was
about to notch an arrow when Poulsen crept toward her.

"Can you use one of these?" he whispered, lifting a sword.

"My pa taught me a few things." She took the sword and
hooked its scabbard around her belt.

Poulsen eyed her steadily. "I hope you won't have to use it."

"Just keep the Flameskins in the clearing and I'll take them
out."

Poulsen's lips quirked into a smile. "If only the rest of us were
as good as you claim to be."

Sol sighed. She had given him sound strategic advice, and he
was mocking her?

Poulsen picked up his own bow and notched an arrow. "You
have to promise me not to die, Hunter, or we'll never find a way
off this mountain."

"I won't."

A dozen Tokken soldiers crouched on the hill overlooking
the Flameskin camp with bows in hand, their position hidden by
the snowy outcropping. A dozen more waited below to rush the
camp with their swords. The Flameskins sat around their camp
in the clearing beneath them, and a couple stood as sentries,

though they were inattentive. There were a few tents, but most of the Flameskins were out in the open, their red uniforms marking them in the snow like drops of blood.

"Ready," Poulsen whispered, and Sol drew her bow.

The largest tent flapped open, and a man emerged. The Flameskins sitting around the camp jumped to attention and saluted.

"Hold," Poulsen said.

Sol cursed silently as she slowly released the tension on the bow. Her heart thumped in her chest, and her body surged with adrenaline. If any of the Flameskins saw them, it would be over. Though their two parties were matched in number, Flameskins made formidable enemies. Their fire could hit long-range targets with deadly accuracy, and at close-range, a human soldier had no hope. Only surprise would give them victory.

Two of the red-coated soldiers mounted horses.

Sol glanced at Poulsen. Sweat beaded his brow, and his cold-nipped face was red. She drew her bow and trained it on the rider exchanging words with another soldier.

"I've got a clear shot," she whispered.

"Don't," Poulsen said. "Let them get away. We'll wait until they let down their guard again."

The two soldiers kicked their horses forward and disappeared behind the trees. They were letting them escape? But what if they rounded back? What if they heard the fighting and returned, or waited to ambush them farther down the path?

Rabid dogs. They couldn't let the Flameskins survive and spread their corruption to another generation.

Sol waited a long time in anxious silence after the mounted soldiers left. Pa had taught her patience in the hunt, but she had never been forced to wait while standing over a Flameskin camp. She was jittery and teeth-chattery, but not from the cold. She kept glancing all around them, expecting Flameskin soldiers to jump out from behind the trees.

It wasn't until the Flameskins returned to their leisurely rest, and the camp grew quiet that Poulsen gave the signal.

"Ready," he whispered.

The twelve archers lifted their bows and fit them with arrows. She took a deep breath as she chose her target and prayed for the demon's soul. Its death would be a mercy.

"Fire!"

Sol loosed her arrow, and the air vibrated with the thrumming of the bow strings. Her arrow embedded itself in a Flameskin's chest, and he toppled backward into the snow. Several others landed shots, but most of the arrows missed.

She grabbed another arrow and notched it in one smooth motion. She let it fly, going more by feel than by sight. The bow was an extension of her body, and the arrows were emissaries of mercy, releasing their victims into the sweet blackness of death.

The Flameskin soldiers shouted, and the injured screamed. Bolts of fire erupted from the demons' fists and sailed into the bank of snow, exploding with a sizzle of fire in ice. Sol ducked as flames poured from the camp at the embankment. The Tokken soldiers rushed the valley with swords flashing.

She strung another arrow and waited for a break in the flames. When fire stopped exploding over her head, she pushed to her feet, found a target, and let her arrow fly. Poulsen abandoned her to run at the advancing Flameskins with his sword.

"For Tokkedal!" he cried as he charged down the hill.

Sol loosed arrow after arrow into the clearing, until black smoke choked the air and obscured her vision. The scene below her looked like the Infernal Pit, and demons raced through it with their burning hands, hurling balls of fire at the Tokken soldiers.

An orb of flames burst over her head, and Sol dropped to the snow, covering her face with her arms. When she looked up, a red-coated soldier was sprinting toward her, a fireball in one hand and an emberstone in the other. He hurled the flames at her, and she leapt aside. Fire exploded at her feet, and she yelped as sparks struck her exposed skin. The edge of her fur coat caught fire, but the melted snow dowsed the flames before they spread.

Sol yanked her sword from its scabbard and faced the soldier. He stood atop a mound of melting snow and refreezing ice, and he held an emberstone in his left hand. This one was a mage, not a Flameskin. If she could get the emberstone away from him, he'd be helpless.

She raced toward him, and the mage let loose another blast of fire. Sol threw herself to the ground and dodged the flames as the mage drew his sword. Their blades clashed and he blocked her attack, but she swung her foot out and they both went down hard on the ice. The emberstone flew out of his hand and into the air and was lost somewhere in the snow.

The soldier growled and got onto all fours on the ice, slipping and falling a couple times before he stood. But Sol was up as well, and she crouched with sword in hand on the icy slope.

The soldier swung and Sol attempted a block. She stumbled backward as the soldier's blade came down and cried out as the tip of his sword sliced open her calf.

Poulsen appeared and rammed into the mage. They parried back and forth until Poulsen disarmed him and ran his sword through the mage's side.

"I told you not to die, Hunter," Poulsen said, panting as he stood over the body.

"I haven't yet," Sol said. She grimaced as she limped toward him. Blood ran from her calf over her boot and into the snow.

"Stick to your bow." He marched toward the battlefield with his bloody sword raised high.

"Poulsen."

He turned.

"Thanks."

CHAPTER 4
KELAN

Kelan yanked aside the tent flap to find chaos. Arrows shot through tents and thudded into the backs of his men. His soldiers screamed as the arrows struck them down and the fire in their hands evaporated.

He ducked, keeping low to the ground, and flames burst out of his fingertips. The adrenaline and the fire around him incited and fueled his pyra, and it pushed flames into his blood.

Now we will destroy, it growled.

"Concentrate fire on the archers!" Kelan shouted. His pyra shoved fire into Kelan's hands, but Kelan willed it back.

Blue-coated Tokken soldiers rushed into the clearing with swords in hand and fire-proofed shields raised to protect their faces. Kelan cursed under his breath. Where were his scouts? How had they been ambushed like this?

A Flameskin soldier beside him let loose a spray of fire at the incoming Tokken soldiers and shoved them into a retreat. The fire melted the snow beneath them, and it refroze immediately, making a wet, icy slush.

Kelan drew his sword and struggled against his pyra's flames. Fire kept seeping out of his fingers.

Let me burn the blue coats, his pyra begged.

Kelan grit his teeth. He couldn't lose himself to it. He had sworn he never would.

A dozen men had already fallen to arrows, and an arrow whistled over Kelan's head. "The archers!" Kelan shouted. "Kill the archers."

But his men were a mess. None of them were wearing armor, and half of them didn't have their swords. And the Tokken foot soldiers distracted them from the real danger: the bowmen raining death from above.

Kelan curled a ball of flame around his hand and hurled it at the archers, melting the snow that hid them. What was the point of resisting his pyra if he was going to die?

Yes, his pyra hissed. *You need me.*

He found a protected position behind a stand of trees and fired at the archers every time a head popped over the snowbank. Fire raced through the camp, flying from his soldiers' hands into the ranks of Tokken soldiers, and burning the enemy's skin and hair and blue uniforms. The flames spread to the tents, then the trees, and black, putrid smoke filled the air.

He breathed it in as he fought his way with sword and flame through the Tokken soldiers. The smoke tasted sweet to his burning lungs, and his pyra swelled within him, urging him to tear the camp apart, but Kelan still resisted its pull.

Kill, Kelan. Kill them all. They're murderers. They hate us. They deserve to die by our flame.

Kelan roared as he swung his sword. Fire rippled up the blade and clung to his free hand, refusing to be contained. The only thing that kept his pyra at bay was the fear that crept over him. Nothing terrified him more than losing himself to his pyra.

"Retreat to the trees," Kelan shouted. They had to get into formation. His Flameskins and mages could outfight Tokken soldiers any day, but not if they were separated and surrounded, and not if the archers picked them off.

Kelan stumbled through the smoke, slipping in the ice and slush. The smog was so thick he couldn't see where his men were. Flashes of red and blue coats passed between the pillars of ash, but the fires surrounding Kelan cut him off from his men.

Someone coughed in the smoke to his left and Kelan whirled around, raising his sword.

A man stood behind him, wreathed in smoke and wearing a thick coat, his face nearly concealed by his furs. He held a longbow with an arrow notched and pointed at Kelan's chest.

"Drop your sword," the man ordered.

Kelan stiffened, and his hand tightened on his sword's hilt. The man's eyes flicked toward his burning hands and he scowled.

"Flameskin." The archer said the word like it was a curse.

Burn his bones to ash, his pyra hissed. Kelan drew fire into his hands, but another Tokken soldier appeared at the archer's side, startling Kelan and breaking his concentration. The Tokken soldier stopped short when he saw Kelan.

"Don't shoot, Hunter," the Tokken soldier ordered.

"He's a Flameskin," Hunter said. "He's better off dead than alive."

The Tokken soldier lifted his sword to Kelan's throat. "Call off your men."

Kelan glanced around him at the chaos of their camp. Dead men littered the ground, most of them his own. Fear gripped him tight, and the flames in his hand sputtered and died.

Don't let them take us, his pyra hissed. *Let me destroy them. I could save us.*

But his pyra's voice was weakening, and the fear made Kelan shiver. As the fire died in his veins, so too did his desire to destroy and to burn.

Without a pyra manipulating and twisting Kelan's thoughts, his true desires became clear: survive and resist the pyra.

Kelan sighed and dropped his sword.

CHAPTER 5
SOL

Sol peeled back the bandage and winced. Her leg throbbed and ached. She had tried her best to stitch her calf closed, but the wound was angry and messy. It was a hand's length, and deep, running along the side of her calf. Her muscle hadn't been severed, but it hurt infernally nonetheless. Pa would've given her dant leaf for the pain, but every dant plant in the mountains was covered by ten feet of snow.

Her hand lingered on the pocket of her coat and the emberstone she had sewn into the lining. Emberstones could summon fire, but they could also heal wounds and illnesses. But using an emberstone would betray everything she had ever believed about fire and would turn the Tokken soldiers against her.

Sol sighed. What had she been thinking, bringing the emberstone? She should've left it at home or tossed it into a river long ago so it wouldn't be a temptation.

She bit her glove-covered hand against the pain as she rubbed snow into the wound, trying to clean it. The touch of ice on her leg felt like fire.

Poulsen crouched next to her and frowned at her leg. "Looks bad. If you're not careful it'll get infected."

"There's nothing we can do about it. I know which herbs to use, but we don't have any."

Poulsen sighed and swore. "I should've been more prepared than this. I should've anticipated a Flameskin attack. We've got too many wounded already."

Sol looked around the camp as she rewrapped the cut. Seven badly wounded and six dead. And then there were the four mage prisoners they had taken, and the demon lieutenant.

Sol glared at the demon. She should've killed him when she had a chance. Why had she hesitated? Pa wouldn't have. A demon was too dangerous to let live.

"Can you walk?" Poulsen asked.

"Of course I can," Sol snapped. She stood and limped toward the horses. She was getting her pay for this journey, and if they didn't give her a medal, too, she'd be outraged. She balled her fists as she walked, trying to ignore the stabbing pain in her leg.

"But those are my dresses!" Lady Isabella was saying. "You can't leave them here." Isabella clung to the packages the soldiers had dropped onto the ground, as though they were martyrs left to die in the snow.

Sol stomped toward her. "Lady Isabella," she said, making her words gravelly. "We need these horses to pull stretchers with the injured men. We can return next spring and bring your dresses back."

Two shining tears had frozen on Isabella's cheeks. "But, what will I wear when I meet Prince Turullius?"

"People have just died to protect you, and you're worried about what you're going to wear?"

Isabella rose, her fur-lined face turning red. "Maybe you think it's silly, but I'm the one who has to leave Tokkedal forever to marry that Cassian prince. I'm the one who's making all the sacrifices."

"You cinder-eating nobles think you know suffering? You know nothing."

Isabella gasped, and her bright green eyes went wide. "How dare you! How dare you say such things, Hunter!" Her eyes filled with tears once more and she dashed away.

Poulsen grabbed Sol's arm. "Leave her alone. She has a delicate constitution."

Sol scowled at Isabella, who now wept into the arms of one of her maids. "Delicate constitutions are not inherited, they are indulged."

She turned on Poulsen. "I told you it was a fool's errand to come into the pass this late. I say we turn back. We don't know if there are more Flameskins waiting to kill us on our way to Olisipo."

"We must try. There are more lives at stake than ours. We're doing this for the good of all Tokkedal."

"Have the prisoners said anything?" Sol asked.

The four mages sat against a bank of snow with their hands tied in front of them, but the demon sat apart, watched over by his own guard. Now that the mages and the Flameskin had been stripped of their fire sources, they shivered in their thin red coats. The demon wore a glowing manacle on his wrist. The metal shackle was fitted with a red emberstone pressed flush to the demon's skin. The emberstone absorbed his pyra, and while he wore it, the demon couldn't even spark.

"They say there aren't any more Flameskins waiting to attack us in the pass, but who knows if they're telling the truth," Poulsen said.

"What're we going to do with them?" Sol asked.

"Bring them with us, I suppose."

"But not the demon, surely."

"He's their commanding officer. He'll know more than the rest, and we can interrogate him once we get to Cassia."

"Why not interrogate him here and dump his body in the snow? I'm not bringing a demon along with us."

"That's not your decision. You're our guide, nothing more, Hunter. We're bringing him with us, and I'll let Commander Jahr decide what to do with him when we get to Olisipo."

Sol sighed. "Fine. When are we breaking camp?"

"I think we can get these stretchers finished within the hour."

"Then we'll go as soon as they're finished. Get your men ready."

"Lead on, Hunter."

CHAPTER 6

KELAN

Kelan trudged through the snow and was, for the first time in his life, completely and utterly frozen.

"Is this what it's like to be flameless?" Kelan asked, his teeth chattering.

The hooded hunter beside him didn't respond. He never responded. The hunter was as silent as the woods themselves.

Kelan glanced at the mages marching at the rear of the party. They had been separated from Kelan so they couldn't get access to the emberstone around his wrist. Kelan twisted in his rope restraints and pressed his cold fingers to his bare neck, trying to warm his hands.

Ashes and cinders. How had he let this happen? He had failed. His whole troop had been slaughtered and captured, and Lady Isabella had walked away from it all unscathed. Kelan stomped in the snow muttering curses under his breath. There was no fear of his anger taking over now; his pyra was gone.

He reached inside himself, searching for his pyra, but there was nothing. No inner warmth, no voice, no urges to destroy. It left him cold and empty and weak.

But it was also . . . freeing, in a way. He was just Kelan. He didn't have to fight to remain in control of himself. He would've never touched an emberstone by choice, but it was a blessed mental reprieve not to have to fight against his pyra every time his emotions surged. But without his pyra, he was powerless against the ropes that bound him and the cold that stole his breath away.

"Hunter," Lady Isabella called. "I need a rest."

Hunter stopped short beside Kelan and ground his teeth before speaking in his gravelly voice. "We're almost to the saddle. We'll stop there."

Kelan glanced at Lady Isabella riding behind him. He could barely make out the tip of her nose and two green eyes beneath her hood of furs. Once Isabella made it across the border to Cassia it'd all be over. She'd marry that Cassian prince, and Cassian soldiers would march into Tokkedal and destroy what little army they had left. He had to stop her, kill her if he could.

He reached for his pyra once more, but the emptiness inside him was absolute. He was alone in his own body. Kelan shivered violently. His boots leaked, and his toes were numb, as well as his hands. They had given him a fur hat, which helped, but not much. His coat was thin and was little protection against the chilly wind.

"Aren't you going to give me a scarf or something? I'm freezing," Kelan said.

"Good," Hunter said.

Kelan yanked against the ropes that bound his wrists, trying to slide the shackle they had attached to his arm. If the emberstone lost contact with his skin, he'd get his pyra back, and he'd use it to burn everything and kill everyone. And his toes would finally warm up.

Hunter watched with eyes narrowed as Kelan struggled.

"Once I'm free you're dead," Kelan hissed.

And Hunter would be the first to burn. The hunter had claimed more lives than any other with his deadly bow. Kelan had watched, helpless and horrified, as they had stacked his soldiers' bodies for a pyre. Ten of them had been run through with one of Hunter's black arrows.

Hunter stepped forward and grabbed the ropes that bound

Kelan's wrists, forcing Kelan to stumble backward to maintain his balance.

"Officer Poulsen wants to keep you alive," Hunter growled, "but I'm not so inclined. I'm waiting for you to do something stupid so I have an excuse to ram my knife through your heart and throw your body off a cliff."

"Do it then. I'd rather it be quick than slowly freezing to death."

Hunter stared at him. Like Lady Isabella, there wasn't much of Hunter's face to see other than a nose and two suspicious green eyes. Hunter turned abruptly and released Kelan, then pulled something from the saddlebag.

Was he getting a knife? Burn it all, Kelan! Why do you have to provoke everyone? Kelan fell backward into the deep drift on the side of the trail, and scrambled to his feet again. There was nothing he could do. He couldn't run with his hands tied like this and he had nothing to defend himself with. Hunter did have a limp. If Kelan ran, he might make it down the side of the slope, until Hunter shot him with his deadly bow.

But Hunter returned, not with a knife, but with a thick fur blanket that he threw around Kelan's shoulders. "I'll never have it be known that I treated an animal poorly. Even a cursed one like you."

Kelan yanked awkwardly on the blanket with his bound hands, pulling it tight around his shoulders. "You think I'm some sort of beast?"

Hunter pulled on the horse's lead line, urging it along behind him through the snow. Kelan's blanket fought back the winter and kept out the wind. Kelan wouldn't die today, at least not from cold.

"How can you call me an animal when I look and act like a man?" Kelan asked.

Hunter didn't answer.

CHAPTER 7

SOL

Sol sat heavily into a powdery bank of snow and let herself relax against the cold wetness of it. It had snowed heavily overnight, and while it was easier for the horses to travel through powder than ice, they had been climbing uphill all morning. She was as exhausted as any of them, but she still had to scout their trail for the afternoon. She closed her eyes. The cold bit into her bones and made her shiver. Her body ached all over. She was missing Solstice for this? A cut leg, a demon traveling companion, and a ridiculous noble charge? The gods were surely playing some elaborate joke on her.

She unwrapped her leg and checked the wound again. It hurt unbearably, and the stitching now oozed with puss. Sol grit her teeth as she cleaned it with more snow. Infected. That's what she got for being a hero. She'd have to clean it properly tonight when she had more time.

"That looks bad," Demon said.

Sol scowled at him, though half the look was lost inside her fur hood. He sat near her, wrapped in his blanket. She had given furs to the mages as well. There was no point in bringing them along if they were going to freeze to death, though Pa would've surely disapproved.

Sol hurriedly wrapped her leg once more and covered it with

her wool legging. She stood and winced as she limped toward the other side of camp.

Lady Isabella had already settled into her furs, and one of her maids was heating a pot of food. It would be an hour before Isabella could be convinced to continue on, and at this rate, they were never going to make it out of the mountains.

The party sat on a bluff beside a cliff with Isabella in the center of everything. The wounded had been laid out in their stretchers beside the horses. The mages sat against the cliff face, and the demon stood on the edge of the slope, isolated from the rest of the camp.

Hopefully he'd try to run for it, so she'd have an excuse to put an arrow through his back.

Officer Poulsen gave her a nod as she headed off into the trees to scout. She passed between the pines, switch-backing as she limped her way down the slope.

She had made it a short way from the bluff when there was a loud thump behind her, as though a thick tree had fallen over in the snow. Sol turned and squinted at the peak above the camp. A crystalline slab of snow slid downward off the peak. The falling snowbank struck a ridge and shattered like broken glass, and ice and snow tumbled down the mountainside.

"Avalanche!" Sol screamed.

Her heart hammered in her chest and she ran, the pain in her leg forgotten. Snow roared as it raced toward their camp and over the slope behind her. She cut sideways, trying to get out of its path, but the snow picked her up and carried her with it. Sol swam frantically against the current, struggling to keep herself from getting pulled under.

The snow caught at her legs and dragged her beneath the snow, covering her face. She kicked and clawed at the relentless current, trying to find a way out, but she couldn't be sure of up or down. The snow shoved her upward again and Sol gasped and coughed as she broke the surface. She kept above the snow, swimming upward and sideways against the flood as icy siren hands gripped her legs and tried to drag her under.

The rushing current slowed and fell still, leaving an eerie silence in its wake. Sol's breaths came in gasps and shudders, and her heart pounded loud in the sudden stillness. She lay back against the snow, thanking all the gods she was still alive.

The avalanche had buried her to her thighs in snow, and a sharp panic overcame her when she tried to kick herself free. She couldn't move. The snow was as thick and immobile as granite. She hurriedly dug herself out, scooping away the snow with frozen fingers. But the work was slow and tedious. Her hands shook as she worked, and it was several minutes of digging before she could crawl out of her icy prison.

Her snowshoes were gone, as well as her hat, and Sol yanked her hood over her long, frozen hair. Now that the adrenaline had worn off, her leg ached more than ever, and she was exhausted. Fighting the avalanche and digging herself free had stolen all her strength, and the cold sapped whatever life was left in her. Winter seeped into her bones, and she was past the point of shivering. The snow on her body had melted, soaking her wool leggings and tunic, and ice had formed a crust on the exterior of her fur coat. She stood in a daze, gazing at the mountain above her, her mind fogged from the bitter cold.

The others would need help. She couldn't have been the only one half-buried by the snow.

Sol crawled up the slope with leaden limbs. The snow still shifted in places and she proceeded cautiously, wary of any movement. Each step was painful, and she was forced to use her frozen hands to drag herself up the hill. Her body resisted each effort, demanding that she stop and rest, but the only thing keeping her alive was the warmth that each movement forced through her blood.

When Sol crested the hill, all she saw was white.

The camp was gone.

CHAPTER 8
KELAN

Kelan opened his eyes. Cold whiteness pressed in around him. He tried to move, but it felt as though his body had been encased in stone. He could see nothing but white.

His heart raced and his breathing grew panicked and frantic. He screamed, and when he sucked in a breath, the snow pushed against his mouth, pressing in on him, drowning him with the closeness of it.

"Help!"

He wriggled his body, trying to break free, but he could move nothing but the tips of his fingers. He waited in silent panic, listening, praying.

But there was nothing. No one to hear him. No one to save him.

Only snow.

And silence.

CHAPTER 9

SOL

Sol clambered forward in a numb daze. The avalanche had covered the mountain and buried the bluff and the slopes all around it. The mountain had been torn and ravaged, trees ripped from its face in a long, white scar.

She sank to her knees and covered her mouth with her gloved hands. Gone. All of them.

Thirty people had been buried by the snow, and she had no way of knowing where they were. They could've been dragged down the slope like she was, or buried in snow where they had sat against the cliffs. Even if she had the strength to dig all night, she wouldn't be able to reach them.

She had to find Lady Isabella. If Isabella were dead, there'd be no Cassian Army to come to Tokkedal's aid next spring.

Without her snowshoes, Sol sank deep into the newly settled snow as she climbed the mountain. When she stopped at the top of the mound, she turned slowly, searching for signs of movement, or evidence of their camp, but there was nothing before her except snow, and more snow.

There must be some way to find them and save them. But she could think of nothing. Her mind was as thick and frozen as the snow beneath her, and the cold muddied her thoughts.

Sol swallowed a sob. She was alone now, alone in the Ulve

Mountains with nothing but her soaking clothes and the knife at her belt. How would she survive? She had no means of making a fire to warm herself, no way to melt snow so she could drink it, and nothing to eat. She didn't even have her bow to hunt with. Sol would be as dead as the rest of them when she froze tonight.

Something caught her eye, a slight movement in the snow. Pale fingertips wriggled in the ice, grasping for freedom.

Sol stumbled toward the hands, her heart catching in her throat. A survivor. Thank the gods.

She dropped to her knees and gave the fingers a squeeze. "I've got you," she whispered. "I'll get you out."

They were men's hands. Officer Poulsen?

Sol dug where she imagined his face would be. He needed air, and quickly. His fingers wriggled frantically in the snow, begging her to work faster.

He was buried deep, and the snow was thick and dense where it had settled around him. Her aching body resisted the effort she expended to dig him out, but she persisted. She couldn't give up. She wouldn't.

As soon as she scooped the snow free of his face he gasped and coughed. "Air," he croaked. "More air."

Sol scraped his face clean, then gasped and scrambled away.

The demon.

She shivered violently, both from the cold and from the horror of touching him.

"Hunter?" he asked blearily.

Sol stood and stepped away from him.

He twisted his head beneath the snow. "Hunter, please. You can't leave me here. I can't move!"

She ran from him. If the demon had survived under the snow, surely someone else had as well. He couldn't be the only one.

"Hunter!" Demon screamed. "Hunter come back!"

Sol cringed and scrunched her shoulders against her ears. She didn't have time to waste digging him out if she was going to help the others.

She walked around the base of the avalanche, looking for any signs of movement. A hand. A foot. Anything.

Demon continued to call her name as she traced the edge of the slope. He screamed it and whimpered it, and she ignored his pleas.

She spotted a splotch of dark amid the white snow. She limped toward it and dug at it to discover a horse's flank, but its body had grown cold already. Dead.

Had someone been holding its lead line? She dug with her frozen hands, two icicles attached to her body. Her teeth chattered as she worked, but she couldn't stop, not now. She was running out of time to find people.

Most had probably suffocated by now.

She dug out most of the horse. There was no sign of anyone else near it, and the avalanche had carried the horse far down the slope before dumping it at the base. The horse had broken its neck in the fall.

Sol sat back and stared at the dead horse. She wasn't going to find any others. Officer Poulsen was dead. Lady Isabella was dead. The wounded soldiers, the mage prisoners, Isabella's maids, the Tokken soldiers she had been joking with this morning.

One minute here, the next gone, buried under the snow.

"Please," Demon shouted, "I can help you. Hunter!"

Sol paused. With his manacle on, the demon couldn't use his pyra, but he wasn't helpless. Demon was considerably taller than she was, and broader and stronger. If he took her unaware, he could overpower her.

She turned back to the horse and its saddlebags. Hopefully those packs carried food, and flint and steel. Or a bow. Then there'd be a chance for her to survive. She would mourn the others later, but if she didn't get warm soon, she'd be too dead to care.

She yanked the packs off the back of the horse, though one was still trapped underneath the horse's body. She was too cold to dig it out.

Five of Isabella's ridiculous, flimsy dresses were in one of the bags. Useless. They weren't even good for warmth.

Sol squeezed her eyes shut. Lady Isabella was dead. There was no reason to insult her memory.

Another smaller pack held a bit of jerky. Enough for four days, if she was careful with it. There was a single bedroll of animal skins and furs, and a hat, which she immediately stuffed on her head. There was a bow, but it had been snapped clean in half and the bowstring and arrows were nowhere to be found. The water skin the horse had carried would be useful, if she could find a way to melt snow to fill it. But there was nothing to start a fire with. Any materials the mountains could give her to make a fire were buried in snow.

She fished inside the pocket of the saddlebag and brought out a key. She held it in her hand and stared at it. The key to the demon's shackle, the one with the emberstone embedded in it.

She could take the demon's emberstone. Her pa's emberstone was small and weak, but the emberstone the demon had was large, large enough to be used in battle. If she used the emberstone she would survive; it would heat her blood and warm her numb hands and feet. She closed her hand around the key, her body yearning for warmth.

Death surely was preferable to corrupting herself with its evil magic, wasn't it? But her mind was clouded by the cold, and though she clung to this thought, her determination was slipping.

Sol hauled all of the useful items toward a rocky outcropping where she planned to make camp.

"Hunter," Demon whimpered, his voice weak. "Please. If you're going to leave me here at least kill me quickly. I can't die like this."

Sol approached and drew her knife, the one etched with oak leaves. He was right. She couldn't leave him like that.

Demon's hands were clasped in front of him, his fingers sticking out of the snow. She had excavated his face and neck, but nothing else, and he had been able to do nothing but shake his head and knock more snow into his face.

She stared at his hands, at where his emberstone was buried beneath the snow. Her heart hitched. Survive and curse herself? Or freeze and die?

Pa had been brave, but she could never be like him. She'd take Demon's emberstone and survive. Somehow, she had always known it would come to that, which was why she had taken the emberstone with her when she had left Hillerod. Pa would've been so disappointed.

She'd kill the demon first, then take his emberstone. Sol knelt over him and he stared at the knife in her hand.

"You'll make it quick?" he asked quietly.

A few of his black curls clung to his wet face. He was Tokken, like she was, but his eyes were turquoise, the color of Bruun royalty. His lips were blue, and his teeth chattered.

Sol gripped her knife tightly. He wasn't human. He was a rabid dog, and the only thing that could be done to help a rabid dog was to kill it.

"You won't suffer," she said.

His eyes widened. "You have the key to my cuff?"

Sol closed her fist around the key, hiding it from view.

"Please. I can help you. You're freezing. I can build you a fire."

Sol hesitated. If he built the fire, she wouldn't have to use the emberstone herself.

"If you save my life, I'll owe you a blood debt."

"I don't trust a demon," she growled.

"I swear in Maja's name I won't hurt you."

Sol sat back. She could take the manacle off him for a little bit, just long enough for him to make a fire to warm her with. She'd keep him tied up and he'd be her prisoner.

The Tokken Army would reward her for bringing in a Flame-skin lieutenant. This trip wouldn't have been for nothing.

"You swear it?" Sol asked.

"I swear it."

CHAPTER 10
KELAN

The cold pressed in around Kelan, constricting his chest and his movement, and turning his body to ice. It took every bit of will power not to scream.

"If you kill me, you'll be lost," Hunter said. "I'm your only way off this mountain." Hunter's voice was slurred and labored.

"I won't hurt you," Kelan said.

He'd never forget what it was like to be buried in the snow, to have it press into his face, his mouth, his nose. To know that there was no one to hear him scream. He would do anything to get out. He'd sell his soul to his pyra to be freed.

Hunter glared at him, then slowly dug at Kelan's hands. Kelan let out a ragged breath. Free. Free to move. Free to breath. He resisted the urge to cry.

"If you take off the manacle, I can melt the snow."

Hunter hesitated. Hunter's lips were blue, and his clothes were covered in ice. Every movement Hunter made was jerky and uncoordinated, and it took several tries for Hunter to insert the key and unlock the shackle around Kelan's wrist. Kelan took a ragged, grateful breath as the emberstone fell free. Hunter pocketed the manacle and sat back with knife in hand.

"Well?" he demanded in his gravelly voice, frowning at Kelan in the snow.

Kelan groped mentally for his pyra. There it was, a tiny spark of flame. He had never felt it so small or so weak.

"Come on," Kelan urged, prodding at it. He needed warmth. He needed fire.

Hunter stared at him expectantly.

"It needs time to refuel."

Hunter sighed and started his jerky digging again. "Some demon you are."

Kelan scowled at Hunter, and his pyra swelled, feeding on Kelan's anger.

"Yes!" Kelan said, his anger turning to joy. "Make me angry. Insult me."

"What?"

"My pyra feeds on emotions. Make me angry and it will grow faster."

"They say never to make a demon angry," he said in a slurred drawl. "But you aren't a threat to me. No wonder they stuck you out here in the middle of the woods. Is that where they send their most useless soldiers?"

You did ask for that, his pyra whispered, its voice weak.

Kelan ground his teeth.

"You were the commanding officer, weren't you? I took down your patrol almost single-handedly. I killed ten of your own with my arrows. Right through the heart. And I would've shot you, too, if Poulsen hadn't stopped me."

The snow on Kelan's body collapsed and melted. His pyra swirled in Kelan's rage, heating his body and driving away the sting of his frozen toes and hands.

Hunter scrambled away with his knife gripped tightly in one hand.

I'm back, his pyra hissed. *I missed you, Kelan.*

Kelan pushed through the snow and sat up. He was soaked to the bone in freezing water, but he didn't care. He was free, and he was warm.

Kelan crawled out of his hole as his clothes steamed and dripped water. With one quick burst of fire, the cords that bound his wrists burned and fell away. He met Hunter's green eyes.

"You swore you wouldn't hurt me," Hunter said, limping backward. "And if I'm dead you'll be lost out here. I buried the food, and I'm the only one who knows where it is."

It would be easy to kill him, especially half-mad with the cold as Hunter was. A burst of flames into his haughty face. Or Kelan could do nothing and let Hunter freeze to death. The ice on Hunter's clothes would kill him once the sun set.

Kelan looked around. The only features in the landscape were the endless peaks and the trees. Hunter was right. Kelan had no idea where he was, and without food, he wouldn't last long.

"Where do you want me to build the fire?" Kelan asked, swallowing his anger. He would make Hunter pay in time. Once they reached civilization, Kelan would end him.

Hunter's face relaxed visibly. "In that alcove," he said, pointing. "We'll make camp there."

Kelan gazed at the peak above them. He couldn't even tell where he had been standing when the avalanche had fallen. The whole landscape had changed. Where once there had been a valley, now there was a mountain of snow.

"Were there any other survivors?"

Hunter shook his head. "I searched, but . . . there's too much snow. They're all dead by now, I think."

Kelan winced. Suffocated alone in the cold snow. He had almost met that same fate.

"And Lady Isabella?"

"Dead."

Kelan pressed his lips together. At least they had accomplished their mission, even if it had cost his entire troop their lives.

He and Hunter gathered sticks and pulled dead branches from trees. The wood was wet and frozen, but that had never hindered Kelan before. He got a roaring blaze up in a matter of minutes, and Hunter sat so close to the fire that Kelan was sure he would burn himself, but still Hunter shivered. The ice and snow on his clothes melted and drenched him.

If Hunter was going to lead him down the mountain, Kelan had to keep him alive. And if Kelan didn't want Hunter to stab him in his sleep, Kelan had to make himself useful.

"I can dry your clothes," Kelan said, trying to sound uninterested. Kelan's own clothes had dried long ago, and his boots, too.

"They'll dry here by the fire," Hunter said. His voice wasn't slurred anymore, but his teeth still chattered.

"Not fast enough. Not if you're wearing them."

Hunter narrowed his eyes. "Fine. I'll stay by the fire while you dry my coat." He tossed his soaking fur coat to Kelan. "If you burn it, I'll kill you," he said, flashing his knife.

Kelan frowned. "Did you mean to say, 'Thank you'? Or are all mountain folk as civilized as you are?"

Hunter scowled and hunched over the fire, putting his wet, gloved hands over the blaze. Kelan squeezed the coat and wrung water from it, letting the heat of his hands evaporate what water he could not wring out. It wouldn't be perfectly dry, but it would be better than wearing it wet.

"Now your clothes, too."

Hunter went rigid. "No."

Kelan rolled his eyes. "Then it'll be your own fault if you freeze to death in your sleep."

"All right," Hunter said slowly. "Wait on the other side of the rocks and I'll bring them to you."

"I can do it right here."

"I said wait over there," Hunter growled.

"I'm still waiting for my thanks," Kelan grumbled as he walked around to the other side of the rock outcropping. These mountain folk had an extreme sense of modesty. Kelan had heard as much, but he hadn't believed it.

Hunter tossed wet clothes over the rocks and into Kelan's hands. "Throw them back over when you're done."

Kelan cursed Hunter silently as he wrung water from Hunter's socks and wool leggings and tunic. At least now Hunter wouldn't freeze. His blood debt had been paid, and he would have no qualms killing Hunter once they reached Cassia.

He carried an armload of mostly-dry clothes around the side of the boulder. "I'm still waiting for my gratitude."

Hunter stood by the fire with his back to him. He had absurdly long hair that hung down his back and his bare legs stuck out from beneath his fur coat.

Kelan froze. His face went slack. Those weren't men's legs.

CHAPTER 11
SOL

Sol whirled around. "I told you to throw them back," she growled. She snatched her clothes out of his arms and glared at his shocked face.

"Go wait over there," she ordered.

Demon saluted and disappeared behind the stone outcropping. Sol wiggled into her deliciously dry clothes, glancing every few seconds toward the rocks, but Demon didn't reappear. She shrugged on her coat again, fully dry for the first time in hours.

"You can come out now." There was no point in pitching her voice low anymore. He knew.

Demon peeked around the corner, then sauntered toward her. She scowled at him as she resettled her hat on her head. She used to hide her long hair underneath it, but there was no need for that anymore, either.

"Why do you hide what you are?" he asked, peering at her curiously from the other side of the fire.

"The army asked for a specific hunter, who happened to be a man. And I needed this job."

"But why hide it from me?"

Sol shrugged. "I've been putting on this charade for weeks now. There was no reason to stop. And if we were going to travel together it would've been better if you thought I was a man."

"Better?"

"If you even think about touching me, I'll slit your throat."

"Wouldn't dream of it, sweetheart."

Sol stomped her foot. "Don't call me that. I'm no one's sweetheart."

"Well what's your name then? It can't be Hunter."

"Sol."

His eyebrows shot up. "Were you born on the Solstice?"

"Winter Solstice, yes."

Demon smiled. "How lucky am I, to have a mountain guide blessed by the gods."

Sol scowled at him. It didn't feel like a blessing to have been born on Solstice. It felt like a curse.

The snow beneath Demon had melted, and he now reclined on a steaming horse's blanket. The darkness and the silence of night closed in around them. How was it that they had been the only ones to survive? Why had the mountain chosen *him* of all people?

"My name's Kelan," Demon said. "In case you were wondering."

"I wasn't."

Demon laughed, an irritating sound.

"There's a mountain village not far from here, called Baarka," Sol said. "It's the closest place we could get food. Depending on the conditions in the mountains, we'll either get more supplies there and continue on, or have to stay in Baarka until the snow melts. Then I'll take you the rest of the way to Cassia and collect a reward for turning you in."

"I was there with you, until the part where you turn me in and collect a reward. That's not happening."

Sol pulled the emberstone manacle from her coat pocket. "Put this on."

"Ah . . . no, thanks."

Sol scowled at him. "This is why I saved you."

"No, you saved me because you were going to freeze to

death. I've saved your life now, too. I think that means we're even."

Sol marched toward him, but he sprung up and backed away. "I should've left you buried in the snow," she growled.

"I'm glad you rescued me, but I'm still not going to put that back on."

Sol reached for her knife and Demon's hands sparked with fire. She gasped and stepped back. What had she been thinking, freeing a demon and giving him back his pyra? She'd had cold sickness, she realized. Her memory was foggy even now, as she tried to remember all that had happened over the last few hours. She never would've set the demon free if she'd been fully cognizant.

She would've preferred to freeze to death than to burn to death. She gripped the manacle, her fingers brushing the ember-stone inside it. The stone was warm and tingly with the promise of power. If he attacked, it would protect her.

But using it would betray Pa's memory.

"You should be more careful who you threaten, Sol," Demon said.

"If you kill me, you'll never find that village."

"Maybe I should take my chances."

Sol slipped the emberstone into her pocket. No, she wouldn't use it. She would be strong like Pa.

"Kill me, then. That's all demons do. Kill, and destroy."

She met his turquoise eyes and held his gaze. She tensed, ready to throw her dagger into his heart if he moved.

His face fell into an easy grin. "No, I don't think I'll kill you yet. I'm not hungry enough, and I like my maiden hearts fresh."

Sol recoiled and stumbled away from him.

He laughed. "Ashes, do you believe all the stories they tell about Flameskins?"

She scowled at him.

"I promised I wouldn't hurt you, and like you said, I'd be lost in the mountains without you."

Maybe he needed her, but she didn't need him. She'd get

along fine without Demon now that she was warm and dry, and it was dangerous to keep him alive. But now that Lady Isabella was dead, it wasn't likely the Tokken Army would pay her for her trip to Cassia, and Ma was going to have to take on debts this winter since the Flameskins had burned their field. Sol needed money, and turning the demon in would be a good way to get it. She'd wait until they got close to Cassia, then slip the ember-stone on him while he was sleeping and tie him up.

Sol rolled out the furs for her bed and tucked the bag of food underneath her head, using it as a pillow. If Demon did try to run away, he wasn't taking the food with him. She slid her knife underneath her pillow, in easy reach.

"Good night, Demon."

Piercing cries rent the chill night air, the sound of the winter howling through the icy mountains. Demon sat upright, his eyes wide. "What was that?"

It was a cry no one ever forgot once they had heard it. "Ice wolves. The avalanche must've released them."

Demon's face went pale. "But I thought those were just mountain legends."

Sol grunted. "You don't know anything about the Ulves."

She let him worry and search the trees with anxious eyes as she settled deeper into her furs.

"Should we—?"

"We'll do nothing. They fear fire. They won't come near you or our camp. We have nothing to fear from them."

He frowned at her, searched the slopes once more, and lay down.

CHAPTER 12

KELAN

K elan opened his eyes. The fire was dead beside him, and his pyra pumped heavily in his blood, beating back the cold. And there was a girl nestled against him.

He froze and stared at her, confused and groggy and blinking away sleep. It had been a long time since he had woken up next to a girl.

Oh. The avalanche. Sol.

His lips quirked into a smile. She had snuggled right up next to him in her sleep. The fire was cold, and she would've frozen without his heat. Even now she looked cold. He studied her face, buried deep in her fur hood. She looked peaceful, pretty even. He wouldn't have guessed her to be a murderer.

Kelan turned carefully onto his back. What was he doing putting himself so close to her? She was the enemy. Sol had killed no less than ten of his men, shot them through with arrows. The only reason he wasn't dead was because she had been freezing to death yesterday.

He shivered. The snow. He never wanted to be buried like that again.

He could kill her, but what would it prove? He'd be no different from Markus, taking life just because he could. And if Sol were dead, he'd be stranded in the mountains. When he looked at her, Kelan saw the mountain woman whose house Markus had destroyed, with children clinging to her skirts. Did Sol have children, too? It seemed unlikely any man would want to claim her. He had never met anyone so bossy. She had given more orders to the Tokken soldiers than their officer.

Kill her. It would be easy. She deserves to die for what she's done.

Kelan winced as he shoved away his pyra's voice and stood up. Sol immediately squirmed deeper into her blankets as cold air replaced the heat of Kelan's body. He threw some logs onto the fire and used a small puff of flame to light it.

Each time he drew on his pyra, he felt it creeping in. It was still weak from the emberstone he had worn, but it would regain its strength as they hiked, especially if Sol made him angry. Irritating him seemed to be a talent of hers.

Sol sat up and wrapped her furs around herself. She scrunched her face at him.

"Cold?" he asked and grinned.

"You didn't kill me during the night."

"We're both still alive. Imagine that."

She scowled at him before getting out of bed and rolling up the fur blankets.

"So, what's the plan for today?"

"We'll search the snow for anything salvageable, and then we'll start toward Baarka. That's the town I was telling you about."

"Do we have any food?"

She hesitated. "Not much."

He frowned. She'd been holding out on him. He went to bed hungry last night.

She'll starve us slowly, then take us while we're weak. Better to burn her now.

She opened up her bag and pulled out two strips of dried venison, one for each of them, then she emptied the bag onto her furs. Strips of meat fell out along with a cloth seal from Lady Isabella's house, and the manacle. She divided the food into two piles.

45

"There's enough for two days for each of us," she said, "but the walk to Baarka will take us at least four or five days."

"So, we're going to be hungry."

"No. The horse I found yesterday might have more supplies, and if it doesn't, we're going to skin it and prepare some of the meat."

Kelan grimaced. "Eat the horse?"

"Would you rather starve?"

She lead him through the snow toward the horse, limping as she walked, but she stopped them at the base of the new mound the avalanche had created. She crouched on the ground, inspecting tracks in the icy snow.

"Ice wolves," she said, pointing.

Kelan knelt next to her and peered at the paw print. "I thought it'd be bigger."

"They're plenty big. Trust me."

Kelan met her eyes. "You've seen them?"

She nodded and bit her lip. "Ashes. I should've gotten the horse out yesterday. I was just so blasted tired. They must've gotten to it."

Sol jumped up and they followed the tracks through the snow. There was little left of the horse. A few bones, shreds of its mane and bridle. No blood, as the horse must've already been frozen when the wolves had found it.

Sol's shoulders slumped. "I'm such a fool. That was our best source of food, and I left it unprotected."

Kelan was almost glad. He wasn't going to eat horse meat. He wasn't a savage mountain huntress. "I don't think either of us were in a state to salvage a horse's carcass last night."

She glared at him. "But I'm a huntress." As if that explained anything. She inspected the tracks and followed them in large circles through the snow. "There was a pack of them last night."

Kelan shivered, thinking about how close the wolves had been to their camp, but Sol seemed unconcerned.

"Will they come back?"

"No. They don't awaken often. They probably already went back to the ice."

"Then . . . ?"

"They're made of ice, just like the legends say," Sol said, meeting his eyes again. "Formed from the glaciers. If this mountain has allowed us to survive the snow, she won't hunt us with her wolves."

"She?"

"Tor and Maja aren't the only gods who rule over Nordby. The Ulve Mountains are gods in their own right, and especially in winter. Traveling through the Ulves is never a thing to be taken lightly."

Kelan cleared his throat and turned away from her unnerving gaze. Huntress. She had lived in these mountains her whole life. Was it common to see things like this? Ice wolves and phoenixes and dragons, too? Or had he heard too many tales about the strange monsters that roamed the Ulves? Sol was surely a feral beast in her own right.

She led him to a group of saddlebags that sat apart from horse's remains. The wolves hadn't gotten to them, but Sol had. Lady Isabella's dresses lay strewn in the snow around them and Sol had messily hacked the seal of Isabella's house from a dress's skirt.

"Don't like dresses much?" Kelan asked, eyeing the fine silks.

"They're a useless waste of resources."

"Mountain women don't appreciate the finer things in life."

She scowled at him. "And this mountain woman is your only hope of survival. Now make yourself useful and help me dig out the other saddlebag. I think there's still one in the snow."

She stooped over the pit where the horse had been, and Kelan dug out the snow in melting handfuls.

"Can't you heat blast it, or whatever?"

Kelan sat up. "Yes, I could. But I'd prefer not to. And it's going to take me a long time to do this by myself."

Sol tentatively started digging out the other side. "I thought demons always wanted to burn things."

"Demons, yes. But I'm not a demon. My name is Kelan."

"But you're a Flameskin. You are a demon."

Breathe. He sucked in a breath and let it out. "I haven't been taken possession of yet. My pyra still obeys me and hasn't taken over my body."

Sol paused in her digging and Kelan looked up. "You're like the Saints, then? They say they can't be possessed, that they've overcome the taint of fire."

He grimaced. "The Saints are something else. I don't even think their powers are real."

"They're real. And they're going to destroy the Flameskin Army."

"That remains to be seen." He was sick of hearing rumors about the women called the Saints.

"What happens to you when your pyra takes possession?"

Kelan tapped the button hanging around his neck. "All those things you hear about. They say a pyra is a piece of Maja's soul, a piece of chaos. Once a Flameskin gives in, their pyra can possess their body at will, and it'll destroy anything and everything it can."

"But you haven't been possessed yet?" she asked, narrowing her eyes at him.

"No."

"But, why?"

Kelan sighed. "Why do people keep asking me that? Isn't it obvious why I wouldn't want my pyra to control me?"

Her face flushed. "No, I mean, I thought it was inevitable. That it happens to all Flameskins."

"Maybe. But I'm going to fight it. That's why I don't use my fire. Using its power makes its hold on me stronger."

"Oh." She thought for a while before joining him in the digging once more. "You used your pyra last night."

"Yesterday my pyra was weak, from the emberstone. And I couldn't very well let you die. I wouldn't have known where you hid the food."

She frowned. "I forgot about dinner. I wasn't in the mood to eat last night."

Truth be told, neither was he.

Kelan glanced at her. "You have a family? Children?"

It was a foolish question to ask and he knew he shouldn't, but his conscience wouldn't stay quiet. He had to know. He had to steel himself for when she begged him to spare her for her children's sakes.

"Yes," she said. "Four mouths to feed. That's why I'm here."

He jerked upright. Four? She couldn't be that old, could she? How early did the mountain folk marry?

"How—? How old are your children?" he asked quietly. When he blinked, he saw in his mind's eye that mountain mother again, and that night with Markus that had been branded into his mind.

"Not my children. I have three younger sisters, and my mother."

"Oh." No children, then. That would make it easier.

They finally pulled out the horse's remaining saddlebag, but it was a disappointing find: three bedrolls, a tin of lemon cake, a coil of rope, and seven pairs of lady's shoes.

Sol sighed. "I let Isabella keep two bags of her own things. And we found both of them."

"So, we have nothing to eat."

"It's better to stretch what you have over a few days, so you at least have something each night."

So, he'd get one meal a day? And a small one at that. Ashes. "Let's get going, then. I'd prefer we get to Baarka in four days instead of five."

Sol had gathered up the strips of bridle and lead line she had found in the snow and stuffed those in the saddlebag, then threw the rope over her shoulder. Kelan trudged back to camp beside her with the tin in one hand and a bedroll under his other arm. At least with a bedroll he would be warmer at night, so his pyra wouldn't have to work so hard. It exhausted him to be constantly fighting the cold.

"Are you sure we need the rope?" Kelan asked. "It's heavy, and we can't eat it." And she was likely going to try to tie him up with it later if she got the chance.

"Rope is useful. Always bring rope. That's what my pa said."

"Did he tell you to always bring a Flameskin as well? I'm quite useful, too."

She whirled around, her eyes fiery. "Don't you ever talk about my pa. He would've slit your throat if he'd seen you."

"Sounds like a nice fellow."

She glared at him and turned on her heel. "Rabid dogs. That's what he called Flameskins."

He pushed away his pyra's growing anger. His skin heated and the snow on his trousers melted and steamed. "Rabid dog? Am I even human to you?"

"No."

Kelan swallowed a growl. "It's no wonder people like you murder innocent child Flameskins."

"Better to pull the weed out while it's still young, before it grows roots and multiplies and chokes your fields."

Breathe. Kelan clutched the cake tin to his chest and shoved his pyra away.

She's a murderer. Destroy her.

"You think I'm the monster?" he asked, his voice hissing out from between clenched teeth. "I would never hurt an innocent. But you? You pile up Flameskin bodies in your streets, burn them after you've cut out their hearts. Women, children, infants, none of that matters to you. Your king slaughtered his own wife and daughter. We don't have to do anything wrong, we just have to exist."

She turned when they reached the fire and studied him with her cold, green eyes. "Better than letting them grow up and burn our cities to the ground."

CHAPTER 13
SOL

Sol tugged on the cord, trying to get it as tight as possible. Both of her snowshoes had been lost in the avalanche, so she had had to build four new ones, each made of three straight sticks lashed together with strips of the horse's bridle and lead line, with a bough of pine needles woven in. They would do, for now. Or at least until they got to Baarka.

She shivered as she strapped on her other snowshoe. Winter had laced silvery threads of ice through her body, and she was cold all the time now. Digging in the snow had made her sweaty, but hadn't beaten back the chill, and now her wet clothes clung to her body. Exhaustion made her weary and numb, and they hadn't even started hiking yet.

"Demon," she said. "I need you to come try these on."

When he didn't answer, she looked up. He was sitting on the other side of the clearing, his face blank and turned toward the sun.

"Demon," she shouted.

He jumped and turned.

"Stop being useless and come put these on."

"I wasn't being useless."

"That's what it looked like."

"Do you want me to burst into flames?"

She stared at him.

"I was meditating. When you make me angry, I start losing control of my pyra."

Sol frowned. Demon made it sound as though he could truly resist his pyra's influence. Was that true? "Tie these onto your shoes," she said, setting out the snowshoes. "You'll travel easier with them on."

As he strapped them onto his boots, she lifted her legging and peeled back the bandages around her calf. It made her light-headed just looking at it. The wound was definitely infected now. It oozed and ached and burned. How was she supposed to walk on this? They had four days hard travel until they got to Baarka and she could get a poultice for this wound. She had nothing she could put on it now but snow.

She breathed in sharply as she rubbed it with ice, trying to clean away the infection. Ashes and cinders.

Demon peered over her shoulder. "I'm no expert, but that looks like it hurts."

"I'm fine," she growled and hurriedly wrapped it once more, concealing it from his view.

"Can you even walk? Or am I going to have to carry you to Baarka?"

"Don't you dare touch me with your demon hands," she snapped. She stood too quickly, and her vision swirled. She threw her bag over her shoulder and faced north. "We'll walk in a straight line. You'll follow in my footsteps."

"Bossy. What if I want to walk arm in arm? Side by side?"

"We'll waste energy paving two trails through the snow. It's easier to go one behind the other. Understand?"

He shrugged. "I didn't try to shrink your underclothes when I dried them, but you might want to check and make sure they're not pulled too tight before we leave."

Sol curled her hands into fists at her side and muttered curses under her breath as she stomped down the trail.

The going was hard. The morning was mostly uphill, and they took only a short break at noon, where they each had a single bite of food. The afternoon was a steep uphill climb. Sol limped as she walked, and their pace grew slower and slower. She hated being so obviously weak, but she couldn't walk any faster than she already was. A stabbing ache radiated through her leg each time she took a step. The climb made her sweat, but the snow and the wind were freezing. She wiped sweat from her brow as she shivered.

"It's too bad you're not a Flameskin. You would've been healed by now."

Sol grit her teeth. "I'd never taint myself by using fire."

She could almost hear him rolling his eyes ahead of her. Demon had taken the lead to make the going easier for her.

"I could make you a sling or something and drag you through the snow."

"I said I was fine."

"Well, you're too slow. At this rate we'll run out of food long before we get to Baarka."

Sol hated that he was right.

They had reached a narrow pass along a cliff near the top of the peak, and she collapsed against the cliff face.

"I need a break for a few minutes," she said, closing her eyes. Her limbs shook, and her body ached. She just needed more food and a few minutes' rest, and then she'd be fine. She took a piece of venison out of her bag and allowed herself one bite, so there'd still be something left for dinner.

Demon squatted next to her and tightened one of the straps on his snowshoes. She'd already had to repair his left one twice. When she had some time tonight, she'd remake it, but right now all she could think about was sleep.

"Why don't you tell me how to get to Baarka and I'll wait for you there," Demon said.

She scowled. "If you knew the way you'd burn me up and steal my food."

"I wouldn't attack you when you were helpless like this. I have honor."

"No, you don't. You're a Flameskin."

He glared at her, then stood and walked away.

"Where are you going?" she shouted, scrambling to her knees. If he left, she'd never get her ransom.

"To relieve myself, or is that not allowed?"

She sighed and lay back again. "Don't go too close to the edge of the cliff."

He waved a dismissive hand at her. "You've already told me that a dozen times."

Sol closed her eyes, shutting out the glaring brightness of the white snow.

When Demon returned, he startled her out of a half doze. "Let's go. We're running out of daylight."

Sol groaned as she tried to move, but her limbs were full of lead and ice.

Demon bent over and looked into her face. "I've never seen a girl so sweaty. And trust me when I say I've seen a lot of sweaty girls."

She scowled at him and forced herself up onto her hands and knees, then to a shaky standing position. The thought of taking another step made her want to cry, but she'd never give Demon the satisfaction of seeing that. She took a few limping steps forward.

He started up the trail, dragging his snowshoes through the deep drifts. "You're the oldest of all your sisters, aren't you?"

"Yeah."

He turned and smirked at her. "I knew it."

"What's that supposed to mean?"

"It's why you're so bossy and mean. I bet you're used to ordering your little sisters around all day."

Sol crushed the icy snow beneath her snowshoe. Demon didn't know anything. Ma was grateful to have her around; Ma told her that every day. Now that Pa was gone, Sol had stepped up and taken his place. So what if she was bossy? She kept people alive. Or at least, she'd tried to.

Pa would've known about the avalanche. He wouldn't have

let them camp in such a dangerous spot. If he had been the guide on this journey, would all of them still be alive?

Demon waited for her several dozen paces ahead, his arms crossed over his chest. "We're never going to get off this blasted mountain with your leg like that."

"Well then, you should've told your soldiers not to cut me up."

"I would tell them, except that you killed them." He stomped forward. "Those were my friends. My comrades."

"They were rabid dogs."

The air around him wavered with heat, and the snow at his feet melted.

"You see nothing but the lies you've been fed your whole life. You have no right to call me Demon, no right to call any Flameskin a demon."

"That label is earned. Flameskins raided my village last summer. They burned half the houses and all our fields. My entire village is starving this winter because of you."

"Were you there when they killed the Flameskins in your village?" Demon asked, his voice low. "Where you there when they piled the bodies in the streets? Did you help cut out their hearts? Did you watch them burn?"

Sol recoiled. She remembered that day. The smell of burning hair had tasted like sulfur, and the smoke had clung to her throat and made her eyes burn. When Pa had returned home that night, there had been blood on his shirt.

"Cleansed," he had said, his green eyes dark. "The village has been cleansed."

And Ma had explained how the Jensen family had left the village, and that they wouldn't be returning. A euphemism to help an eight-year-old understand. But Sol had known. And she had bottled the horror of it inside her until she could comprehend why they had done it.

Sol stared at Demon. She feared neither his fire, nor the wavering heat around his body. She gripped the hilt of her knife. "I was a child when they did it, but I'm glad my village had the strength to rid itself of its Flameskin. Demons are a danger to us all."

"The only danger is your ignorance."

He turned from her, and the melted snow slid out from beneath his feet. Kelan yelped and threw out his arms to catch his balance, and landed hard on his shoulder. But his legs slid over the edge, and then he was gone.

Sol rushed as close to the edge of the cliff as she dared. "Kelan?"

There was silence. She got on shaking hands and knees and peered over the edge. Everything was white. Kelan's fall had shaken the snow lose, and flurries of white drifted down, down, down to the bottom of the mountain.

"Kelan?"

Her heart plummeted in her chest, and she took a shuddering breath. He was dead. Not even a Flameskin could've survived that fall.

Something moved on a small landing about twenty feet below. Kelan shook the snow from his red coat and looked up. "You used my name."

Sol growled and sat up. Fool demon. She had told him not to get so close to the edge.

"Sol? I think I need some help."

She knew she should leave him there; that's what Pa would've done. Kelan was dangerous. And aggravating.

"Sol?"

She stood.

Just walk away. She didn't need him.

"Sol!" he said, his voice frantic. "This ledge is made of ice. Sol, please!"

Her heart squeezed in her chest. "Hold on!"

She yanked the rope out of her bag and knotted the end of it. A boulder sat half-buried in the snow a few paces away and she scraped snow and ice away to tie the rope around it. Her head ached and her hands shook as she worked, but she willed away the exhaustion.

"Kelan, talk to me. How much time do we have?" He didn't answer. "Kelan?"

"I'm fine," he said, his voice shaking. "Just concentrating."

"Can you climb this rope?" she asked. "I can't lift you. If we have a few minutes I can put knots in it."

There was a pause. Sol dragged the rope over and was about to throw it to him when he spoke. "Go ahead and knot it."

She sat and hurriedly tied knots at intervals. After a minute of tense silence, she finished and threw the rope over the edge of the cliff.

"Can you reach it?" she asked.

The rope went taut.

"If you burn the rope, Kelan, you'll be stuck there."

He didn't answer. She peered over the edge of the cliff to watch Kelan climb slowly upward. When he reached the top, he sank his hands into the snow, seeking for purchase.

"Sol, help me."

She stared at him. She couldn't touch a demon, not his skin, but she could touch his clothes.

As weak as she was, she grabbed onto his arm and pulled. No heat came from his body. He scrambled up the side of the cliff and rolled onto the top, panting in the snow. The snow beneath him didn't melt.

CHAPTER 14

KELAN

K elan shivered. His veins coursed with ice, not fire.
A pyra fed on its hosts emotions; anger, joy, and grief
all became fuel for the pyra's flame. But a pyra couldn't consume
fear, and fear could quickly smother a pyra's fire.

It was fear that had forced Kelan's pyra and its flames to
retreat when he stood on that ledge of ice. And it was fear of his
pyra that kept it from possessing him.

But if it weren't for his fear, Sol wouldn't have captured him
in the first place. Fear had forced his pyra to abandon Kelan
when he needed it most.

Sol had rolled out her furs and lay on top of them, shivering
and panting. "I told you rope was useful," she murmured with
her eyes closed.

He stared at her. "I thought you were going to leave me
there."

She opened one eye, and closed it again. "I considered it."

"But you didn't."

She sighed. "I didn't."

"Don't sound so torn up about it. You saved my life."

She rolled over and put her back to him.

Kelan lay on his back and looked up at the gray sky. His pyra
returned, slowly, warming first his core then spreading heat to

the tips of his fingers and toes. Snow fell and landed in big flakes on his face. He blinked it out of his lashes, and it melted on his cheeks.

"Come on," he said, and stood. "We should keep going."

He took a few steps forward and sank deep into the snow with each step. "Oh, sorry, Sol. I lost both the snowshoes."

She curled up tighter on the skins, and falling snow piled up on her hat and coat.

"Sol?"

"I'm too tired," she mumbled.

"Is there somewhere we can camp that will be out of the snow and away from the cliff? We can't stay here."

She opened her eyes. Her face was wet with melted snow and sweat. "There's a cave not far from here. My pa and I stayed there once."

"Are you sick?" Kelan asked, peering at her ashen face.

"I'm fine," she snapped. She sat up and tried to stand, but her legs shook beneath her. He reached out to help her up, but she shoved him out of the way.

"Don't touch me, Demon."

He sighed. Prickly as a pincushion lost in a bramble bush. Hadn't she just used his name? And now he had been relegated to "Demon" again. Some people couldn't be reasoned with.

"I hope the cave's close," he said, "because you're not making it far."

He coiled the rope around his arm and quickly rolled her furs up, trying to shake off as much snow as possible. Snow fell thick and fast, covering their shoulders and the tops of their heads with white. Kelan loaded both bags onto his back.

Sol pointed at a gray shape shrouded by falling snow. "The cave's there."

"Come on. We don't want to be buried in the stuff."

She looked up, seeming to finally realize it was snowing. "Oh." Her brow furrowed. "That's not good."

Kelan stomped through the snow, sinking deep into the drifts without his snowshoes, and he had to stop every few steps for her to catch up. The snow fell fast enough that he worried she'd fall into a snowbank and be buried before he could find her again.

He stopped again and turned, sighing as she limped toward him. He took both bags and slung them across her body, and it looked as though the weight would drop her to the snow.

"Get on my back," he said, and crouched. "I'll carry you the rest of the way."

"No. I won't touch a demon."

"Would you rather be lost in the snow?"

She hesitated and Kelan fumed. Why would she rather suffer than accept his help?

But she wrapped her arms around his neck and rested her sweaty cheek against his. He hefted her onto his back, groaning under the weight, and sank to his knees in the snow with each step. Kelan pushed his pyra into his legs and back, strengthening the muscles with fire, but he still struggled to hold both of them upright as he fought his way toward the cave.

"Ashes and cinders. You're so heavy."

"I'm no dainty Lady Isabella," she murmured.

They had reached the bottom of the slope where the cave lay. Sol pointed out the opening to him and he set her down in the snow. He slung both bags over his back again and half dragged, and half led her up to the cave.

It was as cold inside the cave as out, but it was protected from the snow. He rolled out her furs and sat her on them.

"I'll go out to find some firewood."

"No, don't," she said, hanging limply to his sleeve. "You'll get lost out there. You'll fall off a cliff again."

Outside the cave, snow continued to fall thick and heavy. She was right, of course. They'd barely been able to see the mountain in front of them. Why did she always have to be right?

"I guess we'll have to wait out the storm," Kelan said. His stomach clenched. He'd have to make the food last longer as well. He hated being hungry.

Sol shivered in her furs and wrapped them tighter around

herself. He knelt next to her and placed his hand on her forehead. Her skin was as hot as his.

"Don't touch me, Demon," she growled, squirming away from him.

"You're burning up."

She swore and covered her face with her furs. "It's my leg," she said, her voice muffled by the blanket.

"Let me see it."

She turned over in her bedroll, putting her back to him once more.

"Sol, if you die, I'm going to be stuck out here with no way back. Let me see your leg."

She pulled her leg out from under the skins and winced as she unwrapped the bandages. The cut was clearly infected, and the skin around it was red and irritated.

"Bring me snow," she said. "I have to drain it and clean it." When he returned with an armload of snow, she wiped it clean, but it didn't look any better.

"Is there anything we can put on it?" Kelan asked, trying not to look at it. "I don't know anything about wounds. When a mage or Flameskin gets injured we just seal them up and let them rest." Kelan had never been sick before. A pyra burned away illness and infection quicker than any poultice or potion.

"I know all the herbs in these mountains, but they're all buried under the snow." She blinked twice with her bleary eyes. "I'll rest a bit while it's snowing. Then I'll feel better and we can keep walking."

Kelan frowned at her. "Don't die on me."

"I wouldn't," she said, closing her eyes and lying down. "Because then there'd be no one to boss you around."

For one night and one day it snowed, and all the while Sol tossed and turned in a fevered sleep. When she woke every few hours, she could do little more than take a few sips of water.

Kelan sat beside her, staring at the falling snow and thinking about the men he had lost, and about Markus, as he fingered the button on the chain around his neck. His pyra grew restless and insistent.

Leave the girl, it hissed. *She's dying.*

Sol had saved his life. Twice. He couldn't abandon her. But there was nothing he could do for her fever.

The boredom made him hungry and he ate, cursing himself with each bite.

Sol mumbled in her fevered sleep, and once startled him by crying out. "The winds howl with the cries of men! The mountain has stolen their hearts!"

They were words from one of those bardic poems, the one about the dryads, the spirits that lived in the trees of the Ulves. The poem was often sung during Solstice, and he had heard it many times. It was the tale of a man who had come into the Ulves searching for one of the abandoned dragon caves and its gold, but he got ensnared by a dryad, instead. He fell hopelessly in love with her, and she plucked his heart from his chest. He'd wandered the Ulves in search of his heart for the rest of his days.

The snow stopped just before sunset the next day, and Kelan stepped out into the brilliant white. He was lost the moment he set foot outside. The only reason he could tell up from down was because of the sky, but the entire landscape was indistinct drifts of white snow. He wasn't even sure where they had come from or which way they had been heading. If Sol died, he'd be lost.

Kelan emptied her bag. The tin of lemon cake fell out, along with the rope, her food, and the manacle with its glowing emberstone.

He stared at the red stone. Uncle Haldur had once said that most Nordese were mages, with the power to draw fire into their blood from emberstones. But they hid their gift or left it undiscovered. Kelan picked up the manacle, careful not to touch the emberstone locked inside it.

He lifted Sol's limp wrist and snapped the manacle in place, tightening the band until it was snug to her skin. He studied her face, but she seemed no different. She didn't stir in her sleep.

He lifted her blanket and unwrapped the bandages on her leg. Her wound was disgusting, and it stank.

Kelan took a deep breath and drew a tiny flame onto one finger. He lowered it close to her ankle, where the skin was clean and unmarked. He drew it closer, and closer, waiting for her leg to jerk or for the flame to burn her, but she didn't react at all. He wrapped his flaming hand around her ankle and her skin didn't burn.

The hypocrite! Here she was calling him Demon when she was a mage herself. She didn't have a pyra, but with an ember-stone, she had the same fire running through her blood that he did.

Did she know what she was? She must not, or she would've healed her wound already. Kelan grinned. He couldn't wait to see how she reacted when she found out she was a mage.

He pushed fire from his hand across her wound, burning away the infection and the stitches with stinking smoke and sealing her wound closed. When he finished, her calf had only a thin line of red running across it. Though the skin was still mottled and irritated, it already looked better than it had been. Her body would draw a steady stream of fire from the ember-stone and heal her on the inside. Sol would get better, and quickly.

CHAPTER 15
SOL

Sol was at once shivering in the freezing cave and burning in the Infernal Pit. The cold made her body ache, and the heat burned her.

She woke and saw a man through her blurry eyes, and he forced her to drink water. But he wasn't Pa.

No, that wasn't right. She had come into the mountains to hunt, hadn't she? She and Pa had been following the trail of a winter herd. There had been a storm, and they were waiting it out in the cave.

And then she was eight again, walking through the forest with her pa. "Are you leaving again?" she asked.

"Yes."

"Can't I come with you?"

"When you're older I'll take you all over the mountains with me."

"But why do you have to leave again? You just got back."

"I have to hunt so we can eat."

Sol frowned. "But you could hunt closer to home." That's what Ma always said. "Why don't you hunt around Hillerod?"

Pa glanced back at her and studied her face. "The mountains make me restless. And . . . I'm looking for something that I can't find here."

They had arrived at their rock by the river and Sol climbed on top of the boulder to watch the water flow beneath the thin ice.

"You're a big girl now and I need you to take care of my girls while I'm gone," Pa said, and Sol nodded, proud and tall. Ma said she'd be the tallest woman in the family when she was grown. And Pa said she'd be the best huntress in the Ulves.

"Put out your hands," he said.

Sol put them out, palms up. Was this an early birthday gift? What could she fit in two hands? A bow? A new quiver?

Pa placed something in one palm and closed her hand around it before she could see it. He looked into her eyes. His were dark green, like the pines.

"What does it feel like?" he asked.

"Like a rock."

"Does it feel warm?" he asked, his lips tightening.

Sol's eyebrows shot up. "It is warm. And prickly, a little. Like when your arm falls asleep, but not in a bad way. It feels good."

There weren't words to describe how this stone made her body feel warm and happy and tingly all over. Sol tried to open her fist, but Pa kept his hand clamped over it. He had that stern look he got when she had done something wrong. Sol's heart raced. What had she done to displease him?

"Pa?"

"Sol, I want you to focus on the stone in your hand, focus on its warmth, then pull the heat inside you to your heart." He touched her sternum with his finger. "Then push it into your other hand," he said, touching her open palm.

She stared at him quizzically. Was this another of his mind games? He was always coming up with new tricks to keep her occupied during a hunt.

"Can you do that?" he asked.

"I'll try."

Sol imagined the warmth of the stone flowing through her to her hand. A bright orange flame burst through the skin of her palm.

She screamed and wrenched away from Pa. The stone flew from her hand and got lost in the snow. Pa swore loudly, and he kept swearing until he had found the stone again.

She cowered against a tree. There had been a fire in her hand, but it hadn't burned her. What had she done wrong? Had he wanted a bigger flame, or had he not wanted fire at all?

Pa stared at her, his eyes hard. Tears formed in Sol's eyes and glimmered on her lashes.

"I'm sorry, Pa. I don't—"

"No, no, Sol," he said, burying her in his arms. "I'm sorry I frightened you."

She burrowed herself in his familiar warmth and he kissed the top of her head.

"Did I do wrong?"

"No, I'm the one who did wrong. I gave you my curse, Sol."

She sat up. "Curse?" Curses belonged to princesses in stories, not to Hunters' daughters.

Pa sighed. "I had prayed my curse wouldn't pass on to my children, but I suppose the gods didn't listen. You're a mage Sol, just like me."

He turned her in his arms until she was looking into his face. "You must promise me, Sol. You must never touch an ember-stone. You must never let fire taint your blood."

"I promise."

Sol's eyelids were heavy, and her body shook.

"Pa?" she asked.

She sat up and blinked rapidly, sweeping the bleary visions from her mind. Pa had been dead a year now.

It was Demon who had brought her here.

Sol scrambled onto her hands and knees. Where was Demon? He wasn't in the cave. Had he left her there to ride out her sickness? Taken her food and continued on toward Baarka? She rifled through her bag. Everything was still there, except the manacle. She frowned. He'd probably thrown it off a cliff.

She sat back and took a swig from the water skin. He had been there during her sickness. She remembered seeing him at least once, and he was the one who had forced her to drink water.

Sol sighed. He was probably already lost by now. If he'd left during the storm, he would surely be dead already. She could try to follow his tracks, if he had left any in the snow, but what was the point? She had no chance of taking him as prisoner without an emberstone manacle. At least he had left her with all her food.

She felt a twinge of what could be regret, but it was probably just hunger. She was ravenous now that she was feeling better, and she tore into a piece of jerky.

A figure in a red coat appeared at the cave entrance, and Sol lifted her hand to squint at him, blinded as she was by the sparkling sunlight.

"Kelan?" she asked, reaching for the knife at her belt.

He stomped into the cave and shook snow off his boots as he gave her a brilliant smile. "You're awake! I was hoping you'd be better today."

"I thought you'd left," she said, still chewing on the piece of jerky, and annoyed by the relief she felt. Being alone should be better than being with a demon, but somehow it wasn't.

"No such luck," he said, still smiling. He untied the snow-shoes from his feet.

"Look at these!" he said, holding the snowshoes up for her to see. "I made them myself."

His happiness was infectious, and she smiled. The snowshoes weren't bad, actually.

"How do you feel?" he asked, sitting beside her.

Sol blinked. "Surprisingly good." The pain in her leg was manageable and the chills and fever had passed. "But hungry."

She rolled up her pant leg and inspected the wound. It had healed nicely. The infection was gone, and she had a thick, healthy scab running across her calf. But as she stared at it, her stomach dropped.

"How long have I been asleep?" Her wound looked like it had been healing at least a week. Kelan would certainly be starving by now. She was surprised he hadn't eaten her food.

"About a day and a half. Dawn broke a couple hours ago, and the storm ended last night at dusk."

She gaped. "But that's impossible. It shouldn't have—"

It was impossible, unless he had healed her with an emberstone.

"Did you know you were a mage? We should've checked long ago. I could've had you fixed up and on the road—"

"Where is it?" Sol screamed. "Get it off me!"

She could feel it now, the warmth in her blood, the tingle of fire just beneath her skin. How had she not noticed that she wasn't cold?

She yanked up her sleeve and pulled at the manacle. "Get it off! Get it off me!"

"Sol, calm down. I've got the key here."

He looked at her like she was a wild animal. Maybe she was. He had poisoned her with fire.

He grabbed the shackle in one hand and stuck the key in. It fell open with a click and Sol yanked her wrist free. She scurried away from him, crouching at the other end of the cave as she pulled out her knife.

"You tainted me, Demon."

He threw the manacle to the ground and crossed his arms. "You knew you were a mage?"

She scowled at him. "You had no right to do that to me."

"I saved your life."

Sol swallowed the lump in her throat and tried to blink away her tears. She had promised Pa she wouldn't use emberstones, and that she'd never let them touch her skin. She had broken that promise once before, and had sworn never to do it again.

She rested her forehead against her knees and dropped her knife onto the cave floor. "How long was it on me?"

"One night."

She sobbed into her knees. "I don't want to be extinguished."

Mages didn't have pyri, but they could draw fire into their blood and use it without fear of possession if they had an ember-stone. But there were consequences to using emberstones. Emberstones leeched the emotions from their host mage and left them as empty, unfeeling shell.

Flameskins had an opposite and complementary curse. Their pyri manipulated their emotions and possessed them, but an emberstone could sap a pyra of its strength entirely, leaving the Flameskin without any fire at all.

Demon sighed. "Well, you can cry, so obviously you're not extinguished. It takes years of using an emberstone before you start to lose your feelings. One night won't hurt you."

"I hate you," she muttered, clenching her teeth and willing the tears to stop. How had she let herself cry in front of him? She wrapped her arms around her body. Now that she wasn't wearing the emberstone manacle, the cold bit into her, nipping her uncovered face and fingers.

"Fire isn't evil. We all use fire, to cook, to light and warm our homes. Without fire, humankind wouldn't survive."

"But it is evil to use it like this. To be tainted by it. To let it enter the blood."

"I won't apologize for saving your life."

"It's better to die untainted than to let the poison take you."

"Maybe we aren't so different," Kelan said softly. "We're both afraid of what fire can do to us."

CHAPTER 16

KELAN

The hunger was a constant gnawing in Kelan's stomach.
She has food, his pyra said. *Take it.*

Kelan grimaced and shoved its voice away. He focused on the walking, endless walking through the drifts of white, untouched snow. It had been meditative at first, but now it was disheartening. He was exhausted and hungry and footsore, and he had no idea where they were or how far they had to go. But he knew if he tried to complain, Sol would just tease him.

An enemy made a good traveling companion, in a perverse sort of way. They were both getting weak from the starvation and the strenuous climb, but when one or the other started to slow, they could taunt each other into continuing on. It was sort of encouraging. In a way.

Kelan glanced at Sol a few steps ahead of him. They had reached a snow-covered saddle between two peaks and she led them around the edge.

"Why don't we go across the saddle?" he asked, pointing to the open space in the center.

"Because there's a glacier there, and crevasses, probably. You don't want to chance stepping into a crack and falling to your death. The rope isn't long enough to compensate for that level of stupidity."

Kelan closed his mouth. Why did he even ask her questions? She always had some know-it-all answer to make him feel like a fool.

"It's possible we could find some game," she said. "There's a pond on the south side. It's frozen over, but sometimes there're still animals there."

"Where? I haven't seen anything."

"Hunting is all about patience."

Sol barely limped now, but he could tell she was tired. If she kept an emberstone on her, she wouldn't be so exhausted. The fire would strengthen her muscles and heal her, but she refused to touch it.

"Why do you hate fire so much?" he asked. "I get that you think I'm a demon, but what's so wrong about you using fire?"

"I told you. I don't want to be extinguished."

"But it takes years to even dull your emotions. It won't hurt you to use a little. My uncle's a mage, and he wasn't extinguished until his thirties."

She turned and glared. "Drop it, Kelan."

He crossed his arms as they slogged through the snow. She'd given him no thanks for saving her life, but at least she wasn't calling him "Demon." Did she expect him to feel grateful she now considered him partially human? Human enough for a name, at least.

Burnitall, even dogs had names. Rabid dog, that's what she'd called him.

"Do you even consider me a person?" he asked.

She gave him a withering glance and shrugged.

"How can you look at me and not realize that we're the same? If you didn't know I was a Flameskin, you'd see no difference between us."

"Well, you're a man. That's different."

"Then all men are animals."

She paused and smiled. "No, not all of them. But many of them."

"I guess I'm in good company then."

She shook her head, and it wasn't hard to imagine her rolling her eyes.

"Tell me, Huntress," he said. "What kind of animal do you hunt that they gave you that title?"

"Deer, mostly."

"You killed ten of my men, and I would say that gives you the right to call yourself a murderess as well."

"I did not take pleasure in killing them. I wouldn't have killed them, except that I was impelled to. I didn't sign up to become a soldier."

"What does it matter if you kill them?" he asked. "Since we're just animals?"

"Isn't it a mercy?"

Kelan tugged at the button hanging from the chain around his neck. Rabid dog. Mercy killing. He closed his eyes. As much as he fought her prejudice, hadn't he done the same thing once?

"Taking the life of any creature is hard," Sol said. "I won't pretend I enjoy it."

It's not hard for me, Kelan's pyra said. *I'll take your guilt and consume it.*

"Sol—"

She raised her hand and cut him off, her body tense and alert. A chevron of geese flew over their heads and glided toward a section of the frozen pond.

"Blast," she whispered. "I wish I had my bow."

There were six geese that had settled onto the snow and nosed their beaks at it.

"Can you use your fire to hit one?" she whispered.

His stomach rumbled. "Yes. Unlike you, I realize the importance of survival."

She put a finger to her lips, and they advanced. Sol was considerably quieter than he was. How could she move so silently while wearing snowshoes?

She stopped them a few dozen paces from the geese, which still hadn't noticed them. "Can you hit them from here?"

"Yes."

He took a deep breath. This was for survival. This was necessary. He was so hungry he couldn't think about anything else.

Yes. Use me. Let me help you burn them.

He pulled fire into his hands and closed them into fists. Sol immediately stepped away from him. The fire coiled and spun to form two balls of fire, then he focused on the center of the flock and released the pent-up energy. Fire whipped through the air and the geese squawked and took wing, but the balls exploded before they could escape, and two geese dropped.

His pyra snaked tentacles of fire into his mind before Kelan had a chance to restore his mental defenses. His vision tinted orange and red with the fire behind his eyes.

Sol was shouting something, but he couldn't hear her. His body trembled as he fought it back.

"You will not. Take. Control," Kelan hissed, through gritted teeth.

I own you, Kelan.

He fell onto hands and knees. The snow hissed and steamed as it touched his burning hands. When he looked up, Sol was staring at him, her eyes wide and frightened.

Kill her, it said. *She thinks you're nothing more than a rabid dog. Watch her body burn. Turn her bones to ash.*

"Sol," Kelan gasped. "The manacle."

She threw down her bag and emptied it into the snow. The manacle tumbled out and Kelan reached for it, but his pyra pushed fire into his right hand and yanked it back. He roared and launched himself at the emberstone, gathering it up in his other hand. The moment his fingers brushed the red stone, his pyra disappeared.

He collapsed into the snow, panting, his fingers wrapped tight around the manacle. Too close. He had gotten too close that time. His pyra had gotten his right hand, had forced it to obey the flames instead of him.

"Kelan?" Sol asked, her voice uncertain.

"I'm fine," he said. "I just need a minute."

"Was that your . . . pyra?" she asked. "Was it trying to take control?"

He sighed.

"But you didn't let it," she said.

"No. And I never will. I'm not a demon. I refuse to be."

She knelt next to him and her lips quirked. "Maybe not a demon, but you are a man. So that still makes you something of an animal."

Kelan let out a laugh that felt more like a breathy grimace.

He held the emberstone until the cold pressed in around him and made him shiver in his thin coat. When he let go, his pyra immediately sparked to life again. It was angry, but weak.

Sol walked toward him with two slightly-burned geese in one hand. "Here," she said and tossed one to him. "One for you, and one for me."

"One for you, and one for me," Markus said.

He put a berry in Kelan's hand, and they both popped them into their mouths.

Kelan was eight, and Markus, his cousin, was fourteen. And since the time Kelan had moved into Markus' house, Markus had allowed Kelan tag along with him. Markus' friends had abandoned him last winter, and Kelan had become a sort of accomplice in Markus' schemes. Markus had shown him how to navigate the big city of Duhavn, how to cut the strings of purses, how to throw rocks at the palace guards and make them jump and swear, and where to steal the best sausage.

It was spring now, and the horrors of the winter that had brought Kelan to Duhavn, to the house of his cousin, had been cast far from Kelan's childish mind.

"Thieves!" the shopkeeper shouted.

Markus grinned madly and grabbed Kelan's hand. They scurried out of the way as the shopkeeper threw a brick at them. It cracked against the side of a crate of fruit, and berries rolled into the street to be immediately scooped up by other waiting miscreants or trampled by hooves and boots.

Kelan laughed, breathless as they ran. They slipped into an alley and hid in a doorway. Kelan's heart raced wildly.

More chase! his pyra begged. *More danger!*

The adrenaline was exhilarating. He and Markus were always after the next thrill. Fire glimmered on the tips of Kelan's fingers, but Markus' arms were alight, and fire threatened to singe his sleeves.

"Next time he attacks us, we should burn his fruit stand to the ground," Markus said, his voice deep and dark. Whenever Markus' voice changed like that, it meant that his pyra had taken control.

Kelan shifted away from him. Markus' pyra had come into full strength when Markus was twelve, and it had possessed him at thirteen. When Markus was possessed, he was fun and reckless and unpredictable. They burned things. They got into trouble. Sometimes it was fun, and sometimes it wasn't. And the fire that filled Kelan on these escapades was so intoxicating he had a hard time saying 'no.'

"What do you want to do next?" Kelan asked, grinning.

They both jerked up at the sound of footsteps charging through the alley and peeked out from around the corner.

Peder.

Kelan's pyra shrank as fear seized him, and the flames on his fingers evaporated.

"Come out, demons," Peder spat. He was flanked by seven other boys, all bigger and stronger even than Markus.

Kelan shrank away, but Markus had a terrible, terrible smile on his face. "We have an idea," Markus' pyra said, its voice deep and ugly. "We're going to teach our friends a lesson."

Markus stepped out into the alley and Kelan stood in his shadow. "Hello, Peder," Markus said. "So nice to see you."

Markus and Peder used to be best friends, but that friendship had ended last winter. That was when King Anton had slaughtered his Flameskin wife and daughter. That was when the pyres had been lit, and Kelan's mother had been killed. That was when Uncle Haldur had gone to find Kelan and brought him to Duhavn to live with their family, where he would be safe.

Peder and his friends all carried weapons: rods, kitchen knives, a horse's whip. They hadn't come to play nice. Kelan's heartbeat fluttered in his chest.

Markus' arms flared, and he grinned wickedly.

Peder startled backward and tightened his grip on the wooden club in his hand. "You're demons. Both of you. You're cursed."

Markus growled, a sound like roaring fire, and flames shot out of his arms.

"No, Markus. Don't!" Kelan shouted. Markus shoved Kelan to the ground and left a burning handprint on Kelan's shirt.

Streams of fire flew into the ranks of boys, and they screamed as the flames ate at them. Three boys escaped, but the other five writhed on the ground as the fire consumed their clothes and burned their skin.

Markus' face contorted. "Peder?" he asked, his voice quiet and afraid. Markus shook his head, and then grinned. "Does it hurt, Peder? Does it burn?"

CHAPTER 17
SOL

Sol groaned and squeezed her eyes shut. There was nothing worse than waking up in winter, except waking up in winter on a patch of snow in the middle of the mountains.

When she opened them again, Kelan's turquoise eyes stared back at her. She jerked away, clutching the blankets to her chest.

"Kelan!"

He yawned lazily. "What?"

"Why are you so close to me?"

"You do this every night. You always cuddle up to my warm demon body."

"No, I don't."

He sat up and shrugged. "I haven't moved all night."

The fire had died, but he hadn't bothered to start it again. Sol had watched him light the fire last night. He had used one spark from his finger, then immediately put out his pyra by holding the emberstone manacle. Kelan kept the manacle and its key in his coat pocket now.

What would it be like to know your body would eventually be taken over by a pyra? Would the manacle be enough to stop it?

"Why don't you wear the emberstone all the time?" she asked as she rolled up the furs.

"If I did, I'd freeze to death. I don't have warm clothes like you do. But even if I had proper clothing, it's hard to . . . give up my pyra like that, by choice."

"But won't it eventually take you?"

"Maybe not. I've fought it back this long."

She pressed her lips together. It looked like a losing battle. "But why not use the manacle? It would be easier, wouldn't it? You told me you struggle with it all day."

"Without my pyra I'm cold. And my body is weaker. With a pyra I never get sick. I heal quickly. My muscles are stronger. I have greater stamina."

"But are all those things worth your soul?"

He tied a tight knot on his snowshoe strap and stood. "I thought demons didn't have souls."

"I guess they don't," Sol said. "But you aren't a demon. Not yet."

He stared at her, his brow furrowed. She turned away. It was unnerving when he stared at her like that.

They'd eaten the last of the geese the night before, and now they shared a single strip of venison jerky, their last one.

"If we push hard today," she said, "I think we'll make it to Baarka."

He grinned. "Bless the gods! Food! And a bed. And no more hiking."

She smiled faintly. It seemed too good to be true after so many days in the snow.

"You aren't going to try to turn me in, are you?" he asked.

She should. "No. I won't. I'm not happy about what you did, putting the emberstone on me, but you did save my life."

Letting Kelan go free was a foolish decision she would probably come to regret, but she knew she wouldn't be able to turn him over when the time came. If she gave Kelan to the Tokken Army they'd kill him, and she couldn't stomach that.

"Is that your way of saying 'thank you'?" he asked, his eyebrows rising. "I never thought I'd hear a kind word from your lips."

She scowled at him. "Yeah, well, I'm a huntress. We aren't known for being nice."

She stood and slung her pack over her shoulder. Breaking camp was easy. Roll up the bed and tie on the snowshoes. They had nothing else to pack or eat. "I still think you're dangerous. If I let you go free, how do I know your pyra won't take control and kill people?"

"I won't let it."

"But you're still a soldier."

"I've never killed innocents," he said quietly. "And I never will."

"But you'll still fight in the war, won't you?"

"As long as there are people in the world who want to kill Flameskin children, then I won't stop fighting."

Sol sighed and turned toward the trail. He followed her as they started down the mountain. Pa had taken part in killing the Flameskins in their village, including the children, but Sol hadn't even been able to kill a Flameskin trapped in an avalanche, or hanging on a ledge of ice. Pa had lived what he believed, and he was stronger than she would ever be.

They traveled downhill toward Baarka Valley, and made good time. Once they got close, Sol started scanning the trees for people.

"When we get to the village, it would be better if you hid what you are," she said. "We might have to winter there, and it would be easier if the villagers didn't suspect you were a Flameskin."

"How long will we have to stay in Baarka?"

"At least two moons."

"Ashes and cinders. That's too long. Can't we just continue on?"

"It depends on the conditions. Would you rather get caught in a snow storm or buried in an avalanche?"

He sighed. "And what am I supposed to do in Baarka for two moons?"

"I don't know. I'll offer my services as a huntress, and they'll give us some food, and lodging. Once the snow melts a bit, I'll take you the rest of the way to Cassia, if that's where you want to go. That's where I'm going anyway."

She chewed on her lip. Anywhere Kelan stayed in the village he would draw attention, especially with his red coat. She'd have to get him a new one if they were going to make his disguise convincing.

"Kelan," she said and glanced back at him, "you may have to wear your manacle while you're in Baarka."

"I know," he said and sighed again. "What kind of a demon am I? To wear a collar like a dog and obediently wait for the snow to melt?"

"You're not a demon, not yet. And if you were, things would be different."

They could winter in the hunters' cave above the town, where she and Pa used to stay when passing through. Kelan would be safer there, and farther from the villagers' notice. This late in the season there would be few if any Hunters passing through Baarka, and she and Kelan would be left to themselves for the most part. With some supplies from the villagers, she'd be able to set enough traps to get by and supply them for the long trek to Cassia in the early spring.

Sol smiled. She wouldn't get to celebrate Solstice with her family, but at least she could celebrate it in Baarka. There would be no better way to venerate Pa than by bringing in a Solstice meal, like he always used to.

Her smile faltered. But she'd be spending the Solstice with a Flameskin. Pa would never have approved of that.

"You should hide your red coat in your bag. Will you be warm enough without it?"

He laughed. "Warm? I could walk naked in the snow and still be warm."

Sol exhaled. "I'd appreciate it if you didn't."

"You sure?" he asked, and grinned wickedly. When she replied with a glare, he shrugged off his coat and tucked it into his bag.

Sol's pulse sped as they descended the slope. Food. A warm hearth. Someone to talk to other than Kelan.

They crested the rise and got a full view of the valley, and her heart plummeted.

Baarka was gone. It had been burned to the ground.

CHAPTER 18

KELAN

K elan stared at the burned village, at the fingers of black wood jutting out of the snow.

It would have burned beautifully, his pyra hummed. *One day we'll burn a village like this, leaving nothing but ash.*

Kelan pinched his lips together and shoved its voice away.

He and Sol crunched through the snow, passing into the center of the village. Baarka was silent, deserted. How long ago had this happened? It was at least before the last snowfall. Had his Uncle Haldur done this, or a different troop of Flameskin soldiers? Had the village been evacuated before they burned it?

Sol was breathing hard beside him. "You," she said, and turned on him. "You did this. This is the work of demons."

"I didn't—"

She shrieked and shoved him into the snow. "Fire only burns. It knows no mercy. That thing inside you is made to destroy."

"Sol, I'm sorry. I'm sorry for what other Flameskins did, but I didn't do this."

He made to stand but she cried out and leapt at him, her fists flying. He tried to grab her wrists, but she twisted out of his grasp.

"You murderer!" she screamed. "These were good people and you killed them."

"Sol! Stop!" Her fist cracked against his jaw and he threw up his arms to block her.

Anger welled up and burned hot. *She'll burn just as easily as the rest of them did.*

Kelan roared and grabbed her by the shoulders. He threw her into the snow and crushed her arms beneath him, pinning her there with his weight. Fire twisted into his mind and filled his limbs, making him gasp with the effort of controlling it. She screamed and writhed beneath him, and the snow around them sizzled and melted.

Kill her! his pyra urged.

Kelan grabbed the manacle from his pocket and smashed it onto his wrist. His pyra vanished, as well as the urge to kill Sol.

Feel nothing. He breathed in deep and let out a shaking breath, and Sol finally fell still.

"Are you done hitting me?" Kelan asked.

She nodded.

He eased off her, wary of her fists. She sat up and turned away from him, toward the husks of the village homes.

Kelan rubbed his bruising jaw. "You got me good. Your pa teach you how to throw punches like that?"

She buried her head between her knees and her shoulders shook with silent sobs.

Kelan rested a hand on her arm. "Sol. . . ."

"Don't touch me, Demon," she said, her voice muffled and cracking.

He sighed and shifted away. The cold had started to bite, so he unlocked the manacle and shoved it into his pocket again. He wasn't like the others. How could she lump him in with every Flameskin who had given in to their pyra? It wasn't fair. And it hurt because he kept thinking of Sol as a friend, when he knew she never would be.

He stood and walked through the town. The blackened posts of the buildings looked like grave markers, and they probably were. He stopped at one building and looked inside. The front wall of the home still remained, and Kelan stood in the empty doorway touching the brass button on the chain around his neck.

"Let's check this one," Markus said, grinning. His pyra spoke through his lips, its voice raspy and dark. Markus was pointing at a house on the edge of the village, the one with the light in the window.

"Markus, don't," Kelan said. "There's no need."

But there is a need, Kelan's pyra insisted. *There's always more to burn.*

"These villagers killed children," Markus said. "How can we let such a crime go unpunished?"

"The house is probably empty anyway. Let's go. Everyone evacuated hours ago."

Markus ignored him and stomped toward it, and Kelan didn't stop him. What was the point? That man wasn't Markus anymore; his pyra controlled him completely. There was no reasoning with Markus, there was only more fire, more burning, more chaos. Markus could understand nothing else.

The Flameskin troop had arrived an hour ago and already the whole village burned. Red and orange flames painted the sky with black smoke. Kelan breathed it in, and his pyra swirled inside him, energized by the fire.

Markus jiggled the door handle, but it was locked. He gathered an orb of fire in his palm and let it coil there before thrusting his fist at the door and blasting it from its frame. The door flew inward, and the people inside screamed.

"Markus!" Kelan shouted.

He was at Markus' side with a few strides and grabbed his arm. Markus tried to shrug him off, but Kelan held tight. Markus' pyra had always been more powerful, but Kelan was bigger and taller.

A mountain woman and three children were huddled in the far

corner of the room, and the mother buried her children's weeping faces in her skirts. The door had blasted across the floor and broken their table. Berries rolled across the floor and broken crockery lay strewn among the slivers of wood that had once been their door.

"Please," the mother begged. "Have mercy on my children."

Markus scowled at her. "You had no mercy when you slaughtered the Flameskins in this village."

"Please, I had no part in it."

"Markus," Kelan hissed. "Leave them alone."

"They killed our own," Markus said, his hands glittering with fire. "It's only fair."

"No!" Kelan roared. He grabbed Markus and shoved him out of the house. They fell onto the ground, punching and yanking and rolling, trying to force the other into submission. Markus' body sparked and ignited, and fire poured from his hands and arms. The grass beneath him burned and charred to black, and both their coats caught fire.

"We'll kill them," Markus said. "We'll burn their bones to ash."

"I won't let you touch them," Kelan said, shoving him down and pinning him against the ground.

Markus grinned, his eyes wild, as he lurched and fought in Kelan's grasp, then Markus turned toward the house and fire exploded from his fist. Flames struck the roof, and the thatch caught instantly, igniting the home.

Kelan grabbed Markus' throat. No air, no fire. He squeezed. Markus gasped and pulled at Kelan's hands. The fire on Markus' arms died and went out.

How many times had this happened? How many times had Kelan stood by while Markus murdered innocents in the name of this war?

No more. Markus couldn't be reasoned with, and Markus would never stop. He couldn't.

Kill, kill, kill, Kelan's pyra hissed.

Markus' face turned purple and his struggling slowed.

"You're not Markus anymore," Kelan whispered his throat thick. "You're not even human anymore."

Markus fell still between Kelan's hands.

The house was on fire, but the family had already fled. Kelan dragged Markus' body inside and dropped it onto the floor. Berries squished beneath Kelan's feet. Ashes and sparks flew around the room, and burning thatch fell on Markus' body. Kelan's uniform still smoldered, and Markus' uniform was all but gone. One of Markus' brass buttons lay at the center of his chest, attached to the remains of his uniform by a blackened string. The button had melted and deformed from the heat of Markus' pyra, and Kelan tugged the button loose.

Kelan stood in the doorway of the house, squeezing the brass button in his palm until it hurt.

"Goodbye, Markus," he whispered.

But the body on the floor wasn't Markus; Markus had died eleven years ago, when his pyra had taken possession.

CHAPTER 19

SOL

Sol scooped handfuls of snow away from the hatch and grunted as she lifted it. The waning light of day illuminated her path as she descended into the cellar, but she didn't need much light to see. The cellar had been emptied.

She sagged against the wall and sighed. The villagers had evacuated and taken their food with them. That meant they were alive, somewhere.

But it also meant there would be no food for her and Kelan.

She frowned. Kelan. Sometimes she wanted to hate him so much it hurt. She hated everything he was, and everything he represented. He was the disease Pa had tried so hard to cleanse from the world, in his own way. So why was she keeping him alive?

"Find anything?" Kelan asked. He couched above the cellar door, blocking her light with his broad shoulders. He was wearing his red Flameskin coat again.

"No," she said, her voice terse. "There's a few potatoes and onions, but not much else. They must've taken their food with them when they left."

"You think the village was evacuated before it was burned?"

"Yes."

He exhaled heavily. "Thank the gods."

She scowled at him. What did he care? He was a Flameskin soldier. His occupation was torching villages and burning their occupants.

"Burning your home during winter might as well be a death sentence," Sol said. "They would've had to hike the rest of the way through the pass, with the elderly and children."

"And we're going the rest of the way to Cassia, too?"

Sol climbed out of the cellar and pushed past him, her arms filled with what little food the villagers had left for them. "Yes. And if we're going to survive, we're going to have to hunt. Ashes and cinders. I'd give anything for a bow right now."

"Can't you just make one?" he asked.

"No. I don't have anything for a string, and a bow made of unseasoned wood isn't going to be very good anyway. We'll use your fire to hunt."

"I'd prefer not to. Are there any other cellars we can check?"

Sol shook her head. "The snow's too deep for us to go digging around every house. I knew about this cellar because I've been to this home."

"These were friends of yours?"

"All of the mountain folk are my friends. My pa and I used to hang carcasses in this cellar after we brought them back from our hunts. I've spent several weeks in Baarka, when we hunted these mountains. These were good people. Generous. They would've made sure we ate and were warm this winter, and now they're probably freezing in the snow like we are."

Kelan crossed his arms over his chest. "Stop acting like I'm responsible for this."

Sol marched through the snow toward the cave above the village. "I don't know what you wouldn't do in the name of your war."

"I fight only soldiers."

"Don't try to tell me you haven't burned villages like this. You have, haven't you?"

He didn't answer.

She turned and glared at him. "Stop feeding me this ash

about how you're different from them. You're not, Kelan. You're a demon, and you'll always be a demon."

She trudged forward and blinked away the tears that stung her eyes. These had been friends, and where were they now?

When she couldn't hear Kelan's footsteps behind her, she glanced back. He had stopped in the snow and stood there, a red coat silhouetted by white.

Sol stormed toward the cave and threw her bag onto the ground. How dare he act like he cared. How dare he try to make her feel bad.

Let him sulk. Let him pretend his feelings were hurt. She had told the truth and wouldn't apologize for it.

She should've left him in the snow. She should've been strong like Pa and killed him long ago.

The sun set as Sol rolled out her skins and settled into them. She waited in impatient silence, but Kelan never appeared.

She sat up and listened. Was he getting wood for the fire or what? She tried to gnaw at a potato, but it was frozen solid, so she flung it away from her and crossed her arms.

The cave was dark and silent and still. Where had that blasted demon gone? He had left her to freeze to death. She curled into a ball on the ground. Fine. She didn't need him. She had never needed him. As the night wore on, Sol tried to ignore her grumbling belly and the shivers that ran through her, but sleep eluded her.

There was a scuffling noise outside the cave.

Sol sat up. "Kelan?"

An owl called out into the night, but she could hear nothing else. Her pulse quickened. Where was he? Had he actually left?

She abandoned her bedroll and stepped out of the cave. In the moonlight everything was white, but a single spot of color blotted the snow below her.

She trudged toward Kelan, sinking deep into the snow without her snowshoes. "Kelan?" she asked softly.

He looked up, but his features were indistinct in the dim light. "I'm not a demon."

"Kelan—"

"Call me fool, call me Flameskin, call me anything you like, but never call me Demon."

"Kelan, I meant—"

"I didn't choose this. We don't get to choose our parents, or what we're born to. And every moment is a battle for me. You don't know what it's like to have to resist what you are, to fight every day of your life to keep the fire at bay."

He stood over her, his eyes hard, and angry heat radiated from him. Sol shivered and resisted the urge to lean into him. His shoulders slumped and he pulled her in.

"You're freezing," he whispered.

She was stiff in his arms, but she couldn't pull away. She hated how much she craved the warmth of his body.

"I'm not like the others," he said. "What do I have to do to prove that to you?"

"I don't know."

CHAPTER 20

KELAN

Kelan and Sol crouched in the snow and studied the birds in the tree above them. Kelan held the manacle in one hand but didn't touch the emberstone. He took a deep breath and drew on his pyra.

Burn. We will burn them.

He grit his teeth as he pulled fire into his hand and shot it at the birds. The moment flames burst out of his hand, the flock scattered into the sky. The fireball exploded in the branches, flinging snow all around the tree.

"Cinders," he swore. He hadn't hit a single bird.

His pyra stretched a tentacle of fire through his arm and into his right hand. It pushed fire into his palm, creating another ball of flame

Burn the tree. Watch it turn to ash.

Kelan shoved his burning hand into the snow and snapped the manacle onto his wrist. His pyra immediately disappeared.

It was getting worse. Kelan exhaled slowly. He couldn't use his pyra now without leaving it room to take control. First it would be his arms, then his legs, then his mind, and he'd be lost.

Sol stared at him, tense. "It's trying to take you, isn't it?"

"Yes." He stood and unlocked the manacle once more. His

pyra sparked to life and hissed angrily at him, licking his mind with tongues of flame.

You make yourself weak, Kelan. You waste your time fighting me. I will take control. It won't be long now.

He shuddered.

They tramped through the snow to the tree, but no birds had fallen. "Sorry," Kelan muttered, half to Sol and half to his own grumbling stomach.

"We'll get something."

He sighed. But that meant using his pyra again. He hated using it, and especially in front of Sol. He hated the way she looked at him when his hand sparked, all frightened and judgmental.

"Come on," she said. "The trail is this way."

They had left Baarka far behind, and everything they ate now Kelan hunted, but it was never enough for either of them to get a real meal. Sol set a trap every night, too, but they hadn't caught anything with it. They didn't have time for their dinner to walk into their laps; they needed to keep moving or they'd starve before they got through the pass.

Hunger was a constant companion, more irritating even than Sol. Kelan's body was weakening. His pyra compensated for his lack of energy and the shaking in his limbs, but using its strength only gave it more power over him.

Kelan followed her through the snow, straining his ears for noises. Sol was always better at hearing the birds, though, and she knew most of their calls.

"I could teach you how to use the emberstone," Kelan said. "We'd have more luck if you were doing the hunting."

She glanced at him. "Are you being serious?"

He shrugged. It was worth a shot.

"Does your pyra . . . talk to you in your mind?" she asked. "That's what I've heard said."

"Yes."

"What does it say?"

He couldn't see her face, but he wished he could. Was this

the sort of thing that would make her more afraid of him or would finally help her understand?

"It says things like 'kill the pretty huntress' and 'burn the forest down' and 'I'm hungry.'"

She turned and there was almost a smile on her face. "Really?"

"Maybe not the hungry bit. That might just be my stomach talking."

"You think I'm pretty?" she asked.

Blast. Had he said that?

Kelan looked away. "My pyra has its own opinions. Not all of which I share."

She laughed. "Well, there's not much of me to see anyway, except my nose and my eyes."

He bit his lip. He had seen her legs, and they were very fine legs. And then there were those rare moments when she took off her heavy coats. It wasn't hard to imagine the curves of her body beneath her tunic and leggings.

"Does it truly want to kill me?"

"It's not just you. It wants to kill everyone. It wants to watch the world burn."

"Good to know I'm not special, then."

Kelan sighed. Why couldn't they walk side by side so he could see her face, so he could know if she was teasing him or not? She was so hard to read, and he could never tell if what she said was what she truly believed.

"I'm not dangerous," he said.

"I'll be sure to tell that to your commanding officer when I drop you off."

"Sol—"

"How long do you have? Before your pyra takes you?"

He had asked himself that several times. How many more times could he use fire before he lost control of his other hand, and then his legs? A season? A few weeks?

She stopped and turned toward him.

"Sol, if it comes to that I—"

She shushed him and placed a finger to her lips, staring at the trees to the right of them. Her lips and nose were pink, and her cheeks flushed from the hike. Her eyes were green like the fields during spring and her lashes were long and dark.

"There," she whispered, pointing toward the trees. Birds chirped somewhere in the forest nearby. "Quietly this time, slide in your snowshoes instead of stomping. Can you use your pyra?"

He nodded and followed her through the woods, trying to be as quiet as she was. He watched her with silent awe, and wondered, as he often had the last few days, if she wasn't a dryad. The Ulves were a part of her in a way he couldn't understand, and there was a sort of magic in the way she moved through the forest. The trees above her swayed as she passed between them, and it seemed as though they were trying to reach out and touch her with their long, feathery, pine-needle fingers. The wind blew through their branches and the trees whispered to her, *Sol, Sol, Sol,* and then fell into a reverent hush as they watched her.

She stopped them near a tree and Kelan spotted the birds flitting in the branches above.

"Can you make the explosion bigger?" she asked. "Wider?"

He nodded. Kelan imagined where the birds would fly when they heard his fire and focused on shooting his flames in a wide arc.

Burn! his pyra hissed.

The flames struck the tree, and several birds dropped. The rest swirled into the sky in a chattering flurry as the snow melted off the branches.

Kelan's pyra twisted fire through his hand once more, and gathered weak flames there of its own accord. Kelan snapped the manacle on his wrist and the fire died.

He kicked at the snowdrifts as they walked toward the tree. He didn't have much time at all. With one hand already gone, he'd be surprised if he made it to spring.

Sol grinned as she plucked the charred birds from the snow. One was still alive, and she deftly broke its tiny neck.

"They're small, but it certainly beats eating nothing. Good job, Kelan."

He gave her a half-smile.

She cocked her head. "You aren't happy?"

"I hate using my pyra."

He shivered and unlocked the manacle again. He hated needing his pyra. If he could, he would consider wearing the manacle all the time.

How can you say that? How can you refuse the strength I give you? The warmth? Would you be weak like the rest of them?

"I'm sorry I made you use it," she said.

Kelan looked up and met her eyes. "One day it'll take me. Sometimes I think, what's the point of swimming against the current? I'm so tired of it. I can't do this forever."

"Don't give up." She smiled at him, and his heart squeezed in his chest unexpectedly. "Keep swimming, Kelan."

Kelan stared at the starry night sky. Sol had already snuggled in against him, and her slow breathing reminded him of the whispering of the ocean waves he used to hear at night in Duhavn. He resisted the urge to wrap his arm around her, to pull her in closer.

Something had changed. Had it been as simple as a smile? Or was it just because they had spent so much time together, or because they shared a bed every night? Whatever it was, if she knew what he felt she'd push him away.

She didn't even like to touch him. Even if she didn't call him Demon anymore, there was nothing he could do to change her mind about him. She had said as much. He was a source of warmth, and now food, and nothing more.

Sol didn't even see him as human. He had no hope she could see him as a man.

Take her, then, his pyra hissed. *You are larger, stronger. Why must we submit to her weakness? Why must we allow her to insult us and berate us when we could have what we want?*

Kelan clenched his fists and shoved his pyra away, but he was too tired. The hiking had been uphill all day, and the physical toll of the climb and starvation left him powerless before his pyra's whisperings. He had eaten barely enough to keep his hunger at bay, and now after lying awake in bed for an hour, his hunger had returned, gnawing at him, curling and twisting in his stomach, and his pyra gnawed at his mind.

Why not take her as prisoner? You can force her to please us. It is only what is right after all she has made us suffer.

Kelan rolled over and sat up, breathing hard. His pyra had taken whatever he felt for Sol and twisted it into something dark. Something evil. It made him want what was not his and flooded his body with fire.

I could give you everything you want, Kelan, it whispered.

He scrambled to his feet and trudged into the woods, away from Sol. If only he could walk away from his pyra, too, or rip it from his mind and bury it in the snow. He sat on a fallen log and dropped his head into his hands.

She hates us, Kelan. Burn her. Destroy her.

He grabbed the emberstone manacle from his pocket, but his pyra snaked its fire through his arm and into his hand. His hand spasmed, and he dropped the shackle in the snowdrift. Fear gripped Kelan, forcing his pyra back as he dropped to his knees and scrambled in the snow, frantically searching for the fallen manacle. A faint red glow emanated from beneath a layer of snow, and he dug out the emberstone and clipped it over his wrist.

He sank into the snow, letting the cold seep into his bones as his mind and body emptied of his pyra's presence. He reveled in the stillness of his mind, the peace. Without his pyra, his body trembled from exhaustion and hunger and cold, but for a moment he could look up into the stars and just be Kelan. Be human. Would Sol accept him if he wore his manacle all the time? Was he even strong enough to live without his pyra?

He unlocked the manacle and slipped it into his pocket. Warmth spread through his body again as he trudged back toward camp.

Sol sat up on their furs, staring at the sky. He entered the clearing, and she turned toward him.

"You're awake?" he asked.

"Were you trying to run away?"

"I was . . . getting some air."

"You probably got lost and realized you couldn't find your way without me."

"Probably," he said.

He brushed the snow off his clothes and sat next to her. She scooted in close and rested her head on his shoulder, shivering.

"Sorry I woke you," he said.

"You didn't. I got cold."

Kelan let out a quick breath and rubbed his hand through his hair, his heart catching in his throat, then he slid his arm around her shoulder. She settled in against him and his heart raced.

"You were gone for a long time. I thought you had left."

"Where would I go? Like you said, I'd be lost without you."

Her lips twitched into a smile. "That's right."

They should go to bed, but he didn't want to have to let go yet. "Have you ever seen a dryad?" It was one of the many things he'd been thinking about all day.

He couldn't see her face since she was nestled in against his chest, and her voice was guarded. "Why do you ask?"

"Everyone grows up hearing stories about the Ulves and the creatures that live there. I hadn't thought they were true, but then we heard the ice wolves. . . ."

"All the stories about the Ulves have at least a grain of truth."

She was quiet for a moment, and he thought that was all she would tell him, but then she spoke again. "There's a meadow near one of the peaks south of here. My pa took me once when I was a girl, during the summer. There's a lake there that's the same color as the sky and the greenest grass I've ever seen. And in the middle of the meadow there's this beautiful oak tree.

Oaks don't grow that high up in the mountains, but this one does.

"I've never seen another tree like it. There's something . . . alive about it. I don't know how to describe it. It has roots and it can't move, but somehow it seemed like it was dancing through the grass when the wind blew. And I thought I saw a woman's face among the leaves."

"I'd like to see that one day."

"Dryads steal men's hearts. I'd stay away, if I were you."

She lay down and he kept his arm wrapped around her as he lay down beside her. He pulled her in close so their faces were just a breath away as he covered their bodies with the furs.

She went rigid in his arms. "Kelan."

He cleared his throat and slid his arm back to his side. Who had he been fooling? He was warmth to her, and nothing more.

CHAPTER 21

SOL

Solstice. Sol stared up at the sun hiding behind a bank of clouds. Tonight would be the longest night of the year, and the first time she had spent the holiday without her family. Without Pa.

She was nineteen today. There would've been rich venison stew, and Solstice buns, and laughter, and warmth. Pa would've brought in something big, like he always managed to do at Solstice.

The bow he had made her for her last birthday was gone, buried by the avalanche. Now she had nothing to remember him by but the paths he had taught her through the mountains and the emberstone he had made her promise not to touch.

"The first thing I'm going to eat when we get to Cassia is a big watermelon," Kelan said.

He huffed behind her as they hiked. They were both getting weaker. Little birds and a potato weren't enough for them to hike all day. At least today would be a short day, with little daylight, and she would be warm tonight, lying next to him.

"A watermelon? You do realize it's the middle of winter, right? Me, I want a turkey leg. A big juicy one." She looked behind her, hoping to see Kelan smile. He did, and she smiled back.

"Turkey leg. That does sound nice."

Sol forced herself to face forward again. Why did she keep looking at him? Why did she keep wanting to make him laugh?

The crested the top of a rise, and she stopped them at the top.

Beside her, Kelan's shoulders slumped. "The mountains go on forever."

"Not forever. I think it's mostly downhill from here. We've got only a few days left until we get to Cassia."

She sat in the snow and looked down the mountain. Her calf still ached a bit, but more worrisome was the lightness in her head and the way her legs shook and trembled with each step.

Just a few more days. They would make it. And tonight, they'd have something to eat at least. She had set a trap last night and they had woken to find a Solstice gift from the gods: a rabbit. With daylight so short they didn't have time to cook it in the morning, but they would have a kind of Solstice feast tonight.

Sol glanced at the sun again, hanging above the peaks on the west. "We've got about an hour of daylight left. We'll hike a bit more and find a good campsite."

Kelan groaned as he stood. His handsome face was now covered by a short, scraggily beard, and his black, curly hair was ratted into messy tangles. He looked haggard, all the humor and the energy gone from his face.

"You all right?"

He nodded and gave her a half-smile. "Come on. Let's keep going."

He offered her a hand up, and she took it.

Sol lifted the spitted rabbit from the fire and Kelan cut it in half with her knife, right through the middle. He always split everything in half, even though Kelan was bigger than she was, and probably hungrier, too. She wouldn't have complained if he'd taken a slightly larger portion, but he never had. He'd never even asked.

She took off her gloves and lifted her portion of steaming rabbit with her fingers. Her mouth watered as she took a grateful bite, and she savored the taste of it in her mouth before chewing. She had tried to leave as much skin as possible so there would be some fat to the animal, and this was the best they'd eaten in days.

"It's Solstice," she said.

Kelan looked up. "Today? Why didn't you tell me?"

She shrugged. Why hadn't she told him? Because it was painful to think she shared this night with a Flameskin, who Pa hated, and painful to think of being without her family.

"It's your birthday. Blessings to you, Sol. I wish you'd told me earlier. I would've gotten you a turkey leg as a present."

She blushed and took a bite of rabbit. This was why she hadn't said anything, because now he was going to make her feel awkward.

Kelan stuck his bare hand in the drift beside him and grabbed a handful of snow. "We're so lucky to get to spend the holiday this way. Look at these delicious Solstice buns." He sprinkled some snow on their portions of rabbit. "We forgot the icing," he said, and grinned.

She laughed, and it was a real laugh, the way she would've laughed with her family.

"How old are you now?"

"Nineteen." She flicked her gaze toward him. "And you?"

"You're an old maid, Sol. I won't be nineteen until the summer."

She rolled her eyes at him as she cleaned the bones with her teeth. When she finished, Kelan stood and held out a hand toward her.

"Dance with me."

"What?"

"Mountain folk don't dance on Solstice? We used to gather in the square in the city to dance, and everyone came to drink cider and eat Solstice buns."

"We dance," she said hesitantly.

"Please? This can't be my first Solstice without dancing."

"And your first Solstice without a Solstice kiss, no doubt."

He grinned. "No doubt."

She took his hand, and his skin was warm and tingly, as if there were sparks popping in his blood. Did he always feel like this? She couldn't remember touching his skin before. Her cheeks flushed as he lifted her and wrapped his arms around her.

"Your skin is . . . prickly." Touching Kelan was like touching an emberstone.

He frowned and looked away, as he turned them slowly in the trampled snow beside their campsite. "Is there anything you don't hate about me?" he asked after a moment.

"No, I don't hate it. I was surprised is all. I've never touched you before."

"You don't hate touching me?"

"No. I don't." Touching him made her feel warm, and her pulse quicken, and her stomach flutter.

Kelan smiled. "I wouldn't have chosen to spend the Solstice in the mountains, but I'm glad you're here with me. I wouldn't trade this moment for anything."

He met her eyes, and her breath caught in her throat. She felt so close to him now, dancing like this. Closer than they had ever been lying together at night, which didn't make any sense. But there was something about looking into his eyes that made everything seem different. He wasn't just a Flameskin whose body warmed her, he was Kelan.

She cleared her throat, but she couldn't think of anything to say. Being with Kelan wasn't like spending time with her family, but in a way, she was glad she wasn't home, so she didn't have to relive those memories.

And Kelan was . . . kind, and he made her laugh. She didn't know anyone who could have endured this kind of hardship and still found a way to joke about it. And he was handsome, as much as she didn't want to admit it. She liked the amused turquoise of his eyes, and his tall, broad frame, and the strong hands he had wrapped around her.

But every time she looked at him there was that gnawing guilt, the thought that she had betrayed Pa's memory by befriending a Flameskin.

But how could she think about Pa when Kelan was holding her like this, when they were dancing together? She had never felt so warm before. Every time Kelan looked at her, her cheeks flushed, and his skin made her fingers tingle where she held his hand. He started humming, low in his throat, the Song of Solstice.

It was a year ago, Solstice Eve. Sol sat beside Pa, scanning the snow for movement. They had been there for hours, and Sol was cramped and cold, but beneath the cold ran that warm undercurrent of energy from the hunt, and the anticipation of Solstice. Sol glanced sidelong at Pa. She had seen the bow he had been making for her, and it was beautiful. It was impossible to keep secrets from her now that she knew all his hiding places, but she would pretend to be surprised when he gave it to her in the morning.

Pa hummed the Song of Solstice and slapped his gloved hand on his knee. "Well, I guess the gods didn't bless us with a Solstice feast tomorrow. I'll go check the traps to see if we've got anything. We'll head in when I get back."

Sol nodded and settled into her perch. Pa tromped off into the woods, leaving her alone in the stand of trees. Sol kept her eyes fixed on the stream nearby. They never celebrated the Solstice without a big catch. Something would come, and when she took it down, Pa would be so proud.

There was a noise behind her, and she turned. Josef slid toward her in the snow and scowled when she spotted him. He held his longbow in one hand, and an enormous quiver was strung across his back.

"You're impossible to sneak up on, Sol."

She shrugged.

Josef sat next to her and surveyed the forest. "You two catch anything?"

"Not yet. My pa's checking the traps. There'll be something."

Josef grinned. "I caught a big stag a few days ago. I'll share some, if you like. I wouldn't want your family to go hungry."

Sol bit back a scowl. Josef was aiming to be Hillerod's hunter, but he didn't have a chance. Sol had Pa to teach her the trails and the ways of the hunter, and Josef had never had the patience the position required.

Something moved in the forest ahead of them. Josef had an arrow notched and the string pulled back before Sol had even looked up.

"Stop!" she shouted.

Josef loosed the arrow, and his target crumpled to the ground.

"Pa!"

Sol ran through the snow. Pa lay on his back in the drift, an arrow protruding from the right side of his chest. His body hitched and fell in painful bursts as he tried to breathe, and his clothes and furs were red with blood. He coughed blood onto the white snow around him. Sol dropped to her knees beside him, her whole body trembling.

"Oh, gods above," Josef said behind her. "What have I done?"

"Get help," she growled, and Josef took off toward the village.

Sol's hands shook, and her mind froze. Her breath was as flighty as Pa's.

"Pa," she moaned.

He gripped her hand. "Sol," he said, his voice gurgling. Every breath was a struggle. He was drowning.

Sol pressed her hands to her mouth and tears ran down her

cheeks. What could she do? She wasn't thinking straight. Her mind was as numb as her fingers.

The emberstone. The emberstone could heal him.

Josef reappeared, out of breath and with tears streaking his cheeks. "Hunter," he said, "help is coming."

"Wait here," Sol snapped.

She ran toward their house at the edge of the town and stormed inside, banging open the door. She dragged the heavy chest across the kitchen, knocking off the oakwood bowl and scattering beans on the floor. She climbed on top and reached for the emberstone hidden atop the central roof timber.

Ma made an annoyed sound. "Sol, what—"

"Pa's hurt!"

Her fingers found the emberstone and her skin tingled as she touched it. She jumped off the chest and tore out of the house with the emberstone in her hand. Ma ran after her, not even bothering to put on her coat.

Josef's father knelt next to Pa and had turned him onto his side. The arrow had gone clean through his chest and its tip stuck out his back.

"Elo!" Ma wailed his name. She collapsed beside Pa and cradled his head in his hands. "Elo, Elo."

"Josef," his father said, "run and get bandages."

Josef's father put a hand on Sol's shoulder. "Keep him on his side. I'm going to get the matron. When Josef and I get back, we'll carry him to your house."

Sol gave Josef a hateful glare. It was his blasted fault Pa was hurt.

Josef and his father ran toward the village, and Sol knelt beside Pa again. She put the emberstone in his hand.

"It can heal you. I know you know how to do it," Sol said.

She had heard the stories about the miraculous healings mages could do with the help of an emberstone. Pa's emberstone was small, the size of a small pebble, but it must have enough fire to do something.

Pa dropped the emberstone into the snow. His breath hissed in and out of his mouth. "No, Sol."

"Pa! Please! You'll die."

She picked up the glowing stone again, but Pa shoved her hand away. "If I die, then I die pure. Not tainted by fire."

Ma swept hair away from Pa's face. "Don't leave us. You can't leave us."

He pressed his hand to the front of her dress above her heart. "It was always here." He coughed blood into the snow. "All those years searching, and I never realized my heart was here with you, and the girls."

Ma wept and pressed his hand to her face. His hand was bloody and had left a red handprint on the front of her dress above her heart.

A sob rocked Sol's body.

Kelan's humming stopped abruptly. "What's wrong?"

She buried her face in his red coat, cursing herself for the tears. She had promised herself she was done crying, and she hated crying in front of Kelan.

"Have I offended you?" he asked quietly.

She squeezed him hard as the sobs shook her shoulders. Why? Why did Pa have to die? Why did the gods take him on Solstice, of all days? Why did she let this demon touch her? Why couldn't she be strong like Pa had been?

"Sol," Kelan murmured. "I'm sorry, whatever I've done."

She stepped away from him, her face streaked with tears. "It's what you are," she shouted, her voice cracking. "A demon."

She clamped a hand to her mouth. He stiffened and she turned away. She hated him, and she hated hurting him. But that was all she ever did, take out her anger and her fear and her loneliness and her grief on him. And she hated admitting to herself that he didn't deserve it.

But he was a Flameskin. Of course he deserved it.

How could she celebrate Pa's memory like this? Dancing with a Flameskin? It was wrong.

Sol wiped her wet face with the sleeve of her fur coat. "My pa died last year on Solstice."

"Sol, I'm sorry." He stepped closer, hesitantly, until his heat warmed her body. "Can I do anything for you?" he asked, so softly she was forced to look up and meet his eyes.

Her heart roiled within her, every emotion all tangled up and raw.

He took her hand and her bare fingers tingled at his touch. "Your pa would've been proud, you know, that you've kept us alive in the Ulves. You're a true huntress."

She blinked rapidly, fighting back the tears. Then she looped one arm around Kelan's neck and pulled him in, meeting his lips with hers. His lips were hot, and kissing him was like tasting the first scents of spring after a long winter, it was the heady exhilaration of the hunt. He held her close, wrapping his arms around her waist, and the warmth of his body enveloped her. She pressed herself against him, hating how much she wanted his warmth, how much she wanted him.

His kiss was scorching, pulsing heat through her in a quickening rhythm that matched the beat of his heart. He cupped her cheek, then trailed his burning fingers down her neck. Everywhere his hand touched her skin, it burned in a way that was intoxicating and horrifying.

What was she doing?

She broke away and shoved him hard in the chest. He staggered back, his lips still parted. They were both breathing hard and staring at each other with wild, surprised eyes.

"I hate you, Kelan," she growled

"Then what was that?"

"A mistake."

His hands fell limp at his side. She stomped toward the bedroll and pulled the blanket of skins over her head, blocking out the dim firelight, and the night sky, and Kelan.

She closed her eyes and tried to slow her breathing. Why had she done that? And why had it ached so much to pull away from him?

He lay down next to her, and she stiffened, but he didn't try to touch her. He didn't say anything. She curled up into a ball and set her jaw.

"Good night, Sol," he said softly.

She squeezed her eyes shut. Kelan was a demon, and that's all he would ever be.

CHAPTER 22
KELAN

F eel nothing. Feel nothing.

Kelan repeated this mantra as they hiked, but every time he looked at Sol, his heart hitched, and his pyra bloomed hot in his chest.

The kiss hung over them, and the air tasted like its memory. It was all he could think about when he looked at her, the way her lips had brushed his, hesitant at first, then how she had pressed up against him and wrapped her fingers in his hair. He had pushed his hands beneath her coat and finally traced the curve of her waist he had so longed to touch. All he could think about was the moment the kiss had changed, how it had grown earnest and hungry and full of fire.

Why did she reel him in only to shove him away? It was maddening. She'd been angry all morning, stuffing her bedroll into her bag and stomping through the snow ahead of him. Her usual nagging, "watch out for that cliff. I don't want to have to rescue you again," was more insistent than usual. She ignored most things he said to her.

They had both taken off their snowshoes to hike carefully down a steep, icy slope. Kelan crunched through the snow, stepping in the path Sol made. He was weak and hungry and tired and angry. She couldn't treat him like this, like he was less than human, like he was just something she could toy with. Kiss one moment and curse at the next.

He exhaled slowly. Anger would only feed his pyra.

Feel nothing. Feel nothing.

Kill her. Be rid of her, his pyra hissed, growing hotter with the frustration it consumed.

Kelan shoved his pyra away, but its voice was as insistent as Sol's.

"Icy patch here," she said. "If you slip and break your leg, I'm not carrying you the rest of the way to Cassia."

Kelan gritted his teeth and stomped hard in the snow, crushing it beneath his worn boots. He had no idea he could hate someone so much.

"Sol, why did you—"

"More ice," she said, and crouched low as she moved, using her hands as supports.

"Stop ignoring me."

"I'm not."

"You can't kiss me and then tell me you hate me. It's one or the other."

"Fine. I hate you."

He stopped and stood still, trying to slow his breathing.

Feel nothing. Feel. Nothing.

Ashes! Heat rose to his head, and his pyra pushed angry fire through his arms and slipped trickling fingers of flame into his mind.

We'll watch her body burn. We'll make her suffer for what she's done to us.

Kelan's voice was low, and his breath caught in his chest as he tried to contain his anger. "Hate me, then. Because I hate you. You've never given me a chance to be anything but a demon. You see someone and you think you know them, but you don't know me at all, Sol. And I'd never—"

She yelped as her feet slid out from under her, and she tumbled down the slope. She rolled and twisted, throwing out her arms and legs trying to catch herself.

"Sol!" His heart squeezed in his chest as he watched her fall, and he tromped across the ice toward her. He slid and caught himself a few times as he raced down the slope.

When she hit the bottom of the hill, she finally stopped rolling. Her body lay still. Kelan's heart lodged in his throat as he scrambled toward her.

"Sol!"

She didn't answer. She didn't move.

"Sol, are you all right?" he asked, kneeling over her.

She groaned and rolled over. Her cheek was bloody where the ice had rubbed it raw.

"Can you sit up?" he asked and grabbed the gloved hand she offered.

"Ow," she whimpered.

"What hurts?"

"Everything. I don't know."

"Is anything broken?"

She bit her lip and rubbed her calf. "I don't think so."

Kelan found her hat in the snow and brought it to her. She gingerly pulled it over her hair and wiped her eyes with her sleeve.

"I'm just so tired, Kelan. I can't do this anymore."

"You can. We're almost there."

She looked up and met his eyes.

"We have to keep going," he said. "And when we get to Olisipo I'll buy you a big turkey leg."

She tried to laugh, but winced, instead.

"Do you want the emberstone?" he asked.

"No," she snapped.

Kelan sat back and sighed. Prickly Sol had returned already. That hadn't lasted long.

"I'm sorry about . . . what I said," she whispered.

Kelan sighed again. "Does your cheek hurt?"

She touched her cheek and stared at the blood on her fingers. "A little."

"You did tell me you were going to find the fastest way down the hill, but I hadn't imagined it'd be quite like this."

"Me neither."

He took the bag off her shoulder and pulled out the snow-shoes she had stowed inside. "Can you keep walking? I'll help you put these on."

She cautiously stretched out her legs and he fastened the snowshoes to her boots and his. He made to stand, but she snagged his hand with her gloved one.

"Wait, Kelan."

He turned toward her, pressing his lips into a hard line. At this point he wasn't sure whether to expect a kiss or an insult.

"I don't hate you."

"Lucky me."

She scowled. "I don't know how I'm supposed to feel about you. I know I should hate you, but . . . ." She met his eyes, then looked away and shrugged.

"You realized I'm human and it conflicts with your world view? Sorry to ruin your opinion of Flameskins, but it turns out not all of us are worthy of death in our infancy."

"Stop it, Kelan. I said I was sorry."

"Well, you've told me you hate me enough times that I've started to believe you."

Her face fell. "But I don't. I don't hate you."

He stood. "I don't know what to believe anymore."

He held out a hand to help her up, but she glared at him and pushed herself up without accepting it. She limped forward, muttering under her breath, and he watched her, searching for signs of injury, but her gait smoothed out after a few paces.

They hiked for a long time in silence, long enough for Kelan's anger to pass. Sure, Sol was as fickle as a spring storm, but maybe it was understandable. They had both been pushed to their physical limits, and a few weeks ago, they had stood on the opposite lines of a battle.

But it hurt because Kelan could never be sure if she did hate him, or if that kiss had meant something to her like it did to him. When they got to Cassia would she be glad to be rid of him?

If he weren't so hungry, and if the traveling wasn't so hard, he might've wished they could spend the whole winter together, just to see where things could've gone. Once they parted, would they ever see each other again?

"Sol, do you think—"

She held up a hand.

"Stop ignoring me," he said, his voice rising.

"Quiet," she whispered, stopping in her tracks. "I hear something."

He strained his ears. They hadn't heard any birds today, and the snare had been empty this morning. There'd be nothing to eat tonight if they didn't catch something, but he wasn't looking forward to using his pyra to hunt.

There was rustling in the woods, and figures stepped out from behind the trees. Kelan gaped at them. People. Other human beings. It'd been three weeks since they'd seen another soul in these mountains.

Sol stepped back and took his hand. "Bandits," she hissed.

Kelan tensed. It was a group of five men, all armed with swords, and two held bows at their sides. They were Cassian, with light-colored hair poking out from beneath their fur hats.

One of the bandits stepped forward. "You two traveling from Baarka?" He spoke Nordese with a thick Cassian accent.

"Baarka's gone," Sol said. "Burned to the ground."

The bandit swore. "What you got in your bags? Let me see."

Kelan stood straight and squared his shoulders. "I'm a Flameskin soldier. Leave us alone."

The bandit spat on the ground. "Where's your sword then? You ain't a Flameskin. That's some ratty stolen uniform."

The bandit lifted his sword as he advanced. "And if you are a demon, then it's my duty to kill you before you get to Cassia."

"Please," Sol said, her voice faltering. "We're just passing through. We have no food. We have nothing worth taking."

"That's not true," the bandit said and grinned. "A woman always has something worth taking."

The other men laughed, and Sol pressed herself into Kelan's side, breathing fast. Kelan's pyra bloomed hot in his blood, and heat surged through him.

Kelan pushed Sol aside. "Stand back."

She fell into the snow behind him, her eyes wide. The air around him wavered with heat, and fire sparked and flared on his fingertips. The snow around him melted and gathered in a puddle beneath his feet.

Kill them. Consume them with our fire.

Tentacles of flame pushed at Kelan's mind, and a pulse of fear made the fire on his hands falter.

"Kelan?"

The archers lifted their bows. "Kill the demon," the bandit said. "We'll take the girl."

CHAPTER 23
SOL

"No!" Kelan roared, his voice twining with the crackle of the fire inside him. He sounded otherworldly. Demonic.

Sol scrambled away from him through the snow. The air around him sparked, and fire wound around his hands and burned the sleeves of his coat. The archers drew their bows, but two bursts of fire flew from Kelan's hands and exploded into their chests, dropping them to the ground.

The three other bandits charged them. The Cassians swung at Kelan with their swords, but he forced their retreat with walls of fire that poured from his hands.

One bandit broke away and ran after Sol. She fled in the other direction, but he grabbed her pack and swung her backward. She screamed as he shoved her into the snow, raising his sword over her.

"You're not going anywhere, girlie."

She yanked her knife from her belt and shoved it into him, cutting through his thick coat and stabbing him in the gut. He swore and kicked her in the ribs. She lost her hold on the knife and it got caught in his coat. He ripped the dagger away and tossed it into the snow.

A burst of flame exploded into his back, and he yelped and dropped on top of Sol. The man's coat had caught fire and Sol wriggled beneath him, trying to push him off, but she was buried deep in the snowdrift.

Two burning hands grabbed the man and yanked him upright. The bandit screamed as the flames ate at his clothes and caught his yellow braids on fire. The air tasted of sulfur and death.

"She belongs to us," Kelan growled. But the voice wasn't Kelan's. It was a dark, hissing voice, a voice that made Sol's insides recoil and a shiver run down her spine.

The bandit twisted in Kelan's grasp and slashed upward with his sword, cutting through Kelan's dirty red coat and slicing through the skin of his abdomen. Kelan roared and blasted the man backward with an arc of fire that struck his face and chest. The bandit fell into the snow and lay still.

Kelan turned toward her, and the twisted grin on his face disappeared. The fire on his hands sank beneath his skin. His coat and tunic were cut wide open, and blood ran in steaming rivulets down his body.

"Sol," he whispered.

He sank to one knee, then dropped into the melting snow beside the dead Cassian.

"Kelan!"

She tried to run to him, but the air around Kelan seared like the heat of a roaring bonfire. His face was pale, and his eyes were closed. Each breath looked like a labored agony. When he coughed, blood speckled the snow.

"No!" Sol screamed. "Kelan!"

It was happening again. Kelan was going to die just like Pa. Sol's panicked breath caught in her throat.

She yanked Pa's emberstone out of the lining of her pocket and grasped it in her fist. Touching it made her immune to the searing air around Kelan. She dropped onto the wet earth beside him and ripped open Kelan's tunic. Too much blood. The bandit had sliced him across his abdomen, and the blade had sunk deep into the flesh beneath his ribs.

Sol gripped her emberstone in her left hand and tried to calm her choking breaths. She imagined fire running from the stone, through her arm, and into her other hand. She had never done this before, but she had to try. She couldn't let Kelan die. Not like this.

She pressed her burning hand against Kelan's wound and winced, expecting him to scream or cry out, but he barely stirred. Heat pulsed beneath her hand, and his skin tingled. When she lifted her hand, the edge of his cut had sealed together where the flames had touched it.

It worked similar to stitching a wound then, by closing the skin together. Her heart beat faster. She could do this. He wouldn't bleed out here. Kelan would live.

She pressed the skin of his wound together with one hand, covering herself in his blood, and with her other hand she slowly stroked the wound, coaxing fire into his skin to seal it together. When she finished, she splashed melted snow over Kelan's chest, washing away the blood and checking to make sure he wasn't bleeding anywhere else. His ragged breathing had slowed to a regular hush.

She pressed a hand to his cheek. "Kelan," she whispered, her voice shaking. "Live, Kelan."

He would live, wouldn't he? But when he woke would he still be Kelan, or had his pyra taken full possession? When he had spoken, it hadn't been his voice.

She pressed her fists to her chest. He had lost himself to save her, and he had done it believing she hated him.

But she didn't hate him. And now it was too late to tell him.

The bandits.

She jerked upright and quickly scanned the clearing. The air stung her eyes and tasted of fire. There were five bodies lying in the snow, all of them blackened, and the snow around them melted. Kelan had killed them, burned them to death with his fire. She shuddered, trying not to breathe in the scent of ashes and death.

She gazed at Kelan again. When he woke, if it was only the

pyra left inside him, would he try to kill her, too? If it came to that, would she be able to kill the demon wearing Kelan's face?

She stuffed the emberstone into her pocket, shivering as the cold hit her again. Every time she touched the emberstone she was reminded of the power, of the warmth that would be hers if she kept it on her always, but she had already used too much of it. She had tainted herself with it to save a Flameskin.

She unrolled the skins they used for their bed and laid them out on the ground. There might be more bandits, and neither of them were in a state to fend them off. They needed to hide and lie low while Kelan healed. He had said Flameskins healed quickly, and she hoped that was true. Until he could walk again, they'd be stuck there without food.

With some effort, she pulled Kelan's unconscious form onto the furs and dragged him behind her through the snow. It was hard going, and Kelan was heavy, but at least the path was smooth, an untouched blanket of icy, white snow. She dragged Kelan until she thought her legs and arms would give out, then she left him on an overhang above a small gulch. They were far enough from the road that no one would see them, but the tracks were visible. She covered Kelan with skins and listened to his quiet breathing for a moment before heading out again.

She tromped to the road and searched for her dagger. It was nowhere to be found, so she took one of the men's swords. Both bows had been destroyed in the fire, and the bandits had nothing else salvageable on them. Kelan, or his pyra, had been thorough. Her stomach roiled as she looked at the bodies. How did she keep forgetting that Kelan was a trained soldier? That with a single blast of flame he could kill?

She would have to return later to bury the bodies under the snow. She didn't want to draw attention from any travelers that might be in the pass.

She found the bandits' camp and was elated to find their food. Sol laughed as she dug into their packs and pulled out dried meat, bread, raisins, and a wedge of cheese. It was a feast. She stuffed food into her mouth until she thought she would be sick, then she gathered up the remains into her bag to carry back to their own camp. She'd need to return to bury the bandits' campsite, too, but she didn't want to leave Kelan alone for so long. She needed to be there when he woke, to know if he woke as Kelan or as a demon.

She followed the tracks to Kelan, and doubled back twice, making two false trails in the snow. He was still sleeping when she got there. The light was getting dim. She could light a fire, but the smoke would draw attention, and she'd be warm enough lying next to Kelan. Her stomach ached with the richness of the meat and the cheese, and she didn't dare eat any more, even though her body ached for more food. In the morning she'd eat more, and hopefully Kelan would wake and eat, too.

And hopefully, she wouldn't have to kill him.

CHAPTER 24
KELAN

K elan opened his bleary eyes to the blinding whiteness of snow. He groaned and tried to roll over, but his body ached, and his stomach twisted with pain when he tried to move.

The Cassians.

Kelan jerked upright and gasped as the sudden movement stabbed his ribs. What had happened? Where was Sol?

His pyra thrummed in his blood, but its attention was centered at his ribs, focused on numbing the pain and too spent to bother him.

He turned and found Sol sitting behind him with her back against the stone cliff and a sword in her hand. She woke from her doze and met his eyes.

She gasped and staggered to her feet, lifting her sword. "Kelan?"

He tried to speak but coughed instead, and his spit was mingled with blood and tasted of metal.

"Are you Kelan or the demon?" she asked, her voice trembling.

"It's me," he said, his voice weak. He dropped onto his back again and groaned.

She threw the sword into the snow and knelt beside him. She

touched his cheek with her gloved hand. "I thought you were gone forever."

"I tried to keep it away," he rasped, "but when I knew they wanted to hurt you . . . ."

She took off her glove and grabbed his hand. Her fingers were icy. "How are you feeling?"

"Not good. What happened?" He remembered losing control, he remembered the fire behind his eyes and his pyra roaring out of his throat, but not much after that.

"You killed the bandits, but one of them cut you pretty bad. I think he got your lung."

Kelan threw aside the blankets covering his body and pulled open his coat. A cut ran across his abdomen and his ribs on the right side, but it had scabbed over already. "How long ago was this?"

"A day."

He looked up at her. "You did this. You healed it?"

She pressed her lips together and nodded.

She had used fire to save him. She wouldn't do it to save her own life, but she had done it for him. "Thank you."

"Can you eat something? There's food. Lots of it. Eat as much as you can."

Kelan gratefully accepted the cheese and dried fruit she pressed into his hands.

"It's the bandits' provisions. The bread is only a few days old, and they had just enough food for a couple days each, so I'm thinking we must not be far from the city. One or two days at most."

He nodded as he chewed, and his body let out a grateful sigh. He had missed food. Real food. Not half-charred mouthfuls of strange birds and the lean meat of a starved rabbit.

She watched him intently as he ate, until it made him feel uncomfortable. "What?"

"I thought your pyra had taken you," she said softly. "I wasn't sure who you would be when you woke up."

"It's me," he said, and took her hand. "I promise you it's me. I won't let my pyra take me again."

She let out a pained sigh. "I was so worried about you."

"I bet. Who would you have to boss around if I were gone?"

She frowned at him and he grinned.

"It isn't funny."

"Come here," he said, drawing her toward him.

She lay down next to him and rested her head on his left shoulder. They were close enough that if she leaned forward they would kiss.

Not that he held out any hope she would. She had seen what he was now, the power that he fought against.

"You saved my life," he whispered.

"Kelan, I was so scared. I thought the bandits were going to take me and—"

"I wouldn't have let them."

"And then your voice changed, and I thought you were gone, and you were bleeding, and coughing up blood. I thought when you woke up you might try to kill me, too. That it might be your pyra instead of you."

He rubbed her cheek with his thumb. She was right to think that. How many more times would he be able to lose control like that before it took him permanently? If his pyra weren't so busy healing his broken body it might try to take control even now.

"Is the manacle still in my coat pocket? Can you get it for me?"

She sat up and cocked her head, asking a question with her eyes.

"You're right," he said. "I don't have much time left before it takes me. I think . . . I think I should always wear an emberstone."

Her face lifted, and she smiled as she took the manacle from his pocket. He strapped it onto his wrist and his pyra immediately vanished, and throbbing, pulsing, burning pain ripped through his insides. He groaned and twisted, gasping as the full agony of his wound took him.

"Kelan!" Sol said, her voice frantic. "Where's the key?"

She reached into his pocket as he writhed and searched for the key. When she found it, she unlocked the manacle with shaking fingers and dropped it into her lap. His pyra sparked to life once more, and slowly, the pain diminished and his breathing felt less like gasping.

He sank into the furs, exhausted and sick and aching. "I'm sorry, Sol."

She shushed him and lay down again at his side. "Rest, Kelan. That's the only thing you need to do."

"Once I'm healed, I'm going to wear the manacle always and never take it off. I promise you that, Sol."

She pushed herself up onto her elbows and met his gaze. "For now all I want you to do is just to be alive."

CHAPTER 25

SOL

Sol bent over her last snare and sighed. Nothing.

It was a long trek back, and she trudged toward camp with shoulders slumped. When she passed into view of the camp and Kelan saw her, he smiled. He was sitting up now without too much pain, and healing remarkably fast. But even at this remarkable speed, they were still going to be there for at least another day. And then there was a two-day hike to Olisipo. The bandits' provisions were now nearly gone, and the only food they would have was what Sol brought in.

"We didn't catch anything," she said.

Kelan was still grinning, and she couldn't help but smile in return. "What?" she asked. "What're you so happy about?"

"Come here. You look cold."

She untied her snowshoes and sat beside him. He pulled her legs across his thighs and she didn't object. As she sank into the warmth of his body, he wrapped his arms around her. Once he wore his manacle all the time, this would be one thing she would miss: the way his skin tingled when she touched him, and how he warmed her all the way to the tips of her frozen toes and fingers. During the winter, at least. In the summer it would be better if he weren't so hot.

Sol sighed. Summer with Kelan. That was only a dream. In a

few days he would be gone, back to fight his war, and she'd travel home to Hillerod come spring.

"I think tomorrow I can walk a bit," he said.

"That's good. We can plan to go half, or even a quarter of what we usually do. I don't want you to get hurt, but I'm worried we'll run out of food again. When we're this close, it would be silly to starve to death."

He rested his head against hers, and her heart fluttered in her chest.

"We have so little time left," he whispered.

It was something she tried not to think about, how she would miss looking into Kelan's turquoise eyes and imagining they were the color of the ocean she had never seen. How she would miss his little touches, and the way he looked at her. And how she would miss lying next to him each night, enveloped in his warmth.

Sol cleared her throat and sat up. "I want to go hunting this afternoon."

"Hunting?"

She nodded. "If you don't mind me leaving you alone again. Can you teach me how to use an emberstone?"

He gaped at her and she frowned. "Look, when it's a choice between dying or using an emberstone, I guess I've decided I'll use the emberstone. I know I'm a hypocrite, but I—"

"No," he said and smiled. "I'd be happy to show you."

He kissed her cheek casually, as if it were something he did all the time, and her heart caught in her throat. Then he took out the manacle and its key and handed them to her.

She clicked the emberstone manacle onto her wrist and the tingling warmth of fire filled her. What would Pa say?

Pa was dead. And he hadn't met Kelan. Sol loved Pa. Growing up, he had been her world. He wasn't just her father; he had been her mentor and her best friend. But he was wrong about some things. He was wrong to think Kelan was something evil. And if fire was going to keep her and Kelan alive, then she was going to use it.

She nodded. "I'm ready. Tell me what to do."

She half-listened as he explained the basics of wielding flame, his warm breath tickling her neck as he spoke. She was aware of every place where their bodies touched, aware of the tingly sensation of his skin as their cheeks brushed against each other.

He took her right hand and pushed it into a fist. "You have to be careful though," he was saying, "because if you lose concentration, the fire can explode in your hand."

She startled out of her dreamy trance. "What? Would that hurt? I thought I was immune to fire if I had an emberstone."

"You can't be burned, but there's still the impact of the explosion. You can bruise your hand, or even break fingers if the blast is large enough."

"Oh. Maybe I shouldn't try this."

"No, you'll be fine. If you start to feel like you're losing control of the fire, throw it away from you so it doesn't explode near you."

He traced his fingers over the back of her hand, sending warm shivers up her spine. "Are you ready to try it?"

She had drawn fire once before, with Pa, and then again to heal Kelan. She could do it.

She took a big breath and pulled on the emberstone. The fire raced up the inside of her arm, passed through her heart, and flowed into her other hand. She startled when the flames appeared and coiled around her fist, and she flung them from her. The fire sailed through the air and disappeared into nothing.

"What happened?" she demanded.

"Not enough fire. That was a good first attempt, and it didn't even blow up in our faces," he said, and grinned. "Try it again."

This reminded her so much of using a bow—pulling back on the string, resisting its tension while she aimed, and then releasing the arrow. She pulled fire into her fist and let it coil there, winding tighter, and tighter, then threw it at the bank of snow. It exploded on impact, and water sprayed in every direction, leaving a hole in the snowbank.

"Is that how you do it?"

"You got it on your second try?" Kelan asked, gaping.

"Was I not supposed to?"

"It took me weeks to figure out how to get it to not blow up in my face."

"Is that it? Is that all I do?"

He nodded. "More fire for longer distances. A simple move like that should be enough for hunting. Do you want to try it again?"

"No."

She stood up and fished Pa's emberstone out of her pocket. She held it out so Kelan could see it before sticking it into his pocket. "In case your pyra returns."

"You had an emberstone the whole time?"

"It was my pa's. I'll be back before nightfall."

Sol found a spot near a frozen stream deep in the woods and hid herself among the snow and brush. There she waited as the day grew long, and she grew chill from the cold air. If she touched the emberstone, she would be warm, but she didn't dare.

It was sacrilegious to use an emberstone to hunt. The forest had been Pa's temple. Here he had worshiped the gods and had taught Sol to shun the taint of fire. And now she would use Pa's skills to desecrate his memory and the gods he had worshiped.

She sighed and pushed the guilt away, and thoughts of Kelan replaced her thoughts of Pa. She wished suddenly to be with Kelan, for him to warm her with the heat of his body, to kiss her cheek again. Every time he touched her, he betrayed how he felt about her. She yearned for those touches, but hated them, too. He was only making this more difficult. They could never be anything together. Once they left these woods, they would part ways forever, and there was nothing either of them could do to change that.

Even if he wore an emberstone manacle, Kelan would never be safe in any of the five kingdoms. Choosing to be with him would be choosing to join the Flameskin Army, or live a life on the run. That wasn't the life she wanted.

Something crunched in the snow to her right. A doe tramped toward the stream, its ears flicking as it walked. With bated breath, she watched it come toward her, and the hunt sent a thrill of adrenaline rushing through her. She slowly closed her left hand around the emberstone in her pocket, and her body warmed, all the way to her freezing toes.

The doe stopped at the stream and stooped its head to drink. She slowly lifted her fist and drew fire into it, letting it coil around her hand like Kelan had instructed. But she was concentrating on the deer, not on the flames. The fire wobbled and sparked, and she hurriedly flung it toward the deer, but it exploded a few feet from her, melting a patch of snow. The doe jumped and sprinted away.

She yanked energy from the emberstone and wrapped it around her hand. But the flames were wild, as erratic as her breathing. They exploded on her hand, knocking her backward into the snow. She cried out with pain, and the front of her coat caught fire. She rolled into the snow, instantly extinguishing it, but the fur of her coat had burned, and the smell of the smoke was sickening. Her hand ached and she groaned as she clutched it to her body. It felt like someone had hit her palm with a club and kicked her in the chest.

That was her deserved reward for trying to use an emberstone. She swore and wrapped her burned coat tightly around her. This had been a waste of time. She never should've tried to use the emberstone.

She shook the snow out of her hair and started the trek back to camp. The sun would already be set by the time she returned, so she kept a quick pace, and the throbbing in her hand lessened as she walked. She cut across the woods, taking a shortcut along a ridge. As she passed around the peak, she caught a glimpse of the valley below.

Sol gasped. Olisipo lay just a short walk down the slope.

CHAPTER 26

KELAN

"Kelan!" Sol shouted.

Kelan startled and sat upright, but too quickly, and he winced as his skin pulled at the movement.

"What is it?" he asked, reaching for the sword.

But her voice was happy, excited. She raced into the clearing, her eyes shining, and her cheeks flushed. He loved how the cold made her cheeks pink. But the front of her coat had been burned black, and she smelled of fire.

"What happened?" he asked.

She raced into his arms and hugged him tight. He winced, but didn't complain. It was enough to have her close; he'd endure any pain for that.

"We're so much closer than I thought. The city's only two or three hours walk from here. If we leave in the morning, we'll be there before lunch time."

Kelan smiled and sighed. To never be hungry again, to sleep in a bed. And a bath! The gods knew he needed one. They both did.

"Sol, I'm so happy." He squeezed her tighter, ignoring the ache in his heart.

This was it, then. Their last night.

"Do you think you can make the walk? We'll go slow."

"I can do it," he said, trying not to let his voice sound bitter.

"Are you sad?"

He pulled away and sat down on the skins. "I've gotten so used to having you around. Who'll be there to tell me not to slip in the ice?"

Her shoulders slumped.

"What happened to your coat?" he asked.

She shrugged. "I'm not meant to use emberstones. It . . . didn't work for me."

"Did you get hurt?" he asked, his heart catching.

"My hand hurts a bit, but it's not bad."

He drew her into his arms. "Let me see," he murmured. A bruise had already formed on the pad of her palm. "I'm sorry, Sol. I should've had you practice more before you left."

"No, I shouldn't have used it in the first place."

"Fire isn't evil. You can control it with practice."

"Maybe."

He kissed her bruised hand. "Does this hurt?" he asked, looking up and meeting her eyes.

She shook her head, her lips pressed tight together.

He slowly kissed the tips of her fingers. "What about this?"

He brushed his lips across the back of her hand, then raised her hand to his face and kissed her wrist.

She made a small noise of protest and hurriedly stood. "Let me try to wash your tunic again. You can't walk into the city with bloodstains all across your chest."

"I can wash it myself."

She shook her head. "No, save your strength."

"I'm afraid it's beyond help," he said, but obediently stripped off his coat and tunic. The air wasn't cold to his bare skin, but his pyra did have to work harder to keep him warm.

Sol gazed at his chest and Kelan smiled. He stretched casually, hoping three weeks of near-starvation hadn't left him emaciated, and that he still had something to admire.

"It's almost healed," she said.

He sighed. And he had thought she would be looking at the rest of his body. "Feeling much better, thanks to you."

"What's that you wear on your neck?" she asked, staring toward the button on its chain.

He squeezed it. "A reminder not to become what I hate."

He hoped Sol wouldn't ask any more questions, though he could tell she wanted him to say more. But then she knelt on the ground and scrubbed his stained tunic against a stone with chunks of snow and ice.

"You still planning to turn me?" he asked, trying to keep his voice light.

"No. We'll part as friends."

"Part as friends," he repeated, and scowled.

She sat up. "You're a soldier, Kelan, and you have a war to fight. I'm my village's huntress, and my family relies on me for food. We belong to different worlds."

"Don't you wish it could be otherwise?" he asked, meeting her eyes.

"It doesn't matter what I want. That's the way things are."

She scrubbed harder at his shirt, mostly with her uninjured hand. Then she sat back and held it up. The once-white tunic was now a dingy gray where it wasn't rust red.

She sighed. "There's nothing I can do about the hole, either."

"It's fine, Sol. Don't bother with my tunic."

He took it from her and tossed it aside into the snow and took her by the hands. "Your hands are freezing," he murmured.

He pulled Sol into his lap and placed her hands on his burning chest, covering them with his own. She stared at him and her eyes slowly trailed up his body, as if seeing him for the first time. He smiled. So she wasn't immune then, like she pretended to be.

But having her so close made his body ache. His heart raced in his chest beneath her fingers.

"I'm not going back to the army," he said and met her eyes. "I still want to protect Flameskins, but I don't want to lose myself fighting this war."

"Where will you go?" she asked, breathless.

"Where do you want me to go?"

He swept his hand along her neck. As he brushed his lips against hers, her breath caught. She pushed away and shed her heavy fur coat, revealing the blue Tokken coat she wore underneath.

"Ashes, Kelan," she murmured. "You're so hot."

"I can make it hotter."

She gave him an unreadable look, as if she were trying to decide if he was joking or not.

He wasn't.

"Do you have any plan of what you're going to do once we get to Olisipo?"

"Once I'm healed, I'm going to put on the emberstone manacle and never take it off. I'm going to live an ordinary life."

"But you can't have an ordinary life. You'll always be a Flameskin. You'll always have that emberstone on your wrist, marking you for what you are."

"I'll hide it then, if that's what you're worried about. Wear long sleeves. Or I could get a larger cuff and wear in on my upper arm."

"People hunt and kill Flameskins. You'll never be safe anywhere in Nordby. And not even in Cassia."

"I'll find a place. Sol, you know the mountains. There must be somewhere I could go where no one could find me. Or a village where I could conceal what I am."

She shook her head, her face downcast. "You wouldn't be safe in my village."

He pressed her to him. Her face was flushed, and she fidgeted in his arms, tracing patterns on his chest with her icy fingers.

"I don't want this to end," he whispered. "I'd travel these mountains with you forever if it meant you would always be with me. If I could share my bed with you."

Her head jerked up. "Kelan, please."

He wrapped his arms around her and pulled her closer. "I . . . care about you, Sol. I'm not ready to let you go."

She squeezed her eyes shut. Kelan tipped her face toward his and their lips met. Her hands trailed across his chest, then over his shoulders, and she wrapped her legs around him.

His heart raced, and his pyra soared with the intensity of his emotions. It was distracted from numbing his wound. Pain flared, but Kelan didn't care.

She slid out of her blue coat and pressed up against him, wrapping her arms around his neck as they kissed.

Kelan pulled the manacle from her pocket, careful not to touch the emberstone, and clipped it on her wrist. Then he placed her palm on his chest.

"I want to show you something," he whispered, meeting her eyes. "Draw fire from me like you do an emberstone."

Her eyebrows drew together, and she hesitated. She tried to move back, but he held her there against him.

Flames flowed out of his skin and into her hand. She yanked hard at his pyra, and he gasped and gripped her arm as the pain in his abdomen increased.

"Not so much. Gentle," he said. She was drawing his fire into her blood, and taking too much of it left little to numb the pain.

The flow slowed to a trickle, and Kelan's fire seeped into Sol. Her skin crackled against his with the sparks that they shared.

She stared at her hand on his chest then looked at his face again. "What—"

Kelan smiled. "You're pulling out my pyra. It eats my emotions, so when you take my fire, you feel whatever I feel."

"Your pyra won't corrupt me, will it?"

"No. I'm the only one it can speak to."

Her face was pensive and unreadable. The sparks and the twisting flames that entered her body were filled with the yearning he had for her. She would know that he had never felt for anyone what he felt for Sol.

"No secrets from you now," he murmured. "Here's my heart, laid bare."

"Kelan." Her eyes were lidded as she ran her hand through his curls.

"Whatever it is you want, Sol, I can be that for you." He kissed her lips, then her throat. "But don't tell me we can only be friends."

He laid her on the bed of skins, and she held him tightly. Her breath was cool against his burning skin as he traced the curve of her with his hands and pressed his lips to hers.

Nothing else mattered but Sol and this last night together.

But he would make sure it wasn't their last.

His blood boiled with the fire inside him, and heat pulsed out of him with the rapid beat of his heart. He slid his hand from her waist to the top button of her wool tunic and paused. He met her eyes, his lips parted in a question.

She went rigid and wrapped her arms around her chest.

"What's wrong?" he murmured.

"We can't."

He stroked her hair and kissed her temple. "I won't hurt you. I promised I wouldn't, remember?"

"Stop, Kelan."

He sat up and she pushed herself onto her elbows, but didn't meet his eyes. "Maybe this doesn't mean to you what it does to me, but—"

"It means everything to me," he said, and kissed her again. Was that all she was worried about? "You know how I feel about you. There's no other girl who ever has or who ever could make me feel that."

He had never believed anything so firmly. He needed Sol, not just now but always. Maybe they had once been enemies, but the ties that drew them together now were only the stronger for it.

Her eyes flicked up to meet his. "I always wanted my first to be my last, but you can't be my last, Kelan. There's no future for us together."

Her words turned his heart to ice.

"There's nowhere you can live where you'll be safe," she said. "And I don't want to live a life on the run."

"But I can wear my manacle. I can—"

"Just stop, Kelan." Her eyes glittered with tears. She squirmed her legs out from underneath him and yanked on her coats. She lay down again with her back to him.

He ran his hand over her arm, but she didn't move. How had he even hoped she would want him? And she was right. He had no future, except to be possessed by his pyra or killed by a mob. He couldn't ask her to abandon her home and her family and her way of life for him.

He lay down next to her and nestled in close, resting his head against hers and pressing their bodies together. His abdomen ached from his wound, but more than that, his arms ached to hold her, and his lips ached to kiss her. He listened as the night grew quiet, and Sol's breathing slowed, and she fell asleep.

There would be no sleep tonight for Kelan.

CHAPTER 27
SOL

They were silent as they hiked toward Olisipo. With bandits on the main path, taking one of the game trails seemed safer, even though it was a much longer route. Sol led them along the path she had found the day before, and from there they began a steep descent toward the city.

Olisipo came into view briefly over the ridge, but disappeared again as they descended into a ravine. If they kept at their usual pace, they could've arrived before sunset, but Sol's feet dragged, and their pace slowed as they drew closer to the foothills.

She kept glancing back at Kelan. Last night she had considered leaving everything to be with him. Drawing fire from his pyra had been intoxicating: the crackle of his flames in her blood and the warmth of the love he had for her. His was love deep enough to drown in.

But it was a ridiculous dream. Where could they go? Even if he did wear his emberstone, people would eventually find out what he was. They'd never be able to hide anywhere for long, and while this war was going on, he'd always be hunted. Even after the war, there was no guarantee that Flameskins would have a place in society, especially if the Flameskins lost.

But was this really the last time she was going to see him?

Kelan had stopped in the trail, and she turned around to face him. He stared at the tree line above them with a troubled face.

"Kelan. . . ." She didn't know where to begin. He could show her exactly how he felt about her, but she hadn't yet dared explore the extent of the feelings she had for him.

What was the point? It would only lead to heartbreak. They were born into different worlds. Their paths would never again converge, and they weren't meant to. Soon they would stand on opposite sides of the divide as enemies.

She cleared her throat and tried again. "Kelan—"

"Quiet."

She frowned and followed his gaze toward the ridge. Something was moving among the trees.

"Bandits?" she whispered.

"They're wearing red coats."

She breathed in sharply. Flameskin soldiers?

Kelan grabbed her hand and pulled her forward. "Let's move. Burnitall. I didn't think the Flameskin encampment was this close to Olisipo."

"What? But you told us there weren't any other Flameskins in the Ulves."

"I was tied up. I lied. Which way out of the ravine?"

She pointed, and they stomped through icy sheets of snow as they ran. High, snow-covered walls hid them from view on either side of the narrow canyon, but prevented them from seeing out.

"Did they see us?" she asked.

"I don't think so."

They burst out of the canyon's mouth and into the brilliant sunlight. The snow was blinding white and shot through with red. A dozen Flameskin soldiers waited for them with weapons ready.

Sol stopped short, still clinging to Kelan's hand. The soldiers were a mix of men, women, and adolescents, and several had fire sparking on their fingertips.

Sol reached for her dagger, but it had disappeared in the fight with the bandits. She swore inwardly as the Flameskins advanced. Most of them had crooked, demonic smiles on their faces.

"Why don't we have some fun?" one of them hissed. "Let's see how well they dance." The soldier formed a swirling ball of fire around her fist.

"Stand down, soldiers," Kelan barked. He straightened and strode toward them with a hand on the hilt of his stolen Cassian scimitar. The soldiers faltered, and the woman's ball of fire evaporated into the cold air.

A man stepped forward and drew his sword. "Who are you, giving orders?"

"Your superior deserves more respect than that, Officer Osten," Kelan said. "Now stand down before I run you through."

"Lieutenant Burke?" Osten asked.

Kelan grinned. "Miss me?"

Osten scowled, then sheathed his sword and saluted. "I apologize, sir," Osten said through gritted teeth. "I didn't recognize you with the beard."

"Make that mistake again and I won't give you a chance to apologize before I ram my sword up your—" Kelan glanced at Sol and coughed into his hand.

Sol stared at Kelan. She had always known he was a soldier, but this snappy military version of him seemed so incompatible with the Kelan she knew, the one she called her friend.

"Weren't your orders to stay in the pass?" Osten asked.

"We were attacked. I had no choice but to come here."

"Attacked?"

"Are you all just going to stand there? We've been hiking through these mountains for the last few weeks and we're starving. Take us to camp. I need to speak with the commander."

The soldiers saluted, and their officer motioned Kelan to follow. Sol hung back. Her knees were too weak to carry her forward. What were they doing? Kelan really expected her to walk into a Flameskin camp?

He put a hand on her back and pushed her forward. "Trust me," he whispered.

She met his turquoise eyes. This was madness. She was still wearing her blue Tokken uniform underneath her fur coat. But she had no choice but to follow the soldiers through the snow.

The camp appeared around the other side of the bluff, nestled at the edge of the trees. About one hundred small tents had been erected in neat lines. The smell of smoke clung to the air. Soldiers marched and sparred and flung fire at each other around the edges of camp. Some cackled madly, others hissed as they talked. Only a handful of them wore red coats, the higher-ups; the others wore mismatched and poorly mended clothes. But everyone's sleeves were charred and their hems burned.

Sol stepped in close to Kelan. Possessed. All of these Flame-skins were possessed.

"How do you control all the de—possessed Flameskins?" she whispered.

He frowned. "Pyri have only two directives: self-preservation and destruction. The punishment for most crimes in the army is death, which conflicts with a pyra's central drive. Disobeying isn't an option. We rule our camps with fear. Fear is the only emotion a pyra can't consume, and it prevents the pyra from having too much control over the host."

"Why would the Flameskins even join the army?"

"Because we have nothing else, and because they want to destroy. And it's safer to run with a pack."

She shivered as she watched them. They were little more than intelligent beasts. She couldn't imagine Kelan becoming one of them.

"Is the commander here?" Kelan asked Osten. "I expect he'll want my report."

"No, sir. But he should be back soon. You'll report to Lieutenant Ager for now."

Kelan frowned. "Lieutenant Ager, as in Nilsa Ager?"

"Yes, sir."

He bit his lip and met Sol's eyes. He looked worried, and it made her stomach queasy. She trusted Kelan, which surprised her a little. But even with Kelan on her side, this was still dangerous. People didn't walk out of Flameskin encampments.

"Take us to Nilsa, then," Kelan said, his voice casual, though Sol could see the tension in his face. "And bring us some food. We're starving."

Sol tugged on Kelan's sleeve. "My coat," she hissed.

His eyes went wide, and Sol pulled the two sides of her pa's fur coat tighter around her, hoping there wasn't any blue visible beneath it.

"Any chance we can get a fresh change of clothes first? And a bath?" Kelan asked. "I'd like to look presentable."

Osten stopped. "What about your report?"

Kelan waved a hand. "It's not urgent, is it?"

"You were attacked. She'll want to know right away what the situation is." Officer Osten's eyes rested on Sol. "And who's this?"

Sol gave Kelan a wild, desperate look.

"Sol . . . Jensen," Kelan said. "She's a mage. Newer recruit. She came with me through the pass and is the only other survivor."

Sol saluted the same way she had seen the soldiers do.

Jensen? He couldn't have come up with something less generic than Jensen?

"I don't remember her," Osten said and narrowed his eyes.

"Why would you? You were only at the camp a couple days. She was one of our scouts."

Osten gave Sol a nod and waved them toward a large circular tent that had been erected in the center of the camp. Inside it was dark and sparsely furnished, and devoid of soldiers.

Kelan sprawled on the floor mat as if he owned the place. "So, where's Lieutenant Ager?"

Osten frowned. "She must be meeting with the scouts or gone to Olisipo with Haldur. I'll find out." He saluted and left.

Kelan leapt from the ground and yanked off Sol's fur coat and her Tokken uniform. He crushed the dirty, blue coat in his hands and set it on fire. It burned rapidly and viciously between his fingers, filling the room with smoke. Sol coughed and backed away from him as she pulled her fur coat back on.

Kelan lifted one of the tent flaps in the back to vent the air and smothered the ashes in the snow outside. "Cinders," he swore. "This wasn't supposed to happen."

"What do we do?" Sol asked, trying to keep the panic out of her voice.

"Don't worry. I'll get us out of here."

"Us?"

He stepped closer and took her hand, but the tent door flapped open again. He stepped away from Sol as another woman entered. This soldier looked about their own age, and had brilliant violet eyes. She wore a lieutenant's pin on her red coat that matched Kelan's.

She sniffed the air as she walked in. "What's burning?"

"Something's always burning when I'm around," Kelan said and grinned.

The lieutenant laughed and threw her arms around him, and Sol had the uncomfortable impression that they knew each other very well.

"Ashes, Kelan. What happened to you?" she asked, plucking at his burned and tattered coat.

"Exactly what it looks like. Ambush, avalanche, and four weeks starving in the Ulves."

"Avalanche?"

He smiled and shrugged.

"And who's this one?" the woman asked, nodding toward Sol.

"She's the only other survivor."

"Four weeks alone with Kelan. How was that?" Lieutenant Ager purred and turned her violet eyes on Sol.

"Difficult."

Lieutenant Ager laughed, and Kelan gave Sol a dismayed look.

He misunderstood. The journey hadn't been difficult because of Kelan. He had been the one bright spot in all the hunger and cold and suffering.

"I can't believe it's been a year since I last saw you," Ager said. "And you've been promoted! Does that mean you've been possessed?"

He stiffened. "It's getting closer."

"It's impressive, isn't it?" she said to Sol. "Not many can deny possession for so long, but he'll be unstoppable once his pyra takes him. It's no wonder his uncle promoted him. I can't wait to see what he'll be like."

"What do you mean?"

Lieutenant Ager's eyebrows rose.

"She's a mage," Kelan said quickly.

Sol's heart raced. She was supposed to know these things if she was part of the Flameskin Army.

But Ager shrugged. "The longer someone resists, the stronger their pyra grows, until it becomes more powerful than the host. People who give in earlier work in tandem with their pyra. But people like Kelan become their pyra."

Sol swallowed and Kelan looked away.

Lieutenant Ager walked up to him and tapped his skull. "It'll be just his pyra in there."

Ager looped her arm through Kelan's, and Sol had to swallow a scowl. They were obviously very friendly with each other. Not that she should be surprised. The lieutenant was beautiful and Kelan was . . . Kelan.

"Of course, now he's practically hobbled by the resistance," Ager said, oblivious to the anger burning in Sol's eyes. "It'll be better for him once he lets go."

The tent door parted again, letting in a draft of cold air. A man in a decorated uniform strode inside.

Kelan breathed in sharply and stepped closer to Sol. "Hello, Uncle."

CHAPTER 28
KELAN

Uncle Haldur coughed as he entered. "Who was burning things in here?"

"Sorry," Kelan said. "You know how hard it is for me to resist."

"What are you doing here? Where's the rest of the troop?"

"Dead," Kelan said. He felt a pang of shame and grief as he said it. He hadn't given much thought to his troop since the attack and the avalanche. He hadn't been close with any of them, but they had still been his responsibility.

"I trusted you with their lives," Haldur said.

"We were ambushed. They took some of us prisoner, but then an avalanche killed everyone else."

"Who ambushed you?"

"Lady Isabella's party."

"And where's Isabella now?"

"Dead. The only ones who survived were me and Sol."

Sol saluted Commander Haldur. She had always been level-headed. She was the kind of person you wanted at your back on the battlefield, the kind who could keep her cool no matter the situation.

Haldur strode toward the table in the middle of the room

and sank onto the floor beside it. "Troop Thirty-Seven is gone and so is Lady Isabella."

"Yes, sir."

"How did you get here?" Haldur asked. "Osten and I lost our way a dozen times in this snow. The horses didn't even make it."

"Sol is somewhat familiar with the Ulves." Kelan smiled inwardly. Sol *was* the Ulves.

Haldur looked up and studied Sol's face. "I don't remember her. I didn't know there was another soldier in that troop who knew the Ulves."

"Mage," Kelan said quickly, his heart beating fast. "She's a newer recruit. She comes from an Ulve village."

Haldur nodded absently and let out a long breath. "Lady Isabella is dead. I needed some good news."

Nilsa scowled. "We just got word. Saint Katrine's returned to Tokkedal."

Kelan opened his mouth, but for a moment, no words came out. "What?"

"She's come back from Omdren to fight with the Tokken Army," Haldur said.

"What does that mean for us?" Kelan asked.

"It means the war is over," Nilsa said, her voice sour. "She'll kill us all."

Haldur gave her a look. "It means that we have to regroup with the southern division and defeat her or risk losing the war."

"So, we're leaving the Ulves?" Kelan asked.

He glanced at Sol. She was biting her lip, and he could tell she was trying hard not to smile. To him, the arrival of Saint Katrine was damnation. To her, it was salvation.

"We're waiting for marching orders," Haldur said. "I assume they'll want us back in the valley. We'll have to abandon the raid on the Ulves."

Kelan nodded slowly. At least Sol's village would be spared. He should be happy for Sol, but knowing that Saint Katrine had come to Tokkedal to rid the kingdom of its Flameskins made his blood run cold.

Haldur sighed. "Maybe it would be better if we stayed here. We've put too much work into getting our troops here, and now that you tell me Isabella is dead, Prince Turullius won't be riding to Tokkedal's defense. We need the food the villages will supply us. This is too good an opportunity to give up."

"Of course," Kelan murmured.

"Don't you want to see the mountains burn, Kelan?" Nilsa brushed her hand against his arm.

His pyra responded to the heat that radiated off her body and the prospect of flames and destruction. But he shoved his pyra away before it could seize any part of him. "We have to do what the general orders."

Nilsa scowled. "You're no fun. I'll like you better once you're possessed."

Kelan ignored her. "Uncle—"

"Commander."

"Commander, we haven't eaten much for the last few weeks, and it would be nice to get some fresh clothes."

"Fine, fine. You're dismissed. I suppose there's nothing else for you to report if everyone is dead."

Kelan saluted, and nudged Sol's elbow. She saluted as well. Her face was calm, but he could see the panic in her eyes. He needed to get her away from this camp as fast as possible.

"Lieutenant Ager, find them clothes and places to sleep," his uncle ordered.

Kelan hurried out of the tent with Sol and Nilsa behind him. He turned slowly, taking in the guard posts and fortifications. This wouldn't be easy. The camp was guarded at all times, and deserters were killed.

"I have a larger tent," Nilsa said to Sol. "You can share with me, unless Kelan wants to."

Kelan grinned and put a hand around Sol's shoulders. "I think she'll be wanting to sleep in mine."

Nilsa's eyes narrowed, and Sol blushed a deep red.

"Four difficult weeks in the mountains can really bring

people together," Kelan said, and squeezed Sol's arm hard. How could she have called him difficult?

"Apparently." Nilsa's gaze was cool.

She was angry. He had known her long enough to recognize the signs. But Nilsa could claim no hold on him. He could never love her like he loved Sol. And Nilsa knew their relationship had only been a way to pass the time.

"Clear out a tent for us," Kelan ordered. "I'm exhausted."

They had retired early to Kelan's requisitioned tent and stayed there as the sun set and evening faded into the blackness of night. Sol had fallen asleep as soon as she had laid down. Kelan was exhausted as well, but he couldn't let himself rest, not until they were both safely out of the camp.

They couldn't go to Olisipo. His uncle had spies all over the city, and they would know what Kelan looked like. It would be impossible to hide among all the fair-haired Cassians. If he could find Sol a bow, they could go back to the mountains, and she would keep them fed.

He tried to think of a way to snag them supplies and weapons and clothes, but no solutions presented themselves that didn't end up with the two of them getting executed.

Their priority was to get as far away from the Flameskin camp as they could, as fast as possible. Haldur would try to hunt them down once he knew they were missing.

Going into the mountains without anything to eat wasn't much of a choice, but he'd rather take his chances out there with Sol than give himself back to the army. Returning to the war was a sure road to possession.

He gently shook Sol. "It's time to go."

She rolled over and blearily opened her eyes. "Now? Is it safe?"

"As safe as it will ever be. But we have to hurry. The watch is changing soon, and they'll be distracted for a moment." Hopefully.

Sol pulled on her belt and tugged her hat back onto her head. "If you just get me out of the camp, I can find the way to Olisipo."

"You . . . don't want me to come?"

She fell silent and looked down at her hands. "This is where you belong. This is your army. The commander is your *uncle*." That last word was a jab.

Maybe he should've said something about it before. But he hadn't wanted to mention that his uncle was commander of the Flameskin Army that had terrorized the Ulves for the last five years.

"I don't want to be a soldier anymore," Kelan said. "I want to stay with you. We could go back into the mountains."

"I have to report to the Tokken garrison and tell them what happened to Lady Isabella."

"But after that—"

"If you leave the army, they'll hunt you down and kill you."

"I won't let them find me."

She met his eyes in the darkness. "I don't want to be hunted for the rest of my life."

Kelan opened his mouth, but couldn't speak. His heart shuddered in his chest.

She parted the tent door and peeked outside. "Let's go."

"Sol—"

"You said we had to hurry."

They slipped into the starlit night, past the rows of tents. They avoided the lights of the lanterns and the Flameskins that passed by with tiny fires cupped in their hands, but they couldn't muffle the sounds their feet made as they crunched through the snow. They had abandoned the snowshoes, knowing that would look suspicious, and Sol had brought only what she wore and the seal of Lady Isabella's house, which she had stuffed into her pocket. They slipped past a sleeping guard and began the downward hike toward Olisipo through the woods.

She stopped them not far from the camp. "I can make it from here."

"Let me go with you to the edge of the city at least, to make sure you get there safely."

Please. Please, let me go with you.

She hesitated, but then nodded and set off again. Kelan trudged behind her.

She was right. If he left the camp, he'd be hunted by the Flameskin Army. Sol would find protection in the Tokken garrison, but he had nowhere he could go to be safe.

Their journey together through the mountains was over, and now they were supposed to return to their separate lives. But how could he do that? He could never go back to being satisfied with his life as a lonely soldier, not after knowing Sol.

She stopped again and turned on her heel.

Please, Sol. Don't send me away.

But she was looking at something beyond him. He turned and found Nilsa standing behind them in the snow.

He stepped in front of Sol, his heart thumping. "Hey, Nilsa." He tried to keep his voice light, but panic surged through him in a flood of fire.

Destroy her, his pyra ordered. If Nilsa shouted for help, they'd have a whole camp of Flameskins running after them.

"Out for an evening stroll?" Nilsa asked.

"Yes. Exactly."

"During the change of guard?"

He stepped back, and his foot crunched through ice. Nilsa smiled as she prowled toward them.

"Were you really thinking of leaving, Kelan? You could've at least tried not to be so obvious about it."

"Sol isn't a soldier, she's a huntress. She helped me find my way through the mountains and in return, I promised I'd get her to safety. Just let her leave peacefully."

It was a gamble to tell something so close to the truth, but Nilsa wouldn't let them go if she thought Sol was a deserter.

"A huntress? But she knows the location of our camp. We can't just let her get away."

"I won't say anything," Sol said. "Kelan is here, and I don't want him to get hurt."

"You're staying, Kelan?" Nilsa asked, her eyebrows rising. "I was starting to think you'd leave us for the Hivid Wood."

He let out a long sigh. "The Hivid haven is just a rumor. I'm staying here." Because he had nowhere else to go. Because Sol loving him was an impossibility.

"And when Haldur finds out you helped her run away?"

"He won't find out."

"Is that a threat?" Nilsa asked. Her eyes danced with the fire inside her.

"I'm asking you as a favor to me to let her go. She doesn't belong here."

"So, she really is a huntress? And you lied about her being a mage. Gutsy."

"I am a mage," Sol said softly.

"You could join us," Nilsa hissed.

"Please, Nilsa. Have you forgotten all those times I covered for you while you were out chewing flameweed?" Kelan asked.

Nilsa sighed, then gave them both a twisted smile. "You should go to the Tokkens and tell them where we are," she told Sol. "It's been weeks since I've been in a proper fight, and I'm itching to burn something.

"Be back before dawn, Kelan, or they'll realize you're gone. And if you don't come back, I'll hunt you down myself."

He bowed. "Thank you."

Sol grabbed Kelan's hand and pulled him away into the forest.

Kelan and Sol stood on the edge of the city. The mountains rose behind them and Olisipo stretched before them. Chimney smoke choked the air, and dirty snow lined the streets and covered the brick buildings. It was a far cry from the beautiful open spaces and clear skies they were accustomed to. It was dark, but the starlight reflected off the snow on the gabled rooftops and the ice on the windows.

They both stood hesitantly at the edge of it all, caught between two worlds.

Kelan took her hand. He could barely speak. "I'll miss you."

"I'll miss you, too."

"After the war is over, I'll come find you. I want to see you again."

She swallowed, but didn't reply. She wouldn't meet his gaze.

Sol.

The girl he loved was slipping through his fingers, and there was nothing he could say or do that would make her stay with him. He had to return to the Flameskin camp tonight, and he couldn't ask her to join them. But he wished there was a way forward for the two of them. He wished they could leave this place and never look back.

"I should go. Good luck, Kelan. And be safe."

"Wait," he said, his voice raw. He stepped in and kissed her long and deep, until his hands trembled, and his throat closed up.

When they broke apart, he rested his forehead against hers. "Sol, I love you."

She glanced up and her eyes were rimmed in red. Loving him was a death sentence for her. He knew that. There was no future for them.

"Goodbye, Kelan," she whispered.

She turned and hurried toward the road, leaving him alone in the snow.

Kelan's frozen heart shattered inside him. A thousand shards of Sol embedded in his chest, cutting him apart on the inside.

He braced himself against a tree as his knees gave out. He couldn't understand how his heart could keep functioning, keep pumping blood and fire as though nothing had happened.

Sol was gone.

CHAPTER 29
SOL

S ol sat cross-legged in front of the fireplace, and her smelly, burned coat was draped around the back of a Cassian chair. She lifted her hands and drew them close to the fire. She'd rather have Kelan warm them for her.

All that was behind her now, but it would take a long time before she would stop missing him. She kept turning around, expecting to see him, and it left an empty ache inside her knowing that he'd never sit beside her again. She would lie alone tonight.

She had done the right thing, but knowing that didn't make it any easier.

The door opened and she jerked upright. Two men marched into the room wearing pressed and decorated blue uniforms.

"Sit," one of them ordered.

He was as big as an ox and pulled a chair up next to her and sat in it like a Cassian. She was amazed when the chair didn't break beneath his weight.

"Have they given you food to eat?"

"Yes, sir," she said, sinking uncomfortably into another chair.

"I'm Commander Jahr," he said, and extended a hand. A Cassian greeting.

Sol shook it and unease settled over her. Should she have

kept up her ruse as a man, pretending to be her father? The soldiers had been confused when she had arrived. But if she was going to spend the entire season with the garrison, it would've been impossible to keep that a secret for so long.

"I'm Sol, Huntress of Hillerod."

Jahr nodded. "I thought they hired a hunter. Elo d'Hillerod?"

"My father."

"I see. And where is he?"

"Dead a year now. I am the only hunter in Hillerod, and I traveled with Lady Isabella through the pass from Skive."

"And are you going to tell me where Lady Isabella is now?"

She bit her cheek and exhaled slowly. "She's . . . dead, sir."

Sol told him everything. She told him about the successful attack on the Flameskin troop, and about the avalanche and how it had buried their party beneath a mountain of snow. She told them how she had traveled the rest of the way through the snow without food, and how Baarka had been burned.

But she mentioned nothing of Kelan. Telling the Tokken garrison about the location of the Flameskin camp would mean Kelan's death. It was a betrayal to her country, but she couldn't put Kelan in danger.

As proof of everything she had told them, she gave Jahr the seal of Lady Isabella's house that she had cut from one of Isabella's dresses.

Jahr rubbed his face with a huge hand. "Ashes and cinders."

"I'm sorry, sir. There was nothing I could do for them." She swallowed the lump in her throat. Pa would've known to watch for avalanches. Had he still been alive, Lady Isabella would be, too.

But Kelan would be dead. Pa would've killed him.

"I knew we shouldn't have let Isabella go so late in the season, but what were we to do? There were too many Flameskins in the mountains waiting to kill her if she left any earlier. Sending her at all was sending her to her death. And we all knew that," Jahr said.

"But what do we do now?" the thin lieutenant asked.

"Without the marriage we won't get the Cassian troops we need. We won't be able to defend ourselves once the snow melts. The Flameskins will burn everything."

"Prince Turullius won't be pleased. The wedding is already planned for three weeks from now, and we need those troops."

The lieutenant cocked his head and eyed Sol. "What if it was Lady Isabella who had survived, instead of the huntress?"

Sol sighed. "I would've saved her if I could, but I—"

"No," the lieutenant said, "I mean, Prince Turullius hasn't met Isabella. He doesn't know what she looks like. He only knows he's getting a Tokken bride."

Jahr stared at Sol. "She's pure Tokken. It's obvious in her face. And those green eyes. She's the right age, and she's pretty enough."

Sol turned from one man to the other. What were they talking about?

"No one's coming through the pass for the rest of the season," the lieutenant said, "and by the time winter's over, they'll be married, and the Cassian troops will already be in the pass on their way to Skive."

Sol stood from her chair so fast she knocked it over. Her heart thumped fast in her chest. "No."

"Think what an opportunity we're offering you," Jahr said. "Prince Turullius as your husband? You would never want again. Your family would be well taken care of."

"I can take care of them myself."

Jahr frowned. "Isn't your village on the way to Skive? When the Flameskin armies arrive this spring, they'll pass through and burn it to the ground, like they did to Baarka. If you don't marry Turullius, you're sentencing innocent people to die at the hands of the demon army."

"I'd rather fight the demons with my own two hands than marry some foreign prince."

Jahr scowled at her. "You think Lady Isabella wanted to leave her home? We all must make sacrifices to protect the ones we love."

Sol braced herself with one hand against the wall as her head spun. "But what happens in the spring when people come to visit Isabella and they realize I'm not her?"

"We'll already have the troops we need by that time."

"But what will happen to *me*?" she asked, her voice shrill.

This was too much to ask. Would they expect her to live in some bloated manor eating rice cakes and wearing ridiculous silk dresses? She needed the mountains. She needed the silence and the solitude of the woods. She needed her freedom.

And she needed Kelan.

She shook her head, trying to rid her mind of that thought, but she couldn't stop thinking about Kelan's brilliant smile, those turquoise eyes, and the touch of his fiery skin.

"I think Isabella's father will understand," Jahr said. "He's supportive of the war. It's possible we can convince him to keep this quiet, but even so, I don't know if Turullius will care. All he wants is a pretty bride and access to the trade routes Isabella's family controls."

"So, I'm to be sold off to some prince, so you can have your soldiers?"

"Who knows," Jahr said. "Maybe you'll become the queen of Cassia. Any Cassian prince is eligible to become king, even a prince over such a small city as Olisipo. We're doing you a favor, Huntress."

"Wait," Sol said. This was happening too fast. Her head was reeling. "Saint Katrine. She's arrived in Tokkedal. If she comes, the Flameskin Army will be destroyed." Along with Kelan.

Jahr frowned. "I heard she was in Omdren with the other Saints."

"She's come back."

"How do you know this?"

Sol bit her lip and searched for a lie. "The Flameskin soldiers told us they had just received word Saint Katrine had arrived."

"Even if Saint Katrine is in Tokkedal, she won't make it to the mountains in time. We need the Cassians to march before the snow melts, or we won't have a chance to stop them. We need you to be Lady Isabella."

"But I just want to go home," she said, her voice small.

"To watch your village burn? You'd rather let the demons kill your family?"

She shuddered and closed her eyes. No. Of course she didn't want that.

But what kind of a choice was this?

CHAPTER 30
KELAN

K elan woke from a groggy sleep. He turned over, searching for the shape of Sol in the blankets beside him, but he was alone, and he lay in a bed. His half-remembered dreams of snow and Sol melted as he sat up and rubbed his scratchy cheek.

Sol was gone.

But he was clean, and had new clothes, and he wasn't starving for once. He stumbled out of the bed and into the common room of their rented house. Commander Haldur had brought him to Olisipo to meet with the spies and to search for the deserter.

Kelan had pled ignorance of Sol's disappearance, and Nilsa had kept quiet.

Sol was free now.

A couple officers sat by the fireplace, their voices low. They stood and saluted when Kelan entered the room.

Kelan nodded sleepily and dropped into a chair. He sighed. Sol was free, but he was not. He'd never be rid of the army.

"You got anything to shave with?" Kelan asked.

One of the men pointed out a cracked mirror and shaving implements on the other side of the room.

"So, what're we doing in Olisipo now that Isabella's dead?" he asked as he trimmed and shaved his unruly beard. The blade nicked his skin, but he was too afraid to use his pyra to seal the cut. And he couldn't use his emberstone in front of the other soldiers.

"We were gathering information on Prince Turullius' household, planning to infiltrate and kill Lady Isabella if you didn't kill her in the pass. Now we'll wait here until spring and make sure Turullius doesn't send those troops through."

Kelan splashed cold water on his face and steam fogged the mirror. Back to burning villages and blue-coated soldiers in the name of justice.

Yesss. Fire. Burning. His pyra simmered in his blood. Now that his wound was almost healed, his pyra could dedicate more energy on attacking his mind. It jabbed and prodded him, searching for weakness.

The door of their house burst open and Haldur strode in. "Lady Isabella's alive."

The soldiers around the fire jumped up in alarm, and Kelan whirled around. "What? But that's impossible. She was killed in the avalanche. There's no way she survived."

Haldur could no longer feel anger, since he was extinguished, but there was a tightness about his features that spoke of his displeasure. "There's going to be a bridal procession today, and they're going to parade her through the streets before they present her to the prince."

Kelan ran a hand through his hair. "But I don't understand. We barely made it out ourselves. How is this possible?"

"We're leaving for the parade now," Haldur said. "You're going to identify her, and then we're going to kill her."

Kelan stood among the shivering crowd with his eyes fixed on the procession. Lady Isabella had survived? But how? Going without a daily bath had been a struggle for her. There was no way she had survived in the rugged wilderness like he and Sol had. How had she found the path leading through the mountains? Without Sol, Kelan would've been lost, and he would've starved as well.

The bridal procession was preceded by dozens and dozens of Tokken soldiers on horseback. Their coats were the blue of the sky and had been pressed and cleaned. Kelan sank into his new, nondescript gray coat, and kept one wary eye on the soldiers as they passed. Would Sol be among them, or would they have her waiting on Lady Isabella?

If she were in the carriage with Isabella, she might get hurt. He couldn't stop Haldur from killing Isabella, but he could stop him from hurting Sol. He wouldn't let his uncle take the shot unless it would be a clean one, and only if Sol wasn't sitting too close to Isabella.

If Sol saw the fire, would she think it had been him? Would she call him Demon again? Would she hate him for being a part of it?

But if Isabella survived, it would mean death for him and everyone back at his camp.

He swore under his breath and rubbed the back of his neck. Sol was right to leave him. There was no situation in which he could win. It was fight or die or give himself over to possession.

The carriage turned the corner and Kelan stood on tiptoe to get a better look. It was an open carriage with two fine white horses in front and a driver behind them. Three Tokken women sat side by side in the carriage. Their faces were still indistinct at this distance, and they wore similar outfits of white furs, but the woman in the center had a painted face and her hair was done up and pinned with gold clips.

"That one must be Isabella," Haldur said.

He pushed through the crowd with Kelan behind him.

Kelan squinted at the women in the carriage. They sat too close together. If Sol was in the carriage, he wasn't letting Haldur attack her.

The carriage drew closer. Lady Isabella turned her face toward Kelan, and he gaped at her. No makeup could've concealed who she was. Isabella's eyes met his in the crowd and she stiffened. She mouthed his name with her rouged lips, her eyes wide.

He stared at her, unable to comprehend what he saw.

But this was Sol. Sol the Huntress. He had seen Lady Isabella riding on her horse through the pass, and she was surely dead.

Uncle Haldur touched the emberstone hidden beneath his coat and gathered fire around his fist.

"Wait," Kelan said, yanking his arm down.

"Flameskins!" Sol yelped. She ducked into the bottom of the carriage and pulled the other two girls down with her.

Haldur swore as fire flew from his hand and sailed over the carriage, missing Sol's face and hitting a building on the other side of the street.

The crowd screamed and scattered. Kelan was frozen in place, staring at Sol's carriage. But . . . . All those stories she had told him about her village, about her pa, all that had been a lie?

"Move!" Haldur shouted and grabbed Kelan's arm.

He awakened from his daze with a gasp as Haldur dragged him through the throng and into the streets of Olisipo. Tokken soldiers pushed through the crowd behind them as Haldur led Kelan on a twisting path through the city.

They slipped into an alley, where two Tokkens blocked their path. Haldur released two quick bursts of fire, and flames exploded in the soldiers' chests before the men had a chance to draw their swords. They jumped over the bodies and Kelan ran with his uncle through Olisipo until they could no longer hear the shouts and the pounding footfalls of the soldiers' boots.

Kelan leaned against a brick wall, breathing hard.

"What was that?" Haldur asked. "It would've been a sure hit."

"That woman they had all painted and dressed up wasn't Isabella."

"You don't know that."

Kelan turned on him. "I *do*. It wasn't her. It was someone else."

Haldur went very still. "The girl. The deserter."

Kelan nodded slowly and stared at his shoes. He wasn't sure what the punishment for this was going to be, but it would be painful.

Haldur stepped closer, and Kelan winced. "Who is she?"

"Her name's Sol. She's a huntress from one of the Ulve villages. She was guiding the Tokken Army through the pass."

"And you let her escape?"

"She saved my life. I promised I'd return the favor."

Haldur grabbed Kelan and shoved him up against the wall. "She knows where our camp is, you fool!"

"She won't tell. She hasn't, otherwise the army would've already come and wiped us out."

"Because she's been so busy preparing for her wedding."

Kelan tried to pull himself free from his uncle, but Haldur held him fast. "She's not Isabella. She can't be getting married to Turullius."

"She deceived you. Lady Isabella was the one who traveled with you all the way through the pass and you never knew it."

"I saw Isabella on her horse in her fancy dress and I know she's dead."

"Can't you see? They used a decoy."

"A decoy?"

Haldur rammed Kelan against the wall again, knocking the breath out of him. "That huntress was Lady Isabella all along. They hid her in plain sight. And now they'll keep her far out of reach. It'll be impossible to get to her, even with our inside men."

Kelan couldn't breathe.

Now it all made sense. Why else would she have pretended to be a man? No one would suspect the hunter to be the real Lady Isabella. She had used him to keep warm and to hunt food for her.

Every word had been a lie. Every kiss. Had she ever even

cared for him? Or had she been eager to get to Olisipo so she could send soldiers through the city to hunt him down?

She betrayed us.

Fire flooded Kelan's body and his lips curled into a snarl. "We'll get her, Uncle. We'll find a way."

CHAPTER 31
SOL

The carriage thundered over the cobblestone road and knocked Sol's head against the seat. One of the slave girls was crying.

Sol shut her eyes against the image of Kelan's face, and the confusion and the hurt she had seen there. Kelan had seen her, all covered in this makeup and dressed like a lady. Did he truly think she was Isabella?

She had almost called out to him, almost leapt from the carriage so she could have the chance to talk to him, but the commander had been beside him. And he had tried to kill her.

She and Kelan were enemies once more.

What would become of him? Would the Tokken soldiers catch him? If Sol became a princess, would she have the power to plead for his life?

Everything was so terribly wrong. She should've never left the Ulves. The Flameskin Army had reclaimed Kelan, and she was an imposter in an uncomfortable dress destined for a life without mountains.

The carriage didn't stop until they entered the grounds of Prince Turullius' manor and the gates closed behind them. The enormous walls cut her off from the sky and the mountains behind her.

Commander Jahr extended an enormous hand to help Sol from the carriage. "You're safe here, Lady Isabella."

Jahr had one rule for Sol: remain silent. Lady Isabella didn't speak Cassian, though Sol did. Cassian customs were different from Tokkedal's, and Prince Turullius would overlook her blunders as adjustments to the new culture, not as a huntress pretending to be a lady.

Her two new attendants would help her with the rest. They would paint her face and dress her, and tell her what to do. The two women were Tokken slaves Turullius had bought and trained specifically for the use of his new Tokken wife.

It must have been obvious to them Sol wasn't who she said she was. She spoke and acted like one of the common folk, not a lady. But the slave girls had been blessedly silent as they had attended her and primped her and cleaned her. And Jahr had assured her he would be there to smooth the transition.

Sol stepped out of the carriage into a courtyard of stone. The ground was paved with square blocks, and the manor was made of bricks. This was a home that wouldn't burn.

The manor was larger than any building she had ever seen, larger even than the temple in Skive she had once visited as a child. She had never been to Lady Isabella's manor, but it must've been similarly large and grand. Wavy panes of glass covered the manor's walls and allowed her to see the fine furniture and tapestries inside.

A pair of large oak doors marked the entrance to the manor, and Cassian soldiers in green uniforms and attendants in plain, gray dresses waited on the steps leading up to the door.

A finely-clothed Cassian stood in the center with his arms crossed over his broad chest. His hair and beard were long, as was the Cassian custom, and his beard had many thin braids tied with gold thread. He wore a fur hat over his blond hair, and a thick fur coat rich with red and gold tassels.

Sol's heart caught in her chest and she took a step backward. Prince Turullius. Lady Isabella's betrothed.

Her betrothed.

Jahr caught her arm and dragged her forward. "Behave," he hissed in her ear.

Her heart fluttered in her chest, as flighty as a bird. She wished she were bird, wished she could fly away from here and never return.

Prince Turullius was in his late thirties, and she was barely nineteen. His bearded face gave him a gruff and surly aspect, and his sharp, blue predator eyes didn't help.

She forced herself to meet his gaze. This was her future now. She was going to marry him and save her village. She would be wealthy, and her family would never know hunger again. She was going to be brave and do the right thing. And Kelan—

And Kelan had come to the parade with the intention of killing Lady Isabella. Whatever had happened between them on those cold, snowy nights was over.

Turullius walked forward and held out his arms. He caught her by the shoulders and kissed each of her cheeks with lips that barely stuck out from beneath his thick beard. She stiffened at his touch. He stank of spicy, curried meat, and honey mead.

"My lovely bride," Turullius said in Cassian, his eyes roving her face. "Welcome," he added for her benefit, in thick, clumsy Nordese.

Jahr nudged her.

"Prince Turullius," Sol said and curtsied low, as she had practiced. "I am grateful to be with you." She tried to make her words stick and the sounds come out strange. Lady Isabella was only supposed to know a few words of Cassian.

Turllius grinned and took her tightly by the arm, leading her into the house. It was all she could do to make herself keep breathing as they passed through the oak doors of the prince's manor. Why had she agreed to do this? Her stomach twisted itself into knots just standing next to him.

It was warm and smelled of food inside the manor. One thing she could look forward to, at least. She was always hungry now, though she could eat only a little at a time. Her stomach was still adjusting.

Turullius released her to shrug off his fur coat. Sol's attendants helped her remove the furs they had draped around her shoulders, though Sol protested. The slaves had dressed her in Cassian style, and Sol hated her gown. Nordese dresses were high-necked and practical, and the common folk wore them with leggings beneath and slits up the skirt to facilitate movement. Sol's dress rested off her shoulders and its neckline swooped low, revealing far too much of her chest, and the bodice and skirt were both restricting.

She pressed a hand to her chest and tried to yank the fabric up, but one of the attendants pushed her hand away.

"Can't I have anything decent to wear?" Sol asked.

"When they gave us your measurements, they underestimated how well you would fill out your dresses. We'll have them remade for you," one of the girls whispered back.

"And let out the hem," the other said, staring at Sol's exposed ankles. At least the shoes they had provided Sol had fit her.

"Let me wear my furs," Sol said, trying to take them back from her attendant, but the girl held them out of reach.

"I think this dress looks well on you," Jahr said, his eyes lingering on her neckline. "I rather think Prince Turullius will like it."

She glared at Jahr, but he took her hand and dragged her away from her attendants. He took her into the spacious hall, where Turullius was speaking with a large group of Tokken and Cassian soldiers.

Turullius' voice was loud and rang through the high-ceilinged room. "We'll search the city until they're found. I want to see those Flameskins hung on my wedding day."

Sol's stomach lurched. Kelan. She had to warn him to stay away.

Turullius turned toward her and held out a hand. "Come here, my sweet bride."

She took his hand and tried not to squirm. He pulled her in and kissed her lips. His kiss was gruff and abrupt, as though a kiss was the same as a handshake. It was nothing like the way

Kelan kissed her: slow, and wanting, his lips tingling with fire in a way that made her breathless.

"I won't let anything harm Lady Isabella. We'll double the guards on the manor. And she's to be kept here until the Flameskins are found and killed," Turullius said.

Sol swallowed. Prisoner. There would be no finding Kelan, no warning him. No visits to her mountains.

"I'll find the ones who attacked you," Turullius said, and stroked her hair. "Would that please you, my sweet?"

Sol opened her mouth, but Jahr answered for her. "I apologize, Prince Turullius, but she doesn't speak much Cassian."

Turullius laughed. "No matter. A woman doesn't need words. She needs only a pretty face and a large dowry. And you my dear," he said, pointedly staring at her cleavage, "have a very large dowry, indeed."

She clenched her fists at her side and held her breath. Jahr took her arm and gave her a warning look.

She slowly exhaled. She was doing this for her family and for her village.

During the banquet she ate little and said nothing. Several of the local Cassian nobles had been invited, and the women laughed at the way Sol ate and at her slanted, Nordese eyes, and were scandalized by her dress. The noblemen, most especially Turullius, made lewd comments about their upcoming nuptials.

Her new home was as gaudy and useless as its guests. Trinkets, paintings, and tapestries covered every inch of wall in a suffocating display of wealth.

The food wasn't even good. Too flavorful. She was used to lightly flavored meats, plain rice, and vegetables. The spices in the food overwhelmed her, and she could stomach little of it, especially with Turullius beside her.

She stood to excuse herself when the guests began to leave.

Turullius rose and enveloped her hand with his thick fingers. "Are you going somewhere, Lady Isabella?"

"I am tired," she said haltingly in Cassian.

Turullius' face brightened. "I'll show you to your rooms. Come, my dear."

He took her by the hand and guided her out of the hall toward the staircase. Commander Jahr stood and made to accompany them, but Turullius waved him off. Sol gave Jahr a frightened, wide-eyed look. Jahr wouldn't abandon her to Turullius, would he?

The prince led her upstairs, murmuring sweet things the real Lady Isabella wouldn't have understood and that disgusted Sol. He stopped at the end of the hallway and opened a door for her. A trunk of clothes Jahr had supplied was already waiting for her at the foot of the bed.

Turullius wrapped his large hand around her hip and pressed her to him. "We need not wait until we are married to enjoy the time we have together," he murmured, staring at her neckline.

She tried to twist away from him, but he held her tight. He was squeezing the air out of her, suffocating her. She couldn't breathe. She tried to inhale to scream, but who would come for her? Who would stop Turullius from taking his bride?

He mashed his lips against her mouth and pulled her closer. "I know you can't understand me, Isabella, but I will teach you a language all people know."

"I-I am tired," she said, pushing away from him. Her whole body shook, and her head spun.

He kissed her cheek and released her. She immediately stepped away from him and pressed herself against the wall, watching him warily.

"I forget the ordeal you've been through. Rest, my dear, sweet Isabella. Tomorrow night I will see you properly sent to bed."

He kissed her hand with his bearded lips and strolled away down the hall. She scurried into the bedroom and locked the door behind her. She ran to the desk and rooted through the drawers for a weapon.

One drawer contained a jeweled letter opener. It was dull, but it looked dangerous.

She gripped it in her hand. If Turullius tried to return to her room tonight, she would be ready.

CHAPTER 32
SOL

S ol paced the room, letter opener in hand. She couldn't stay here. She wasn't noble enough to give herself to a beast like that, especially not after knowing what it was like to have someone like Kelan, who cared about her, who would give his life for her.

She fisted her hands and shoved away the thoughts of Kelan. Why couldn't she stop thinking about him when she had her own prince-sized problem to deal with?

She couldn't stay here. Not a single night. She would run. She'd return to the mountains and never look back. Jahr could find another girl to play Lady Isabella if he wanted, but Sol refused to play this part.

And maybe, if she got a chance, she could find a way into the Flameskin camp and warn Kelan. She didn't want to see him hurt because of all this.

She opened the chest of clothes and sorted through them, tossing aside the useless dresses. Jahr had let her keep her old clothes, and they had already been washed and dried, though they were stained and ripped from her travel. It didn't matter. She never cared to wear another dress like this again.

She stripped off the ridiculous dress and threw it on the

ground, then pulled on her wool leggings and tunic, and her burned fur coat as well. Her pa's emberstone was still in her coat pocket.

She took a fur wrap from the chest of clothing and rolled it up with a blanket from the bed. That would have to do as a bedroll. She could sneak to the kitchens after the banquet ended and steal some food, and a bow if she could find one. They had to have an armory somewhere with so many soldiers around.

She sat on the bed and waited until the night grew late and the noisy guests had all left. Then she waited longer, until she was sure even the guards must be sleeping.

She tied her new bedroll around her back and unlocked the door. She padded soundlessly down the hallway. A huntress was always silent on the hunt, except this time, she was the animal being hunted.

The hall led to a landing above the staircase. Commander Jahr sat in a chair in the center of the hall with his long legs stretched across the landing. He was slumped in the chair, asleep.

She paused, listening. Jahr's breathing was even and deep.

She took slow, careful steps, praying to all the gods he would stay asleep. She inched closer and a board groaned beneath her foot.

She froze midstep and watched Jahr's face. His nose twitched, and he scratched it.

She stepped over his legs slowly, carefully. But the hem of her coat brushed his leg.

Jahr jerked upright.

She leapt forward, but Jahr was faster. He tripped her, and she landed hard on her side, then he yanked her upright and had her tightly by the arm before she could get to the stairs.

"I thought you might try to run," he growled.

He pushed her against the wall and pinned her there. She tried to squirm away, but Jahr was as massive and immobile as a tree.

"Where were you going?" he demanded.

"Away. Anywhere but here."

"You have a duty to perform, and I will see that you do it."

"It's not my duty. It's Isabella's."

"And it's your fault Isabella's dead."

"Find some other girl who wants to be Turullius' wife. I won't marry that pig. I won't let him touch me."

"So we let the demons overrun us? Is that what you want?"

"They're not all demons."

Jahr roughly dragged her toward her room, opened the door, and shoved her inside.

"You will do this, or I'll see your family punished. I won't feel obligated to protect your village if its huntress is a traitor to her own people. Think on that, Lady Isabella."

He slammed the door and Sol pounded her fists against it. "Let me go!" she screamed. But Jahr had his weight pressed against the door, and it didn't budge. She whirled around and ran toward the window. She pried at the windowpanes, but the glass was built into the wooden frame of the wall. It wasn't a window that was meant to open.

She threw herself onto the bed and tried not to sob. She should've stayed with Kelan. She wished more than anything to be in the mountains with him again. They could've left all of this, the war, the soldiers, Prince Turullius.

But what would he say now that he thought she was Isabella? Would he hate her? Was there a way to get him a message and explain everything to him? Would be able to rescue her if he knew?

She missed his easy smile. She missed the way he seemed to find the humor in the blackest of circumstances. She missed the way he held her, the way his skin prickled with heat.

A pinging at the window scattered her thoughts.

She looked up as another stone clattered against the windowpane. She stepped toward the window and cupped her hands around her face so she could peer outside.

A man stood outside, silhouetted by the snow. He wore a gray coat, and it was difficult to see his face in the darkness, but she would've recognized the straight edge of his shoulders and the tangle of his curly hair anywhere.

"Kelan," she whispered.

He had come for her. She had wished it and he had come.

He waved at her and she waved back. Would he know she was happy to see him?

But how could she get down? She couldn't get through the window, and Jahr was in the hallway.

She brushed her fingers against the tingly emberstone in her pocket. No, she couldn't burn her way out. She wasn't skilled enough to control the emberstone, and she couldn't risk setting the whole manor on fire.

She glanced around the room, searching for some means of escape, and her gaze rested on the wooden chair near her vanity. Maybe there was a way out.

With great effort, she shoved the dresser across the floor and pushed it against the door, wedging it against the door handle. It wouldn't give her much extra time, but hopefully enough.

She pressed her face against the glass to check if Kelan was still there and waved to him again. Then she picked up the chair and slammed it against the window.

Glass shattered, and the windowpanes smashed to pieces on the ground and cut her hands. Several glass shards flew into her face and sliced her cheeks. But she didn't care. She was getting out.

She used the chair legs to smash open the window, making a hole in the wall big enough to jump through.

"Lady Isabella?" Jahr shouted on the other side of the door. He jiggled the handle and swore. The dresser bumped and skittered, and the door thumped when he threw himself against it.

"Kelan!" Sol shouted through the window.

"I'm here," he said, and her heart thrilled at the sound of his voice. "Jump. I'll catch you."

Her stomach fluttered. She wanted nothing more than to be in his arms again.

She threw her makeshift bedroll into the snow beside him and used the chair to climb up onto the window ledge. Sharp glass cut her boots, and she kicked the window shards away as she balanced on the edge. Kelan stood below her with his arms outstretched, but her stomach flipped as she judged the distance between them. It was a long fall.

Something heavy smashed against her door. Another chair?

She took a deep breath to steady herself and jumped. It was a quick drop, and a yelp escaped her throat as she slammed into him. They fell hard into the snow, and he gasped. But Sol smiled and wrapped her arms around his neck and touched his smooth, clean-shaven face.

"Kelan," she murmured. "You don't know how happy I am to see you."

He took her hands in his and rolled on top of her. He broke away from her kisses and bent upward, pressing her hands hard into her chest.

"You lied to me," he said, his eyes hard.

"No, Kelan, I—"

He clamped a hand over her mouth as Commander Birke appeared above her and tied ropes around her wrists. When Kelan lifted her from the snow, someone else came from behind and gagged her. She stared dumbly at Kelan, unable to comprehend what was happening.

But as the gag was pulled tight over her mouth, she understood.

Kelan was a soldier now, and she was Lady Isabella. None of that time in the woods together meant anything to him. She squirmed and tried to scream, but the gag muffled the sound.

"Lady Isabella!" Jahr shouted from her window. Kelan and her two assailants startled, and Kelan's hands sparked.

"Flameskins!" Jahr shouted. "Guards!"

Kelan hurled a ball of fire at the window, and Jahr ducked inside before it exploded against the house.

Then Kelan turned toward her, an ugly snarl marring his handsome face. His voice was dark and horrible. "We'll burn the manor to the ground."

Kelan had been possessed.

CHAPTER 33
KELAN

K elan led the horse through the snow with Lady Isabella draped over its saddle and lashed to it with rope. Isabella's lashes were wet and icy. Her hair tumbled loose from her head and her hat was gone.

His pyra simmered with pleasure, and it stretched his face into that crooked smile Kelan had seen Markus wear so often. She screamed something into her gag when he looked at her and squirmed atop the horse.

She's ours, his pyra hissed in his mind. *We will make her suffer.*

"She came when you called," Haldur said. "How interesting."

Kelan looked back at her again. But why would she? If everything had been a lie, why did she jump right into his arms? Uncle Haldur had insisted they try to lure her out of the house, once Kelan had explained their relationship, and how she had manipulated him.

Had not all of it been a lie?

"We're as surprised as you are," Kelan said, his voice twinned with his pyra's.

Haldur gave him his best attempt at a smile—Kelan's reward for finally giving himself over to his pyra. Kelan should've been horrified, but he wasn't. Sol had proved to him that no amount of trying could change what he was.

They will always hate us. That's why we must destroy them.

Officer Osten led them at a quick pace, but he kept glancing behind them at their moonlit tracks. "We should slit her throat and dump her in the snow."

"No," Kelan's pyra hissed. "We want her death to be slow. We want to watch her burn."

"The soldiers can't be far behind," Osten said.

"We'll split up," Haldur said. "I'll take the horse and make a false trail. Osten, you go back to the house and tell the men we've got Isabella and that we're leaving. Kelan, you take Isabella, and hide the body when you've finished."

"There will be no body left to hide," Kelan said. The thought gave him a thrill of pleasure. The power to burn anything, to turn even the unbreakable Lady Isabella to ash.

"But, Commander—" Osten argued.

"Those are the orders," Haldur said. He put a hand on Kelan's shoulder. "He's finally given himself over to possession. I think this is fair compensation."

Kelan glanced at Isabella. Her face was drawn and terrified.

Good. Let her fear us. We were meant to be feared.

"Meet back at camp in an hour. We'll leave immediately," Haldur said.

"An hour isn't enough time," Kelan said.

"Make it enough. We have to be out of the foothills before the soldiers start searching for her in the mountains."

Kelan untied Isabella from the saddle and slung her over his shoulder. She was still as heavy as before, but now his pyra had full possession of his body. It pumped fire into his shoulder and his legs, strengthening them so he could barely feel her weight. Isabella thrashed, but her wrists and ankles were bound, and Kelan held her tight. She beat at his chest with her tied hands.

Kelan grabbed her by the throat and squeezed. "Stop," he growled.

Her thrashing slowed as she gasped for air through her gag. His pyra laughed inside him, a sound like crackling fire.

The three of them separated, Uncle Haldur leading the horse

through the snow, Kelan with Isabella, and Osten hurrying toward the city to get the other spies.

Isabella hung limp over his shoulder as Kelan hiked through the foothills. Why had he resisted his pyra so long? He was stronger than he had ever been. A mountain climb that had once seemed daunting was now a welcome challenge.

Once they were out of view of Olisipo, Kelan dumped her into the snow and stood over her, his lips curled into a scowl. The Lady Isabella. She flailed in the snow, trying to get away from him, but he stomped on her chest, pinning her in place with his boot.

She wore that ratty, burned fur coat. It wasn't a good enough disguise to fool him anymore. Isabella yanked with her fingers at the gag around her mouth and pulled it free. Good. He wanted to hear her plead for her life, and hear her screams as he burned her.

"Kelan, please. I'm not Lady Isabella."

"Don't tell us more lies," Kelan said, his voice low and dark and laced with crackling energy. "You always hated us. You used us to get down the mountain so you could call your armies to destroy us."

He yanked off one of her boots. He would burn her from her toes to her head, slowly, so she could feel the flames crawl across every inch of her skin.

"I'm just Sol, just the huntress. I never lied to you. They forced me to take Lady Isabella's place. I was trying to run away. I thought you had come to rescue me." Her voice broke into a sob.

Fire wrapped around Kelan's hand, and he brought it closer to the sock on her foot. He grinned as her eyes widened and she tried to kick away.

Burn her. Burn her!

He had no real control over his own body anymore. His pyra manipulated his hands and spread fire through his veins. It held the flame far enough from her foot not to burn her, but close enough for her to feel its heat.

But his pyra hesitated as he looked over her. *We'll take her, Kelan,* it said. It quivered inside him with the anticipation of pleasure. *We'll take what she owes us. We can burn her after.*

His pyra sucked the fire back into his hand and brought Kelan down onto his knees. He knelt over her, a crooked grin twisting his face. Some part of him resisted, but his pyra was stronger. It wanted to hurt Sol in every way possible.

"Kelan, stop," she begged. "I know you're in there somewhere. Fight back!"

"There's nothing to fight." He unbuttoned her coat with agitated hands.

"You promised," she sobbed. "You promised you wouldn't become this monster. You promised you wouldn't hurt me. You said you loved me!"

He recoiled from her, sitting back on his heels.

She's manipulating us again. Nothing she says matters.

But he still loved her. He didn't want to hurt her.

His head ached and fire burned inside his mind, chasing away his thoughts. His pyra manipulated his memories, twisting them into darkness and pain, and whispered death in his ear. Kelan pressed his palms to his eyes and shuddered as fire ripped through his mind.

"Fight it, Kelan! Don't let it take you."

"No!" Kelan's pyra roared. "Never!"

He crouched over her, breathing hard.

We will burn her to ash and listen to her scream.

And Kelan couldn't remember if he had ever thought he wanted to do anything else. There was only the need to destroy, the need to burn, the need to watch Isabella suffer.

He grabbed her foot and fire shot out of his hands, leaping up her body. Flames consumed her sock and grabbed at the hem of her pants and the ropes that encircled her ankles. She screamed and writhed, but he held tight. His body flooded with euphoric heat as he watched the fire grow.

Everything must burn.

Isabella twisted to the side and tried to yank her foot free.

But he didn't let go. Then she reached for his hand and pressed something hard against his skin.

His pyra evaporated.

He tried to pull away, but she grasped at his fingers, squeezing the emberstone to his skin as she shoved her burning feet into the snow.

"Please still be there," she begged.

He yanked the emberstone from her hand.

"Don't throw it!"

He sank into the snow, grasping the stone tightly, as if it were a lifeline. No, he wouldn't throw it. He'd never let go of it again. The fire left his blood, and his mind cleared, leaving only thoughts of Sol.

He yanked the manacle out of his pocket and snapped it onto his wrist, then crawled toward her.

"Sol," he sobbed. "I burned you."

"I had my emberstone. You didn't hurt me."

Though one leg of her pants was charred, her skin was undamaged. He hurriedly ripped at the ropes and freed her ankles, then moved to her wrists. Once her hands were loosed, she wrapped them around his neck.

"Is it you, Kelan?" she asked, searching his eyes.

"It's me. I'm so sorry, Sol."

She held him tight, and he squeezed her to him as a shudder wracked his body. He had tried to kill her; he had thought she was burning, and he had reveled in her pain.

"Forgive me. I would never have hurt you."

"It's over. You're back," she whispered. She rubbed her wet cheeks against his shoulder.

He kissed her forehead and wiped away a tear at the corner of her eye. "And are you Sol, or Isabella?" It didn't matter. He would've loved her whatever her name was.

"Isabella's dead. They made me take her place and they were going to force me to marry that beast, Turullius. I tried to run away. I was going to find you, Kelan."

He pulled her up to sitting and crushed her to him. "Ashes. How did this happen?"

He kissed her forehead again because he didn't know if she would let him kiss her lips, but he couldn't not hold her and touch her. He needed her. Now that they were together again, he was never going to let her go. He laced his fingers together around her back, beneath her coat. "I'll never take off this manacle again. I promise you that."

"Is that so?" Lieutenant Ager asked.

CHAPTER 34
KELAN

K elan scrambled to his feet, his heart lurching in his chest. Nilsa and Osten stood below them, near the edge of the cliff-side path that led toward Olisipo. Nilsa's face was pulled into a cruel sneer.

"Nilsa," Kelan said, his breath catching. He pushed Sol behind him, blocking her from view. "She isn't Lady Isabella. We were wrong."

"It doesn't matter who she is," Osten said. "Prince Turullius thinks she's Isabella, and he's got soldiers scouring the city looking for her. You were supposed to kill her."

"I won't."

Sol clung tight to his arm. He slipped her pa's emberstone into her hand. At least that would give her some protection against Nilsa's fire. Kelan could unlock the manacle and get his pyra back, but his pyra would try to hurt Sol after it had destroyed Nilsa and Osten, and he had no guarantee he could get the manacle back on again.

The two soldiers walked toward them along the edge of the cliff, following the path toward the bluff where they stood. Fire sparked on Nilsa's fingers, and her eyes burned with the savage fire inside her.

"What has she done to you, Kelan?" she hissed. "Why would you wear an emberstone?"

Sol pulled a jeweled dagger out of her belt and held it in one hand, poised to throw. "I'm a dead aim with a knife."

Nilsa stopped short, but the fire in her hand sparked and swirled tightly around her fist.

"Let us go," Kelan said. "I'll take Sol away from here, where Turullius won't be able to find her." Sol stepped closer to Kelan and reached into his coat pocket.

Nilsa took a few steps forward with Osten advancing tentatively behind her. Fire swirled around her hand and up her arm. "Can't you feel the call to destroy? I can get your pyra back, Kelan. I can help you." She extended one burning hand to him.

"I won't be a demon."

Nilsa snarled and raised her flaming hands. Fire shot over her arms and up her sleeves, burning her coat and sending pieces of ash over the white snow.

"Kill him," Osten said.

Nilsa shoved Osten into the snow with a burning hand, setting his coat on fire. "I don't take orders from you." But she turned back toward Kelan and leapt across the snow, gathering fire between her fingers.

Sol had grabbed Kelan's wrist, and the lock on his manacle clicked open. The shackle fell into Sol's hand as fire erupted from Nilsa's fists.

"No!" Kelan shouted.

His pyra blossomed in his blood, and Nilsa's fire struck his chest, knocking him backward into Sol. He hit the snow with a sizzle of ice and a cloud of steam, but was on his feet before he could think.

His pyra wore his body like a glove, pushing fire into his arms and legs. Flames flickered behind his eyes, turning everything to red and gold. Sol lay in the snow behind him, forgotten, as he stood and turned toward Nilsa.

She attacked us. She will burn.

Kelan advanced slowly. The snow around him melted and

evaporated at his feet. Fire consumed Nilsa. It ate her coat, revealing the leather fire-proof armor she wore underneath. Flames crawled over her legs and her arms, and flickered through her black hair.

Osten got to his feet and Kelan threw out a blast and knocked him down again. Osten was no threat. What mages could do with fire was a shadow of Kelan's powers. Osten pretended he could summon and control fire, but Kelan had been born with it in his blood. Nilsa was his only worthy adversary.

"Come back to us, Kelan. We could burn the world together." Her voice hissed in her throat, and her eyes burned.

Nilsa didn't want him to come back. Her pyra wanted a fight, and that's what he would give her.

He crouched low and gave her a vicious smile. "You always thought you were better than me."

"It's the truth. We'll tear you apart and bring your ashes back to your uncle." She crackled with laughter and sparks danced over her skin. Her face flickered with tongues of fire running up her skin, and all he could make out were her violet eyes. They looked red in the light of her fire.

Flames shot out of Kelan's hands. His pyra moved him into a crouch and then a dive as he leapt to avoid Nilsa's fire.

Nilsa had been possessed early and had worked in tandem with her pyra for a long time. She always used to beat him when they sparred. But now Kelan had given complete control to the monster inside him.

Nilsa didn't stand a chance.

The hill steamed and exploded with flames and ice and splashes of melted snow. Kelan's pyra leapt at Nilsa, taking Kelan's body with it. Fire exploded out of Kelan's skin, but instead of wasting it to let it crawl all over his skin like Nilsa, his pyra kept it tightly controlled inside his hands, two streams of raw energy fueled by his anger and his hate and the joy of destruction. A column of fire shot out of him and struck Nilsa, shoving her backward and dropping her into a roll.

She hissed at him and spat curses, and Kelan smiled.

This is what we were always meant to be.

Nilsa tried to beat him back with flames, but Kelan was no longer human, and no longer limited by his frail mortal frame. Fire burned through every muscle and tendon in his body. He darted toward Nilsa, closing the distance between them, and the panic in her eyes filled him with intoxicating joy.

She will burn.

He gloried in the prospect of it. For every blast Nilsa sent his way, Kelan met it with an explosion of his own. She didn't have the control and the dexterity he did.

"Kelan!" Nilsa screamed. Her human voice had broken through her pyra's control. She had given herself over to her fear and it had extinguished her pyra.

Kelan grabbed the knife from his belt and advanced, fire still swirling over his hands.

Spill her blood upon the snow! his pyra hissed.

Kelan's heart thumped wildly, and his pyra buzzed inside him.

This had always been his true purpose: to burn and destroy and kill.

He was a demon, and he had born to burn.

"Kelan, please," Nilsa whimpered.

He smiled as he bent down and slashed her open.

CHAPTER 35

SOL

S ol watched, horrified, as Lieutenant Ager dropped onto the snow. Dead. Her blood ran over the white snow and froze in rivulets of red.

This was what Sol had wanted, wasn't it? This was why she had released his pyra, so it could save them from the soldiers.

But letting Kelan turn into this monstrous creature had been a mistake.

Kelan laughed as he stood over Nilsa, and he released a burst of fire at her face. It consumed her, and sticky, foul smoke filled the air. Sol covered her mouth with her sleeve and gagged on the smell. This had gone on long enough.

Osten had run off down the hill before Sol could get to him, and he'd return with reinforcements. She and Kelan needed to keep moving or Flameskin soldiers would find them.

Sol slid her boot back on and pulled the manacle and her pa's emberstone from her pocket. If she could get either of those to touch Kelan, the demon would be gone. She just needed to get close enough to him to do it.

Kelan stood near the edge of the cliff, and if she launched herself at him, they'd both go over the edge. She crept carefully around the clearing to get behind him. Then she took a breath and leapt toward him, extending both emberstones at him.

He looked up just as she jumped and hissed at her as he leapt away. She hit the snow hard, and narrowly missed landing on Lieutenant Ager's mutilated body. She swallowed bile as she scrambled away from the body and crouched in the snow, searching for Kelan.

He stood at the edge of the tree line, that horrible smile marring his face.

This creature wasn't Kelan. Kelan was gentle and kind. This thing was cruel, and it took pleasure in pain and suffering. Maybe it looked like Kelan, but its eyes were different, hard where Kelan's were soft. Its mouth was sharp where Kelan's was inviting. Fire still glimmered on its hands, and nipped at the edges of his sleeves.

This was the monster her pa had always warned her about, the one with fire beneath its skin and a voice inside it that whispered death.

The demon circled slowly. Sol was trapped at the edge of the cliff next to Nilsa's body.

"Sol," it hissed, as if testing the name in its mouth. She shuddered at the sound of its voice, a crackling roar of flames inside Kelan's throat.

"Please, Kelan, you need to put the emberstone back on."

It laughed. "Your Kelan is gone. There is only fire left."

It advanced, and she took a wary step backward. Her hands were shaking now, and she closed them over the emberstones. Breathe. She had to breathe and remain in control.

But her heart wouldn't listen. It galloped and pounded madly in her chest as she held the demon's gaze.

Fire swirled around the demon's hand. "How do you want us to kill you, *Sol?*" It said her name like a curse.

"Fight this, Kelan! It isn't you!"

It laughed again and two blasts of flame flew out of the demon's hands. Sol screamed and jumped. She tumbled into the snow to dodge them and picked herself up again, breathing hard.

"We're going to destroy you, *Sol*," it purred. "We will drink your blood and eat your ash."

She swallowed hard and clipped the manacle onto her own wrist, then pulled the jeweled letter opener out of her belt. "I don't want to hurt you, Kelan."

Something flickered in its face and it moved farther back, out of range of her knife. She wished it were a real knife. She wouldn't kill Kelan, of course, but if she could get him down long enough to get an emberstone on him . . . .

The demon growled and fire swirled in its hands again, just long enough to warn her what was coming. Orbs of fire flew toward her, and she threw herself to the side, but he was too fast, and it was too hard to maneuver through the snow. One of them hit her head, and it felt like he had taken a club to the side of her face. The blast knocked something loose inside her. She fell back into the snow groaning, and her vision swam.

"Get up," the demon hissed. "Get up and fight us."

She rose unsteadily to her feet.

"You tried to prevent us from becoming what we were meant to be," he said, gesturing to his body with his burning hands.

"Don't listen to it, Kelan."

"You're a murderess," it hissed. "For our trust you gave only lies and blind hate. For our love you gave only pain."

Love.

She stared at the monster occupying Kelan's body. Wasn't love supposed to be the answer? In the old legends about the Ulves, wasn't it love that turned dragons' hearts to gold, and melted the frost wolves, and forced the dryads to return their stolen hearts? Love was supposed to be stronger than any curse.

She searched the demon's face for anything of her Kelan, the Kelan she had kissed, the one she used to curl up against to stay warm, the one who liked to tease her, and who smiled at her when he thought she was wasn't looking.

That was the Kelan she loved, the one she wanted back.

"Kelan, I love you."

His hands fell to his side and the grin on his face faltered.

Sol took a hesitant step forward. "I know you're still in there. You can fight this. I'll help you."

But then he smiled, a cruel, twisted, horrible smile, and the flames on his arms and hands spiked. "You think anything you say matters to us?"

She yelped as he hurled more fire at her.

Kelan was gone.

She let out a sob as she stumbled through the snow. This wasn't a fairytale. Love was conqueror of no one and nothing. He was going to kill her. He was going to watch her burn just like he'd said.

She drew fire from the emberstone at her wrist and gathered flames in her hand the way he had taught her. Then she stood and faced him.

"Go on," it goaded, grinning, "just try to hurt us."

She coiled the fire, trying to control it, but it was as unsteady as her shaking hands and her frantic pulse.

"Your death will be our greatest triumph," the demon hissed. "Your ashes will taste like victory."

She stared hard at the demon, and the snowy cliff and the pale dawn sky behind it. The flames on its arms lit the snow and his face with orange light. The air tasted of burning hair and oily smoke.

She hurled the flames at him. The orb wavered in the air, half-formed and unsteady, and sunk with a hiss into the snow at the demon's feet.

It laughed, but then the snow shifted. The demon's feet slipped backward. He threw out his arms as he lost his balance and he fell forward, sliding over the ice at his feet toward the edge of the cliff.

Sol ran through the snow and launched herself at him. She grasped his arms, pressing the emberstone around her wrist to his skin as she did so. The fire on his body evaporated and Kelan shouted as his feet slid off the edge.

They both screamed as Kelan's body dropped. His chest hit the cliff face and his legs dangled in open air.

They clutched each other's forearms desperately. Sol tried to wedge her feet into something so they'd stop sliding, but the ice was slick from Kelan's flames. She grunted and sobbed as she pulled on him, but he kept slipping farther. Each moment brought her closer to the edge. He was going to pull both of them over the cliff.

"Let go!" Kelan shouted.

"No!"

She looked into his face, into turquoise eyes now full of terror. She wedged the toe of one boot into a crag of ice and they finally stopped slipping.

"Climb up!"

He tried to twist and bring his legs up to reach the ledge, but the movement dislodged her hold and yanked her closer to the edge. She cried out, and his arms slid between her grasp.

She sobbed as she met his eyes.

"I love you, Sol," he whispered.

She shook her head, fighting back tears and tugging on his arms.

He loosened his hold on her forearms and hung limp, his arms sliding between her sweat-slick hands.

"Kelan!"

"It's time to let go, love."

"No! Stop!"

She couldn't lose him. Not now. She wouldn't.

She pulled on the fire in her emberstone, letting it rush into her and through her arms. He winced as her skin warmed, and heat came off her in blistering waves, but she could feel the flames pooling in her arms, her shoulders, her back. She tightened her grip with her flame-strengthened hands and pulled, trying to slither backward. She grunted as she yanked on him, and used her knees to slide them backward, pulling him upward first one inch, then two.

She would not give up. She would not let him go.

He gripped her forearms tight, despite the burning of her skin, and once he was high enough, his feet found purchase on the frozen cliff face and he propelled himself upward.

She hauled him over the top and into her arms where they lay panting, their limbs intertwined. She quickly unlocked the manacle on her wrist and clipped it onto his.

That was never coming off again.

He wrapped his arms around her as he pressed his cheek to hers.

She shuddered in his arms.

This was Kelan.

Kelan.

Not the demon.

But it was hard to look into his face and forget that a moment ago he had been trying to kill her. The terror of this endless night had left her raw. Her head still ached from his blow and her thoughts were tangled and sharp-edged.

She wedged her hands beneath his chest and shoved him so hard he tumbled backward. She pushed herself to her feet and scowled down at him. "Don't you ever do that again."

He stood and faced her. "I never wanted that. You were the one who unlocked it."

She shoved him again, and her voice broke as she shouted. "Don't you ever give up on yourself like that! Don't you ever let go. Don't ever leave me."

He caught her wrists and held them tight. "You were the one who left me."

She swallowed a sob. "I know."

How could she have done that? How could she ever have imagined herself as the wife of Turullius?

She needed Kelan, like the way she needed the mountains and the trees and a bow in her hands. He was as much a part of her life now as the mountains were. Why had it taken so long to realize that? Why had it taken almost losing him to see what he meant to her?

She just wanted things to back to the way they were, before they came to Cassia.

He picked up the lost letter opener from the snow and she stuffed it into her belt. He crossed his arms over his chest. The emberstone glowed on his wrist, turning his pale skin red as he shivered. His sleeves were burned to the elbow and offered no protection from the cold.

"What do we do now?" he asked. "The Tokken and Flameskin armies will be hunting us."

"And Turullius' army, too. He said he wanted the Flameskins hung on his wedding day."

Kelan's eyebrows rose and he gave a strangled laugh. "You're going back for the wedding?"

She scowled at him. "Don't. I'm going back to the mountains."

She was already considering which trail they could take that would best hide their tracks and what terrain would give them the best cover. But her stomach clenched at the thought of the hunger and the cold and the depravity that awaited them.

Kelan shifted. "Are you going alone, or . . . ?"

She shoved him again. "No, you idiot. We're going together."

He scowled and rubbed his shoulder. "A few days ago that wasn't the case."

"Well it is now."

"Sol, what you said before. I need to know what—"

"We're not having this discussion now. We need to move."

"Wait." He reached out to touch her and she instinctively stepped away. Her heart went into a wild panic. His eyes darkened with hurt, and he pulled his hand back.

"You shouldn't have unlocked it," he said. "I never wanted you to be afraid of me."

"I'm not." She tried to reach out and grab his hand, but she was shaking too badly. She wanted all of this to be over. She wanted to make a fire and curl up next to Kelan and sleep.

There was noise below the cliff that startled both of them.

Shouting, and the *crunch, crunch* of soldiers marching through icy snow.

She steeled herself and grabbed his hand, then pulled him into the woods beside her.

CHAPTER 36
KELAN

K elan trudged through the snow. He was past shivering.
The cold locked up his limbs and made his movements
stiff and slow. Sol had switched coats with him, but even her pa's
fur coat wasn't enough to stave off the winter.

They had been following the main road through the pass that
had already been tramped down by other feet, making the going
a bit easier. Sol seemed confident that the trail hadn't been
paved by any of their enemies, though Kelan didn't know how
that could be possible. There wasn't a single person in the world
who didn't want Kelan dead, except Sol.

And even that felt still up in the air.

Sol had stopped on the trail above him and waited for him to
catch up. Dawn had broken hours ago, and the broad, generous
morning sun lit the snow in a glittering carpet of crystal.

When he reached her, she pointed to a mound of sparkling
snow. "That's where the bandits are."

Kelan looked around. This was the clearing where they had
been attacked? Everywhere in these mountains looked the same
to him. Just trees and snow and boulders. How did Sol always
know where she was?

"Can you melt it?" he asked. "If I can't fight with my pyra, I'll
need a sword."

Her face was blank. She looked tired, worn around the edges. "You think we'll have to fight?"

"I'd rather be prepared than not."

He instructed her on how to melt the snow, and she used her emberstone to push heat out of her body, melting a large swath of the snowdrift and sending a river of water rushing down the hillside. The bandits lay in a neat pile, though their scorched faces and chests and clothes were not as tidy. They had been perfectly preserved by the ice, frozen in the same horrible positions they had died in.

Kelan grimaced. His pyra had done that. His pyra had killed Nilsa and it would've killed Sol, too. He regretted Nilsa's death. They had once been friends; she hadn't deserved to die like that.

He sent up a prayer for her soul as he loosened a bandit's scabbard with his numb fingers. Sol kept a silent watch beside him, her eyes fixed on the trail.

She had been silent on their walk, but it was a loud kind of silence, the kind that felt like one long continuous scream.

She was silent because she was afraid. Because she had seen his pyra and spoken with it. Because it had hurt her.

He was horrified at what he had done, but in equal measure he was angry. Angry at the Flameskin Army for turning him into this beast, angry at the world for denying him peace, and angry at Sol for releasing his pyra.

Why had she taken off his emberstone? Hadn't she just seen what he would become? Why would she make him into that monster?

The questions pulsed with anger that was hot and fresh. All those shards of his broken heart still cut him up inside, and it was worse when she looked at him with those wide, frightened eyes.

She said she loved him, but how could she when she was afraid of him?

He pulled two hats off the bodies and two pairs of gloves, and a scabbard and sword. He tried not to look at or think about what he was touching as he worked. The men had been ruthless bandits, intent on hurting and killing them. They probably would've tried to sell Sol into slavery if he hadn't ended them. He wasn't sorry for what he had done.

Some people deserved to die by fire.

When he shoved one of the frozen bodies to unravel a scarf beneath it, he found a knife lying in the melting snow. The curling oak etched onto the blade and the dark handle were familiar.

"Sol."

She looked up and he tossed the dagger to her. "This yours?"

"Where did you find it?"

He gestured to the bodies and she grimaced. "Keep it on you. You might need it if I ever lose my emberstone." The words came out more bitterly sarcastic than he had intended. She turned away from him.

Kelan gathered up the hats and gloves he had found and kicked snow over the bodies so he wouldn't have to look at their faces, frozen in the agony of death.

Sol had already sheathed her knife and had that jeweled dagger in her hand, poised to throw into the woods.

He grabbed her arm. "Wait!"

She gave a strangled cry and stumbled away from him in the slush. Her eyes were dark with terror. Kelan let go of her hand, and she took another step back.

"I'm not going to hurt you." Her fear cut like a dagger. "That wasn't me. You know that, don't you?"

She didn't answer.

Those shards of his heart cut deeper, making him bleed on the inside.

So, this was how it was going to be. Fine. They had played this game before, the huntress and the soldier. They could work together just fine and still hate each other.

He stuffed one of the bandit's hats on her head and took the jeweled knife from her. The blade was far too dull for any practical use, but it was sparkly. "Don't throw it. You can use it to buy food if you ever get to civilization again." He brought it close to his face to inspect the gems. "Are these real sapphires?"

She shrugged.

"Was this a gift from your beloved Turullius?"

She snatched it from his hand. "Say his name one more time and see what happens."

He studied her eyes, the same green of the forest, of which she was the queen. "Were you really going to marry him?"

"They forced me to become Lady Isabella."

"Maybe, but I've never seen anyone succeed in forcing you to do something you didn't want to do."

"But I ran away!"

That was the part that didn't make sense. If she had abandoned Kelan to the Flameskin Army, if she had never loved him, if they had offered her a prince, why had she smashed through her window and jumped into his arms?

But then, nothing Sol ever did made sense. Why had she said she loved him when he was fully possessed? Sol would say she hated him, then kiss him and look at him with those green eyes, and then hit him and curse his name.

He was tired of it. He was tired of everything. These blasted mountains, the snow, the cold. Beautiful, cruel, heartless Sol. The ice in her heart couldn't be melted, buried deep as it was beneath the mountains.

"You let them dress you up and put you in that carriage and parade you through the streets as his new bride. Don't tell me you didn't want that."

She scowled. An admission. At least she was being honest.

"Why are you even here if you're afraid of me?" he demanded. "Go back to your prince."

She stomped her foot. "Because of you, the Flameskins will destroy Hillerod."

"Because of me? I'm not the one who jumped out of a window."

"I trusted you!"

"You deceived me."

"You promised you would never hurt me."

"You knew what I was when we first met. You've always known what I would become."

"But you were supposed to resist!"

"I tried. I tried and I failed. Why did you take off my ember-stone? Why would you turn me into that thing?"

"I had no choice."

"Did you mean what you said? That you love me?"

She fell still, hesitating. He looked down at her small mouth, puckered with uncertainty, her cheeks and nose red with the cold, those green eyes the color of spring and better days.

Those better days had never included him in them.

She was right. She was always right.

There was no future for them.

Sol was like the mountains, an unchanging part of the land. Eternal and unbreakable. And he had broken himself against her, smashed himself to pieces trying to change her, to bend what could not be moved, to change nature itself.

"I don't know," she finally said.

He clenched his fists and exhaled heavily. He should've known she could never return his love. Loving Sol was like loving the wind that cut through him, chilling him to the bone. Or loving the sky that was too far away to touch. Or loving a river as he drowned in it.

He sighed and slumped against a tree. "Go back to your mountains, Sol. I'm done with this."

She breathed in sharply. "What?"

"Go back to your life. I don't want any part of it."

"You don't want to come with me?"

"Why would I? You hate me. You're afraid of me."

She was breathing heavily now, with the jeweled dagger tucked under one arm as she wrung her hands. "But I left Olisipo because of—But I—But where will you go?"

He shrugged. There was a place Flameskin deserters could go, at least, there were rumors of such a place. Really only something to give hope to those who didn't want to fight anymore.

Maybe it would've been better if Sol hadn't saved him from the cliff. He already felt like he was falling. Maybe it would be easier for him to slip into an abyss and be forgotten.

She was pacing now in the melted snow as rivers of water ran beneath her boots. She looked like an unraveling ball of yarn. "We're just exhausted. We just need some rest and food."

He shook his head. He was spent, a candle guttering out. Maybe rest would help with that, but it wouldn't do anything to fix his shattered heart or her fear. It would do nothing to change unbreakable Sol.

"I'm not going without you," she said. "I'm not letting you give up like that."

"Don't pretend like you care."

She stepped in close and curled her hands into fists. "Stop it, Kelan."

"No, you stop. I'm done with your games. I'm done with your lies."

"I'm not lying!"

"You pretend we're friends, but we never were."

"We are friends, Kelan. More than friends."

"How can we be friends if you're afraid of me? If you hate what I am?"

She was silent, and he stood over her, shivering. The hate and the rage curled and grew, and there was no pyra to consume his anger and turn it into fire. Instead, it welled up inside him, making his whole body quiver with the deep, erratic note of his pulse.

She reached a hand toward him, and he lurched away.

"Kelan—" She turned and faced the tracks they had left in the snow behind them. She went absolutely still, and Kelan could hear the wind blowing through the pines in the silence. Then she grabbed his hand. "We have to hide. Soldiers are here."

The trees here were sparse, and running away through the snow would leave tracks.

She pulled him toward the bandits' bodies and scooped at the snow. The drifts were in deep layers here, and she used her emberstone to carve out a tunnel for them in the snow. She pushed Kelan inside and crawled in after him, then dragged a body over the hole in the drift.

"I don't think this—"

"Quiet," she whispered.

She rested her head against his chest, and he wrapped his arms around her. The tunnel glowed a bright red with the light of his emberstone, and he buried his hand in the ice to smother it.

He closed his eyes to block out the walls of ice and snow around him. It was too much like being trapped by the avalanche, with the snow closing in around him. He struggled to keep his breathing even.

Outside their hideout, the snow crunched, and the murmur of men's voices filtered in.

"Look!" a man shouted. "There's someone in the snow!"

Kelan's blood turned to ice as the soldiers' footsteps pounded toward them.

CHAPTER 37
SOL

Sol held her breath as the soldiers crunched through the snow and the river of frozen meltwater.

"More bodies," Commander Jahr said. Sol squirmed at the sound of his voice. "This is the work of that demon. They've all been burned."

The footsteps came closer and stopped just outside their tunnel. "They're Cassians. Do you think they're some of Turullius'?"

The voice was so close it made Sol's pulse thrash in her ears. Kelan shivered and exhaled shakily. She clamped her hand around his arm, willing him to be silent.

"They don't have uniforms," Jahr said. "Looks like they're travelers."

"That monster."

"Isabella's body isn't here. Do you think she's still alive?" another man asked.

"If we haven't found the body yet, then we have to hope," Jahr said. "We continue on. No time to waste."

The footsteps retreated, but Sol didn't dare breathe again until they were far in the distance.

Kelan shivered and rested his head against hers. They both exhaled and relaxed against the chilly ground. Sol brushed her fingers against the emberstone in her pocket and warmth filled her body once more. Kelan pulled her in tighter. She pushed more warmth out until her tiny emberstone went empty. It wasn't large enough to hold much fire.

"Is it safe to go out now?" he asked.

"I don't know. That was Commander Jahr from the Tokken Army."

She shivered as the cold encroached again. Her eyes were drooping. She was exhausted. They couldn't continue on like this. Her empty stomach gnawed at her, and all she wanted to do was rest.

They were smashed together in the tight, dark tunnel, and he had to twist his arm to get it out from around her back.

"Here," he said. He held out the glowing emberstone and she put her fingers on it. Warmth flooded their little ice cave, and water dripped from the ceiling onto Sol's face and down her neck. The emberstone bathed the icy walls in red light.

"When we get out, we'll find the bandit's camp," Sol said. "There were extra bedrolls and packs there."

"And food?"

"No. But I set up all those traps when we were camped out here. They'll still be there, and I think at least one of them will have something in it by now."

Kelan pressed his icy cheek against hers. They were both soaked in meltwater and sweat, and covered in snow, but at least she was warm.

Kelan would always be cold. "Where will we go now?" he asked, his teeth chattering. "There're rumors I've heard about a place called the Hivid Wood. They say it's a refuge for Flameskins who want to live in peace away from the world."

"But I have to go to my family. I have to warn them about the coming Flameskin raid."

He nodded. "We'll go to Hillerod, then."

She bit her lip. "And maybe there's a way you could . . . we could find a way to keep an emberstone on you so people couldn't see it . . . ."

"If the people from your village knew what I was, they'd kill me."

"They won't find out. You could live there in Hillerod. You could be safe there."

He was quiet for a moment, his eyes searching her face. "How long would that last? And what happens when they throw me out or try to kill me? You would never leave the Ulves to be with me."

"That's not—That's—" Her cheeks burned because she couldn't deny it. Leaving the mountains was unthinkable. "I'll find a way for you to stay."

He shook his head and closed his eyes, then shivered again.

She pulled off her glove and put a hand to his face. "You're freezing."

"To death."

She pushed a gentle wave of heat toward him, and he winced as he placed a soggy glove over her burning hand. "Do you remember when I showed you how to draw on my pyra?"

She blushed, as memories of his kisses flooded her mind. "Yes."

"If you take off my emberstone—"

"No."

"If you absorb my pyra it can't possess me. The fire will pass through me and make me warm, but I won't be able to use it."

"I'm not taking off the manacle."

He shut his eyes again. "You don't trust me."

"I do, Kelan. I trust you. Just not your pyra."

He slid the knife from her belt with shaking fingers and put it in her hand, then guided its point to his chest, holding her gaze as he did it. "If my pyra takes me, you can just kill me. Then it will all be over."

"Stop being an idiot."

She tried to tug the knife out of his hand, but he resisted. When she let go, the knife point jerked toward him and pierced his coat.

She gasped. "Kelan!"

He winced and let her take the knife from his hands. Then she unbuttoned his coat to find a small spot of red forming on his tunic. The knife had cut a small gash across his sternum.

"Are you going to heal me?" he asked through gritted teeth.

She swore as she unfasted the buttons of his tunic and took the key from her pocket.

"If you kill me, I'm going to haunt you," she muttered.

"You already do haunt me. Every waking hour all I can think about is you. And at night I dream of you."

She paused with key in hand and looked up at his face and his glazed eyes.

Cold sickness?

Neither of them were thinking straight at this point. Especially not her. Hours after he had tried to kill her, she was already unlocking his manacle again.

She put her hand on his chest over the cut and unlocked the manacle. The tingle of fire sparked beneath Kelan's skin the moment the emberstone fell away. She pulled on that fire, her whole body tense, and it flooded her body with warmth, the same way an emberstone did.

She used the flames to heal his cut, and Kelan let out a long, long sigh and gave a small smile. A real smile, not a demon's smile.

Then the flames inside her started taking shape like they had before, wrapping themselves around her heart.

There was a wave of relief, not hers, and then anger and grief and hopelessness, but it was blunted. He was still angry at her, too, and she didn't want to feel it.

She tried to retract her hand, but he caught it and pressed it to his chest. "Don't. If you let go, my pyra will come back." His eyes were earnest now.

"You're angry at me."

He sighed and let his hand travel over the side of her body. "I'm angry at myself."

The warmth and the tingling fire made her drowsy and she struggled to keep her eyes open.

"We can't stay here," she said, mostly to herself.

He wrapped his arms around her, squeezing tighter, and brushed his lips against her temple. She shivered, not because she was cold, but because she wanted. She wanted Kelan, and she wanted to stay here where it felt safe, even though she knew it wasn't. She wanted to hide away from the world and stay in these mountains where they couldn't be found.

She was just so tired of fighting and struggling. They both were.

She rested her head against his shoulder and was lulled to sleep by the soft hush of his breathing.

CHAPTER 38

KELAN

K elan woke to the metallic snap of his manacle closing over his wrist. The fire in his body sputtered and died. He opened his bleary eyes and saw Sol lying next to him, her face tense.

"We fell asleep," she said.

He nodded. It hadn't been enough sleep. He could sleep for a week without waking. The sun was going down and cast long shadows across the white snow.

She frowned, her lips pinched tight. "You weren't wearing your manacle."

Now he was awake. "Ashes, Sol. I'm such a fool."

"What would've happened if you had woken first?"

He shook his head and shuddered.

She squirmed out of the tunnel, pushing away the snow that had fallen in around them and shoving aside the frozen bodies.

When he crawled out, she was already stripping one of the bandits of his boot laces. "Help me make snowshoes," she said.

And just like that they fell back into their old rhythms.

They pilfered packs and supplies from the bandits' camp and found food waiting for them in Sol's traps.

And just like that they were traveling the mountains, but now their journey was a frantic flight. And it was overshadowed by the uncertainty of what waited for them at the end of their journey in Hillerod. These were cold nights for Kelan, and he was warmed only by the kisses they shared. But these kisses felt like wishes.

That's what Kelan was doing, wishing. But he couldn't stop. Not while Sol held his hand as they walked, her fingers woven through his, or their pinkies linked like a promise. Not while his fire flowed into her and she knew how he felt. He couldn't hide it and he didn't try.

It was dangerous to have him free of his manacle, but Sol insisted they travel like that so he wouldn't freeze. Most of the day he was free of his manacle, though he never again slept without it. His fire flowed into her, and he was warm without the taint of his pyra.

They traveled north along the Cassian border. Sol pressed them hard and ran them ragged, leading them through streams and across craggy hillsides where their footprints were easier to hide.

They were taking a different path through the mountains back to Hillerod, one which Sol had assured him the Tokken soldiers wouldn't be able to track them on. But they had to move quickly, sometimes traveling past sunset with a flame in Sol's hand to light their path.

They traveled a week this way, hand in hand. And at night when she lay beside him, he would ask her the questions he was afraid to speak in daylight under the harsh gaze of the mountains.

"What will happen when we get to Hillerod?"

"I don't know," she would whisper back. "I just don't know."

Sol knew how he felt, and he was too full of wishes to risk speaking them aloud. His wishes were fragile things, and he knew when they got to Hillerod, his wishes would be crushed by the reality of what he was and the cruel, unyielding mountains.

He didn't belong here in the Ulves. And he could do nothing more than hold Sol close and wish.

Their path led them to a Nordese village near the border of Cassia called Vodskov. Kelan had clipped his emberstone manacle onto his wrist long before they arrived, and he had pulled the long, furred coat sleeve over top of it. The coat Sol wore, the one that had once belonged to Kelan, was in tatters. The sleeves came only to her elbows and the edges were singed, an obvious sign it had been worn by someone playing with fire. They looked like they felt: travel-worn and exhausted and hungry.

"We can stay here for a couple days if we're careful," Sol said.

"What do you mean by 'careful'?"

"I mean, if no one recognizes who I am or sees the emberstone on your wrist."

Kelan tugged on his sleeve again.

"It would be nice to rest for a little bit, and get supplies," she said, her eyes fixed on the inn's welcoming windows, the warm light of a fire lighting the inn within.

He let out a long sigh. Rest. A bed. Food. There had been only a couple nights of that in Olisipo before he and Sol had tramped off into the wilderness once more. The four hares Sol had trapped at their campsite near Olisipo were long gone, and the only thing they'd eaten since then were a few potatoes they had dug out of the garden of an abandoned farm.

Sol pulled her hat down over her eyebrows and pulled up the collar of her coat. "Try not to be to memorable. And don't look up too much. Your eyes are too foreign. And don't mention Hillerod or say my name. If people find out who I am, word could get back to Commander Jahr."

"What am I supposed to call you?"

She shrugged.

"Isabella?"

She scowled. "Anything but that."

She pulled the pack off her back and found the jeweled

dagger at the bottom. "I suppose we'll be pretty memorable with this."

"Do you think they'll take it?"

"I don't know. I'd be leery of travelers with something that was obviously stolen."

He sighed as his wishes for warmth and food and a bed slowly faded. Those had been fragile, too.

He and Sol were fugitives now. As much as she insisted that they'd find a place that was safe for him, he knew that was only a vain wish, too. Nowhere was safe for him anymore.

Sol pulled open the door to the inn and they let themselves in. He shouldn't have been surprised that there were only one or two other travelers inside, but it unnerved him all the same. There was no crowd for them to disappear into. They were supposed to be inconspicuous, but what was more conspicuous than a girl with burned sleeves and a stolen letter opener traveling the mountains in the dead of winter?

He took her elbow. "Maybe we should leave."

Her shoulders deflated. "I'm just so tired, Kelan. I just want to sleep somewhere and eat something." She leaned against him and he put an arm around her shoulder.

A man bustled down the stairs. "Sorry to keep you waiting. Welcome, welcome." He bowed to them and ushered them inside.

He had an apron tied around his waist and was as warm and welcoming as his inn. He was a mountain Tokken like Sol, with brilliant green eyes and a prominent, straight nose.

"Here, sit," he said, leading them to one of the tables crammed into the narrow room.

Kelan kept his head down like he had been ordered, and his mouth watered as he passed a table where a lone traveler was eating.

Rice! What he wouldn't give for a bowl of red beans and rice. He seated himself eagerly, but Sol was still standing, her body tense.

"We're looking for lodging for a couple nights and supplies for our journey," she said.

"You can get all that here."

"But we don't have any money. We only have this." She held up the jeweled dagger for the innkeeper to see.

But the innkeeper wasn't looking at the dagger, he was staring into her face. "Sol?" he asked. "Sol d'Hillerod?"

Kelan swore under his breath, and Sol's face went taut.

"Is that really you?" the innkeeper asked. "You've grown so much! You're a woman now! Anna! Look who's come! It's Sol d'Hillerod."

"No, please, I'd like to keep this quiet," Sol said, but her voice was drowned out by the clatter of a woman coming down the stairs.

Anna grabbed Sol in a hug. "Sol! It's been years. How are your parents? And little Carol?"

Kelan watched the exchange with a little bit of awe. There was no one he could think of who would greet him like this. These were her people. Kelan had never belonged anywhere like she belonged in the mountains.

"My sisters are well," Sol said quietly, "and my ma's holding together, I think."

"We expected to see Elo this winter, and you with him, of course," said the innkeeper.

Sol stiffened. "He—He passed, last Solstice."

"Oh, Sol! But he was so young," Anna said. "Did the plague reach Hillerod, as well, last winter?"

"No, we were spared. It was a hunting accident."

Kelan straightened in his seat on the floor. Hunting accident? Was that why Sol was so haunted by her father's death? Had she played some part in it?

"I'm so sorry, dear. So sorry," Anna said, patting Sol's hand.

"This is very hard news. Everyone will want to see you and offer their condolences. I'll send for Marge and Agnes. They'll want to send well wishes for your ma, I'm sure."

Kelan stood. "Please, we'd prefer no one knows we're here."

The innkeeper and his wife looked up at him, as if realizing he was there for the first time.

"Who's this?" Anna demanded. Her voice sounded distrustful. "A city boy?"

Kelan looked down, keeping his eyes lidded, but it was too late now. They'd seen he wasn't one of them. But he had to convince them to keep this quiet, and so the obvious conclusion was—

"I'm her husband," he said and bowed, and prayed that Sol wouldn't kill him for this later. "Kelan Burke. Very pleased to meet you."

When he came up out of his bow, the innkeeper looked at him with newfound respect, his wife looked disappointed, and Sol looked like she *was* going to murder him.

Love always had casualties.

It hurt that she was so angered by this. Obviously, Sol had never even imagined it. She wasn't wishing like he was.

But he turned from her to meet the innkeepers' eyes, drawing himself up to his full height as they sized him up. He knew he was wanting. She was made of granite and winter, and he was made of nothing but fire and lies.

But he could imagine, if only for one evening.

"You from Skive?" Anna asked, her words simmering with disapproval.

"Duhavn," Kelan said. He stepped in closer to Sol. "We're on our way to Duhavn now, actually. We've eloped."

"Eloped?" the innkeeper asked with a wide grin.

"Does your ma know?" Anna asked Sol.

Kelan put his arm around Sol and brushed his fingers through her hair like she really was his. "She knows, of course. Only, since Sol's pa has been gone, the boys in Hillerod have been very protective of her. And since she had so many suitors, we decided it might be best to leave the mountains for a while. You know how these things are."

Sol was staring at her boots, blushing hard.

"Well," Anna said, her eyebrows rising. "Well, isn't that something."

The innkeeper laughed and clapped his hand on Kelan's back. "Ha! Love always blooms in the strangest of places."

Kelan looked at Sol's face, and she glanced up at him, holding his gaze for a brief moment.

"Yes, it does. Doesn't it?" he whispered.

Anna took Sol's hand. "Does married life suit you, dear?"

"It does." Sol's voice was quiet, but the mountains had never had to be loud to be heard. Her voice was sure, and her blush gone.

The wishes were making Kelan see things that weren't there.

But her hand was warm and alive and his to hold. He ran his thumb over the back of her hand, and she squeezed his in return.

"Sit!" the innkeeper ordered. "You're tired and hungry! Anna will prepare a room for you, and I'll get you some food."

Sol offered the letter opener to him, but he shook his head.

"I'd never dream of taking anything from Elo's daughter. He saved Oscar's life, you know."

"I remember."

"Wedding gifts should be kept and treasured," Anna said, gently pushing Sol's hand away.

Kelan snorted. That was a gift from the wrong husband, and from a wedding neither of them wanted to remember.

Glorious food arrived from the kitchen in steaming bowls. Kelan reached up to take his, and the emberstone on his wrist cast a faint red glow on his hand. He yanked at his sleeve and looked up at the innkeeper, but the innkeeper was already bustling back toward the kitchen. "Drinks for the newlyweds!"

If he was ever going to live in Hillerod, he needed a better way to wear the emberstone. It would be a difficult secret to keep.

Anna clattered down the stairs again. "Your room is ready. Oh, Sol, how long do I have to wait until I can tell everyone that you're married? This is absolutely the worst thing I've ever been asked to do. Keep a secret like this!"

Sol considered for a moment as the innkeeper pushed two large cups of ale toward them. "Wait until summer, please, Anna. Josef had it in his head that he was going to marry me, and you know what a good tracker he is. I'm don't want Kelan to get hurt."

"The demon!" Anna cried, and Kelan choked on his drink. She leaned in. "I would take this secret to my grave if I had to."

It seemed unlikely she'd make it through the end of the week. This was probably the best piece of gossip this side of the mountains.

But this food! He couldn't remember food that tasted this good. He downed his ale in a few swallows, and the innkeeper arrived with a smile and another full cup.

"Easy," Sol whispered as he drained his second.

"Who's Josef?" he asked.

She made a face.

Interesting.

"How long have you and Josef known each other?"

She rolled her eyes at him as she picked up another dumpling.

The second mug of ale was starting to affect him. Usually his pyra just burned the alcohol off. It was really hard to get drunk as a Flameskin, and he had never really known how potent alcohol could be. His mind fuzzed and sleep called to him. Maybe that was good, since Sol was going to carve into him tonight.

It was worth it.

He put a hand around her waist. She had taken off her burned coat and there was nothing but a thin wool tunic between his hand and her skin.

These wishes were as intoxicating as the drinks.

When they had finished the blessed meal, the innkeeper led them to their room. "If there's anything you need, Sol, we're just down the hall."

"Thanks for everything, Johan." She closed the screen door behind him and locked it. Then she turned and faced Kelan.

He leaned against the wall and blinked slowly a few times, waiting for her to start shouting. He was exhausted. He regretted immensely that third mug. His whole body was starting to feel blunt, like the letter opener. Not really useful for anything, but pretty.

"Eloped," was all she said. He couldn't see the anger yet, but sometimes it simmered for a long time beneath the surface before she exploded.

He grimaced. "It was the best I could come up with."

She looked different, standing there in front of the painted screen doorway. She didn't look like she was made of the mountains. She looked like a girl again. The granite and the cliffs and the snow-covered peak were gone. Maybe it was just because she wasn't wearing all her winter gear. It made her seem smaller. And showed off all her delightful curves.

"Anna said she filled up the tub," Sol said.

The humid, bathtub air made him drowsy. "You're not angry?"

"At first, maybe, but then . . . ." She shrugged.

Kelan swayed a little on his feet, then dragged a blanket from the bed to the ground. "I'm exhausted. I'm just going to bed down for the night."

"You can sleep in the bed with me. I'm used to it."

She had stepped closer and now took his hand. He wasn't too blunt-edged to feel that, or to see the way she was looking at him. He reached up to brush her cheek and was pleasantly surprised that his hand responded, that it hadn't had to blunder its way toward her. Ashes, this alcohol. It blurred the edges of everything.

Was this real or just another wish?

She wasn't speaking. She pressed her hand to his chest. He wasn't wearing his fur coat anymore, only his tunic. Where had the coat gone? Sol would kill him if he lost it.

She looked up. Her cheeks were pink. It took her a moment to find her words. "You should bathe, and then we should get to sleep."

Right. He sighed again. He had almost wanted to sleep on the floor just because he was too exhausted to think of doing anything else. Ashes and cinders, he was so tired.

Kelan found the bath behind the screen in the corner of the room and stripped down. The water was deliciously warm. It was a struggle to stay awake in there, and speed was his only ally. Anna, bless her, had left clean clothes for both of them to wear so theirs could be washed the next day, and when Kelan had finished, he sloughed off the water and pulled on a pair of clean, wool pants.

He shook water from his curls as he emerged from behind the screen. Sol sat on the edge of the bed, her long hair loose down her back and over her shoulders, and she wasn't wearing shoes. For Sol that was practically naked. He blinked at her a few times, his shirt still in his hand, enjoying the few inches of her bare ankles and the sight of her body without its multitude of furs and coats. He forced himself to focus on her eyes. Her eyes and her lips. Ashes, those lips.

Then he tucked that wish back inside him and started to put his arms through his sleeves, but Sol crossed the room toward him and slowly pulled his shirt away and dropped it on the ground. She smiled at him, but it was a shy smile, an uncertain one. One he had never seen before.

She put her hands on his chest. His heart came alive at her touch. The exhaustion retreated, if only for a few seconds.

He looked at her face. His vision was too clouded to read her expression. What—?

And then her lips were against his.

This he understood.

Ashes, why was he so exhausted? Why now? Why of all nights had he drunk so much?

But his fingers fumbled their way to her waist and his lips worked well enough to do what they were supposed to—though they were a little numb.

She broke away and looked up at him again, breathless. "I'm going to bathe. Wait for me?"

216

He smiled and kissed her lips again. For a thousand years he would wait, if he had to.

She squeezed his hand once before disappearing behind the screen.

He flopped onto the bed. He didn't know what would happen to them when they got to Hillerod, if there would be a way he could stay, but he wanted that more than anything.

He smiled and hope sparked in his chest. Maybe he could be a part of her future. Then he rolled over and fell asleep.

CHAPTER 39
SOL

Sol's cheeks burned hotter than the water. She scrubbed soap through her hair and her face and all over her aching body. But she could feel nothing but the buzzing in her veins and the pounding of her heart.

Love blooms in the most unusual places.

He loved her. He had loved her for a long time, and she had loved him, too.

Seeing him with Anna and Johan was like looking into a possible future. He had been his usual, enigmatic self, and no one had guessed what he was.

They could do this. They could have a life together, and he'd live with a hidden emberstone on his arm.

She wanted him to be something more than just a friend. She wanted him, and the promise of tomorrow. Too many times he had almost slipped through her fingers, but she wasn't letting go now.

These were her mountains, and she was master of them. She would find a place for them. They would return to Hillerod, and no one would know any different.

They would find a way.

Sol stepped out of the bath and wrung out her hair, then slipped on her clothes.

When she peeked around the screen, Kelan was lying on the bed still without a shirt on. She tiptoed toward him. His eyes were closed.

She laid a hand on his arm, then ran her fingers across his chest. "You can open your eyes. I'm decent."

But he didn't open his eyes.

She shook his arm. "Kelan?"

Completely and utterly asleep.

She sat on the bed next to him as the sparks in her blood fizzled and died.

She scowled at him, trying and failing at not being frustrated. She had all these things she wanted to tell him, and he had fallen asleep when she finally felt brave enough to say them aloud.

A knock at the screen door made her jump. She scrambled away from him and grumbled as she unlatched the screen. Didn't they know not to bother weary, married travelers at night?

She slid open the screen door and found Johan, who pushed into the room brandishing a knife. She stumbled back from him with a shout.

Kelan didn't stir on the bed.

Johan gave Kelan a wary glance before sighing. "You're safe now, Sol."

"Safe? Safe! What did you do to Kelan?" She shook Kelan's arm, but he didn't move.

"Sleeping draft. He shouldn't wake up for hours. Help me tie him up." Johan unslung the rope from around his shoulder, and it landed on Kelan's body with a thud.

She thrust the rope back into Johan's arms. "Don't touch him."

Johan turned, his face pinched. "Do you know what he is?" He pointed to the manacle on Kelan's wrist. It glowed red in the dim candlelight. "Do you know what this does?"

"Of course, I do." She stepped in front of Kelan's body, shielding it with her own. If the village found out who he was they'd kill him, and he was helpless like this. "Who else knows?" she demanded. "Did you tell Anna?"

He shook his head. "But if you know what he is, you know what must be done."

"Kelan isn't like the others. He's not a demon."

"There's a reason he's wearing that manacle."

"Yes! He put it on himself. He's harmless like this."

"But his blood isn't. Is he really your husband?"

"No, but—"

She stared down at Kelan, at his scarred body and his wet curls. She wished the bonds that held them together were stronger than the memories they shared. She wanted more. She wanted so much more.

Johan must have seen the look in her face because he made a disgusted, strangled noise in his throat and stepped away from her. "How could the daughter of Elo love one of those?"

"Kelan isn't a monster, and I'll defend him with my life. Consider that carefully before you do anything else."

His shoulders sagged. "Sol, Sol, this is—You can't love him. Your children would all be—"

They'd all be Flameskins, if they weren't mages. All cursed with fire.

"How did you find out?" she asked.

"I saw the emberstone on his wrist downstairs."

She let out a slow, shaky breath. She'd been a fool to think that life they had pretended to have downstairs, with Johan and Anna, could be theirs.

"My father saved your son's life," Sol said.

"And that's why I determined to save yours after I realized what that thing was," he said, jerking his chin at Kelan. "I owe Elo a debt after what he did for Oscar."

"Spare Kelan's life. Let us pass though Vodskov and tell no one that we were here or what Kelan is. You'll never have to see us or hear from us again."

His face crumpled. "Oh, Sol."

"Please. Please, Johan. I'm begging you."

He glanced at Kelan, his shoulders sagging. "You have to

leave in the morning. I don't know how long Anna can keep this quiet."

"You can't tell her what Kelan is. You can't tell anyone."

"I won't. But are you sure about this? We can help you. You have friends. We can get you back to Hillerod."

"I know my own path." She crossed the room and fished in her bag for the jeweled letter opener. "We need supplies for our journey. Food and a bow, if possible."

He pushed it away wearily. "Keep it. Let me repay my debt. I'll get everything ready for you to leave in the morning."

"Thank you."

"I don't condone this."

"I know."

"I wish you would change your mind. We can have him sent to Olisipo. They have people there that would take care of it."

She shivered. "I won't change my mind."

He nodded and started for the door.

"He'll wake up, won't he?"

Johan gave her a strained smile. "I use that particular mix to help especially rowdy travelers settle down. He'll wake up in the morning."

He slid the door shut behind him, and she latched it. She slumped against the screen. Her heart was still pounding erratically. Had Kelan lived his whole life like this, jumping from one near miss to another? Was this what her life would be like from now on if she stayed with him?

She sank onto the bed beside him and laid her head on his chest. His heart thumped inside him as she ran her fingers over his scars.

She wanted so desperately for him to be part of her life in Hillerod, but Johan had found out what Kelan was only minutes after meeting him. It would be an impossible secret to keep, but they had to find a way. If her neighbors found out what he was, they would drive him out, if they didn't try to kill him. A life without Kelan and without her mountains would be unbearable.

She shivered and wrapped an arm around him. She listened

to his heart thump in his chest a long time before she could fall asleep.

They would find a way. They had to.

Kelan and Sol left the inn with full bellies and full packs. When they set off into the mountains, they weren't cold.

Each day was filled with the bright, winter sun glinting off the white carpet at their feet, and the touch of Sol's warm hand. And each night was starlight and fire and kisses and laughter.

Winter tightened its hold on the Ulves, and then like a sigh, it let go. As they descended the mountains into Tokkedal once more, streams thawed and swelled with snow melt. Trees stretched their branches, their heavy boughs now unburdened by snow.

With a bow in Sol's hand, they were never hungry for long. And with her leading their path through the mountains, they were never lost and their pursuers, if there were any, would never find them.

They had reached another saddle in these endless, beautiful mountains. Sol held his hand, pulling the darkness from his pyra and leaving him with just the warmth.

Kelan looked at her as she stared at the valley beneath them and brushed a strand of hair off her cheek. Maybe they could travel these mountains forever, live like dryads or sojourners. Never stopping, always moving. It wouldn't be an easy life, but they had both already accustomed themselves to it. They could be safe this way, far from the reach of any army.

He could travel anywhere with her by his side. He never wanted it to end.

"We're here," she whispered.

CHAPTER 40
SOL

Returning home had the unsettling quality of a dream, familiar and yet strange. Everything about her life had changed dramatically, and yet Hillerod was the same.

The valley was dotted with patches of green where the snow had melted, and grass was coming through. The spring birds had returned and twittered in the trees. Her neighbor, Oscar, had finally fixed the hole in his roof and had new shingles to keep out the snow, and her Aunt Saffi had already set up a terrace for her peas to climb and constructed supports for her tomatoes.

Sol's house stood on the edge of the woods and seemed to lean toward the forest, as if the logs that the house had been built from wished to return to their native home. The ivy that curled over the walls was dead, but it would soon put out new buds and grow once more. Everything was almost exactly as she had left it.

Her heart caught in her chest when her eyes snagged on her sister, Carol. She stood out front of their house with an ax raised over her head, chopping wood.

"Carol!"

Carol dropped the ax and whirled around. Sol tore free of Kelan's hand and ran to her.

Sol grabbed her sister in a tight embrace. She pushed at the tears that tugged at her eyes. She had missed Solstice. She had left Ma and Carol and the girls alone to fend for themselves while she had been running for her life and struggling to survive in the mountains. Every day she had worried and wondered what was happening to her family.

"Where have you been?" Carol demanded, squeezing her fiercely.

Sol measured the question. The tone wasn't one of anger or hurt, but more of despair and worry. She pulled away and looked at Carol's face. It was thinner than she remembered. They hadn't been eating well enough. Carol had surpassed Sol in height last year and was even taller now, but as thin as a pine in a dense wood, grasping for sunlight.

Carol was looking at Sol, too, studying her eyes. What would she see? The danger and fatigue of their journey, or the fire beneath her skin, or how she had betrayed Pa?

"Have you been eating?" Sol asked, trying to deflect Carol's penetrating gaze.

Carol's chin lifted in a very familiar way. "Of course, we have. I've been feeding them. You weren't the only one Pa taught to use a bow."

"And Ma and the girls, they're all right?"

"You told me to take care of them and I did. Ma! Come see!" she shouted at their tiny house.

Sol turned expectantly toward the door as Carol turned to look up at Kelan. "Wait, who's this? He came with you?"

He bowed low. "Kelan Burke."

Carol's eyebrows rose.

Sol met Kelan's eyes and reached for his hand as her stomach fluttered. They had talked about this. It didn't matter what her family thought. She had told herself that a thousand times. But now standing before Carol, she wanted so much for them to love him, for them to accept him.

Carol's eyebrows rose to her hairline as she stared at their joined hands.

The door flew open, and Lisbet d'Hillerod stepped into the sunshine. Sol ran to her mother and threw her arms around her as Josef d'Hilledrod and Commander Jahr stepped out behind her.

"Sol!" Kelan shouted.

Sol was able to do little more than take a ragged breath and drag her mother away from them as Commander Jahr smirked at her.

"Hello, Sol."

She stuffed a hand in her pocket and grabbed her ember-stone. Ashes and cinders. Her bow and arrows were tied to her pack and not in easy reach.

"I thought you were lost to us," Ma murmured, and brushed Sol's hair away from her face.

Sol pushed her mother behind her and grabbed the knife from her belt as Kelan pulled his sword from his pack. But Sol wasn't sure who she was supposed to attack first.

She turned on Josef. "I told you if I ever saw you again, I'd kill you."

Josef backed away, bumping against the wall of the house. "I was only trying to help. They said you had been kidnapped." He looked meaningfully toward Kelan.

"No need for weapons," Jahr said. "You're outnumbered here."

Josef had already strung his bow and notched an arrow in it, but his eyes were uncertain

"Aim for his head or his heart," Jahr ordered, pointing at Kelan. "Nothing else will kill a Flameskin."

Flameskin. The word sent a chill through the air. Carol stumbled away from Kelan. Through the trees, Tokken soldiers in blue coats appeared. Sol's little sisters, Dorit and Grete, stood in the doorway with pale, frightened faces.

"Get inside, girls!" Lisbet said, her voice shrill.

Carol slowly reached down and picked the ax up from the ground. "Sol, what's going on?"

"Lay down your weapons," Jahr said, his voice edged but calm.

Jahr had all the cards. Sol felt the panic rising as she and Kelan drew closer together, Sol with her knife, and Kelan with his Cassian scimitar. Ten of Jahr's blue-coated soldiers surrounded them, their swords raised, and Josef held the same bow that had taken the life of Elo d'Hillerod.

Jahr advanced slowly. "We don't want anyone to get hurt. Don't forget that your mother and your sisters are here, Sol."

"I haven't." She was struggling to keep her breath even.

After all this. After all the time they had spent hiking through the wilderness struggling to survive, she had thought they were finally free of this.

"Sol," Jahr said, his voice sharper now. "Put down the knife. Is that any way for a lady to behave?"

"I'm not going anywhere with you."

He scowled at her. "I want that arrow pointed at the boy's head," he told Josef. "Think about what you're doing."

Josef met Sol's eyes, his face uncertain, then slowly, his bow inched up from Kelan's chest to the level of his face.

Kelan's breath hitched. Sol's knees wobbled. Josef wouldn't miss if he loosed that arrow. And at this range, Kelan would die instantly.

Sol stepped in front of Josef's bow, staring down the arrow into his eyes. "I won't let you kill another man I love."

"Sol!" Ma cried. The same anguished tone she had used that night her husband had died.

A shudder ran through Josef. His arm jerked, and he turned the arrow at Jahr's enormous chest, instead. "You told me Sol had been kidnapped."

"That man is a Flameskin! A soldier in their army! They stole her from Prince Turullius' house."

"Do I look kidnapped to you?" Sol spat. "I ran away."

"Is he a Flameskin?" Josef asked, his eyes flicking toward Kelan.

"Does it matter?"

Josef's lips curled into a snarl. "Of course, it matters."

Sol took the emberstone out of her pocket. "Does it matter if I'm a mage?" She drew on the emberstone and orange fire lit her fingertips.

Josef gasped, and his bow dipped. Jahr leapt at him, tackling him to the ground in the melting snow. The soldiers charged. Lisbet screamed. Carol swung her ax at one of the Tokken soldiers, and the soldier deflected it with his sword and wrenched it from her hands.

Kelan swept his scimitar through the air, trying to block the attacks of four different soldiers at once. Soldiers grabbed at Sol. One took her arm, and she drove her knife into his leg. He dropped with a cry, but two other soldiers grabbed her arms. She screamed and thrashed as they yanked the knife from her fingers.

Jahr kicked Josef aside and grabbed tiny Dorit, who was frozen in the doorway. He yanked her forward by her hair and rested the tip of his sword against her pale neck. "Enough!"

Lisbet moaned. She had fallen to her knees and had her hands pressed to her mouth.

Sol twisted against her captors' hands to see Dorit. One soldier held each of Sol's arms. Her knife lay on the grass, covered in blood.

Kelan was surrounded by soldiers and had a cut on his arm. Blood ran down to his wrist and dripped on the body of a fallen Tokken soldier. Another soldier had Carol's hands pinned behind her body.

"Put down your weapon, Flameskin," Jahr spat.

Lisbet let out a small moan.

Kelan slowly lowered his sword.

"Kelan," Sol sobbed.

They were going to kill him. They were going to run him through and make her watch. Her happiness was bleeding onto the snow with every drop of Kelan's blood. He held her gaze with mournful eyes.

"Tie them both up," Jahr ordered.

One of the soldier's shoved Kelan down, and he hit the ground with a grunt. Soldiers tied their hands with rough cords.

Josef stood and stared at Sol in open-mouthed silence.

Traitor. He had killed her pa, and now he would kill Kelan, too. Josef was the one who had led Jahr through the mountains to Hillerod.

Sol twisted her wrists against her bindings, and the cords cut into her cold-chapped skin. If she could just somehow get the emberstone off Kelan. But then what kind of destruction would he cause? She had her own emberstone, and she might be able to burn the ropes, but then what would become of Dorit? Jahr still held her sister with his sword against her neck.

"Let them go!" Carol screamed. The soldier holding her cuffed her cheek, but she struggled against him, and he almost lost hold of her.

Two soldiers lifted Sol off the ground as Jahr approached, still dragging Dorit with him.

"Corrupted," he said, scowling at her. "We can't let Turullius find out she's a mage. We'll bring her back dead. That'll be enough to convince Turullius to ride with us. He'll want his revenge."

Lisbet fell to her knees. "Please. Please let my daughters go."

Jahr released his hold on Dorit, and she wailed as she ran into her mother's arms. Sol closed her eyes against the sight. She never should've come back. When she jumped from that window in Olisipo, she should've known she was saying goodbye to her family forever. Coming here had only put them in danger. How could she have ever thought Jahr would give up the chase?

"And the Flameskin?" one of the soldiers asked. Kelan's coat sleeve was hitched up by the cords, and his emberstone glowed a brilliant red on his skin.

"He's harmless with the shackle on, but make sure you cut out his heart before you burn the body."

"No!" The scream tore out of Sol's throat like a living thing made of horror and ashes. She tried to lurch away from the soldiers, but they held her tight. "Kelan!"

They picked him up from the ground. She couldn't stop screaming. Her body shuddered.

"And you, Hunter," Jahr said, whirling on Josef.

Josef had been staring at Sol's face, frozen in place as he watched her scream.

"You're leading us back to Olisipo. We'll leave first thing in the morning. Turullius is waiting for his bride."

Josef startled, as if coming awake. His eyes flicked to Jahr and back to Sol's. Then he slid his arrow onto his bowstring. The arrow flew into the air with a twang and embedded itself in Jahr's chest before Sol could blink.

Jahr gave a dying gasp as another arrow slid from Josef's quiver and into his hand in one effortless motion. Two more soldiers fell before they could react, arrows protruding from their thighs. The other soldiers rushed him. Carol tripped the one who had been holding her and yanked the knife from her belt to hold against his throat.

The other soldiers launched themselves at Josef. He fired into the chest of one, dropping him beside Jahr, and hurled his bow at another as he yanked his knife from his belt. A soldier cut a bright line of red across Josef's arm as he thrust his dagger into the soldier's belly. He yanked it out, covered in the soldier's blood. The last soldier stopped, his sword still raised as he faced Josef.

"Put it down," Josef said, his voice trembling.

The soldier dropped his sword and stumbled backward. There were a half-dozen soldiers moaning and injured on the ground, and a few more dead or dying.

Josef looked down at Jahr already dead on the ground. "I don't take orders from monsters like you."

Then he walked toward Kelan with his blood-slicked knife and madness in his eyes.

"Josef, no!" Sol screamed.

He brought his knife down and cut through the bindings on Kelan's wrists, and Kelan scrambled away from him.

Carol ran to Sol and cut her free as well.

Sol and Kelan collided, and she buried her face in his chest.

"Sol," Josef said.

She turned.

Josef had his bow in his hands once more. There was an arrow notched and ready to fly, but he hadn't taken aim yet. "Why did I just kill two Tokken soldiers?"

CHAPTER 41
KELAN

K elan sat at the kitchen table beside Sol. Her hands were still shaking.

He used to get like that after battles. He remembered that ragged edge that was left over when the adrenaline had worn off, and there was only the gore and the realization of what you had done, and what you had almost lost.

But he had seen so much death in his lifetime. He was ashamed to admit that it rarely affected him anymore.

His shackle lay on the table, making the worn, wood surface glow red. He had slid out of his bloody tunic and coat, and Sol now traced her burning fingers over the cut on his arm. Her family and the hunter watched with wary eyes.

Hillerod's matron was binding up the wounded soldiers outside the house, but Sol had taken Kelan inside to heal him. She hadn't wanted her neighbors to see.

The hunter leaned against the wall, one hand on the knife at his belt. "I followed you all the way from Olisipo, and someone in Vodskov told me you had passed through."

Sol scowled. "Johan?"

"No. Johan and Anna wouldn't tell me anything. There was another hunter at the inn who thought he had seen Elo's daughter." The hunter swore under his breath. "Jahr told me you had been kidnapped, but I should've known no Flameskin could take you. There would've been signs of distress if you wanted to be found. Ashes. I should've just let you disappear. I lost your trail after Vodskov and then we came straight here. Jahr convinced me that your Flameskin was coming to Hillerod to burn it down. We came through Odslov's Pass and only beat you by a couple days."

Sol finished sealing Kelan's cut and handed him his manacle. Kelan sighed as he strapped it on his wrist again. It would've been nice to have it off and dull the pain a bit, but he understood. He didn't want her family to be afraid of him.

But Carol wasn't afraid. She sat at the table beside him, watching with interest. Her face was narrow, like Lisbet's, instead of soft and round like Sol's. Carol was made of the mountains, like Sol, and had leveled an ax at a trained soldier's head. He wished he could have the opportunity to get to know Sol's family and the place where she grew up. He wished they didn't have to leave again. But now the whole village knew what he was; they wouldn't let him stay.

The hunter ran a hand through his hair. "And what now? I've got blood on my hands, Sol. All to save that filthy demon."

"You'll always have blood on your hands," Sol snapped.

The hunter looked sick.

"Josef, go get your pa and bring him back here. I need to speak to him," Lisbet said. Sol had inherited Lisbet's commanding tone. Lisbet wasn't a woman to be questioned.

"My pa won't see me. I've been banished from Hillerod, and doubly so, now that I've shot our own soldiers."

"So, you're Josef," Kelan said, studying him. The suitor Sol had warned Johan about. Josef seemed a likely candidate. Sol saved her most potent hatred for the people she liked best.

Josef glared at him. "Shut up, demon."

Sol shot up from her seat on the floor and grabbed the front of Josef's shirt. She slammed him against the wall. "You will not call him that."

Kelan stood, unsure whether he should intervene on Sol's

behalf or Josef's. It warmed his heart to see Sol turn her considerable rage on someone else for once, and on his behalf.

Josef yanked his shirt out of her grip and slid away. "I can't just let him walk away from this. He's a Flameskin, Sol. He's dangerous. Your pa would've—"

"My pa is dead because of you."

The kitchen fell silent. Lisbet took a sharp, painful breath. Kelan tried to piece together what this meant and came up with a fuzzy understanding of what had transpired. A hunting accident. Josef. That wickedly fast draw. Josef hadn't even blinked when he had shot down Jahr. It had happened so fast Kelan hadn't even been able to react.

Josef slumped against the wall, eyes downcast. "I think of it every day. You don't know how sorry I am."

"Sorry won't bring him back," Sol said.

"I know."

Kelan took Sol's hand and put an arm around her waist. There was grief behind the anger, and she was close to cracking.

"A life for a life," she said quietly. "Let Kelan live, and the blood you spilled is forgiven."

Josef met Kelan's eyes. There was murder in Josef's gaze. Kelan had seen that look in the eyes of every soldier who had ever lifted a sword against him.

"And what about me? I've killed two Tokken soldiers now. They'll be after my life," Josef said.

"Your life is your concern." Sol's voice was like ice.

There was a knock on the door, and the matron stepped inside Sol's home. She had gray hair and a face as craggy as a mountainside. Her clothes were stained with the soldiers' blood.

"I've finished," she said. "They will all live, except the two that have already passed."

Josef bowed. "Thank you, Matron."

She frowned at him. "You have done a great harm to Hillerod. The Tokken Army will not look kindly upon us for this."

Josef let out a long breath, and his eyes flicked toward Kelan.

"I'll take full responsibility for it. And I'll take the soldiers back to their camp in Skive once they've recovered."

"And Sol?" the matron asked turning toward her.

"I won't go back to Cassia."

"No," the matron said gravely. "You belong to the mountains. We will protect you, even if it must be from our own army."

"But what of Hillerod?" Josef asked. "If the Cassians don't march to our aid—"

"That's why I came back here," Sol said, "to warn the village about the Flameskins."

"We've always known they would come," Lisbet said. Her eyes were hard, made of the same stone as the mountains.

"And what will we do?" Carol asked.

"What we've always done. Survive."

"Saint Katrine has arrived in Tokkedal," Kelan said. "She might be able to come to your aid before the Flameskins arrive."

"The demon speaks," the matron said and scowled at him.

"He's not a demon," Sol insisted.

"He has the face of a man, but he has no humanity. Do you forget whose daughter you are? You dishonor Elo's memory."

"I never forget whose daughter I am," Sol said. "I never could, not as long as the mountains stand. But my pa was wrong about Flameskins."

"Wrong?" the matron demanded. "Who destroyed Baarka? Who has burned our mountains and killed our people?"

"But—"

"No. They are all the same. They are not human, however much they may look like us."

Sol stepped in front of Kelan, clinging tight to his hand.

"You know what must be done, child." The matron turned to Kelan. "Will you come quietly, or must we use force?"

"No! You can't hurt him," Sol cried, her voice twisted with pain. They had backed up against the wall. Kelan had no weapons, but how could he hurt any of these people, Sol's family and friends? If her village turned against him, what could he do but give himself into their hands?

"He's not human, Sol," Lisbet said. "It is no sin to end his life. It's a mercy."

"Mercy," Sol hissed. "It's murder. He has a heart and a soul just like any of us."

"You would call Elo a murderer then?" the matron asked.

Sol breathed in sharply.

"He did what none of us had the courage to do," Lisbet said softly.

Sol shook her head. She was breathing fast. Kelan held tight to her.

"Twelve Flameskins he killed," the matron said, her voice low. "Twelve that were corrupted beyond redemption, tainted by fire. Twelve hearts he cut out. And when his arms grew too tired from the cutting, he held the others down so Oscar could finish."

Sol pressed a hand to her mouth and gasped.

Kelan swallowed. "Sol's father killed Flameskin soldiers?"

The matron scowled. "We thought they were our own, but they were tainted like you. Demons. Faces of children and mothers and friends, but they were cursed with flame. They were not like us."

Sol's father had killed Flameskin children.

Kelan gaped in horror at the dark faces of Sol's mother, Hillerod's matron, and the hunter. They would do the same to him, hold him down while he screamed and cut his heart out so they could burn his body.

"It's a blot on Pa's memory," Carol said, her voice thick. "Sol says Kelan is not corrupted, and I believe her."

"A blot?" the matron cried. "He was braver than any of us. You are too young to understand. Too young to remember. You were a child when this war began."

"But why must they be killed?" Carol demanded.

"King Anton Bruun was widowed thirty years ago, and his daughter, Princess Vara, was left motherless. The grieving king remarried, a beautiful woman with a heart of black. She bore him but one child, Princess Ingrid, a sister to his own heart-sick Vara."

The tale spun from the matron's wrinkled mouth like a well-worn path, smooth from frequent use. It was one Kelan had heard many times, but now it came from the enemy's lips.

"Twenty years the queen kept her secret as her heart burned black within her. Twenty years she hid her pyra from her king and kingdom. But a heart as black as that could not be hid forever. In a fit of passion, her pyra overcame her. Her beauty turned to burning, and King Anton and Princess Vara nearly lost their lives."

"If the queen had been allowed to wear an emberstone, her pyra could have been controlled," Kelan said.

"There is no controlling the fire inside a Flameskin," the matron spat. "Fire knows only destruction; it breeds only corruption. Princess Ingrid was tainted by the same fire as her mother."

"King Anton slaughtered his own wife and child!" Kelan shouted. "He could've saved them, but instead he killed them."

"There is no redemption for Flameskins," the matron said, her green eyes dark. "That was why the king ordered killed any man, woman, or child that bore the corruption of a pyra."

"The children had no choice in their heritage. They didn't deserve death."

The matron scowled. "Your kind rose up like the plague they are, washing through our land like a wave of flames. Burning everything in their path."

"We had no choice. You would have me give myself to you to be killed? You'll cut out my heart and watch me burn. How could we not fight back?"

"Now all of Nordby burns, all five kingdoms. And it's because we weren't strong enough to destroy you when we had the chance. Not like Elo. He heard the king's decree and he did what we could not."

Kelan shuddered. "You couldn't kill them because you knew in your heart it was wrong."

"But the gods heard our prayers and gave us the Saints," Lisbet said. "They will destroy you, all of you. The Burning War will be over."

Kelan shivered. Maybe it really would be over. Haldur and Nilsa had both thought so.

"I will not let you take Kelan," Sol said.

The matron turned to Josef, but he only sighed. "I can't. I've already taken too much from her."

He slid out of the house without a backward glance and the matron huffed after him. "Josef!" A cold wind snapped at the curtains and girls' skirts until they could get the door closed again.

Sol let out a heavy breath and squeezed Kelan's hand. Kelan's life had been bought with her pa's blood. What a strange twist in the lines of fate.

Sol turned to her mother. "Let him stay here one night."

"Never," Lisbet snarled.

Kelan sighed inwardly. He had hoped . . . . No. He had never had grounds to hope that her family would accept him. Sol seeing him for who he was had been nothing short of a miracle.

He brushed his thumb along her jaw. "I'm used to sleeping out there. I don't mind."

One of Sol's younger sisters threw her arms around Sol's waist. "Don't go again. It's so hungry when you leave."

Kelan's heart tore in two looking at them and their gaunt faces. They needed Sol. If he took her away from her family, what would happen to them?

But what would become of him without his mountain queen?

Sol knelt and hugged her littlest sister. Kelan swallowed, trying to keep his heart from lodging in his throat. He had never had a family like this. He had never had a home where he was wanted and missed. Maybe once, but that had been stripped from him as a child.

Lisbet threw the door open. "Get out."

Sol moved in front of Kelan. "No."

Her mother stared at her for a long while as the cold wind blew into the house and whipped her hair.

"You are not my daughter," Lisbet hissed. "I always knew you were not of this world." She stalked out of the house and slammed the door behind her, leaving them in an aching silence.

Sol's face crumpled as Carol ran to her and wrapped her arms around her.

He was making Sol sacrifice all of this for him. And her family would suffer without her.

It was selfish. He knew it. But wasn't love always a little selfish? He would give anything to be with her, but he wouldn't settle for anything else.

"She doesn't trust me," Sol said.

"I've found that it takes a long time to earn the trust of a mountain woman," Kelan said.

She made a face.

"I don't want to cause any trouble for your family."

She sighed. "You can stay here tonight, and my ma can sleep over at my aunt's. But tomorrow—"

He nodded. This was their life now. Never staying in one place for long. "I know. Tomorrow morning, we leave. I'm sorry we can't stay." This would be a difficult goodbye for her.

She bit her lip and stared at the floor.

"We'll come back, once the war is over and it's safe for us," he promised.

He wasn't sure what that would mean, for the war to be over. It would end either when the Flameskins found a way to destroy the Saints and repaid the innocent bloodshed with fire, or the Saints finally destroyed the last of the Flameskins. But neither of those outcomes led to him being welcomed back to Hillerod. And if the Saints triumphed, he would be hunted. Would there ever be an escape for him?

Carol threw her arms around Sol with a sob.

"Oh, Sol," Kelan murmured. It broke his heart to see this. He had to believe that they'd come back, that this wouldn't be forever.

She pulled away from her sisters and buried her face in Kelan's shoulder. "What will happen to them if I leave? There must be some way you can stay."

"You know I can't."

"No," she sobbed.

He wiped the corner of her eye with his thumb. Please don't make me go alone. Please don't let this be our last night.

But what else could be done? He would be killed if he stayed, and the mountains owned Sol. They had stolen her heart long before Kelan had arrived. He could no sooner take her from the mountains than he could pluck a cloud from the sky.

His heart plummeted. He had known this would happen, despite his desperate wishes. He and Sol were never meant to share the same path.

Sol would travel these mountains for the rest of her life, but not with him. She would lie alone beneath the snow-burdened canopies and the star-strewn sky where they had once lain together. She would walk alone in the brilliant light of the winter sun, treading through the diamond carpet of ice at her feet with no one beside her.

He trapped her against his chest, holding her tight. He hoped she would never forget. That she would remember each night spent next to him, each place they camped, the clearing where they danced, the place where the bandits had spilled his blood onto the snow.

Because he would never forget.

He pulled away from her to look into her face. "When the war is over and it's safe, I'll come back."

Her eyes went wide and her breath caught. "No."

He turned his head. "I can't take you from them."

She gripped his arms tight between her hands, forcing him to look up into her burning green eyes. "No, Kelan. You keep telling me to let go, but I won't. Not now, not ever."

His mouth opened, and he couldn't speak.

Her shoulders sagged, and she turned to meet Carol's gaze. "I know I promised Pa I would take care of our family, but I have to go with Kelan."

"I know," Carol said. "Don't worry about us. We'll manage."

Kelan ran his thumb along her jaw and ensnared his fingers in her hair. "You would give all of this up for me?"

"If they won't let you stay here, then I won't stay, either."

"Truly?"

"Are you even listening to me? We have bags to pack and clothes to wash, so stop being an idiot, and—"

He pulled her in against him, and their lips met. One of her sister's let out a little gasp, and Kelan smiled as he kissed her, pressing his hands tighter against her back.

She wasn't letting go, and he wasn't, either. Because she loved him, enough to leave her family and her mountains. Enough to dig her heart out of the snow and give it to him to hold. Enough to thaw the ice that ran through her veins and make room for fire.

The door slammed open, filling the room with cold air once more. They broke apart. She was flushed and beautiful, and he couldn't look away from her. But then her smile wavered as her eyes darted up. A cry escaped her lips as a pair of hands grabbed Kelan from behind.

CHAPTER 42
SOL

"Stop!" Sol screamed. Kelan was torn from her arms, and she scrambled after him, trying to catch his hands.

He struggled against his assailant and smashed his head against the low table as he was wrenched toward the door. Two more neighbors appeared in the doorway and grabbed him as he thrashed. Sol ran at one of them, a burly woodchopper named Oscar, the same woodchopper who had kept their fire burning all winter after her pa had passed.

And now Oscar was wrestling Kelan across the grass toward the pyre he had built in front of their house.

She grabbed one of Oscar's arms, digging her nails into his skin. "Let him go!"

Oscar knocked her aside, and she landed hard in a patch of dirty snow. But she was up on her feet again and running toward them. Other men had come to help. Kelan kicked at them and shouted, but they grabbed his arms and legs, stretching him out and pinning him to the ground.

Oscar drew a heavy knife from his belt.

"No!" Sol threw herself across Kelan's body, clinging tight to his neck. Her chest heaved as she held back a sob.

"Sol!" Kelan cried. "Don't! They'll hurt you!"

Oscar grabbed Sol's arm and yanked on her, but she held

tight. Her mother looked on, her features curled with disgust, her arms crossed over her chest. The matron's face was set in hard stone.

"Josef!" Sol screamed. He was the only one whose features had not been carved from granite and ice. His frown wavered, and he stepped toward them. Carol rushed to Sol's side and shoved the man that held Kelan's left arm.

"Let him go. Do you want to hurt Sol?"

Josef stepped closer and put a hand on his knife hilt. "Leave her."

The men shifted back, their eyes downcast. Kelan sat up, and Sol held him tight.

"He's a demon," Oscar said gruffly.

She buried her head in Kelan's shoulder. How could he have thought to leave without her? This was all that awaited him if he were alone. He would have no one to stand beside him and fight for him.

Oscar left out a heavy breath. "Sol—"

"I won't let you hurt him. You'll have to kill me first."

She glared at each of the men in turn, daring them to turn their blades and their large hands against her. Josef turned on his heel and left. Her mother followed. One by one the villagers shuffled away. Even Oscar sheathed his knife with a sigh and returned to his house.

Kelan dropped his head into his hands and took a ragged breath.

She placed a hand against his cheek. "They're gone. You're safe."

He gripped her wrist hard and met her eyes. "I won't use your body as a shield."

"But it was the only way to—"

"I will not let you sacrifice your life for mine."

"I told you, I'm not letting go."

"You have a life and a home. You have a place to come back to. If something ever happens to me—"

"I won't let anyone hurt you." She put an arm around his

neck and brushed the curls away from his forehead with her other hand.

"There's nothing for me if you're gone."

"Don't say that."

He brushed his thumb across her lower lip. "You know it's true. You saw what I left behind. It was nothing like this." He gestured to her house, to her sisters standing in the doorway.

"Wherever our journey takes, even if it be to the City of the Dead, I'll go with you."

He took her hand and kissed her palm. "I'm honored, love. But I can't allow that."

"Kelan—"

"I'm a Flameskin. I don't know what this war will bring. How it will end."

"We'll fight together if we have to."

He took her face between his hands. "No. If it comes to that, promise you'll let me go."

"I won't."

Carol braided Sol's clean, wet hair while Kelan bathed in the next room. Dorit had already fallen asleep in Sol's lap, and Grete was nodding off on her seat beside the fireplace.

Carol laid her head on Sol's shoulder when she finished. "I'm going to miss you."

Sol squeezed her eyes shut. It was an impossible choice, to give up her home for her heart, her past for her future. Already she ached knowing that she would leave them so vulnerable. "I've let everyone down. You and the girls. Pa. Tokkedal."

"You haven't let us down."

"I abandoned you for Solstice, and everyone's been starving here. I was supposed to keep us fed and safe, and I failed. And now I'm leaving."

"I've been feeding them."

"Then why is there no food here?"

Carol let out a frustrated breath. "My traps were bad at first, but they're getting better. I can take care of our family just fine."

Sol wrapped her arms around Carol and rested her chin on Carol's shoulder. The firelit kitchen was filled with all the familiar sounds of her sisters sleeping. "I wish they would let him stay."

"Me, too."

"How could they have wanted to kill him? They're wrong about Flameskins. Pa was wrong, too." She shivered. Her pa had committed an unthinkable crime.

Carol sighed. "Pa was wrong about a lot of things. I think you were the only one who thought he had no faults."

Heat rose to Sol's cheeks. She really had. She had grown up believing Pa could do no wrong. She had always taken his side, always obeyed without question, always listened when he spoke. He was the reason she had fought her feelings for Kelan for so long.

Kelan emerged from the bedroom in a pair of her pa's clean clothes. His turquoise eyes were bright, and her heart swelled at the sight of him.

"Where should I sleep?" he asked.

"Take him to the loft," Carol said, and picked Dorit up from Sol's arms. "The rest of us can sleep in Ma's bed."

Sol slid open the screen door to her parents' tiny bedroom—Ma's tiny bedroom—and Carol carried Dorit inside. Sol climbed the ladder, lifted the trap door, and pulled herself into the girls' bedroom in the loft. The room occupied the entire second floor, and the steep pitch of the roof made it impossible to stand anywhere except beneath the central roof timber. Kelan climbed in after her, and Sol lit a candle for him with the pinch of her fingers. She should've gone down to light it with their candle downstairs, but she was getting careless with her emberstone. It was so convenient.

Pa would've been so disappointed. But she found she cared less and less.

The girls' shared bed lay along one wall, and their clothes and

Dorit's toys and their belongings were strewn across the rest of the space. Everything was so familiar here, as familiar as her own pulse. This was where she had grown up. This was where she had slept since she had grown out of her parents' bed. This was the sacred and sometimes war-filled space she shared with her sisters. It was a place without secrets or pretense or misery. It was a place she belonged so wholly she ached to see it after such an absence. How she would miss it.

Kelan drew her in, one hand at her neck, the other at her waist. His lips met hers in the darkness. She reached up and ran her fingers across his temple and into his curly hair. It had gotten long and shaggy again after their travels. He smelled of the lavender soap she and Ma had made last summer.

"I'm sorry to take you away from all this," he whispered. His breath was hot against her cheek.

"We'll come back after the war is over."

He pulled back, and his face was pensive. "I don't know if I can promise you that. I know I can't promise you safety, or a normal life, or anything close to what you deserve."

"You're all I want." She kissed him softly, then met his eyes. "I love you."

He pressed his forehead against hers and laced his fingers behind her back. "I've loved you since Baarka."

Her mouth fell open, and her heart fluttered. "So long?"

"When I realized how much I wanted you to really see me, to see I wasn't like the others, I knew I was falling for you."

He smiled and kissed her surprised lips. She leaned into his kisses and fumbled for the manacle's key in her pocket. She wanted to be warmed with his love; she wanted it to flow through her veins.

But then his hands slid to her hips, pulling her in against him. His hands were gentle, coaxing her closer as his body moved against hers. He pressed kisses along the length of her neck, and her heart pounded loud in her chest, beating against his.

She didn't want to pull away—her body resisted the thought. She was desperate to lose herself in this, but—

"Sol," he murmured.

She broke away. "We should—we should get some sleep. We have to leave early tomorrow."

He pressed his cheek against hers and hesitated before letting her go. "I know." He pecked her cheek and blew out the candle. "Goodnight, love."

She felt her way to the hatch in the darkness and climbed down. Carol had banked the fire, and the embers gave a soft glow from the fireplace. She made her way across the kitchen, running her hand along the wooden shelf, gently touching the ceramic jars filled with fragrant herbs, the wooden plates, the beautiful oakwood bowl. Saying goodbye.

She squeezed into the bed alongside her sisters. From the soft rhythm of Carol's breathing, she could tell she was already asleep. Sol lay there for a long time at the edge of the pallet, warmed by the closeness of her sisters and thinking of all that she would miss.

But sleep eluded her. Kelan's kisses had filled her with fire, and the burning wouldn't stop.

But they couldn't. Not tonight. They had to wait until—

Until what?

There would be no wedding feasts, no bridal gown, no wreath of juniper or crown of holly. There would be no home for them to call their own, no hearthstone to lay or cellar to dig. There would be no gifts or well wishes from the neighbors, no sleigh to carry them to the temple altar with bells jangling in the frozen air.

She and Kelan would have none of those things.

No.

The mountains would be their altar, the furs her gown. The trees would be their wedding party, and ice would make her crown. In the morning, they would depart into an unknown road, tying their fates together more tightly than any knotted wedding veil.

Her heart beat fast as she slipped from the bed and silently slid open the screen.

And there he was, standing outside the door with his hand raised to knock on it. She could barely see his outline in the darkness, but she didn't need the light. She knew his face so well and loved the slope of his eyebrows and the curve of his jaw, and those enchanting turquoise eyes.

"I'm not used to sleeping alone," he whispered.

She wrapped her arms around his neck and pulled him toward her, pressing her lips against his. He stumbled over her, and they lost their balance. He grappled and caught them, one hand shoved up against the wall, the other arm encircling her waist. He pressed her up against the wall, pushing his body against hers. His hands found the skin at her waist.

Winter rattled its last cries on the wind outside, and cold tendrils of air snuck in through the chinks in the wooden slats, but she was warm against his body. She was burning.

She led him up to the loft. The faint glow of his emberstone lit their faces as he lowered her onto the bed and pulled her close.

She unhooked the buttons running across his chest, and his shirt fell open. The token he wore around his neck brushed her skin as it swung back and forth on its chain. She ran her fingers over his scars and guided his hand underneath her tunic to her waist. She sighed at the touch of his fingers on her skin.

When she removed the key and her emberstone from her pocket, he pulled back.

"What are you doing?"

She pressed one hand to his chest and unlocked the manacle. The moment his emberstone came off, his skin came alive. Sparks burst beneath the surface.

"I want you like this."

She pressed her cheek to his and gripped his fiery skin with burning fingers, leaning in against him. His lips stretched into a smile she couldn't see in the darkness, but that she could feel.

When he kissed her again, it was the kind of kiss that was heavy with desire and impatient for more and yet wanted this moment to stretch on forever. All of her was burning now. Every inch of her skin was filled with his fire.

His want flooded her with sparks, but this fire had already been burning for a long time inside her. She could no longer contain it. It ran like wildfire through her veins.

Kelan's pyra burned hot and bright and fierce. She thought for a moment she wouldn't be able to contain all the fire inside her, but hearts were made to expand. Sol's blood surged with both her joy and his, the exultation and the flames and the intoxication of it. There were only the sparks inside them, and his breath on her skin, and his burning hands on her body.

And then Sol's eyes pricked with unexpected tears.

Something had been gained, but something had also been lost.

"Did I hurt you?" he asked. Worry and fear bled out of his heart and into hers.

She shook her head, trying and failing to speak.

"What's wrong?" he asked, more anxious.

She didn't understand the tears. She was happy. She had never been happier.

But this was her last night at home. This was the end of her childhood. This was the end of four sisters in a bed in the loft, the end of hanging clothes from the rafters to make a castle and dancing around the table after dinner. The end of summers spent swimming in the creek beside the house and making lavender soap in the kitchen.

He swore quietly and rested his cheek against hers. "I shouldn't have."

She took his head in her hands. "No. This is what I want. Only, I'll miss all of this. And this place. Life was so good here for my family, and I want that for us."

"I'll find a way to give you the life you want."

"No. We'll find a way. Together."

CHAPTER 43
KELAN

I t hadn't been a dream.

Kelan woke to find Sol nestled in the bed beside him.
The morning light coming in through the small rice paper
window illuminated her form. His shackle was on again, but he
was warm. He put an arm around her waist, trapping her against
him, and his whole body came awake as he brushed his fingers
across her skin.

His mountain queen.

The legends said that dryads slept with men and then
plucked their victims' hearts out of their chests. The dryads
would disappear into the mist and the trees and never return,
leaving their lovers to wander the mountains in search of their
hearts.

No. Sol's skin was warm and soft. She was real. This was real.

But she had fallen asleep with tears in her eyes, and that was
because of him.

If he loved her, should he have set her free and let her hide in
these mountains and forget him?

If he loved her, shouldn't he do anything to remain by her
side?

She was giving up everything to be with him, and he loved

her the more for it. But he didn't want her to resent him for everything she had lost.

Even if he couldn't bring himself to regret what they had done, he couldn't be sure of what she would think this morning when the fire that had warmed them all night was banked, and all that awaited them was the cold reality of the journey before them.

Sol stirred and woke, and his heart raced within him.

Please, please still love me. Please don't disappear into the woods.

She turned and met his eyes. "Oh," she gasped as she yanked at the blankets to cover her body.

He hugged her to him. "Morning, love."

He kissed her forehead and her cheek and her lips and her stiffness softened.

"How do you feel?" he asked.

Her cheeks pinked. "I'm fine. I'm better than fine."

"Are you really?"

She sighed. "I just—Yesterday was a lot. Soldiers and coming home, and Josef, and—"

He cut her off there with a kiss. "Don't be sorry about anything." His hands trailed over the curves of her waist and her hip.

She put her hand over his heart. His heart still beat inside his chest; she hadn't plucked it out.

"I just wish everything about this didn't have to be so difficult."

"Maybe we'll be hungry, and maybe the journey will be long, but I'd travel any distance and climb any mountain to be with you."

She smiled and kissed him.

Sol.

This mountain queen was his.

CHAPTER 44
SOL

Sol wasn't sure how her heart could be so full and so broken at the same time. She spun in a slow circle, memorizing the line of the mountains, the colors of their peaks, the pale morning sky and the frost-laden trees. She breathed in the smell of the pines and the woodsmoke.

Ma hadn't come to say goodbye.

Carol was helping Kelan pack Sol's bag with food she insisted they didn't need, but Sol knew they did. Sol was grateful anyway.

"You'll smell the smoke before the Flameskins arrive," Kelan was saying. "That should give you one- or two-days' warning before they come. Make sure you have a place in the woods to retreat to with most of your food stores, because if they do come, they'll burn down the house."

"Will they come looking for us?" Carol asked.

"No. The only people that ever get hurt in a Flameskin raid are the ones who fight back."

"Maybe we should fight back."

Kelan's eyes were lidded. "The only thing you can do is hide and wait until it's over."

Sol's heart twisted within her. She was leaving her family while the Flameskins marched on their heels. It would be years before she and Kelan would be able to return.

Kelan grabbed Sol's pack and pulled out the jeweled letter opener. "Would you be able to make good use of this?" He dropped it into Carol's waiting hands, and she stared at it with wide eyes.

Sol smiled. "Take it to Skive. You'll get a better price for it, and a better price for seed, too."

Carol closed her hands around the gift. "I'll take care of them, Sol. I swear it."

"We'll miss you," Grete said. "I don't care what Ma says about you."

Sol tried not to let the words sting. She could guess what Ma had said.

"You're really not our sister?" Dorit asked.

Carol pulled Dorit away. "Hush. That's not true."

Sol clenched her fists. "She's disowned me?" Lisbet had said as much yesterday, but Sol had prayed she hadn't meant it.

Carol bit her lip and wouldn't speak.

"Carol—"

"No, it's not that. She said—It doesn't matter. She was just angry. She'll miss you."

"Carol, tell me."

"She told us you weren't her daughter," Grete said. "She told us you were left on the doorstep in that oakwood bowl. The one with the leaves carved on it."

Sol breathed in sharply and took a step back. "That's not—"

Carol grabbed her in a fierce hug. "It's a lie. Please come back, Sol. She won't be angry forever."

Sol let out a long breath and tears stung her eyes. Why would Ma have said something like that, even if she was angry?

"We know the truth. You're our sister," Carol said. "I'll light a candle for you in the temple when I go to Skive."

Sol gave Carol another fierce hug, and buried her tears in her sister's black hair. "I'll come back."

"Where will you go?" Carol asked.

"There's a place called the Hivid Wood. Maybe it's only a rumor, but they say that Flameskins are sheltered there."

"Sol," Kelan said in a warning voice.

"You can't tell anyone where we're going," Sol told Carol.

"I won't."

Sol took Kelan's hand and squeezed it. "Let's go."

Then she framed in her view her sisters and the house that Pa built and the village of Hillerod and the mountains she called home.

She would be back.

The descent from Hillerod to the foothills near Skive took only three days on foot, but each step away from her home was laborious. The mountain sucked at the soles of her boots as she walked. And her ma's parting lie still stung. Kelan didn't say anything about it, and she was grateful for that. She didn't want to think about it.

The path they took was an old, narrow game trail that hadn't been used yet this spring, and new growth threatened to conceal it completely. Spring had already come to the lower hills, and the vibrant greens of new shoots and leaves, and the yellows and whites and violets of wild flowers filled the mountains. The air was fragrant with the smell of blossoms and choked with insects. Sticker bushes lined the path and kept catching at Sol's clothes and tearing her tunic and skin.

She got snared yet again in the grasp of briars, and Kelan had to carefully disentangle her from the branches. He pulled thorns from her hair and her pants.

He kissed her cut hand. "I'm sorry, love."

"I've never seen anything so overgrown. We'll have to find another way down."

It hadn't looked like such a difficult path from above, and none of the thorns ever caught at Kelan and trapped him.

He frowned as he wiped blood from a cut on her arm. "It's like the mountain doesn't want to let you go."

She yanked another thorny branch from her sleeve. "The feeling is mutual."

She unhooked a clawed branch from her pants, and it immediately swung back and reattached itself to her clothes. Kelan ripped at the branch, but the moment he let go, it wrapped itself around her leg once more.

She met Kelan's eyes. A tremor of something like fear passed through her. It was difficult not to believe the impossible when she stared it in the face.

"Has this ever happened before?" he asked. His voice was strained.

"Never. I've left the mountains before. This didn't happen when we went to Olisipo."

"Why won't it let you go this time?"

She ripped at the branch. "No. They're just overgrown brambles. The Ulves don't trap people here."

"Is it me? Do they not want you to go with me?"

"No. If the Ulves didn't like you, you'd be dead."

He yanked at the thorns and pulled her loose. "You're the queen of these mountains. They don't want to let you go."

"The queen? Burnitall, Kelan. What are you talking about?"

She tried to walk forward, but the undergrowth stretched more tightly around her, tripping her up and clinging to her arms and legs. She yelped as she was ripped from Kelan's grasp and hauled backward.

He grabbed her arm and pulled, but her arm was streaked with blood from the cuts and she slipped between his fingers. He stumbled backward and the brambles parted for him, but twined more tightly around her. The wind whispered through the trees, and the rustle of the leaves almost sounded like words.

"Help me!" She ripped at the vines and the branches and the thorns that clawed at her, but they snaked around her torso and held her in place. Leaves tickled the back of her neck as branches descended on her.

This didn't make any sense. Why was this happening?

He pulled the vines, trying to disentangle her, but they

slapped at his hands, and a tree branch swung forward and slammed into his gut. Kelan grunted as he was thrown to the ground. Above them a tree creaked.

"Watch out!" she screamed.

He jumped to his feet and threw himself into the brambles beside her as a tree crashed down in front of them, hitting the ground where Kelan had been. Clods of dirt and sticks pelted and cut them. Dust flew into their faces and they both coughed and blinked it out of their eyes.

The more she struggled against the trees and the brambles, the tighter they twined around her. She had always known there was magic in these mountains, but she had never seen it act like this. A vine twisted around her palm, wrapping itself tight around her skin and covering her hand. She couldn't reach her knife to cut herself free. The mountains had taken her captive.

"Use my emberstone!" Kelan said.

He pressed the glowing stone to the tips of her fingers, which were barely visible beneath the leaves. She drew on the stone and fire exploded out of her other hand, burning her sleeve and the brambles that caught at her skin. Kelan yanked on her other arm and kicked at the vines around her legs as fire consumed them. The branches slowly unwound themselves from her feet.

She fell free of the thorns and landed on top of Kelan with a grunt. He grabbed her cool hand and yanked her to her feet. Vines and twigs and leaves trailed in her wake as she ran. She still had a vine wrapped around her arm and leaves threaded through her hair. Behind them, there was another whoosh as a tree crashed to the ground.

"Run!" she shouted. "Don't stop until we're in the valley."

They bolted through the woods and leapt over bushes as their packs bounced on their backs. Brambles snagged her legs, and branches swung out and caught her as she ran. They climbed over fallen trees that tried to block their path and jumped over a ravine that opened at their feet.

The trees slowly thinned, and the mountain gave way to the

gentle slope of the valley, but they didn't stop. They ran until they were breathless, and the trees were far, far behind them.

Sol slowed and dropped to her knees in the grass. "I think we're safe," she gasped.

The trees of the Ulves quivered, and the wind blew mournfully through their leaves, but nature had ceased attacking them.

"What in the name of Maja was that?" Kelan demanded. "I thought we weren't going to get you free." He grabbed her and held her tight. His eyes were wild and afraid.

"I don't understand it, either."

He stroked her black hair. "Sol, about what your mother said—"

"Don't." She curled up in his arms. He held her the same way her pa used to, and she laid her head on his chest.

Except Kelan had a heartbeat.

She had never heard her pa's pulse.

She scrambled upright and stared at the mountains. Her hands flew her mouth. "They're *not* my sisters. Lisbet isn't my ma."

Kelan held her tight. "They're still your family."

"You knew."

He cringed. "I didn't. But I've never seen anyone move through the woods like you do."

She clutched her hands to her chest. "My pa's heart was stolen. He fell in love with a dryad. Oh, saints. Saints!"

She dropped to her knees.

What did this make her? Something less than human? Something made of oak and malice and magic? Something made to steal hearts and flit through the misty trees?

"It doesn't matter," Kelan whispered.

"But it does! What am I?"

"You're as human as I am, Sol."

She was still covered in twigs and vines, and she pulled at them frantically, trying to rid herself of the trailing fingers of the mountains that still wanted to drag her back.

"Sol, it's fine." Kelan pressed his forehead against hers and kissed her softly.

He gently unwound the vine still wrapped around her right hand. When he pulled the ivy free, there was a large red acorn in her palm.

He brought her hand to his face. "What is this?"

"An acorn?" It was like no acorn she had ever seen. It glowed red and was about the size of a cherry. Touching it was like touching an emberstone; it felt alive, filled with energy and possibility.

She stared at the mountains. "Why would they give this to me?"

Kelan was staring at the mountains, too. "If you can't stay in the Ulves, maybe they want you to bring the mountains with you wherever you go."

"What do you think it will grow?"

He closed her palm over it and kissed her. "Something beautiful, like you."

CHAPTER 45
KELAN

They traveled off the road most of the time, both to avoid soldiers and to increase their likelihood of finding greens and game to fill their bellies with. They never rested, and they stopped only to sleep and to prepare the food Sol had caught. They were following a trail of rumor and hearsay toward the Hivid Wood, and neither of them knew what they would find when they got there.

Though they avoided people and villages as much as possible, they couldn't stay away from civilization forever. The terrain and the roads were unfamiliar, and neither of them knew the exact location of the Wood.

They had arrived at a town called Rodding. Kelan tugged constantly at his sleeve as they walked through the streets, pulling it down low over his emberstone. He wasn't going to make the mistake of letting it be seen again.

He and Sol had talked about remaking the band so that it wrapped around his upper arm and could be more easily concealed. But reshaping it themselves would give it an imperfect seal on his skin. They would need a metalsmith to do it for them. But letting someone see his cuff had risks of its own. He had been wearing it for weeks now and it chafed his wrist, but he didn't dare remove it.

Kelan watched the road anxiously for soldiers as they passed through the town. The streets churned around them with vegetable sellers and peddlers, but no soldiers. They passed a woman pulling noodles at a table on the street. Cooking noodles swam in a simmering pot of meat broth beside her. Kelan's mouth watered at the smell. There were so many things he hadn't eaten in ages: dumplings, shrimp, noodles, rice, seaweed. He wanted all of it.

Sol laughed when she saw his face. "I'll get us some dinner, if I can." She had a neatly-folded deerskin in her pack, along with a bundle of brightly-colored feathers they had collected to trade.

"Can we get you a new pair of shoes, too?" he asked.

She looked longingly toward a cobbler's shop. She had worn through her soles and covered the holes with folded deerskin scraps. All their clothes and supplies were ragged from use.

She linked her arm through his and pulled him toward the trading post. "I don't know what they'll give me for the deerskin, but hopefully they'll at least give us some directions."

She opened the door, but Kelan pulled away. He had another errand to do.

"You're not coming in?" she asked.

"Just give me five minutes. I want to look at something."

"But, Kelan." Trouble had a way of finding them, and it compounded when they were apart.

"Just five minutes, then I'll come straight here. I'll be fine."

She frowned.

"Trust me."

She rolled her eyes. "I trust you. Just be careful."

She entered the trading post and once the door closed behind her, Kelan hurried off down the street. He retraced their steps and slipped into the metalsmith's shop he had seen earlier.

The interior was warmed by the dying fire of the smith's workstation. Kelan's palms sweat as he approached the counter, but not because of the heat.

"Looking for something in particular?" the smith asked, his eyes roving over Kelan's stained and dirty clothes, and the ragged pack on his back. The walls of the smith's shop were covered in shelves with utinsels, weapons, pots, and vessels.

"Do you work in silver?" Kelan asked.

"I can."

Kelan unhooked the chain around his neck and slid the brass button into his pocket before laying the chain on the counter.

"Could you melt this into a ring for me? It's silver. You could keep the excess." If he still had his pyra he could've done it himself, but it would've been a crude thing. He wanted Sol to have something beautiful.

The jeweler picked up the chain and inspected it. "It'd be a shame to melt down a nice chain like this. I'll trade you for it."

Kelan sighed as the smith placed his mother's chain in a wooden box. He had hoped the chain could've been melted down, so it would still be close by, even if it were in a different form. But he only had five minutes before Sol would start to worry.

She had given up so much for him; he could make this one sacrifice for her.

"This for a you or for a girl?"

"A girl," Kelan conceded.

The smith grunted and rummaged on shelves for another box. "This is the only one I have to fit a girl's finger."

The smith dropped it into Kelan's palm. The small band had been etched with leaves, like her dagger. "It's perfect."

He wanted to make Sol his in every way. It was only a silver band, but maybe it would ground her. She would always have it to remember him, even if he couldn't be with her. He wouldn't be able to bear it if she disappeared one day and returned to the mist or was reclaimed by the trees.

"You getting married?" the smith asked.

"We were married recently."

Kelan grinned. They had gotten it completely backward. First, they had eloped, then he had met the family, and now he was finally getting the ring.

"Let an old man indulge himself in a piece of advice: She's

always right."

Kelan laughed. "I've already learned that one."

"Smart boy."

He nodded and bowed as he slipped the ring into his pocket. "Thank you." He turned toward the door, but paused. "Could you give me some directions? Do you know how to get to the Hivid Wood?"

The man stepped away from Kelan with a scowl. "The Hivid Wood? That's a dangerous place. The wraiths eat anyone who enters. I'd stay away if I were you."

He sighed. "Never mind."

That was the only thing most people knew, that wraiths had overtaken the forest. He wouldn't have believed the rumors a year ago, but after what he had seen in the Ulves . . . .

As Kelan turned toward the door, there were several shouts outside. Through the small window of the shop he caught a glimpse of dozens of people and torches pass by.

"What—?"

"Trouble," the smith growled. "That's what that is. Trouble for Rodding and trouble for you. Stay far away from it."

Kelan bowed again and left the shop.

The crowd had already passed down the street, taking the peddlers and the shoppers with them. Kelan hurried through the empty street toward the trading post and yanked on his sleeve again to make sure it was covering his emberstone.

Sol was already in the street, and she ran to him when she spotted him. "Cinders, Kelan," she scolded and scowled at him. "Don't you ever leave me again."

"What? What's happened?"

"They've taken some Flameskins."

Kelan's blood went cold.

"Demon! She's a demon!" the mob shouted.

Sol clung tight to Kelan's arm. "Let's get out of here."

"Who have they taken? Did you see?"

She pulled on his arm again. "It doesn't matter. There's nothing we can do for them."

"Tell me."

"Please, Kelan. Let's just leave. I don't want you to get hurt."

He was not going to walk away and allow another atrocity to happen. She shivered when he took her hand, but she let him lead her toward the crowd in the town square. Above the shouts of the crowd came a woman's scream that pierced Kelan to the core.

A pyre had already been lit in the square, and smoke blotted the blue sky. He pushed through the writhing mob trying to get closer, but it was slow moving for two people with large packs on their backs. The woman continued to scream, and her cries rang in Kelan's ears.

He moved more frantically, pushing people aside, trying to get to her. The crowd was suffocating, so many people brushing up against him, spewing hatred and brimming with violence. Smoke blew toward them, stinging Kelan's eyes and making him cough.

The woman's screaming ceased abruptly, sending a chill through him.

He shoved someone aside and stepped into the square.

Blood pooled on the street. The woman's heart torn out and left half-submerged in a puddle of red-tinted rainwater.

Kelan recoiled and Sol was there to catch him when his knees gave out.

They had already thrown the woman's body onto the pyre and flames licked at her hair and her clothes.

Kelan swallowed bile.

Rage burned hot inside him as his head spun. If he had his cuff off, he'd burn Rodding to the ground. He'd make every one of these people suffer for what they had done.

Sol yanked on his arm. "Let's go. There's nothing we can do."

He was standing on his own now, but he couldn't move. He could only watch the flames consume her.

Sol pressed a kiss to his cheek and tried to pull him back into the crowd. "Kelan, please."

"Mommy!" sobbed a voice. "Mommy!"

Kelan turned.

The mob had its hands on another victim, a girl no more than five, with tears running down her dirty cheeks. Her black hair was mussed and tangled in the ropes they had wound around her body.

Two men held the girl taut between them. The child, even if she was a Flameskin, was powerless against them. Fear had undoubtedly drowned out her pyra long ago, and at that age, the girl's flames had only just started appearing. She wouldn't know how to use her pyra to protect herself.

A man stepped forward with a knife in hand to cut out the girl's heart.

Kelan couldn't move. He couldn't scream. He could only watch, horrified and transfixed like he had been that day so long ago when he had been that child. It was the same tragedy played out over and over again. This is how it would always be for Flameskins.

The man raised his knife and an arrow struck it and knocked the blade from the man's hand. Both knife and arrow skittered across the ground.

The crowd hushed and turned from the Flameskin child to the huntress. Sol stood in the town square beside the pyre with another arrow already notched on the string.

Kelan gasped for breath as he came out of his trance. He threw off his pack and drew the sword he had stashed inside it.

He stood beside Sol and gave her a weak smile. Sol. He had never loved her so well.

"Put down the child," Sol ordered, aiming for the face of one of the men.

But the men didn't release her.

"What right have you to tell us how to do our business?" one demanded.

"To kill innocents like this is to bring the wrath of the Flameskin Army," Sol said. "I've seen what they can do to a village."

"Saint Katrine is riding with the Tokken Army. The Flameskins are no more."

A chill ran down Kelan's spine. Everywhere they went the rumors of Saint Katrine grew more numerous and hopeful. Saint Katrine had come to redeem Tokkedal and wipe every Flameskin from the face of the land.

"Don't sully your hands with a child's blood," Sol said. "Let Saint Katrine kill her."

One of the men dropped the sobbing girl's arm and picked up the dented knife from the ground. He took a few tentative steps toward them. "Flameskin sympathizers aren't welcome here."

"Give us the girl," Kelan said.

Sol shot him a wide-eyed glance.

"We're traveling south," Kelan said. "We'll take the girl to the Hivid Wood."

The crowd grumbled and there were hissed cries of "demons" and "wraiths."

"Flameskin sympathizers are just as bad as the Flameskins themselves," the man said. He gave them an ugly scowl as he advanced toward them. "Perhaps we need a bigger pyre."

Sol loosed her arrow, the man cried out, and the arrow struck the cobblestone in front of his foot. The shaft broke, showering him in splinters of wood.

"I'm getting tired of this," she said as she notched another arrow. "Give us the girl. The next arrow goes straight through your chest."

The man's hands shook as he dropped his knife. The crowd protested and shouted and raged, but no one stepped forward to challenge the huntress.

Sol nudged Kelan with her elbow. "Go get her, then."

Kelan strode forward with his sword in hand and took the sobbing girl from the mob's hands. He ripped the ropes from her body and left them in the bloody street, then he picked her up and carried her back toward Sol, still holding his sword.

Then, slowly, they retreated away from the mob and the still-burning pyre. Ash of the girl's mother rose up into the air and followed them as they returned to the forest.

CHAPTER 46
SOL

T hey had done the right thing.

Sol kept telling herself that as she banked the fire and prepared for bed.

But taking in the girl wouldn't make the journey any easier. They would travel twice as slow as before with her in tow, and she was another mouth to feed as well.

The girl had already curled up in one of their bedrolls and fallen asleep. They still didn't know her name. She had cried all afternoon and they had taken turns carrying her until their arms ached too badly to continue on. They had found a campsite in the shelter of a grove of aspens and now sat exhausted on the ground.

Kelan had been silent all afternoon. They had witnessed many terrible things during their time together, but she had never once seen him freeze up like that.

She still couldn't get the sight of it out of her mind. The heart lying on the ground in a pool of its own blood. The woman with the carved-out chest tossed onto the fire to burn. How could her pa have committed such a horrible crime? Even if the woman were a possessed Flameskin, how could they have considered giving the same punishment to her daughter, a child?

They needed to get to the Hivid Wood where all of them

would be safe, where they could hide from mobs and from Tokken soldiers and from Saint Katrine.

Sol moved in beside Kelan, and he put his arm around her. The dim glow of the coals and the starlight illuminated his moist eyes.

She put a hand on his cheek. "Kelan."

He rubbed at his eye and cleared his throat. "The world is too cruel to children."

She sighed. Her childhood had been a thing of dreams and sunshine and warm, winter nights. How was it that some were blessed to be born into happiness and others born into misery?

"Thank you, Sol, for what you did earlier. You don't know what it means to me that you stood up to them."

"A year ago I would've joined them. I'm grateful you've taught me to be better than that."

He ran his fingers through her hair and kissed her softly. "I'm glad I fell in love with the kind of girl who would risk her life to save another's."

"It wasn't my life I was risking; it was yours." Her stomach twisted as she thought again of the mob passing by the trading post, and the terror that had gripped her, thinking it had been Kelan they had taken.

He sighed and pulled her in, hugging her to him. "We saved her. That's what matters." His eyes were fixed on the girl, trapped in a fitful sleep.

They watched her for a while as Kelan stroked Sol's hair.

"That was how my mother died, too," he whispered.

"Your mother?"

"I watched them cut out my mother's heart, and they would've done it to me, too, if one of my neighbors hadn't inter-vened. He was able to hide me until my uncle came to get me."

"I'm sorry, Kelan."

"Bringing a Flameskin child into the world is a sin," Kelan whispered. "I used to wish that I had never been born. We're all miserable. Every Flameskin in Nordby."

Sol's heart twisted. Any child born to her and Kelan would be a Flameskin as well, if not a mage. Not that it was likely they would have children in the near future. Their journey was far too arduous for her to expect she could conceive. But the thought frightened her nonetheless.

Kelan's brows drew together. "I'm sorry, love. I didn't mean to scare you. I'm not miserable, not since I met you."

She laid her head on his shoulder. "I know what you meant."

"Oh! I almost forgot." He pulled a shining object from his pocket. Then he took her hand and slid a small silver ring onto her finger.

"This is beautiful. Where did you get it?" she asked, admiring the band with its lovely filigree leaves.

"Today, in town. Do you like it?"

"Did you steal it?"

He frowned. "I'm not a thief. I traded for it." He tapped his collar where the chain and its brass ornament used to hang.

She stared at his bare throat. He had always worn that chain, as long as she had known him. "That was important to you."

He kissed her cheek. "It was. But you've given up much more for me."

She ran her fingertip over the band. She had never seen anything so beautiful. Her heart swelled. "You didn't have to get me a ring."

"You don't like it?"

She kissed him. "No, I love it. Thank you. It's the most beautiful thing I've ever owned."

He smiled and brushed his lips along her cheek and whispered in her ear. "Now you're officially mine."

"I've always been yours."

"Not always. And now the mountains will know you belong with me, and that they can't take you away."

Sol forced out a laugh. "You're still worried about that?" It had shaken both of them, but Kelan especially. She had started to think he wouldn't let her go back to the Ulves.

"Nothing will ever separate us," she promised.

He took her hand and kissed her knuckles. "My wife," he

whispered, and met her eyes. A shiver of pleasure ran through her.

"Can I call you that?" he asked.

She nodded. Their life was so hard sometimes, but she had never known anything so wonderful as being with him.

When she laid down, he pulled the blanket over them. They were squished tight in a single bedroll since the girl had taken the other one, but Sol didn't mind. She loved being close to him and feeling his heartbeat beneath her fingers.

"You are my queen," he whispered between kisses.

That always made her smile.

A crash startled Sol from sleep. She woke to blinding, orange light and heat that singed her skin. A burning tree branch had crashed to the ground nearby and thrown sparks into the air. She coughed as smoke filled her lungs and burned her eyes.

Fire.

She grabbed the emberstone from her pocket. The moment she had it in her hand, the burning heat abated, and she could breathe easier in the smoke.

"Kelan!" she shouted over the crackle of the flames.

He lay still beside her in the bedroll. She swore and her shaking, panicky fingers searched for the key in her pocket to unlock his manacle.

"Kelan!" She shook him roughly and unlocked the manacle. She took one of his hands to draw the fire from his pyra and could feel the sparks underneath his skin. He was still alive. She crawled out of the bedroll and started dragging him away from the flames, but the blanket caught on the prickly forest floor. The fire roared as it snapped and popped, throwing sparks over both of them.

She coughed and shouted his name and shook him again, and finally, finally his eyes flickered open.

"Get up! Fire!" She dragged him upright as he coughed and

blearily took in the scene around them. The trees north of their camp were burning, and the fire had spread to the grass. Smoke filled their little clearing, and sparks leapt onto their bags and bedrolls.

She put Kelan's hand on her arm so they wouldn't break contact and threw their bags over her shoulder, then she picked up the girl.

"Don't let go!" she told Kelan over the crackle of the flames. He clung to her as they hurried away from the fire. Smoke still billowed around them, and she coughed it out of her lungs. The girl woke and clung groggily to Sol's neck.

Sol and Kelan were both coughing. They had inhaled a great deal of smoke in their flameless states. When Sol doubled over again, Kelan took the girl from her arms and threw her over his shoulder, then took Sol's hand in his.

The fire raced after them, leaping from tree to tree. The wind hurled sparks at them, and little fires started on the grass beneath their feet. They tripped over fallen logs and tore their way through bushes to get out.

They didn't stop moving until the smoke and the fire were far behind them, and they had come out on the other side of the forest.

Kelan set the girl down in the grass and took Sol up in his arms. They both sank to the ground. Sol's head and limbs ached. Both of them were still coughing.

"You all right?" he asked as he coughed.

"I'm fine. I don't know what happened." She coughed again. "I thought I banked the fire properly, but I guess not."

"I don't think we started it. Look." He pointed toward the forest behind them. An enormous portion of it was burning now, and it looked like it would continue to spread through the night. It burned all the way to the edge of Rodding, the town they had just left.

"You think it's more Flameskins?" Sol asked.

"No. They were trying to burn us out. They knew we would be here tonight."

"But that's madness. They'd burn down their own forest to kill the girl? And risk their town catching on fire?"

Kelan's face was dark. "You haven't seen what people are willing to do to destroy Flameskins."

Shapes approached from the darkness. Men with torches and shining weapons.

Sol struggled to her feet and yanked the bow from her bag. She coughed as she searched for her string and arrows.

She gasped and jerked upright.

She had broken contact with Kelan. She wasn't absorbing his pyra.

Kelan stood and slid his sword from his bag.

Sol grabbed the girl and scrambled away from him, swearing under her breath. She had gotten careless. She had known eventually this would happen and Kelan's pyra would escape, but why did it have to be now?

Her mind was foggy from the smoke. She smothered a cough as she struggled to string her bow.

But Kelan's pyra must have been consumed by rage at the pyre they had witnessed yesterday because it ignored her and the girl entirely. He strode soundlessly through the tall grass toward the advancing mob. His scimitar looked like a wicked crescent moon in his hand.

Sol finally got her bow strung and threw her quiver over her shoulder. "Stay here," she told the girl. The girl nodded and curled up beside their bags.

Sol stole forward, keeping a safe distance from Kelan. She didn't want to have to hurt him, but he'd forgive her for sticking an arrow in his leg to get him down. She could do it without hurting him too badly, but they'd have to lie low for a few days while he healed.

She knew what she had to do, but still her fingers trembled on the string. She couldn't look at that thing wearing Kelan's face. It had the twisted familiarity of nightmare.

Kelan had stopped before the mob. There were about ten men, armed with the weapons of villagers: axes, a shovel, daggers, a pickax, and an old sword. It was the man she had shot at earlier in the village who carried the sword. He had that same cruel look on his face.

"Give us the girl," he ordered.

Kelan raised his scimitar. His voice was dark and angry. "You almost killed us."

"You brought fire on yourselves when you aligned with Flameskins," he spat. "Give us the demon child so we can end this."

"Leave now with your lives," Kelan hissed.

His voice sent a shiver down Sol's spine.

The man roared and swung with his sword. Kelan knocked it away with a practiced blow and thrust his sword through the man's side. The man fell with a cry onto the ground and the villagers beside him shouted and charged as Kelan slid the sword free and the body dropped.

Kelan barely moved. He didn't even need fire for this fight. His scimitar carved the air, a vicious streak of silver moonlight. He blocked ax heads and knives and dropped three more men.

Sol was rooted in place. Her hands shook. She tried to pull back the bowstring, but her strength failed her.

The six remaining villagers retreated with their axes and their scythes. "What have you done?" one man gasped.

A shudder ran through Sol. This was what Kelan became without his manacle. She raised her bow and strained as she pulled back the string.

Kelan lifted his sword again toward the mob. "Get out of my sight."

The men lurched backward and scrambled over each other as they fled.

Kelan lowered his sword tip to the ground and slowly turned in place until he faced her. He dropped his sword and stumbled backward when he saw the arrow pointed at him. "Sol, what—"

It was then she saw the manacle peeking out from beneath his sleeve, bathing his hand in red light.

She dropped her bow.

That hadn't been the demon at all.

That was all the work of Kelan the soldier.

How often she forgot who he had been, and what he was capable of, even without his pyra.

He sank to his knees beside the bodies and pressed his palms into his forehead. Sol ran to him and threw her arms around him.

"I thought you were possessed. Are you hurt?"

"I can't blame you for thinking that," he said, his voice dark. "I am a killer. Not any better than they are."

"You protected us."

"These men had families and lives of their own. Why did they have to fight me?" he asked. He was shaking. They were both shaking.

"You did what you had to," she whispered, but the words tasted wrong in her mouth. Why did he have to kill them? Couldn't he just have wounded them, instead?

He took her by the shoulders and looked into her face. "I never asked to be a soldier, and I never wanted to fight. But for you, I'd fight every day of my life if I had to. I'll do anything to protect you."

CHAPTER 47

KELAN

The girl didn't speak a single word as they trekked through the forest away from Rodding, leaving bodies and ashes in their wake. The girl didn't complain about the long days and how sore her feet must have been. When she got tired, she just sat down in the road with silent tears, and then Kelan and Sol would take turns carrying her as far as they could go.

Kelan's heart ached for the girl. He had been that child once.

The girl clung to Sol's neck as Sol carried her on her back. "Do you have a name?" Sol asked for the hundredth time. "What did your ma call you?"

In answer, the girl closed her eyes and rested her head on Sol's shoulder.

"We can't keep calling her 'the girl,'" Sol said.

"We could guess her name. Is it Isabella?"

The girl shook her head and Sol made a face at him. "Very funny."

Sol stuck out a hand and swiped a flower off the side of the road. "This is an azalea. What if I call you Azalea, too?"

The girl crushed the flower to herself and gave a brisk nod of assent.

"Azalea. It's a pretty name for a pretty girl," Sol said and smiled at her.

Azalea had long black hair that Sol braided with flowers and tied with string. She had haunted green Tokken eyes, and nothing they said or did could lift the darkness from Azalea's face.

Azalea didn't slow them too much, though, and they arrived at the Hivid Wood a couple weeks after they'd found her. They had entered the Wood on the highway, but it was soon so overgrown that it was impassable. And they had been warned by locals against traveling on the abandoned road.

The terrain was vastly different from that of the Ulves. The coastal forest was dominated by enormous redwood pines, and clover flourished in the shade. The trees towered over them and trapped the ocean mist that permeated the Wood. It was beautiful in the silent, mysterious way of forests.

Azalea still hadn't spoken, but she seemed more relaxed beneath the cool boughs of the trees. She clung to Sol's hand whenever Sol wasn't carrying her, but she permitted Kelan to carry her on his back.

But for all its beauty and tranquility, their travel through the Hivid Wood had been a disappointment so far. Despite all the rumors of Flameskins and wraiths, they had seen nothing but trees. Sol had been following tracks that led them deep into the woods, but it had rained last night and erased any evidence that a trail had once been laid.

She passed by a redwood shoot and plucked at a broken branch with wilting pine needles. She pointed out several deer tracks beneath her feet in the soft soil at the tree's roots,

"We're not the only ones here, but maybe the only humans," she said.

Kelan wasn't sure Sol was human. But to be fair, he had never really been human, either.

"Do you think there really are wraiths in these woods?" she asked.

He shrugged. "About as likely as a refugee Flameskin camp. All I know are the rumors."

It was called the Last Haven. The only place where Flameskins were still welcomed and protected.

"Well, if the Flameskins are here, we'll find them."

"And if they're not?"

"Then this could be as good a home as any. Maybe we could hide in these woods until the war is over. It's easy to get lost in here, and no one passes through here anymore because of the wraiths."

But if he had heard and believed the rumors about the Flameskin refugees in the Hivid Wood, then he wasn't the only one. Eventually soldiers would come through these woods, either Tokkens looking to destroy the last of the Flameskin Army, or the Flameskins looking for new recruits. He had heard his uncle mention plans to go to the Hivid Wood a few times.

"I don't know if it's the safest place," he said.

"But if the Flameskins are here, they're very well hidden. I haven't seen anything."

"Which is why I doubt there's anything here at all."

"I'm not giving up hope yet."

She nodded in another direction, and they kept moving through the trees, over fallen logs and around boulders and beneath the whispering pines accompanied by the haunting sounds of the birds concealed in the mist.

Even if they did find the Flameskin camp, would it be a safe place for them? Would the Flameskins be like him, possessed entirely because they had resisted so long?

He hated to make Sol use her emberstone more than she had to, knowing that it would slowly extinguish her ability to feel. Living among possessed Flameskins would require her to wear her emberstone always so she wouldn't get burned, and she would become heartless like his Uncle Haldur. And if he always wore his manacle, he would be susceptible to burns, as well.

Azalea stopped and sat down on a rock with a sigh, so Kelan lifted her and carried her on his shoulders. Sol paused before the trunk of a large tree and pointed to the pile of pine needles at its base. "Look at that."

"The leaves?"

She crept forward carefully. "They're not matted down. They've been moved recently."

How did she notice things like that?

She quirked a smile at him. "I wonder if we can't find the Flameskins because we haven't been looking low enough."

"You think they're underground?"

She brushed her hand through the brown needles. "This soil's been turned by a spade. You can see the marks the shovel made."

She took a step onto the needles and a strange thing happened. One moment Sol was smiling at him, then there was a snap and the hiss of rope, and she was gone.

"Sol!" His heart plummeted even as she was launched into the air. She yelped as a rope net tangled around her and hauled her upward. She swung crazily beneath a branch high above his head. Azalea screamed.

"Hold on, Sol!"

He set Azalea down next to the tree and searched for a way to get her down. There was a rope knotted to a root at the foot of the tree. The knot was too weather-worn to budge when he tugged at it. He threw down his pack and pulled out the Cassian scimitar he had hidden inside. He sawed at the rough rope as Sol dangled and spun above him.

"Don't! I'll fall."

He stopped and followed the line with his eyes to where she hung above him in the tree branches.

"I'll catch you."

"Not if you're all the way over there. There must be some sort of counterweight, or a way to lower me. I don't know how this trap works. I've never made one like this."

Kelan searched the ground for more rope, but found nothing.

"They must not like visitors," Sol said. "This is obviously a trap meant for humans. We must be close to the refugee camp."

"That or the wraiths have gotten a taste for human."

"That will be much funnier when I'm back on the ground."

Her voice was strained. Sol never liked being helpless. "I think I can cut myself out and climb onto this limb," she said.

"Just give me another minute." He didn't want to risk her falling. It was too far of a drop.

Kelan paced the clearing, searching the misty canopy for a way to free her.

There. Up in the great redwood were more ropes, and it looked like they could be unwound to lower her. But the nearest branch was far over his head.

He hoisted himself up a foot and put a hand on the bark to test it with his weight. The bark crumbled between his fingers and he dropped to the ground again.

"Kelan." Sol's voice was edged with fear.

"I think I've figured it out. I just have to get up this tree."

"There's something up here."

He froze.

There were shadows among the mist and the boughs of pine needles, shapes that moved and jumped from branch to branch, shaking dead leaves onto their heads.

"Cut me loose!" she shouted. "Now!"

He ran for the rope at the foot of the redwood, but an arrow thudded into the trunk beside it. He whirled around. The shadows had taken shape. Human-shaped forms with cracked, brown skin the color of the earth, and clothes made of leaves and grasses. Their hair was formed of dead leaves that trailed over their shoulders and faces, obscuring everything except their bright eyes.

Azalea screamed and ran to Kelan's side where she clung to his leg. "I want mommy!"

Kelan lifted his scimitar. "Let my wife go."

The wraiths in the trees cackled, and the leaves shook around them.

"Cut her loose," one crooned. "Watch her drop. Break her bones."

Laughter rustled through the treetops above him, seemingly everywhere at once. He couldn't tell how many wraiths there were. Five? Twelve? Twenty? Two of them remained stationary with their feathered bows drawn, one arrow aimed at Kelan and one at Sol.

"Please," Sol pleaded. "We are friends of forests. We mean no harm."

"No harm, no harm," sang a voice from atop another tree, and the others laughed.

Kelan slowly edged forward until he was standing beneath Sol. "Drop the key," he said, staring at the wraith archers.

How long would it take his pyra to return? Too long. He'd need to hurl two fireballs at once to take out the archers, and before they realized what he was doing. But who knew how many more wraiths had arrows pointed at their heads.

"Kelan."

"Drop the key, Sol."

"You made me promise."

He let out a shaky breath and swore. Either way they were dead. But if he kept his shackle on at least he wouldn't be the one to kill her. He tightened his grip on his scimitar.

"You come to leave the child with us," one of them crooned. "They always give us the Flameskin children."

Kelan put one hand on Azalea's head. She had burrowed her face in his leg. "We're not giving her to you."

One of the wraiths descended to a lower branch and hung upside down. "We'll take good care of her."

"Such good care," another added and cackled.

A chill ran down Kelan's spine. All those rumors about children being left at the doorstep of the Hivid Wood . . . . This was what happened to them? Taken and devoured by these creatures?

"Is there a Flameskin haven here?" Kelan asked. "Can you take us to it?"

The wraiths hissed in the trees.

"Flameskins," one spat. "There are no Flameskins in these woods."

"They're soldiers," another said. "The man has a sword."

Kelan slowly lowered his sword to the ground. It wasn't doing him much good anyway, when his enemy was so high above him in the trees.

"What do you want from us?" Kelan asked.

"Blood and bones, blood and bones!" one cried and the others laughed.

"Pretty bracelet! We want the glowing bracelet," said another.

Kelan had rolled up his sleeve and his emberstone glowed red against his skin. "You can have it if you let her down."

The trees rustled, and the wraiths whispered to each other.

One wraith stepped forward. His cheeks were streaked and cracked like bark on a tree. "We'll take only the child." His voice sounded more human than any of the other wraiths.

"We stay together," Kelan said. He hadn't saved Azalea from a mob just to hand her over to hungry wraiths. He couldn't imagine a worse fate.

He glanced up at Sol dangling above him, and dust fell into his eyes. She was sawing at the ropes that bound her.

The wraith slid down a trunk and then swung from branch to branch until he reached the ground. "Why do you wear the manacle, Flameskin?"

"I don't want to hurt people anymore."

The wraith was tall and willowy, and beneath the dirt and the leaves there was matted hair and a pair of curious, violet eyes. From afar, his skin had looked covered in bark, but now Kelan could see it was nothing but cracked mud.

The wraith touched Kelan's emberstone manacle and then Kelan's skin with one dirt-caked finger, then peered up into Kelan's face. Kelan shifted and tried not to flinch away as the wraith inspected him.

"Turquoise eyes," the wraith murmured. "Interesting. What's your name?"

"Kelan Burke."

"Not Bruun?"

"What?" Kelan asked. That was the surname of the royal family.

The wraith patted Azalea's head. "Is she your daughter?"

"No, but we've been taking care of her." Kelan frowned. Beneath the dirt and the grime this boy looked human.

Another wraith dropped to the ground, this one female. "What are you doing, Silas? Slit their throats and be done with it."

Silas sighed and unslung a coil of rope from his shoulders. "I'm sorry about this, but we have rules here."

The girl snarled as she snatched the rope from Silas, and one of her hands sparked with angry fire.

CHAPTER 48
SOL

S ol and Kelan were marched through the Wood with their hands bound in front of them and their eyes blindfolded. The wraith named Silas, who she was fairly certain was human, gripped Sol's sleeve and pulled her forward. She stumbled over a root and Silas tugged her sideways.

"Oh, root there. Sorry."

"Kelan?" Sol asked.

"I'm here," he said, somewhere to her right. Azalea clung to the back of her tunic and didn't say a word as they hiked through the forest.

The blindfold scratched against her eyes and her face. The crude rope chafed her wrists.

Sol had nearly cut herself free from her rope net by the time they had lowered her to the ground, but it wouldn't have helped. She wouldn't have been able to climb to the branch above her, and they would've shot her down if she had tried.

Her feet scuffed on the ground as she walked. The world was conspiring to tear her and Kelan apart. Kelan was right. There was nowhere safe for them. Life was so fragile, as easily extinguished as a candle.

"We're going to the left. Walk carefully here," Silas said, pulling on her sleeve.

"This would be much easier if I could see," Sol said.

"Would you rather we gouge your eyes out?" asked the female wraith.

Sol pressed her lips together. If she got a glimpse of the night sky and could get her bearings, she'd be able to find a way out of the forest. She was a huntress. She'd get them out alive.

At the end of their long march, Silas stopped Sol and removed her blindfold. The wraiths, who were really just dirty adolescents, had halted at the base of an enormous tree. There were a dozen of these wraiths, with leaves and wildflowers and twigs laced through their hair and mud smeared artfully over their skin. It was a convincing disguise, from a distance.

Silas looked to be about her own age, but the other wraiths were younger. One boy looked no more than twelve. A few of them wore shards of emberstone set into rings or around their wrists like Kelan.

They were all Flameskins.

Silas pulled aside a curtain of leaves to reveal a hollowed-out trunk of an enormous redwood.

"Marta, tell Master Rask that I'm bringing him a present," Silas said, nodding to the girl who had tied them up. "And someone go find Ingrid."

"Rask is going to tear your head off for this. No one's allowed to see the haven," Marta said. She crossed her arms over a tunic covered in crow feathers.

"But look at his eyes," Silas said, pointing at Kelan's face. "Turquoise!"

Marta shrugged. "The last ones you took pity on ended up running off and we had to hunt them down, or did you forget already? I say we end them now before they cause us any trouble."

"If they do try to run, they won't get far." Silas directed this comment at Kelan.

Sol stepped in front of Azalea. "I thought you would be better than this. How can you kill a child?"

"We'll take care of the child," Marta said. "But adults we kill on sight."

"I won't let you touch Sol," Kelan growled.

Marta grinned wickedly. "Try something. See what happens."

"They're our own age," Silas said. "And I'd hardly call you an adult, Marta."

He shoved her into the hollowed-out tree, then extended an arm to Sol. "Shall we?"

He laughed when she held up her bound hands and gave him an annoyed look.

He leapt into the fire-blackened interior of the redwood, and Sol peeked inside. The tree had been hollowed-out by a fire, and a spiraling staircase had been built around the interior edge of the trunk. Slits in the tree had been cut to make windows, and faint light filtered through the dusty space, illuminating a staircase into the mist.

Sol climbed the uneven steps behind Silas. As they ascended, the mist surrounded and embraced them. It muffled the sounds of the wraiths, and droplets clung to Sol's black hair like a crown of dew.

Marta stood guard at the top of the staircase, fingering the handle of the knife on her belt. Behind her was a platform built out over the tree branches, but the mist was too thick to see beyond it.

"I told Rask you're coming," Marta said. "He told me to make sure your pets don't piss on the rug before you wring their necks."

Sol shot Kelan a look. He stood close to her, and brushed her waist with the back of his bound hands. His lips were pressed into a grim line.

They had taken Sol's knife and her emberstone and her bow. She had nothing to defend herself with. Though their kidnappers were young, they were all armed. And if the stories about the wraiths of Hivid Wood were true, they knew how to use those weapons. Many of them had scars on their arms and faces and their bare calves. These children were dangerous.

Silas rolled his eyes at Marta and waved Sol and Kelan forward. At the end of the platform they found a rope bridge that spanned the gap between their redwood and another tree. The bridge swayed crazily beneath Sol's feet when she stepped onto it. She grasped hold of the railing with her bound hands as her stomach dropped and rolled with each movement of the bridge.

She and Kelan slid sideways and clung to the rope supports as the children bounded and ran around them, laughing and chattering. Silas took Azalea by the hand and led her across, and Sol's heart lurched at the dizzying distance between them and the ground. How was this a safe place for children?

Sol caught glimpses of the tree city around them as they traversed various bridges. Impossible-looking dwellings had been built out onto branches and limbs, with ladders and precarious scaffolding connecting the trees. Children lazed and played and patched clothes and fired arrows among the leafy treetops. None looked to be older than Silas, and she spotted only two adults among them. Some of the younger children were tied with harnesses to the railing of their platform, and several of them came dangerously close to the edge to wave at Sol.

"If this is a refuge for Flameskins, how can you kill people who come to you seeking asylum?" Sol demanded. Her wrists were still tied in front of her. She had to balance carefully as she walked across a creaking wooden platform toward another bridge.

"It's not up to me. We'll take you to our leader, Master Rask, and he'll decide what happens to you," Silas said.

Sol whirled around and yanked on Silas' leafy shirt with her bound hands. "That's not good enough. We didn't risk our lives to come all the way here just to be slaughtered by children."

Silas ripped his shirt free. "I'm eighteen. And I take offense to that. I'm also the one who saved your life, so I'd appreciate it if you were a little nicer."

"Sol," Kelan said, his voice a warning.

She turned and caught sight of Marta, who had sparks

dancing on her fingers. "Touch Silas again, and I'll kill you," she hissed. Her pyra deepened her voice.

"Let it go," Silas told her. "It's not like they can do anything."

He was right. Sol shuffled in closer to Kelan and tried to keep the despair at bay.

"So, you only allow children to live here?" Kelan asked.

"There are adults, a handful of them, but they were living in the woods long before the Burning War began, and King Anton murdered his wife," Silas said. "They all wear cuffs, like you."

"And what happened to your parents?" Sol asked. "Did they leave you when they went off to fight the war?"

"I don't know anything about my parents. We're all foundlings. Left at the edge of the forest to be raised by the wraiths of Hivid Wood. Or eaten by them. The stories vary."

"Are there wraiths?" she asked, searching the dirty faces that peered down at her.

Silas grinned. "We're the wraiths of Hivid Wood. Isn't it brilliant? That's why the haven hasn't been found yet."

"And that's why we have to kill intruders," Marta said, scowling at Sol.

"How many people live here?" Kelan asked.

"There's a dozen of the old-timers, and more than one hundred foundlings at last count," Silas said.

"So many?" Sol asked, incredulous. How could people have abandoned their children to the woods? It was unthinkable.

"We're the lucky ones," Silas said. "A pyra doesn't start to manifest itself until you're three or four years old. We're the ones whose parents didn't immediately turn us over to soldiers or strangle us. They brought us to the Hivid Wood in the hope that the stories were true."

They had arrived at a large dwelling built around the trunk of another redwood tree. Its windows had curtains of dry grasses, and its walls were made of uneven planks. Mist curled over the mossy roof. Silas opened the door to reveal a dim interior. Sol and Kelan and Azalea were pushed by many small hands through the doorway.

An older, heavy-set man sat on the ground inside. White and gray laced his black hair and overgrown beard. He wasn't dressed like a wraith, and his skin was free of dirt and grime, but he didn't look pleased to see them. There was a metal band with a shard of emberstone strapped around his upper arm, and the emberstone glowed like a hot coal on his skin.

Rask scowled at Sol and Kelan. "What have you brought me this time, Silas?"

Sol edged closer to Kelan so they were standing side by side, and Azalea clung to Sol's shirt again. There were a dozen wraith adolescents packed into the small room around them, and they watched them with bright, curious eyes.

Silas bowed low with an elegant flourish of his hand. "I brought you two responsible adults. Probably responsible. I'm not sure how responsible it is to wander into Hivid Wood."

"I told you no more," Rask growled.

"I know, but look!" Silas said, pointing at Kelan's face.

Why was he obsessed with Kelan's eyes? Sol wished she had her hands free so she could slap that boy's finger away.

"It doesn't matter what color his eyes are. You have a responsibility to protect our camp and you've violated it," Rask said.

"But I blindfolded them!" Silas insisted. "They don't know where we are."

Sol smiled to herself. They didn't know who they were dealing with.

"Get rid of them," Rask growled.

"I claim the girl's boots!" Marta said.

Another girl shoved her. "They're mine. I saw her first."

Sol pressed up against Kelan as her heartrate accelerated. She searched wildly through the room for something she could use as a weapon.

A woman, the first Sol had seen, pushed her way into the room. "What's going on here?" Her dress was made of silk scraps, and she wore an elegant braid crown around her head.

"Silas brought us tasty morsels to eat!" one of the boys cried, and laughter crackled through their ranks.

Silas shoved his way through the crowd of youths and dragged the woman to the front of the room. "Ingrid! I found your brother!"

The woman peered up into Kelan's face at his eyes, then stepped back to take in his full form. She wore an emberstone set into a ring on her pinky.

"We came here seeking asylum with the Flameskin haven," Kelan said.

"We take only children. You can leave your daughter with us, and we'll take care of her. And this boy's not my brother." This last sentence she directed at Silas.

"But he has the eyes," Silas insisted

Ingrid, Sol now noticed, had Kelan's same turquoise eyes.

"She's not our daughter and we can't just leave her with you," Sol said. "We stay together."

Ingrid ignored Sol as she stared at Kelan's face. "But the shape of his face is all wrong. He doesn't look a thing like King Anton."

King Anton Bruun? The king who had murdered his Flameskin wife and started the Burning War? Sol gaped at Ingrid.

"You're the princess. The Flameskin princess," Sol said.

Ingrid frowned at her.

"But they said she was killed," Kelan said, his eyes going wide.

"Obviously I'm not dead," Ingrid said and scowled. "I escaped."

Sol struggled to wrap her mind around it. She had grown up hearing the story about the Flameskin queen with the burning heart, and here was her daughter. It was like something out of a fairytale.

Ingrid was still studying Kelan's face "I'm thinking you must be a cousin. Maybe Nikel's son? Who are your parents?"

"My mother was named Marina. She'd dead now. I never knew my father."

"But you must have some idea who he might be."

"I know my mother worked as a scullery maid in a manor

near Duhavn before I was born. I assume she met my father there."

"Duhavn. Must be a Bruun then. Your mother was a Flameskin?"

Sol stared at Kelan. He was truly related to the royal family? He was related to this banished princess?

"She kept it secret for a while, but it possessed her when she was twenty-eight."

Silas whistled. "She must've never used a spark in her life to have lasted that long."

"I never saw her use her pyra before she was possessed." Kelan's eyes were pained, and it hurt Sol's heart to see it. This was the most he had ever spoken about his mother.

Ingrid turned to Rask, who sat hunched on the floor with his chin in his hand. "Rask? What do you think?"

He waved a hand at her. "It doesn't matter what I say. You always end up doing whatever you want. But let it be known I don't condone this, especially not when we're so close to freedom. And besides, it's two more mouths to feed."

Marta shoved Silas. "You shouldn't have brought them. They're too dangerous. If they tattle on us to the Flameskin Army, it's over."

"Back off, Marta," he said and shoved her in return.

Marta growled, and her fingers sparked.

"Marta!" Ingrid barked. The girl winced, and her face contorted the same way Kelan's did when he fought his pyra. "Get hold of yourself or we'll have to put you in containment."

One of the other wraiths slapped Sol's pebble emberstone against Marta's skin, and her face relaxed.

"An emberstone?" Ingrid asked.

"It's hers," the wraith said, pointing at Sol. "She's a mage."

"A mage," Ingrid muttered. She drummed her fingers on a branch that poked through one of the hut's walls.

"And the prince has a full emberstone. I told you this was a good find," Silas said.

Sol stared at Kelan. The prince?

"And this!" one of the little girls said, holding up Sol's acorn.

"That's mine!" Sol snapped. She was filled with a sudden, vicious urge to protect Ulve's seed. She had to keep it safe. She hadn't known it had been taken from her pocket.

Ingrid picked up the glowing acorn and turned it over in her palms. "It feels so alive. What is this?"

"The Ulves gave it to me when I left. I don't know what it is."

Ingrid's eyebrows rose. "And why is a mage from the Ulves here in Hivid?"

Sol brushed her bound hands against Kelan's. The ropes bit into her skin and Kelan wrists were red. "We've been running since we met, and since we were married. There was nowhere else we could go where we could be safe."

Silas grinned and leaned in. "Milk it. Ingrid is a hopeless romantic."

Sol blushed. She had thought she was past blushing over Kelan, but it turned out she just hadn't had enough opportunities to talk about him around other people.

Ingrid lifted Sol's hands and studied the silver ring on her finger.

"The only thing we want is to be together," Kelan said.

Ingrid sighed and dropped Sol's hand. "Are either of you aligned with those who could harm us? Tokken or Flameskin soldiers?"

"I was a soldier, but I left the army after I met Sol. I have no desire to return."

"They hunt deserters. Are they looking for you?" Rask asked.

"No," Sol said quickly. "They lost us in the mountains long ago."

Ingrid nodded. "Untie them. They'll stay here until Vara can meet them, at least."

Silas grinned triumphantly, and Rask let out a string of curses under his breath.

"Rask," Ingrid hissed. "There are children in this room."

"You should hear him when you're not around," one of the boys said and sniggered. Rask cuffed his ear.

"We are guardians of the last haven for Flameskins on this continent," Ingrid said as Silas untied them. "If you try to leave, you'll be killed on sight."

CHAPTER 49

KELAN

S unlight poured in through the hole in the roof and woke Kelan. He groaned and yanked the threadbare blanket over his head. He really needed to finish fixing that roof.

He rolled over and wrapped an arm around Sol beside him.

She smiled sleepily and kissed the tip of his nose. "Morning, love."

His heart bloomed hot in his chest as he kissed her. Sol. He had thought waking up beside her every morning was the best that life could give him, but waking up beside her in a *bed*, albeit a lumpy one, was heaven.

They had spent a few blissful weeks together in the Flame-skin haven. Weeks of waking up warm beside her and basking in happiness. The long journey was over. They had finally found a home.

He drew her closer and trailed kisses along her neck and shoulder.

"I don't think we're alone," she whispered as he slid his fingers beneath her shirt.

He sighed into her hair. "Are we ever?"

She gave a miserable laugh.

"Well then, any creature in this bed who isn't Sol will surely suffer a horrible fate." There was a laugh somewhere nearby, smothered by the blanket.

Sol gasped. "I think there are wraiths in our bed." More spatters of muffled laughter from beneath the blankets.

Kelan sat up and pulled Sol in next to him. "Don't worry. I'll protect you."

He grabbed the blanket and yanked. The three lumpy forms at the foot of their bed were revealed to be three very dirty and very naughty children: Dotti, Lotti, and Silas II, a foundling discovered and named by the original Silas.

They pounced on Kelan and Sol laughed as he wrestled them out of the bed. "I told you not to come in our bed anymore!" he cried.

But they were all laughing now as the children wiggled out of his grasp. Kelan grabbed Silas II and threw him over his shoulder. Azalea hung back shyly, half-hidden by the darkness, and Kelan beckoned to her. She grinned as she jumped onto the bed and threw her arms around Sol.

Sol's eyes glowed with delight, and it filled Kelan with warmth to see her so happy. Was this what it was like to have a family? Was this what it was like to have a home, where laughter and smiles and love were served in buckets instead of teaspoons?

"They're going to keep coming back if you keep playing with them every morning," Sol said. She wasn't really scolding.

He tackled Sol, and she laughed as they tangled themselves in the blankets and the children jumped on top.

Kelan would never turn the children away, even if it meant giving up time with Sol. He knew what it was like to grow up without parents, and if these girls wanted Sol to mother them, he'd never force them out.

He kissed Sol's cheek. "I'm glad they come, but it would be nice if we could have *some* time to ourselves."

She put her arms around Lotti and Dotti and Azalea and Silas II. "Maybe we'll just adopt them."

"Well, one or two children is fine, but four all at once? Isn't that a bit much?"

She blushed and something in his heart overflowed at the sight of it. "You want children, Kelan?"

His mouth went dry, and his mind emptied of all its contents. They hadn't talked about this yet.

Someone scurried across the rooftop, and Marta's face appeared above them through the hole. "You two awake yet?"

This definitely wasn't the time to start talking about it.

The cascading curtain of leaves that made their door parted, and Silas the First stepped inside. Kelan sighed. He was going to fix the roof and make a door. Today.

"Knock first," Sol said, scowling at Silas.

"It sounded like you two were decent in here." Silas' eyes roved the wreckage of their room, the makeshift bed of moss and blankets, their weapons leaning against the side of one wall, and the branches overhead that made it impossible to walk across the room without stooping multiple times.

Silas' eyes landed on Lotti and Dotti lying in Sol's lap. "If the others find out that you're letting the twins sleep in your bed, you're going to wake up with half the camp in your room."

"They're not allowed. They don't sleep here. Right?" Kelan said, giving Dotti a look. She pouted.

Sol combed her fingers through Azalea's hair to braid it. "Does Ingrid still want to go out this morning?"

"Yes. She's waiting for you," Silas said. He knelt down in front of Silas II. Though Silas II was only four, he had already mastered Silas the First's complicated handshake, and they performed it now at the foot of the bed.

An emberstone flashed on Silas' wrist as his hand moved through the air. Kelan's emberstone had been cut into fourths and divided among the Flameskins that needed it most, and Kelan had been left with only a small shard. He really only needed a speck of emberstone to extinguish his emberstone, but a piece any smaller wouldn't fit in his manacle. And he didn't want to risk losing control.

"I'll have to check my traps before we go," Sol said.

"Already checked them," Marta said. "And look!" She dangled a very dead rabbit through the hole in their roof.

Kelan and Sol both made a face. "That belongs in the kitchen," Sol said.

Marta laughed maniacally and slid off the roof.

Sol tugged on Azalea's braid and stood up. "Let's go."

Kelan stepped out of their low hut onto a platform built out over several tree branches. Children scampered across the rope bridges and climbed off the top of their house as they emerged.

It was a rare, bright morning in the Wood. The sun had burned off the fog. The redwoods creaked in the wind, and the air smelled of pine sap and sawdust.

He and Sol had only been living in the Flameskin camp for a few weeks, but it already felt like home. With Sol beside him, he had everything he needed. And his heart had swelled unexpectedly to include this new family as well, made of wild, untamed foundlings that danced through the trees.

He laced his fingers through Sol's. Could this be her home, too, or was she still yearning for her mountains?

"Are you coming with us to forage?" she asked.

"Yes. But I can't stay out too late. I need to finish fixing the roof."

"And build us a door, I hope?"

He nodded, and she grinned. Then at least they'd be able to shut the wraiths out for a few moments.

They climbed down the rope ladder to the forest floor and found Ingrid waiting for them at the foot of their tree. Sol had been a queen in the Ulves, and it was no different here in the Hivid Wood. She had quickly made herself indispensable to the Flameskin community, teaching them how to make animal traps and build better arrows.

Sol took an ambling path through the forest followed by her motley crew: Ingrid in her tattered dress, Marta with her bow and her watchful eyes and that horrible dead rabbit hanging over her shoulder like a prize, swaggering Silas the First, and Kelan with Azalea on his shoulders. Sol bent down at intervals to dig up plants and show them to Ingrid and Silas. Then she would hand them to Azalea, who dropped them in the pack on Kelan's back.

Traffic through the Hivid Wood had dried up, along with the Flameskin's main source of food. Without merchants and traders to steal goods from, and without the freedom to farm, they had no way to feed themselves. With each passing day, they relied more heavily on Sol and her expertise.

Sol took Kelan by the arm and pulled him ahead of the group as Silas and Marta squabbled. Sol glanced up at Kelan with those green eyes of hers. Her voice was hesitant. "About what you were saying earlier. . . ."

Kelan's heart raced in his chest. "I didn't say anything earlier." He shifted Azalea, who was getting heavy on his shoulders.

Sol chewed on her lip.

What did she want him to say? There were more than one hundred children living in the haven and they already struggled to feed and care for them. But he should've known Sol would want a family of her own. He had promised her she could have the life she wanted, but this wasn't the time. There would probably never be a right time. The panic inside him felt like a small, vicious animal tearing out his insides.

Kelan swallowed. "What I meant was—It's just that—"

She shook her head and blushed. "It's fine. You've never really said anything about it, so I was just surprised is all."

Kelan let out a heavy breath. "Yeah. Me, too." It took a long time for him to stop feeling like he was about to have a heart attack.

She stopped them at a bush with small white flowers and waved Ingrid forward. "These flowers are edible as well as the roots, but the name of it escapes me." Sol plucked a flower and tucked it behind Kelan's ear. She laughed when he stuffed it in his mouth.

Even if this wasn't her home, they were both happy here, and he didn't want anything about this to change.

"The roots might go well in a soup with something else, as

they're quite bitter alone," Sol told Ingrid. "But if you dig up the whole plant, it won't be here for next year."

"We only need food to last us through the rest of this year," Ingrid said.

"And then what?" Kelan asked.

Ingrid pressed her lips together, and he frowned. Ingrid and Rask were planning something, but they wouldn't say what yet. Though Kelan and Sol had won over the children's hearts, they hadn't yet earned Rask's trust.

Kelan hated not knowing. Why wouldn't they need to think of a future here in the Hivid Wood? That was all he thought about now, his present and his future with Sol at his side, a real roof over their head and a door to keep out the wraiths. This was all he ever wanted.

"How long have you been living here in the Wood?" Sol asked Ingrid. "I'm surprised you don't know any of the plants."

"Oh, it's almost been ten years now, and Rask has been here twenty, but none of us knew anything when we came. We've had to teach ourselves how to live out here."

"And you lived in the palace before that?" Kelan asked.

"I escaped after King Bruun—after my mother died." Ingrid was very tight-lipped about her life in the palace. Each detail was unwillingly given, and Kelan pressed for more.

"The king never knew you and your mother were Flameskins until then?"

"No. My mother and I would eat emberstone dust every morning, a little pinch of that in your body to keep your pyra at bay. I didn't know what it was we were doing. I never even knew I had a pyra until the day we ran out of emberstone."

"What happened?" Kelan asked. Her story echoed inside him with a certain familiarity.

"Same thing I suspect happened to your mother," Ingrid said, and he looked away. "It's impossible for us to hide what we are for long."

Ingrid called Marta over. Marta had been wandering behind them with her bow trained on a songbird. "Pick these flowers and then I want you to dig up the roots. Go back to the haven for a spade, if you have to."

"But you need me as lookout. Aren't you worried about the Flameskins?" Marta asked.

"Which ones? You?" Ingrid asked.

"No. The soldiers. Aya told me that Mie found two Flameskin soldiers in the pits this morning."

Kelan whirled around. "Flameskin soldiers?"

"Aya likes to invent stories," Ingrid said.

"But Mie would never lie about something like that. If she saw them it must be true," Marta said.

"Have you asked Mie what she saw? Does Rask know?" Ingrid asked.

Marta shrugged. "I don't know. I had to go check the traps, and then you wanted me to come out."

Kelan swore. It was so easy to forget how fragile this new home was. They often found Flameskin scouts wandering the woods and searching for their hideout. The ones they caught were killed or left to wander into traps they had laid. If the Flameskin Army found the haven, they'd press all these children into service.

Kelan fingered Markus' button in his pocket. He couldn't let the army turn these wraiths into monsters like Markus.

"It's probably nothing," Silas said, but his eyes darted back and forth, surveying the trees.

"We shouldn't be out here if there are soldiers in the Wood," Ingrid said. "Let's go back. I need to speak to Rask."

"Ingrid!" cried a voice. A girl tore through the woods shouting Ingrid's name. "There are soldiers at the haven!"

CHAPTER 50
SOL

S ol yanked out her emberstone as she ran, and her quiver and bow bounced on her back. She was glad she hadn't been fool enough to leave her bow at home.

Kelan sprinted beside her with Azalea clutched to his chest. Her heart snagged on the image of the two of them, and the fear in Azalea's face.

Would it always be like this? Would they always be running and fighting for their lives?

"Ingrid!" Kelan shouted. "Is there somewhere else you can take the littles?"

"Marta, take Azalea to the lookout tree by the river. You'll be safe there," Ingrid said.

Marta peeled off from their party with Azalea in her arms, and the others raced toward the haven. Sol and Kelan were the first to come up over the rise. Two female soldiers in blue uniforms stood beside the redwood staircase, flanking a woman in an elegant coat and skirt, cut in a military style.

Though the woman wore no crown, Sol recognized her face, which had been stamped on every coin minted during the last five years of her reign.

It was Vara Bruun, Queen of Tokkedal, and Commander of

the Tokken Army. Daughter of the murderer, King Anton Bruun.

Sol shoved her dagger into Kelan's hand and notched an arrow in her bow. They both crouched low behind a log. The soldiers hadn't spotted them yet. With each rapid breath Sol's lungs filled with the scents of rotting wood.

"Do you have my key?" Kelan asked.

"We're not that desperate yet."

There were only two soldiers accompanying the queen, but there would be more soldiers close by. They wouldn't leave their queen unprotected.

Sol took a breath to ground herself and came out of her crouch. If she knew anything about Tokkens, it was that they had no tolerance for fire. There would be no mercy from the Tokken queen.

Silas and Ingrid raced up the hill behind them and gasped when they spotted the queen, then took a knee. Wraiths started pouring out of the haven's staircase and bowed low to the queen.

Silas the First tugged on Kelan's trousers. "Bow, you idiot."

"I will not bow to a queen that slaughters Flameskins."

"She's with us," Silas hissed.

With us? What did that even mean?

Sol stared at the queen, and as Vara Bruun's head swiveled toward them, she fell onto one knee and dropped her bow on the ground. Still close enough to pick up if she needed it.

Queen Vara smiled brightly at their little party. "Ingrid! There you are!" She strode toward Ingrid and embraced her.

Sol blinked at them as realization dawned. "They're sisters." They had grown up together. Though they had different mothers —one of them not quite human—it didn't change that they were family.

Just like Sol. She loved her sisters no less, even knowing that they didn't share a mother.

Queen Vara had eyes the same color as Kelan's. Turquoise was the color of Bruun royalty. Which meant Kelan *was* related to this queen, the one who had ordered the death of so many Flameskins.

And Ingrid welcomed her to their haven?

Ingrid was smiling. "When they said there were soldiers at the haven, I didn't know they meant you!"

Kelan took Sol's hand as they stood, and they both watched the queen warily. How could Vara slaughter Flameskins on the battlefield and embrace Ingrid?

Queen Vara turned and frowned at Sol and Kelan. "I haven't seen these before. Newcomers? I thought we agreed you wouldn't harbor any but children."

"They're hardly more than children themselves," Ingrid said, "and they've become a part of the family already."

"I found them," Silas said with a grin.

Sol and Kelan bowed stiffly when then queen approached.

"I believe the boy is one of Nikel's," Ingrid said.

The queen's eyebrows rose. "My cousin, Nikel?" She studied Kelan's face with interest and then gave a long sigh. "Ashes. He looks just like Nikel." She sighed again. "So many mistakes have been made in this family."

Fiery heat rose to Sol's cheeks. "Kelan is not a mistake." Kelan hadn't chosen who his parents were. He wasn't at fault for what he was.

The queen's turquoise eyes were hard. "The mistake was my father killing Ingrid's mother instead of saving her. The mistake was him declaring war on Flameskins and slaughtering them on our soil. *That* was the mistake."

Sol stepped back, unable to reply. The queen regretted the Burning War?

"We've heard that Saint Katrine has returned to our shores. Is this true?" Ingrid asked, drawing away the queen's piercing gaze.

"Come," Queen Vara said. "We have much to discuss."

To Sol's surprise, Ingrid insisted that Sol and Kelan be present at the meeting with Queen Vara. Rask relented with only a few curses and sulky scowls. Only the adults that had been invited to meet with Queen Vara, as well as Silas the First, who was the oldest of the foundlings. The Flameskin men and women left their posts watching the haven's children to meet with their queen.

Queen Vara settled herself into Rask's usual seat on the floor, and Sol and Kelan sat on a low branch that stuck through the wall. The other adults found seats on the floor, and Silas crouched in the eaves to push away spying wraiths who tried to press their ears against the holes in the ceiling.

"What you have heard is true, Saint Katrine has returned to Tokkedal, and she rides at the head of the Tokken Army now," the queen said.

Hope and fear twisted through Sol simultaneously. What was deliverance for her family in the Ulves was death for her and Kelan.

"The Saints convened in Omdren and have come to an agreement with the four other kingdoms of Nordby. They want to create a new empire so they can stand as a united front against the Flameskins. The kings have abdicated and handed their crowns to the Saints in return for protection."

"But why would they do that?" Rask asked. "The Saints are creations of Maja, too. They have fire in their blood just like we do."

Queen Vara sighed. She looked tired. "I've known Katrine for five years now, and I've seen what she can do. Fire obeys her in ways I never thought possible. She can't be possessed. She can control the pyri of other Flameskins. Emberstones enhance her abilities, instead of stemming them. She's not a Flameskin. She's something else entirely. I really believe she was chosen and blessed by Maja to end the Burning War."

The room fell silent.

"You really think the goddess would intervene in the affairs of mortals?" Ingrid asked in a hush.

"I know she has. She was the one who gave Katrine her powers. And now Saint Katrine has come to accept my abdication and take my place as ruler of Tokkedal."

"But you won't abdicate," Ingrid said.

"Yes. I will. And very soon."

Ingrid jumped to her feet. "You can't! You can't give Tokkedal to them! You can't abandon us."

Vara sighed again. "I must. Without the Saints, Tokkedal will burn. Only she can stop the Flameskin armies. I'll have nothing left to rule over but ashes, if I don't."

"And what of us?" Ingrid demanded. "We just give up? Saint Katrine will come here, and she'll find us. She'll kill all of us. The children, too."

"I know all of this! You think this was an easy decision to make? But I have an entire kingdom of people to think of, not just you."

"You said you would protect us."

"And I will. I won't abdicate until I've seen you all safely evacuated from Tokkedal."

Evacuated? Sol looked up and met Kelan's troubled eyes.

"They've found a place for us, then?" Rask asked, and his voice had an unfamiliar note of hope in it.

"Yes," Vara said. "But it's not in Tokkedal. You have to leave the continent. We've found an island for you, and it should be big enough to support a colony."

Sol gasped aloud.

That's why Ingrid hadn't been concerned about next year. They had always planned on abandoning Tokkedal.

Sol's mind spun, but Vara was still speaking. Everyone else was oblivious to the way the universe had tilted.

"The ship will arrive in four weeks. I've already loaded it with supplies, and the crew is made up of a family of mages who will join your colony. One of their own is a Flameskin."

Sol gripped Kelan's hand. She would never be able to return to the Ulves.

Silas had floated down from the ceiling in a dreamy fog, and now he threw his arms around Ingrid. All of them were cheering and rejoicing. Sol knew she should be happy, but all she could think about was Hillerod and Ma and her sisters and the familiar peaks of the Ulves.

Kelan pulled her in, and she rested her head against his chest as she shuddered.

"We don't have to go," Kelan whispered.

But when she looked into his eyes, she could see the hope and the want there.

"Of course we're going." The words were painful.

She twisted the ring on her finger. The gods had given them a chance at a future, and she wouldn't squander it. But leaving the Ulves was never supposed to be permanent. She had promised to return.

Queen Vara had pulled out a map and pointed to a place on the Tokken coast where they would find the ship. "You'll have plenty of supplies in the ship so that you can plant something this summer, and still have seed for next spring."

"Is the island far from here?" Silas asked.

Vara nodded. "It's an island in the Archipelago. It will take several weeks to get there."

"And once we leave, we can't come back?" Kelan asked.

"No, you can't," Vara said. "I've taken great pains to keep this whole operation a secret."

Kelan hadn't needed to ask that question. Sol had already known the answer.

"Has Saint Katrine already marched on the Ulves?" Sol asked.

It was nearly summer now, and the Flameskins would've started their march through the pass long ago. They could've already passed through Hillerod and burned it down. Her family could've been killed, or if not, their house and their field would be gone.

"She won't make it to the Ulves. She'll stay along the coast for now to push out the main Flameskin Army."

Sol couldn't get her breath under control. Her heart was beating too fast, and she couldn't inhale fully.

Kelan took her hand and squeezed it. "Let's get some air."

She pushed him away and faced the queen. "My family is in the Ulves."

The queen turned her steely turquoise eyes on her. "A Cassian prince lost his bride to the Flameskins, and he's ridden out with his army to drive them from the mountains. The Ulve villages are safe for now."

Sol sank against Kelan.

But the queen had now leaned in and was looking at Sol. "What was it you said your name was?"

"I don't think I introduced them," Ingrid said. "Sol and Kelan Burke. They've been with us now for a few weeks."

"And which village do you hail from, Sol?"

"Baarka," Kelan said quickly and pulled Sol in closer. Both their hearts were beating fast.

The queen narrowed her eyes at Sol. She knew who Sol was. Sol could see it in the queen's face.

Isabella's ghost had chased Sol all the way to the Hivid Wood.

CHAPTER 51
KELAN

Kelan held tightly to Sol's hand as they crossed the rope bridges back to their home. He wasn't sure if the wind in the trees would knock her over or transform her into a hurricane, so he clung to her to keep her grounded.

He parted the leafy curtain, and their room was blessedly empty. There weren't even any children on the roof. The novelty of a queen in Hivid Wood must have drawn them off to other parts of the haven to play or to eavesdrop.

Kelan studied Sol's face. "Tell me what you're thinking."

"The queen knows who I am."

"And she's sided with Ingrid and the haven. I don't think she'll turn you over to Prince Turullius."

She wilted onto the bed. "I just want all of this to be over. I keep thinking that finally we've made it, then everything comes crashing down again."

He gathered her up in his arms and kissed her forehead. "I know."

"I promised my sisters I would go back. I promised the mountains I would return." She let out a sob and swallowed hard.

Kelan had to force himself to take slow, steady breaths. If Sol was going to fall apart, he had to keep himself together.

She had pulled the acorn out of her pocket and ran her thumb over its glowing surface. She did this often. It was drawing her back. Next time they tried to leave the mountains, he knew the Ulves wouldn't let her go.

He put his hand over hers, hiding the acorn from view. "Maybe that's why the Ulves gave you that seed. They knew you were leaving, and they wanted you to take a piece of the mountains with you."

She sucked in a ragged breath. "No. That's not true. This was never supposed to be a permanent thing. We were supposed to go back home after the war."

"But I can't go back. You think your ma would let me? You think your neighbors wouldn't attack me again? Sol, this war ends when all the Flameskins in Tokkedal are dead. I have no choice but to leave or to give myself up to Saint Katrine."

"I know." She blinked twice, and a fast tear rolled down her cheek.

He let out a long, long sigh. When he had fallen in love with Sol, he should've known the mountains would always claim a piece of her. She couldn't stray from them for very long without withering.

He wanted to shout and rejoice. They had finally found a home and a chance at freedom.

But he had to pretend he was sorry to be leaving Tokkedal.

He wasn't sorry.

He was anxious to leave behind the war and the memories of blood and ashes. If they left Tokkedal, they'd finally be safe. And the Ulves wouldn't be able to reclaim his bride.

She had to understand they had no other choice.

"If we don't go with the others, where will we stay?" he asked. "Where can we hide from the Saints?"

"Don't be a fool. We're going. Of course, we're going." She pressed her hands against his chest to shove him away, but he caught her wrists and pushed her onto the bed beneath him.

"I'm a fool only for you."

"Stop it."

He kissed her. She tasted like dappled sunshine and the bubbling creek they had waded across this morning.

She was quiet for a long moment. He brushed her hair away from her eyes and ran his thumb over her tear-stained cheek.

Sol.

Leaving Tokkedal wouldn't break her. She would recover. It was no wonder the mountains were loath to give her to him. There was no woman more beautiful, no woman more passionate or strong.

She sighed. "I just wish I could see them one more time. And the mountains."

He sucked in a breath. He wouldn't be getting Sol back if they returned. The Ulves would steal her away from him, wind vines around her to drag her away. And four weeks wasn't enough time to get there and back.

She was blinking tears out of her eyes again. Kelan's heart ached. She wouldn't even get to tell her family goodbye.

"What if . . . What if we wrote them a letter. You could tell them we were leaving. You wouldn't be able to say where we were going, but they would know you were safe."

"I don't know how to write."

He blinked. "You don't?"

"You do?"

He opened his mouth, but words failed him. How had he known her and loved her for so long and not known she couldn't read?

"Does anyone in Hillerod know how to read?" he asked.

"The matron and her daughter know a few characters. Will you write a letter for me, Kelan?" She sucked in a breath and let it out. "At least then Carol will know that I'm still alive."

He pressed his cheek against hers. "Yes, my love. I'll write a letter for you."

"But how will it get to them?"

He lowered his voice and glanced above them for eavesdropping wraiths. "We can go into the town on the other side of the

Wood. They'll have paper there, and they can send it for us. It will only take us a couple days to get to town and back."

"But Rask and Ingrid won't let us leave. You know how strict they are about it."

"We leave tonight. We won't tell them."

She wrapped her arms around him. "Thank you, Kelan. It would mean so much to me."

The boards outside their dwelling creaked, giving them warning that an adult was approaching. There was no warning before wraiths appeared.

If they had a real door, people would at least start knocking. Not that it mattered anymore.

"Kelan?" Ingrid asked.

"We're here," he said as he rolled off Sol.

Ingrid parted the curtain of leaves and stepped inside, followed by the queen. He caught a glimpse of the queen's two guards outside.

The queen stooped beneath their low roof and found a seat on a branch. Ingrid sat on the end of the bed, and she looked cross.

"Sol d'Hillerod, isn't it?" the queen asked.

Sol stiffened, and Kelan took her hand.

"You didn't tell me you were a fugitive," Ingrid said, glaring at Sol.

"We're all fugitives here," Kelan said.

"Tokkens have been scouring the country looking for you," Ingrid said. "Imagine if they had caught wind you came here."

"But they didn't. I made sure of that," Sol said.

"You destroyed a treaty that was years in planning," the queen said. "And if Turullius hadn't been so incited by his loss, the Ulves would've burned, and I would've been powerless to stop it."

Sol hung her head.

"And I suppose you are the Flameskin accused of kidnapping her?" the queen asked, turning her sharp eyes on Kelan.

"It isn't kidnapping if she came willingly."

"You were a soldier in the Flameskin Army?" Queen Vara asked.

He shifted under her gaze. "Yes."

"What was your office?"

"I was a lieutenant."

"A lieutenant? They promote them so young."

"We die young, too, Your Majesty."

"And I suppose you both know what happened to Commander Jahr in Hillerod."

Kelan's heart thumped loud enough in his chest that he was sure the queen could hear it. He couldn't breathe. He'd take the fall for Sol. He deserved as much for all the Tokken lives he had ended

The queen sighed. "At least now the search is finally over."

"You can't take her back to Turullius," Kelan said.

"Of course not," the queen snapped. "The only thing I can imagine being worse than having your bride kidnapped by a demon is having her leave you for one."

Kelan flinched.

"Turullius is a monster," Sol said. "I'd rather be dead than marry him."

Queen Vara scowled. "Yes, I suppose you would know how to judge a monster. And I'll have you know that Commander Jahr was a friend of mine, and a talented leader."

Did Vara know that Jahr had threatened the life of Sol's sister? Kelan couldn't find it in his heart to be sorry for Jahr's death. Jahr had tried to force Sol to marry against her will and had wanted to drag her corpse back to Turullius. If there ever had been a monster, it was Commander Jahr.

"Cousin," the queen said, meeting Kelan's gaze, "you will tell me everything you know about the Flameskin Army, its positions and its numbers."

"So, you fight some Flameskins and save others?" he asked.

"We've both fought in this war, Lieutenant. I've only ever raised my sword against those who have burned my country and killed my people. If you'd like to join your dead brothers, please," she said, gesturing to Kelan's scimitar. "I'd like to repay the favor."

Sol clung to Kelan's arm. "He didn't kill Jahr and neither did I."

"I know that. I presided over the hunter's trial."

"Josef?" Sol asked, her voice small.

"He was hanged for his crimes against Tokkedal."

A strangled cry escaped Sol's lips. The death stung Kelan as well. A reminder of how little power either of them had, and how fragile their existence was.

"I ask again, Lieutenant," Vara said. "I don't want to see more people hang. You will tell me what you know."

Kelan exhaled slowly. The Flameskins were dead anyway. Maybe it was better this way. The war would be shorter. But it was painful to think that every one of his kind would be slaughtered, and that he had contributed to it.

"I don't know how much of what I know is still accurate, but I'll tell you," Kelan said.

"Good, and I will keep your secrets in return. When I see you both at the disembarking, I will ask another favor of you."

"What kind of a favor?" Sol asked.

"The kind you cannot refuse." The queen rose and knocked her head against a low-hanging branch. She scowled at it before turning to Kelan. "Let's take a walk, cousin. I want you to tell me everything."

CHAPTER 52
SOL

The rope ladder creaked as they descended, and the wooden rungs slapped against the tree trunk. Every sound felt like a thunderclap in the darkness. Stealth was nigh impossible in the tree haven. Everything creaked and rattled and groaned, and there were sleeping children sprawled across every surface.

They reached the ground, and Sol waved Kelan forward. The moonlight barely touched the forest floor, and Sol was tempted to light a flame in her palm. But there would still be wraith scouts in the trees.

She and Kelan walked in silence, tripping over the roots and stumbling over rocks hidden beneath the dead leaves. Mist filled the air and beaded on their skin. The forest smelled of damp tree rot.

There was a rustle in the trees above them. Sol grabbed Kelan's arm and put a finger to her lips. They both froze, listening, and she searched the treetops for movement.

"Kelan."

They both jumped as Silas the First appeared from behind a tree with Marta beside them. The wraiths both had their bows notched, but hadn't pulled back the strings.

"So, you're leaving," Silas said. "Rask said you would."

"How could you abandon us?" Marta demanded. "You were supposed to come with us to the colony. You were our family."

The wraiths advanced on them, and Kelan held up his hands. "We're coming back."

Silas drew his bow, but it was still pointed away from them. "We trusted you, and all along you were working with the Flameskin Army. You going to send them after us now?"

"No!" Sol said. "Of course we won't."

"Then why are you leaving us?" Marta demanded.

"My family lives in the Ulves. I just want to send them a letter to tell them goodbye."

"And give away our position?" Silas asked.

"No. We would never do that. We're going to the town on the highway and then we're coming straight back," Kelan said.

"It's too dangerous for you to leave the Wood," Marta said.

"Kelan and I will be fine. We managed before we got here."

Marta threw her arms around Sol. Silas sighed and threw his bow down so he could clap Kelan on the back.

"Don't stay away too long," Silas said. "We need you two, Sol especially. She's the only one in this camp who knows anything. We would've starved this summer without her."

"We'll only be gone a couple days," Sol said.

"Rask is going to kill us when he finds out you're gone," Marta said. "I think he's afraid he's going to have to do some work when we get to the island. He's hoping Kelan will do all the heavy lifting."

"We'll walk you at least as far as the pits," Marta said. "I talked to Mie earlier, and she said there really are Flameskin soldiers there."

"There was no warning before Queen Vara showed up at the haven," Sol said. She was still bothered by this. The haven was so vulnerable. They had a dozen scouts out all the time, but they couldn't be expected to cover the whole forest.

"Queen Vara knows her way, so she moves fast," Marta said, and made a face. "But I guess we need to do better."

Sol squinted at a couple blinking lights in the distance. They were orange lights, like lanterns. Queen Vara and her retinue? Wraiths?

"Kelan," she murmured, pointing at the lights.

"I see it, too," Silas whispered. "I had thought Queen Vara would be long gone by now." He pulled a leafy hood over his head and made a silent gesture to Marta. They sped toward the light before Sol could stop them.

She and Kelan unslung their packs and drew their weapons. Kelan pulled them both behind the trunk of two conjoined redwoods. Sol's heart beat fast. Kelan rubbed her arm with a clammy hand. The wind swirled the fog around them, obscuring their view.

It was probably nothing. A traveler who had gotten lost. A woman leaving behind an unwanted Flameskin child. But at night the Wood was dark and strange. This wasn't the Ulves, and the trees and the sounds were unfamiliar.

Kelan had his sword in his right hand, but pulled her in with his left. "I hate this. I hate always being in danger. It's still four weeks before that boat gets here."

She, too, had somewhat forgotten what it was like to be out there in the world, where everyone was an enemy. Even here they weren't safe. What would it cost her to leave the Wood to send a letter to her family? She had too much to lose now.

"Maybe we should stay here," she said.

A scream pierced the air. Silas'.

Sol gasped into her hand as Kelan hugged her to him. She peered around the tree trunk, and a shape hurtled toward them in the darkness. Sol fumbled with her bow, but Kelan was ready. He stepped out from behind the tree and lifted his sword.

Marta skidded to a halt. "Silas!" she sobbed, pointing toward the approaching lights.

"What happened? Who are they?" Sol whispered.

"Flameskin soldiers. They grabbed Silas. We didn't see the ones behind us."

"How many?" Kelan demanded.

Marta shook her head. "I don't know. A lot."

Sol grabbed Marta by the shoulders. Marta was shaking badly and had lost her bow. "Go back to the camp and warn the others. Run!"

Marta took off in the direction of the haven, and Kelan followed after her, but stopped when Sol didn't follow.

"We have to hide," he said.

"But, Silas—"

He took her hand and pulled her toward the haven. "There's nothing we can do for him now."

Sol tried to keep her breath steady. They had taken Silas. There had to be some way to save him.

"The pits!" she said. "We can lead them to the pits and trap them there."

Kelan's face twisted painfully, but then he nodded. He let her lead him in the direction of the pit traps.

The lights were close now: flames cupped in hands that illuminated the faces of the Flameskin soldiers. Silas kicked and screamed somewhere behind them. The noise ricocheted inside Sol, each sound making her wince.

She drew her bow and aimed at one of the lights, then released her arrow. There was a scream and the light went out.

"Archers!" one of the soldiers cried.

"Let's give them something to follow," Sol said. She pulled her bow over her shoulder and took her emberstone from her pocket. She lit a flame in her hand and held it aloft.

Then they ran.

"There!" someone shouted. "After them!"

Panic surged hot in Sol's blood, twining with the fire in her veins. The flame on her hand flickered and wavered as they ran. The emberstone wasn't large enough to sustain fire for long, and once it was gone, they would be plunged back into darkness. If they weren't careful, she and Kelan would be lying at the bottom of the pits instead of the soldiers.

Comets shot out of the darkness and exploded on the ground around them.

"Get down!" Kelan shouted. He launched himself at her as

more blasts erupted through the trees. They rolled across the mossy forest floor as fire flew over their heads. Kelan crawled on top of her and covered her with his body.

A fiery orb struck Kelan's side and tossed him across the forest floor. He cried out as he rolled and his clothes and skin burned.

"Kelan!" Sol screamed.

She dropped to his side and beat out the flames as he writhed. His left arm had been badly burned, and the skin was black and red and horrible.

"The manacle. Get it off!" he cried.

She fumbled for the key. She had to heal him. The air brightened around them, glowing orange and crackling with heat. She whirled around and threw up her hands, calling on the fire inside her emberstone.

Fire burst out of her palms, striking the fireball that soared toward her. The flames from her hands deflected the spinning orb of fire and it hit a tree above them, showering them with sparks and scraps of bark.

But her emberstone was empty now. She was as helpless as Kelan.

Kelan had inserted the key into his shackle. It clicked open and her heart stuttered in her chest. She saw the change in Kelan's face as his eyes darkened and his lips twitched.

"Run!" he shouted at her. He hissed as he put a hand to his burned arm and ran fire across the burn, sealing some of the mutilated skin.

She took a step backward. Soldiers appeared through the trees in their red coats, fire glittering in their hands. The tree above them had caught fire, and burning debris rained down on them. She threw her hands over her face as cinders fell onto her head.

"Sol."

Her heart shuddered.

Kelan had stood and stared at her, his lips quirked in a smug smile. His voice was dark and unnatural. This wasn't Kelan anymore.

The demon took a step toward her, and she stepped back. Its face contorted again.

"Run, Sol!" It was Kelan's voice again.

"Fight it!"

But in answer, fire exploded out of his fingertips. She screamed and covered her face. Fire struck the ground in front of her. Kelan poured a line of fire across the ground and separated them.

"Kelan!" she shouted.

The wall of fire surged, growing higher and stranding her on the other side of the flames. He had cut her off from himself and the Flameskin soldiers.

Balls of fire shot through the flames and Sol rolled to the side as they struck the ground. She couldn't breathe. She couldn't think. Her hands shook as she pushed herself up to her feet again.

"Kelan!"

She screamed his name as the wall of flames crackled and consumed the ground at her feet.

Someone hissed and she was grabbed from behind as a hand clamped over her mouth.

CHAPTER 53
KELAN

Kelan clutched his arm and poured fire into his wound. He clenched his teeth against the pain as he retreated toward the wall of flames behind him.

He'd had several revelations over the last few minutes, and the first was that burns hurt worse than he'd thought.

The Flameskin soldiers advanced, and he was backed up against the wall of fire. Sol screamed his name again, and the sound of her voice tore his heart in half.

That was his second revelation: He'd never see Sol again.

She shouted again on the other side of the flames, and soldiers hurled balls of fire toward the sound. Kelan swore as he threw a deflective burst into the air and blocked most of the fireballs.

Run, Sol. Please, go.

Her emberstone was exhausted by now. He couldn't let her get burned. He was lost, but it wouldn't be for nothing if she got away.

He pushed more fire out of his hands, and the wall of flames surged behind him. There was plenty of grief and anger to fuel his pyra now.

And that was his third revelation: He wasn't possessed.

It had tried to seize him when the shackle first came off, but it had failed. And now his pyra was there, but it wasn't as strong as it had been before.

He didn't know if it was the prolonged use of the emberstone manacle or his injury, but he had complete control over his pyra once more.

The Flameskin soldiers approached slowly. They could see he was trapped and wounded.

He glanced behind him at the wall of flames, but he couldn't hear or see Sol. The fire ate at the damp forest floor and licked at the trunks of trees. She had to see there was nothing she could do.

Let her burn. His pyra wanted Sol gone. Sol was the one who had shackled him and cut off his flames and who drew off his pyra so that it couldn't control him.

The Flameskin soldiers closed in around him. Several had flames sparking in their hands and the others drew their swords. There were at least two dozen of them, and a pair of soldiers held Silas' limp form.

A man pushed his way through the ranks.

Kelan breathed in sharply and took another step backward.

"Hello, Kelan," Officer Osten said. "Did you miss me?"

CHAPTER 54
SOL

Someone had grabbed Sol from behind. She bucked and yanked her knife from her belt.

"It's me!" Marta hissed.

Sol jerked her mouth out of Marta's grasp. "You were supposed to go back to the haven to warn the others."

"I did, and then I came back to help you. Now let's go."

"But Kelan—"

"There's nothing we can do. Don't waste Kelan's sacrifice."

Sol put a hand over her mouth and sobbed into it. How could Marta say that? Kelan couldn't give himself up for her. She couldn't let him die.

Kelan's wall of flame flickered and receded as proof of Marta's words. Soldiers moved through the flames and used their hands to beat out the fire singing their uniforms.

"There!" a soldier shouted and pointed at them.

Marta tugged on Sol's hand, and Sol stumbled after her into the darkness. Sol couldn't think. The only thing keeping her moving was Marta yanking her forward. They ran through the forest and sprinted through the banks of mist.

But they were too loud, crashing through the underbrush and giving away their position. The soldiers chasing her and Marta kept close behind them. The flames in the soldiers' hands marked the soldiers' positions in the darkness. Every time Sol glanced over her shoulder, she could see the tiny flames and the manic faces. The lights were closing in around them.

Sol ran. Three steps for every ragged breath. No thoughts but fear and anguish.

Kelan.

Leaves and mud squished beneath their feet and roots conspired to trip them. Branches whipped at her cheeks and flicked dew in her eyes.

Kelan was gone.

The soldiers were closing in on them, drawing in on every side and herding them like sheep.

She had left Kelan.

The lights flickered in between the trees at her right. Marta veered left and pulled Sol with her, and then there were lights ahead of them, too, floating demon eyes that winked at them between the trunks of the redwoods.

Everywhere there were lights. The orange glow illuminated the soldiers' red coats and their devilish smiles and their dark eyes.

Marta and Sol were gasping for breath. They turned round and round and round. There was nowhere to go. The soldiers were everywhere.

Sol saw an opening in the trees and yanked Marta toward it. Trees whirred past as they jumped down into a small ravine and ran up a slope thick with fallen trees and exposed stones. Mud caked her fingers as she scrambled upward.

The soldiers' footsteps were muffled by the moss and leaves underfoot, but Sol could hear them. Too close. The orange light cast long shadows at Sol's feet and illuminated her path.

"Don't you want to see what we're going to do to your friends?" a soldier called, just behind them.

They had killed Kelan.

She yanked the dagger from her belt and launched herself at the soldier just as he was gathering fire in his hand. Sol rammed the dagger into his heart, just the way his words had cut through her heart.

They had taken Kelan. They had taken everything.

Sol fell along with the body and sat quivering on the ground beside it.

Marta grabbed her shoulders. "We can't stop!"

They were bathed in orange light. Soldiers shouted. Marta yanked Sol backward, and they both tumbled into the rotting carcass of a dead tree. They were half-submerged in soil, and everything smelled of rot and earth. The smell crawled its way into her nostrils and mouth. It buried her in decay and darkness. Marta pulled Sol in deeper, and entombed them in the moist, sloping soil and rotting wood.

There was a chink in the trunk that gave Sol a sliver of a view, and it let in the brilliant orange light of a soldier's flame.

The soldier approached and shouted when she saw the body. Sol still held her oak leaf dagger, dripping with the man's blood.

Kelan was dead because of her. She had let him give himself up for her and had done nothing to help him. Everything they had fought for had been undone in a moment.

The soldier stepped closer, her boots at the same level of Sol's eyes. The Flameskin turned slowly, and her flames illuminated the ground. Marta quivered beside Sol and they were both held their breaths, waiting.

The soldier drew her sword slowly. Took another step.

The light went out.

Sol was blinded by the darkness, and panic set in. The darkness. The closeness of the earth. The flurry of Marta's heartbeat against her side, and the drumming of her own pulse in her blood.

The soldier's boots scuffed against the ground outside their hiding place, moving away from them.

Marta blew out a long breath and rested her head against Sol's sweaty back.

The wood splintered above them, and a sword blade crashed

through it. Pain shot through Sol's leg as the blade sliced her calf. Marta screamed.

Sol crawled out of the trunk and limped to her feet. The soldier was still trying to get her blade back, but it had caught in the wood.

But Sol was ready. She grabbed the front of the Flameskin's coat and plunged her dagger into the woman's chest.

The Flameskin collapsed beneath Sol and fell onto the ground with a thud. Sol yanked the dagger out and stumbled to her feet, breathing hard.

She would not rest until she had cut every one of their hearts out.

Just like they had done to her.

CHAPTER 55

KELAN

Kelan's head drooped as he panted. His hands were shackled behind him around the narrow waist of a tree. Blood dripped over his eyebrow, and he blinked at it, trying to keep it from getting into his eye.

The pain in his arm was nauseating. Every time his skin brushed up against his shirt or the bark of the tree, it felt like it was burning all over again. He hadn't had long for his pyra to heal him before they had stuck another emberstone on him.

A shadow fell over him.

He looked up through his bleary eyes, and Haldur stood over him, blocking the morning light.

"Where is the haven?" Haldur demanded.

"I don't know."

Haldur growled as he backhanded Kelan across the jaw. His ring cut Kelan's lip.

Kelan spit blood out of his mouth. "I don't know my way around the Wood. I don't know where it is."

It was the truth. He had never needed to know where he was with Sol at his side.

Haldur grabbed him by his hair and pressed his bruised skull against the rough bark. Kelan twisted against his uncle's grasp, but he was shackled in place and had no flames to fight with. His arm was in agony.

"Silas, the other boy, knows," Kelan gasped. "I don't know anything."

Haldur let go, and Kelan slumped against the tree and glanced at Silas as waves of pain rolled through his body. He and Silas were both chained to trees at the edge of the Hivid Wood.

A Flameskin Army stretched out in the meadow beyond the Wood. A thousand soldiers sprawled out in the dry summer grass. A pitiful number. All that was left after years of struggling and war.

Silas' emberstone had been removed, and Silas was in stasis, asleep, as his pyra healed his body. He had been horribly burned, all along his chest, right shoulder, and arm. New skin was growing over the mutilated flesh, but it would be a long time before he would be well.

But it was better that way. If Silas were awake, they'd be torturing him as well, trying to get answers.

Osten approached and saluted Commander Haldur Burke. "Sir, we followed the girls' trail as far as we could, but it disappeared. We couldn't find the haven."

Kelan tried to smile, but it came out as more of a grimace. Sol had gotten away. Sol was safe.

Haldur swore under his breath. "We need those soldiers from the haven."

"There *are* no soldiers in the haven," Kelan said. "You're wasting your time."

"Then where have all the deserters gone?" Haldur demanded.

"Dead, probably."

"You're hiding an army in there. I know it." Haldur turned to Osten. "How far is Saint Katrine from our position?"

"She'll arrive in two days, sir."

"Katrine?" Kelan asked.

"She's coming to kill us all. The rest of the Flameskin Army and any Flameskins you've got hidden in there."

Kelan's mouth went dry.

But Vara had promised to help them escape.

Haldur kicked Kelan in the ribs. "How many Flameskins are in this Wood?"

Kelan had to spit blood out of his mouth again before he could reply. "They're just children."

Haldur kicked him again, and Kelan gasped as all the air was forced from his lungs. "The rumors say hundreds. Thousands."

"There's no secret army in the woods."

"Lies," Haldur spat. "We've been sending scouts into the Wood searching for the refugees for two years now, and none of them ever come back."

"Your scouts were killed by traps or Tokken soldiers."

Osten stepped forward. "Sir—"

"This is our last stand," Haldur said. "If we join our armies together, we'll be able to survive against Saint Katrine."

This was insanity. Haldur had pinned his last hopes on something that didn't exist. If Saint Katrine was coming, they were all dead. He could only hope that Sol and the others would see the fires and they'd have enough time to escape.

"Take his emberstone off," Haldur ordered, nodding to Kelan.

Kelan wasn't sure if he should be relieved or terrified. His pyra would heal him, but maybe that was what his uncle wanted. He was going to push him so close to death he would need his pyra to stay alive.

"Please, Uncle. I don't know where it is," Kelan begged. "Sol always took me where we needed to go."

Haldur's eyes flicked up, and Kelan winced. "Your huntress? She's here?"

Kelan stared at his bloody spittle clotting in the dirt at his feet. He shouldn't have said anything.

Haldur grabbed Kelan's burned arm and scraped it against the rough bark of the tree. Kelan screamed as bright, cutting pain lanced through him.

Haldur paused, and Kelan gasped, trying to catch his breath.

"Is the huntress here?" Haldur asked again, his voice cool.

"Yes," Kelan gasped.

Haldur dropped Kelan's arm. "She was the reason you left the army."

Kelan didn't answer. He couldn't. He could barely breathe.

"She's the one you were trying to protect last night."

Kelan closed his eyes.

Ashes. He just wanted this to be over, to be dead so he couldn't hurt anyone else. If they found her because he had given them some bit of information, he would never be able to forgive himself.

Sol.

If he had known that yesterday would be his last day with her, the last time to see her smile, to touch her skin and to kiss her lips—

Osten bent down and reached for the emberstone bound to Kelan's arm, but Haldur held out his hand. "Wait."

Osten stood. "Sir?"

"The huntress would know the way to the haven."

"Do you want me to send out scouts again and look for her?" Osten asked.

"No. If she followed Kelan all the way here, I bet there's not much she won't do to get him back. When she comes back to reclaim her lover, she'll lead us straight to the haven."

Kelan took a ragged breath. Ingrid and Rask wouldn't let Sol come back for him.

But since when had Sol ever done the reasonable thing?

He couldn't help but hope there was some chance she would. To see her one last time was all he wanted. But he didn't wish that at the expense of her life or the safety of the haven.

He groaned and laid his head against the tree. She needed to stay in the haven where it was safe.

Or maybe it didn't matter. Saint Katrine was coming and would kill all of them.

"Station guards here," Haldur said, "but keep them out of

sight. And have someone exchange the metal shackles with a rope. Same with the boy. Keep them both drugged."

"No," Kelan moaned.

Haldur bent down and met Kelan's eyes. "We'll find out how true her love is, won't we?"

Haldur took Kelan's skull between his hands and smashed it against the tree. The world was pain and blackness.

CHAPTER 56

SOL

"Absolutely not," Ingrid said. Her eyes were furious, and her body was stiff. If she wasn't wearing an emberstone, she probably would've sparked at the edges.

Marta stopped her foot. "Kelan and Silas will be killed if we don't—"

"They might be dead already," Ingrid said.

Dead. Sol squeezed her eyes shut.

Ingrid shook her head. "No. You've already put us in danger. You don't know that they didn't follow you back to the haven."

"We aren't fools," Sol said. She leaned against the other wall in the shadows, not looking at any of them. "I made sure we weren't followed, and we took the long way back. We didn't leave a trail."

Rask scowled at Sol. "She should be executed for trying to leave the haven."

"I believe she's already received punishment enough," Ingrid said.

Punishment.

Yes, that was what it was. The gods were punishing her for squandering what she had in exchange for a past she couldn't let go of.

She and Kelan should've been in their bed last night, asleep.

If she hadn't wanted so badly to say goodbye to her family, Kelan would still be alive.

"Come on, Marta," Sol said, and grabbed Marta's hand.

Marta wrenched her wrist free and turned to Ingrid. "How can you just abandon them like that? You love Silas!"

Ingrid sank onto a branch beside Rask. "I love all my children. And I won't endanger all of them to save one."

"It's a betrayal. If you had been taken, Silas would've come for you. He would've come for any of us."

Ingrid stood. She wore her grief with an erect spine and anger burning in her eyes. "You will stay here, Marta."

"I won't. You can't force me to stay. I'm going after Silas."

"Then you can't come back. If you lead them back to the haven, you'll get all of us killed."

Marta grabbed her bow from the ground and stormed out of Rask's dwelling. Sol trudged behind her.

They passed between rows of wraiths who hung off the eaves and leaned against the railings and straddled the tree branches. Everyone was there. They had all listened. There were few secrets in the Flameskin haven.

"Silas is really gone?" one girl asked, her lip trembling.

Azalea pushed through the crowd and grabbed Sol's legs. She burrowed her face into Sol's mud-streaked pants.

"I'm going after him," Marta said. She grabbed a quiver from one of her companions and looped its strap over her shoulder.

"You said Silas was already dead," Sol said.

"But we don't know for sure. How can you just give up on Kelan?" Marta demanded.

Sol strode away, taking the rope bridge back toward her dwelling.

"Sol!" Marta chased after her, along with an entourage of Flameskins.

Sol ignored Marta. Her head was pounding. She was numb. She couldn't think. She couldn't breathe.

She reached their home and stopped outside to stare at its

broken roof and the crumbling curtain of leaves that served as their door.

They were supposed to make a new door together yesterday.

She dropped onto her knees outside the door and muffled a sob.

"He wouldn't have given up on you," Marta said.

"He gave himself up!" Sol shouted. She stood and whirled on Marta. "You were the one who convinced me to leave him."

"That was last night. We were outnumbered, and your emberstone was empty."

"And how is it any different today? There's an entire army camped on the edge of the Hivid Wood."

"If they have Silas, and if he's still alive, it's only a matter of time before they find us," Marta said.

"And if they catch any of the rest of us trying to rescue him, it's the same thing. We can't risk exposing the haven."

"We have to rescue Silas."

"You just told me he was dead!"

"What if there was a chance Kelan was still alive, and you let him die because you didn't come for him?"

Sol took in a ragged breath as she twisted the ring around her finger. No. She couldn't start hoping. She couldn't hope and then have to grieve him again.

He had taken off his emberstone. Even if he was still alive, he was possessed. He would try to kill her if she found him.

Her Kelan was gone.

Marta unhooked the emberstone manacle around her arm and threw it onto the ground. She smiled a horrible smile.

"I'm going after Silas. And if he's dead, I'm going to burn their camp to the ground."

Another boy her age stripped his emberstone off as well, and a girl drew her dagger.

Sol sagged against the doorframe. "What happens when they catch us? They'll use us to find the haven."

Marta drew an arrow from her quiver. "Anyone who gets caught gets shot."

"I'm not going to shoot you," Sol said.

"We're all just demons. What does it matter anyway?"

"You're not a demon. Stop this."

Marta turned toward the crowd. "Who's coming with me?"

Several of the children stepped forward, raising bows or knives or hands that glittered with fire. Marta turned to Sol, but Sol only shook her head.

"I won't make Kelan's sacrifice meaningless." He had sent her away. He had put up a burning wall and stranded her.

She remembered that last glimpse she had of him. The orange light of the fire had cast ghastly shadows over his body. But the face he had worn was the same one he had made when they were falling off that cliff: *It's time to let go, love.*

She slammed the tip of her oak dagger into the doorframe. Why did he always have to give up so easily? She would've found a way if he had just let her help him!

"There's an army waiting to invade the Wood, and eventually their scouts will find us," Marta said. "We have to fight back. We have to protect our haven and our family."

"But there's just a handful of us," Sol said. "And they're trained soldiers."

"Are you a huntress or are you the prey?"

Sol took in a ragged breath. The moment she left Cassia and stepped with Kelan back into the Ulves, she had become the hunted. She had been chased across Tokkedal and been forced to flee her home and her family and her mountains. And now the war had finally found her here in this final haven.

She was finished running. There was nowhere left to run to. And without Kelan, there was nothing left to protect except this new family gathered around her.

If they were marching into battle, so was she.

"I'm a huntress," Sol whispered.

Marta smiled and her voice went dark. "Then hunt."

CHAPTER 57

SOL

Sol pulled the red Flameskin soldier's coat over her tunic. The coat had been taken from a body in the pit and was streaked with dirt, but it should pass.

One of the boys handed her a large leather packet filled with powder, and she tucked a second smaller packet in her pocket. Beside her, Marta did the same.

Fire buzzed in her veins. She had her emberstone clutched in her hand, and the flames were eager to be used. She could imagine what it was like to have a pyra. She wanted to destroy the Flameskin camp. Her hatred swirled and surged with the fire inside her.

Sol glanced at Marta, who was fastening the buttons on her Flameskin coat. "If you get taken—"

Marta patted the smaller packet at her hip. "I'll eat it. I swear."

Sol let out a shaky breath. This was a suicide mission, but it was their best chance at destroying the camp. She just had to pray she would have the strength to take her own life if she got caught. If they took her alive, it would all be for nothing.

Marta saluted the wraiths, and a few embraced her and Sol.

"We'll be back," Sol promised. But her voice wavered. She

hoped she would be back, and Marta, too, but there were no promises when sneaking into a flameksin camp.

The wraiths slowly melted into the forest and climbed back into the trees. They had weapons strapped across their hips and over their backs. They would attack the Flameskin camp tonight, if Sol's plan succeeded.

"Are you ready?" Marta asked.

Sol nodded, and they set off in opposite directions through the forest. Her hands sweated as she clutched the leather packet of poison to her side.

The wraiths had spent all morning grinding and preparing enough powder to contaminate every water source in the camp.

At least, she hoped it would be enough.

As the trees of the Hivid Wood thinned, the camp appeared before her. Tents and horses, men and women. An army preparing for war. They sharpened weapons and polished armor, cut down trees and sawed wood to construct barricades and defenses.

Sol stepped out from between the trees toward the nearest tents. Everyone seemed to be occupied, but she couldn't tell if there were soldiers patrolling and watching this portion of the Wood.

"Hey," a man shouted.

Sol jumped as he rushed toward her. She froze, and her heart thundered inside her.

"No one's allowed in the forest except scouts," the soldier said.

Sol took a deep breath and stood straighter. She was a Flame-skin now, and she needed to act like one. She deepened her voice and let it become gravelly. "I was taking a piss. You got a problem with that?" She pulled on the emberstone in her hand and sparks ran over her knuckles.

He sighed and waved her on. "Stay out of the woods. Don't you know the rules?"

Sol gave him a good scowl and hurried away, her heart skipping inside her. She couldn't get caught. She didn't want to consume the poison in her pocket.

She strode purposefully through the camp with her head down, but her path was aimless. She passed dozens and dozens of soldiers, multicolored tents, and tired animals. There were so many people here, and so much going on. She had no idea where to begin.

Anvils clanged, and she paused to watch a man melt a hunk of metal between his hand and use his hammer to shape it into a sword.

She wandered toward a large pot of rice boiling over a fire. A cook stood nearby, salting a cow's bloody haunch.

Sol crept forward silently and took a small handful of powder from the larger packet and dropped it into the rice. The bubbles popped over the sparkling powder, dispersing and submerging it in the starchy water.

A hand grabbed her wrist. Sol yanked back, but the cook held tight. Her hand shook as she reached for the poison in her breast pocket.

"What do you think you're doing?" the cook demanded. "Food's not ready yet."

He shoved her away from the rice, and she landed hard on her tailbone. The cook turned back to his meat and she scurried away with a gasp.

She and Marta had talked about poisoning the water and wine in the camp, but Sol realized that poisoning the army's lunch would be much more effective. The wine might or might not be drunk for a while yet, but the food would be eaten immediately, while it was still hot.

There were people cooking all over the camp, and they seemed accustomed to the appearance of soldiers in their kitchens looking for snacks to sustain them between meals. They took little notice of one more Nordese girl in a red coat.

She wandered the whole length and breadth of the camp until her heavy packet of powder ran empty. And all around the camp lunch was being served to oblivious soldiers. They ate tainted rice, meat sauce, and soup, and Sol took a grim satisfaction from it.

The Flameskins had come to the Hivid Wood wanting to strip away the wraiths' freedom. She would protect the haven with whatever means available to her. Even stooping so low as this.

She knew she should get back to the forest, but her feet dragged as she walked. She wasn't here to look for Kelan, but he was the reason her feet refused to carry her back to safety.

But the camp was enormous, and her search was futile. It was just like she had told Marta: impossible. He could be held in any of the hundreds of tents in the camp and she could search all of them without finding him.

She had reached a place near the center of camp where a high and wide tent had been erected. The tent door flapped open and a large group of soldiers strode out.

One of them was horrifyingly familiar: Haldur, Kelan's uncle.

Sol bolted, dodging people and tents as she fled and prayed that Haldur hadn't seen her.

But people stared at her as she ran. Someone shouted. Soldiers didn't run in their own camp.

She slipped in between two tents and stood there for a few minutes, regaining her breath and burying herself in the folds of the thick cloth. She patted the packet of poison.

Running would get her caught.

Getting caught would mean eating the remaining poison.

She had to keep her head. She could still walk out of this alive. Kelan would want her to keep living and do what she could to protect Azalea and the haven. She just had to get out of the camp.

She took another deep breath and strode out from between the tents.

Officer Osten stood waiting for her. "Hello, Isabella."

Sol yanked the oak dagger from her belt and Osten threw up his hands. "Wait!"

She launched herself at him, and he jumped into the tent to

evade her. She tumbled into the tent, striking out blindly as her body tangled with the cloth door. Osten had fallen to the ground inside and scrambled away from her, but Sol was faster.

She landed on top of him and pressed the edge of her knife blade to his throat.

She should kill him.

She knew she should.

That night they had taken Kelan she had killed Flameskin soldiers. But this was a new day. Osten's lips trembled and his hands shook.

"Let me go!" he squealed. "I'll tell you where Kelan is! That's what you're here for, isn't it?" He squirmed underneath her as she hesitated. He tried to slide out, and she pressed her blade against his neck. He cried out, and her blade coaxed a single drop of blood from beneath his skin.

"Where is he?" Sol demanded.

Osten swallowed. "He's in the southernmost point of the camp, at the edge of the Wood. He's tied to a tree there. Him and the other boy."

Sol shoved hard with her knee in his chest, making him gasp. This was a trap.

"I swear it! He's there! He's alive!"

"Why would you help me?"

"Because Kelan is my friend. I don't want to see him hurt."

She frowned at him. That was a lie. There was nothing friendly between them.

"Who did you tell I was here?" Sol asked.

"No one. I saw you near the command tent and followed you straight here. I swear it."

Osten still struggled to get free beneath her.

If there was a chance Kelan was alive, she would take it. She patted the packet of poison to make sure it was still there.

This was a trap. But even if it was, she didn't care. Even if she only got to see Kelan one more time, it would be worth it.

She slid the tiny packet of poison from her pocket.

"What's—"

The moment he opened his mouth, she poured a mouthful onto his tongue. She got up, and he tried to spit it out of his mouth, but it was too late. He quivered for a moment, then fell still.

She knew how to make a proper poison.

There was still enough of it left to kill her as well, though not as quickly. She shook herself and peeked out of the tent. No one took notice of her.

It appeared that Osten had been telling the truth, in that regard at least. He hadn't told anyone else she was there. But why?

She went south, and passed more blacksmiths shaping horseshoes between their hands, and lieutenants running drills, and food that Sol hadn't had a chance to poison.

Hopefully, Marta had gotten to it.

Hopefully, Marta was still alive.

As the Wood grew closer, the tents were spaced farther apart. The Wood loomed over the camp, casting a long, misty shadow. She thought she caught sight of movement among the treetops, but it was difficult to tell with the shifting darkness and the wind sifting through the branches.

Sol caught a glimpse of something at the edge of the trees. There, tied to trees at the edge of the Wood, lay Kelan and Silas.

She gasped into her hand and broke into a run.

Kelan.

Gods above, it was Kelan.

He lay inert on the ground, and whether he was unconscious or dead she didn't know.

She stopped short when she got close and looked around hurriedly, but could see no one else around. It was quiet here; the silence of the Wood invaded this space and muffled the clamor of the camp. She took a step toward Kelan, watching, waiting, but there were no guards. Why were there no guards?

Sol took another step toward Kelan. Bruises had bloomed on his cheek and his forehead and his eye, and his lip was split.

Blood had run down his chin and dried there. His burned arm looked horribly painful.

But his chest was still rising and falling. Kelan was alive.

Every sense warned against approach, but her aching heart couldn't bear the sight of him like this.

Maybe Osten really had wanted to help him. And she had killed him for it without a thought.

Shouts behind her. She pressed herself against a tent wall and tried to lose herself in the folds of cloth.

More shouting. She caught snippets of the words and smiled. The Flameskin Army had realized something was wrong. Hopefully, they wouldn't understand what had happened until everyone had eaten their fill of contaminated food.

Someone grabbed her arm. Sol gasped and tried to jerk away, but when she looked up, she found Marta beside her.

"Stop scaring me like that," Sol hissed.

Marta shushed her with a finger to her lips.

"Did you know Kelan was here?" Sol demanded.

"Mie just spotted them. Did you finish?" she asked, eyeing the leather bag tucked into Sol's belt.

"Yes." Sol tried to get up, but Marta pulled her back.

"Wait. The wraiths are coming to help us."

They crouched in silence, half-hidden behind the fold of a tent wall. Sol watched Kelan's chest rise and fall and rise and fall, and watched the wind pull at his bloodstained tunic. She itched to touch him, to wake him, and see his turquoise eyes and hear his voice again.

There was a bird call from the trees. Sol looked up at the treetops to find shadows there with bright eyes and dirt-caked faces.

"They're ready. Get Kelan," Marta whispered.

Sol rushed toward him. She took his face in her hands and pressed her lips to his bruised forehead. She allowed herself only one blessed moment to hold him, then hacked at the ropes around his wrists.

He was unresponsive to her touch, but he was warm and alive

and breathing. His captors had tied an emberstone to his arm and she ripped it off. Fire sparked underneath his skin as she hoisted him over her shoulders and stood. She drew on the emberstone, and fire surged into her legs and her back, giving her the strength to lift him.

Marta had pulled Silas over her shoulders as well, and together they ran for the trees.

Kelan was almost twice her weight, and his long legs and arms dangled over her body. She couldn't move fast, but the emberstone helped. The wraiths followed above, jumping from limb to limb.

There was another bird call. A warning.

Sol couldn't glance behind her with Kelan on her shoulders, so she turned quickly when she crested the hill. The soldiers crept between the trees, but their red coats made it impossible for them to hide. Dozens and dozens of soldiers had filed into the forest and followed behind her and Marta.

Bows twanged in the trees above Sol, followed by crackling laughter. An arrow thudded into a Flameskin soldier's side, and she dropped. The soldiers shouted and drew their swords.

Sol sucked fire from the emberstone and bolted into the trees with Kelan thumping on her shoulders as she ran.

"Go to the haven, Sol!" one of the wraiths shouted above her as she passed beneath the trees.

But they weren't supposed to go to the haven. They couldn't lead the soldiers to it.

The forest filled with the shouts of war. The wraiths rained arrows on the Flameskin soldiers, and fire exploded through the treetops. The mage soldiers tried desperately to strike at the shadows, but the wraiths moved like mist from limb to limb as they scurried above the forest floor.

Sol glanced back once more. The red-coated soldiers were gaining on her and Marta.

A dozen wraiths dropped from the trees and stood in a line, laughing and shrieking. They were dressed in leaves and grasses and smeared with mud.

The soldiers faltered.

"Do not taunt the wraiths of Hivid Wood," one of them screamed.

"Do not enter into this cursed forest!"

The wraiths held out their hands and gathered fire from their pyri. They sent a wave of flames rushing at the advancing lines of soldiers. The Flameskin soldiers screamed as the fire ignited their clothes and skin. More than half of them succumbed to the flames, the half that had eaten the tainted food. The other half fell to arrows from the treetops.

It only took a single speck of emberstone to extinguish a pyra, and the poison Sol and Marta had poured into the army's food was made of emberstone dust. While the Flameskins had specks of emberstone in their bodies, they were as susceptible to fire as anyone else.

Fire crackled on the trees, eating at branches and limbs and sending sweet pine smoke into the air. The wraiths marched forward, pushing fire toward the Flameskin camp. Flames leapt from their hands toward the grass and the tents. Horses and people screamed, and smoke choked the air and blackened the sky. A bugle sounded in the Flameskin camp and was joined by other horns.

The hunt had started. But this time, Sol was not the prey.

CHAPTER 58

KELAN

Kelan blinked awake to the steady thump of his body crashing against a pair of bony shoulders. There was the pounding of a pair of running feet and the crackle of fire. His arms and legs slowly regained their feeling, and as he lifted his head, he caught a glimpse of Sol's face.

Sol.

His veins were buzzing with fire again, and the flames sparked as he caught sight of her face.

Ashes.

Everything hurt. But Sol was with him, and he didn't care about anything else.

He lifted his hand to touch her, and she jerked sideways.

"Kelan?"

She swore and stumbled. Kelan slid off her shoulders and onto the ground. He groaned as he rolled.

Burnitall, this arm. He pushed his pyra into his arm to help dull some of the pain.

Sol's emberstone had fallen from her hand and dropped onto the pine needles. She scrambled after it and cast a wary glance at Kelan as she picked it up from the ground.

He rubbed his face, trying to reorient himself. Sol

approached cautiously, holding out the emberstone. She looked afraid.

"It's just me," he said. He tried and failed to sit up, and instead lay groaning on the ground.

She took a step toward him. "You aren't possessed?"

He shook his head in answer, and his vision spun.

She threw her arms around him and smothered him with a kiss. He clung to her even as he struggled to breathe. She was back. They were together again. Nothing else mattered. Not even breathing.

"What are you doing? You're supposed to be running!" Marta shouted. They broke apart, and Kelan looked up to see Marta with an unconscious Silas on her shoulders.

Sol pulled Kelan to his feet. "Can you run?"

He wasn't sure if he could even walk. "If you help me."

He straightened and took stock of his body. Bruises, cuts, and burns, but everything still seemed to be in place. His pyra was there, but absorbed in healing his arm. And he wasn't possessed.

He took Sol's hand. "Tell me what's going on."

"We came to burn the Flameskin camp, but then—"

"But then we found you and Silas," Marta said. "And we caught sight of the Tokken Army."

"The Tokken Army?" Sol asked. "They're here?"

An explosion of fire sent the three of them scurrying in different directions. Silas fell onto the ground as fire struck the trees and the ground around them. Marta sent balls of fire toward their attackers and tried to deflect the blasts.

"Go!" Marta shouted at them. "I can hold them off."

A wraith dropped from the tree above them and picked up Silas. But a volley of flames knocked Marta off her feet and sent her sprawling.

Kelan took up her position. Marta didn't have the practice he had, and he expertly wielded his pyra. For every burst of flame the soldiers sent toward them, he replied with one of his own.

The air erupted with sparks and fire as Kelan deflected the blows.

Through the flames on the ground emerged the soldiers, all mages, who held their emberstones aloft in their hands and drew swirling fire around their fists. They cast flames at the wraiths, dropping them from the trees and knocking them off their feet.

Marta winced as she picked herself up off the ground. "Why are they attacking us?"

"They think we're hiding an army in the Wood," Kelan said. He launched another explosive wave of flame from his fingers. "They think we'll be able to push back Katrine."

"They're insane!" Sol shouted.

"They're desperate." Kelan intercepted the attacks and gave the wraiths a chance to regroup. His pyra grew in strength as he used it, but it didn't try to overpower him. It was content to let him block the attacks and send fire and cinders exploding through the trees.

Sol grabbed a bow and arrows that had dropped from one of the trees and shot the mages, dropping them onto the forest floor. Many of the red-coated soldiers lay on the ground, inexplicably suffering from burns.

"How are the soldiers burning?" Kelan asked. He had to shout to be heard over the explosive crash of fire and the screams of men and women, and the crackle of fire licking its way up the tree trunks.

"We fed them emberstone. Their pyri have been extinguished, for now."

Clever girl. Ingested emberstone would be difficult, if not impossible to expel. And it left them completely vulnerable.

Sol raised her bow and shot another soldier who had gotten too close to the top of the hill. But there were too many soldiers for her to hold them all back.

Kelan widened his stance. This was what he had been trained to do—hurl flames and fight.

The first soldier reached the crest of their hill and swung with his sword. Kelan stepped in front of Sol and sent a blast of fire into the soldier's chest, igniting his red coat and sending him to the ground. Kelan wrestled the sword from the soldier's hand. He slashed the soldier's chest, then swung his new sword upward to meet another blade.

Kill. Kill. Kill, his pyra hissed.

Kelan struck down soldiers one by one, distracting them with flames and cutting them open with his blade.

His whole life he had been doing this. He had joined the army at ten, alongside Markus and his uncle. And now he turned everything he had learned against the people who had raised him.

The forest burned. Kelan's injured arm ached, but he couldn't let it distract him. Sweat ran down his arm and stung his wounds. Whenever Kelan's blade faltered, one of Sol's arrows felled his foes.

He slashed at a soldier who went down with a cry, and two more took her place. Sol's bow twanged above him on the rise, and the soldier fell. Kelan used the distraction to run the other soldier through.

The flames crept up the hill in the wake of the soldiers. Sol coughed as smoke choked the trees.

A familiar figure strode through the smoke and the fog. Uncle Haldur.

Haldur advanced slowly, almost casually through the trees. His soldiers passed him and ran at the wraiths, hurling fire and getting felled by arrows. The number of advancing soldiers was diminishing. The flames that now consumed the forest created an impassable barrier for the poisoned Flameskins.

"Kelan," Haldur said, drawling out the word.

Kelan raised his sword. "Call off the attack. This is my home, Uncle, and I won't let you take it from me."

"I gave you a home. I was the one who took you in when my sister was murdered."

Nearby, Sol was doubled over and coughing again. Black pine smoke drifted as thick as the mist.

Haldur tried to kill us, his pyra hissed. *Now we will kill him.*

"You betray your own kind," Haldur said. He stopped in front of Kelan and drew his sword.

"I don't want to kill soldiers. I just want to protect the people I love."

"Flameskins that won't fight with us don't deserve our protection."

Haldur swung his sword without warning, forcing Kelan to step backward to block it. Their blades clashed and rang through the forest as sparks flew around them.

Haldur was the one who had taught Kelan to use a sword, and his uncle had always been the better swordsman.

But he doesn't have a pyra.

Kelan drew on his pyra, sending fire into his arms and his shoulders to strengthen the muscles. He slammed his blade against Haldur's, each blow pushing his uncle backward down the burning hill. Haldur's face was slick with sweat, and the heat intensified, coming out in blistering waves as the flames leapt through the trees.

Kelan kept Haldur on the defensive. Kelan's attacks grew heavier and faster with his pyra strengthening his body. Sparks flew from their blades and Kelan's hilt began to glow with the heat of his hands.

Haldur threw a blast of fire at Kelan's face, temporarily blinding him, and in return Kelan sent out a wave of flames from his hand. Haldur knocked Kelan's sword from his hand. Kelan scrambled backward, trying to get away from Haldur as he regained his bearings.

Haldur had picked up Kelan's sword from the ground and held both of them as he circled. "Join with us, Kelan. It isn't too late. The Tokkens are here, and we need soldiers."

"I won't be a weapon anymore."

Haldur sighed. "I always did wish you were more like Markus."

"Makus is dead."

Haldur blinked. "What?"

"Markus was a monster, but you could never see that. He wasn't a soldier. He was a murderer."

"What did you do?"

Kelan clambered to his feet.

"What did you do?" Haldur shouted. His face changed. Haldur was extinguished; he could no longer feel grief or anger or happiness, but something had triggered inside him.

Haldur threw himself with a roar at Kelan. Kelan raced toward a fallen soldier and grabbed his sword from the ground. He tumbled backward, and Haldur's sword struck the trunk of a tree just above Kelan's head.

Haldur slammed his swords at Kelan, and now their positions were reversed. Haldur forced Kelan downhill toward the fire and the fallen Flameskin soldiers. Kelan could barely keep track of Haldur's two flashing swords. His pyra quavered, and his strength diminished as fear threatened to take him.

Sol followed close behind, but her quiver was empty. She stooped to yank an arrow from the back of a dead soldier.

Haldur slammed both swords at Kelan, and Kelan lost his footing. Kelan stumbled back a step and tripped on a root. He fell. Haldur had the opening. He could thrust in his sword and end Kelan's life.

But instead, Haldur turned and charged Sol. He threw a blast of fire at her and knocked her down. She cried out as she fell, and Haldur lifted his sword over her head.

"No!" Kelan screamed. He hurled flames at Haldur, catching him in the side just an arrow struck Haldur's back.

Kelan's flames blasted Haldur sideways into the dirt. Haldur's chest heaved once, and then he was still.

Kelan scrambled to his feet and ran to Sol's side.

He beat out the flames burning her red coat and helped her up from the ground. "Are you hurt?"

"No. Are you?"

He shook his head as she wrapped her arms around him. She didn't hold him too tightly, and he was grateful for that. Everything hurt.

He ran his hand over her long, black hair and brushed his fingers across her soot-streaked face.

Sol. He closed his eyes as smoke billowed around them, and didn't release her until she began to cough.

"Keep drawing on your emberstone. It will help with the smoke," he said.

She nodded as her eyes watered. He took her hand and led them away from the fire that raced up the trees. But he paused when he caught sight of the body.

Haldur had an arrow protruding from his back, and fire still smoldered on his red coat. His skin and his hair had burned.

This was the uncle who had saved him from the mobs, who had raised him since he was a boy. The uncle who had taught him the art of death and destruction, who had turned him into a weapon, who had encouraged him to give in to the darkness.

Sol edged toward Haldur, and turned away after she had gotten a glimpse of him. "I'm sorry."

He let out a heavy sigh. "I'm not. He would've killed you if he could've. He knew that was the best way to hurt me."

"But he's your family."

Fire had taken every member of his family in the end. His mother and his aunt had been lost to the pyre, and now Markus and Haldur had been burned as well.

Kelan let out a long sigh. "It's over now."

Marta had slid down from a tree branch above them. "No, it's not. The Tokkens have arrived."

CHAPTER 59
SOL

"The Tokkens are in the Wood?" Sol asked. She clung tight to Kelan's hand, not wanting to ever let go again. She was also a little leery of him without his emberstone. How was he not possessed?

"Come and see," one of the wraiths shouted from above.

She needed to get up there and see what was going on, but she hesitated. "Do you need the emberstone back?" she asked Kelan.

"I don't think so."

All this time they had spent worrying about what would happen if he was without his emberstone, and now he didn't need it?

But she trusted him.

Her eyes watered, and she coughed as she climbed. Up there the air was thick with smoke. She could peek through the boughs at the Flameskin camp beyond the forest from the canopy. The fire had spread across the camp, leaping from tent to tent. The Flameskin soldiers were in complete disarray. Many of them were burning and dying. Their contaminated food was doing its work and keeping the Flameskins from using their pyri.

Beyond the sea of fire and red coats came a wave of blue across the grass. Tokken soldiers marched toward the camp and began their own version of destruction with steel. At their head stood a woman wreathed in flames that shot a frothing sea of fire into the Flameskin Army. As she stormed through the camp, the flames burning the tents bent toward her, as if being sucked in by her breath, then she blasted the fire outward at the Flameskin soldiers.

Marta had followed Sol up the tree and hung from a branch beside her. "They're going to destroy the entire Flameskin Army, then they'll come for us."

"We'll have to hide," Sol said.

Marta shook her head. "We can't hide from her. Haven't you heard the stories? She can summon fire from our bodies without touching us. She can find us by our heat."

Other wraiths had gathered at the base of the tree. The Flameskin Army had abandoned the attack on the burning Hivid Wood to face the advancing Tokken Army.

Sol climbed down to the forest floor and the wraiths gathered around her. Kelan rested his head against her shoulder, and she put an arm around him. Kelan wasn't the only one injured. Many of the wraiths had cuts and bruises, and all of them had drooping, tired eyes and were covered in soot.

How were a handful of youths supposed to stand against a saint?

"They say the goddess made her immortal," one of the wraiths said. "There's nothing we can do to stop her."

"Even if she can heal, arrows will slow her down," Sol said.

They gave her uncertain looks. "Slow her down, maybe, but not stop her," one muttered.

"Were any of ours killed?" Sol asked.

"Mie is dead," one boy said.

Marta let out a strangled cry and the boy put an arm around her. Sol let out a long sigh. Hopefully there would be time to mourn the dead at the end of this, if they didn't all perish in the fight.

"There's a couple missing, and some of us are hurt pretty

bad," said the boy who had carried Silas. Silas lay inert on the ground nearby among the bodies of Flameskin soldiers.

"Take Silas and whoever's been injured back to the haven," Sol said. "The rest of us will stay and fight. We won't let Saint Katrine take our home."

Kelan ran his thumb across Sol's cheek. "Our home," he murmured.

"Kelan, you should go back with Silas. You can barely stand," Sol said.

"Didn't you just see me fighting?"

"I know, but . . . ." He looked ragged around the edges, and he was obviously in a great deal of pain. He winced every time he moved.

"I'm not leaving you again," he said. "We stand or we fall together."

"Kelan." She sighed and kissed the corner of his mouth, careful of his healing lip.

He grabbed her hand and pulled her closer. "No. Kiss me, Sol."

She kissed him, and tasted the smoke and the fire and the desire and the hope on his lips.

"We have to find a way to survive. I don't want this to be the end."

Silas was carried off to the haven along with the other wounded, and Sol led a retreat deeper into the woods away from the fire. It looked like the whole forest would burn. The redwoods resisted the flames, but they weren't immune to them, and the elms and the oaks were already crackling with fire. Flames devoured the bed of pine needles on the forest floor, and burning limbs rained hot coals on their heads.

The wraiths took up a position near the haven and climbed the trees. From there, Sol got a view of the Tokken Army pushing through the burning camp. Flameskins fell by Tokken swords, and Saint Katrine led their charge. She absorbed the flames at her feet and created a path through the fire for her army.

Katrine stopped her soldiers at the edge of the forest and sent them fanning out in every direction to destroy the camp. Then she turned toward the Wood and stretched one hand toward the crackling flames that curled up the trees. The flames wavered, then leaned toward her. The fire flowed from the trees into the air and sank into her open palm.

On each of her arms were several dozen circular ember-stones. As the fire entered into her body, she touched each of the stones running up her arm. They glowed brighter as she filled them with fire.

She reduced the fire in the Hivid Wood to a smolder, and all that remained were the black, dead coals, the ash beneath Katrine's feet, and the smoke that lingered in the air.

Then she gathered a small retinue of soldiers around her and started her advance through the Wood.

"She's coming," Sol hissed at the wraiths below her.

Kelan hid behind a tree with his sword in hand, alongside a few other wraiths. More wraiths were in the trees and they each drew their bows.

In the bright light of the emberstones on Katrine's body, Sol could make out the faces of the soldiers around her: Queen Vara, with a braid woven through a gold circlet on her head, and the two female guards who had come with her before to the haven.

Saint Katrine leaned against the queen, apparently for support. Queen Vara led the saint into the forest and took her on a direct path toward the haven.

Sol's shoulders slumped.

All of Vara's promises had been lies.

In the end, Queen Vara was just like all the others. She had sold them out to Katrine.

Sol drew her bow and aimed for Katrine's heart, but the trees here were too densely grown to get a clear shot

Saint Katrine reappeared from behind a tree and Sol released her arrow.

One of the soldiers shouted and threw up her shield. The arrow embedded itself in the leather.

Vara drew her sword. "Cease fire!"

"You betrayed us!" Sol shouted at her from the trees. "We trusted you."

Katrine pushed herself away from Vara and her lips curled. "Flameskin," she spat.

She held out a hand, and Sol jerked forward. The energy in her emberstone was yanked through her and shot out of her hand. Fire burned the cuffs of her stolen Flameskin coat as Katrine jerked Sol's flames from her body and into her fingers.

Sol had no control over her body as fire was forced from her, squeezed out of her like water rung from a rag. Sol's bow fell from her hands and she swung out her arms wildly, searching for something to hold on to, but the flames yanked her forward into the air. She tumbled off the branch and out of the tree.

"Sol!" Kelan shouted.

He leapt out from behind the tree and broke her fall with his body. They both hit the ground hard, and he gasped as he smashed his shoulder into the ground. Sol bounced off him and hit the ground, and still the fire flowed out of her hands and into Saint Katrine.

Kelan gasped as Katrine wrenched flames from his body, as well. The wraiths fired on the Tokkens, but Katrine incinerated the arrow shafts with fire. One stray arrow grazed Queen Vara's arm.

Katrine put out both hands, drawing flames from all the wraiths in the trees. She immobilized them and sucked them dry. Kelan rolled over to Sol and ripped off the emberstone she had tied to her arm with a leather band. He clutched it in his hand and fire ceased flowing from their skin. They were once again flameless.

"Enough," Queen Vara shouted, grabbing Saint Katrine's arm. Fire stopped draining from the wraiths' hands, and Katrine sagged against the queen. The ground was littered with wraiths, several of whom had also fallen from the trees.

"That girl is wearing a Flameskin soldier's uniform," Katrine said. She trod unsteadily toward Sol, who crawled backward and away from her. Kelan scrambled to his feet in front of Sol and lifted his sword.

"Leave us in peace," he said. "There are only children who live here, and we have no desire to attack Tokkedal."

Katrine frowned at him. "Put down your sword, boy."

"The ship is already here, waiting to take you away. Katrine's going to accompany you to the shore," Queen Vara said.

"The ship is here?" Marta asked.

"The Flameskin Army marched on the Hivid Wood, and I had to act or lose the haven entirely." Queen Vara stripped off her coat. Blood ran down her arm from the cut on her bicep. She rested a hand on one of the emberstones on Katrine's arm and then traced the cut with a burning finger.

The queen was a mage.

"You aren't here to kill us?" Marta asked the saint.

"My desire is only to end the war, not kill Flameskins," Katrine said. "All Flameskins left after the war is over will be brought to the empire's new capitol, to be protected there."

Queen Vara gave a bitter laugh as she slid her coat back on. "Protected? Is that what you call it? Imprisonment is what it is."

Katrine's face darkened. "I have sworn to do what I can to protect Nordby. I know as well as any how dangerous Flameskins are."

"Is that where we're going then? The capital?" Sol asked. She held tight to Kelan's hand.

"No," Katrine said. "Vara has bought your freedom with her crown."

Vara sighed. "I refuse to abdicate until the haven has boarded that ship."

"And I'm here to ensure no Flameskins are left in Tokkedal."

CHAPTER 60
KELAN

They walked through the night to reach the distant coastline. Kelan was too bloodied and burned to manage carrying any of the children, but Azalea clung to his hand and walked the whole way herself. Everyone who was well enough and old enough to handle the weight was carrying some toddler in their arms or on their back. Sol made Lotti and Dotti take turns riding on her back. Even Saint Katrine carried a child in her arms as they trekked across the forest.

It was a long walk, and Kelan's body ached, but he had his pyra to strengthen him and dull the pain, and he was buoyed by his hope.

"I just don't understand it," Sol said.

"Ingrid was Vara's half-sister and they grew up together. Vara gave up her crown to save us," Kelan said.

"No, your pyra. How are you not possessed?" she asked.

"I don't know. I don't understand it, either." Was it just the passage of time? He hadn't taken off his emberstone since Nilsa attacked them at the Cassian border.

But if it was time that had reduced his pyra's power, why couldn't Ingrid and Rask remove their emberstones without becoming possessed? No, it had to be something else.

They crested the last hill and the ocean came into view

before them. Beside him, Sol gasped. The dawn had painted the sky with fire, and the sea sparkled blue and gold. It was a breath-taking view.

Just beyond the beach, a ship waited for them in the swells.

The wraiths whooped and shouted and raced down the hill toward the beach. Even Azalea joined in.

Kelan took Sol's hand.

"The ocean is so beautiful," she murmured. "I've never seen anything like it."

They hurried down the hill with their fingers intertwined. Sol scooped up a handful of sand and laughed as it trickled through her fingers. The air was briny from the seaweed strewn across the beach, and Kelan tasted salty air for the first time in years.

Azalea returned to them with wet shoes and a handful of mussel shells that shone an iridescent purple. "Look!"

The first rowboat full of Flameskins had already set out for the ship, and Marta cheered from the stern.

Saint Katrine stood close to Queen Vara and watched the proceedings with an impassive face. "This banishment to the island is permanent. Should any of you return, you will be hunted down and taken to the capital."

"They know," Queen Vara said. "They won't return to Tokkedal."

The ship's captain had come ashore and handed Saint Katrine a heavy basket. Katrine peeked inside it before sighing and handing it to Queen Vara. Then she rubbed her red eyes and retreated to the other side of the beach with her arms crossed tight over her chest.

Queen Vara set the basket at her feet and waved Sol and Kelan over.

They approached cautiously and bowed. "We are indebted to you," Kelan said.

"I can't right all the wrongs of my father, but I've done what I can." She glanced at the basket. "If you remember, I said I would ask a favor from you both on this beach."

"What is it?" Sol asked. She held tight to Kelan's hand.

The queen nodded toward the basket at her feet. "This is my favor."

Sol knelt and lifted the blanket covering the basket. "What—?"

There was a baby with cherubic cheeks and a fluff of dark hair on its head. It slept soundly, lulled by the sound of the breaking waves.

"I don't understand," Kelan said. What did Vara want them to do with it?

"She'll go with you to the colony," Vara said.

"Is she a Flameskin, too?" Sol asked.

Queen Vara glanced away. "We won't know until she's older, but I believe she'll be a Flameskin, or perhaps something more."

"Something more?" Kelan asked. He followed Vara's gaze. She was staring at Saint Katrine.

Kelan gaped. "It's Katrine's—"

"She's yours now. You'll raise her as your own child. That is my favor. And it is my wish that she never know you two weren't her parents."

Kelan stared at the baby. At least the other children in the haven could walk and communicate. This thing was helpless. When they got to the island there would be houses to build and fields to plant. How were they supposed to take care of a baby as well? There were already too many children on this ship.

"We'll do it," Sol said.

"Sol," Kelan whispered. "Are you sure?"

"Ingrid will help us. And we can't very well refuse."

"But this is different. This is pretending she's ours. This isn't like taking care of Azalea, like we've been doing."

"Who else then? Why shouldn't this baby have parents?"

Kelan sighed. Sol had a habit of jumping through windows without thinking through the long-term consequences.

Sol turned back to the queen. "Does she have a name?"

"No. You can name her."

"We'd be honored to have her," Sol said and smiled. Kelan

rubbed his forehead with his palm. Honored? That's what she called getting a baby dumped on them?

"Thank you," the queen said, looking relieved. "Her mother —" the queen's gaze flicked to Katrine again. "I'll tell her mother she is in good hands. I wish you luck in your new life on the island, and a safe voyage."

The queen bowed low and turned to walk away.

"Wait," Sol said. "My family, in Hillerod. They don't know that I won't come back."

"I will ensure they receive word you are safe and well."

Sol's face was pinched. "Thank you."

The queen strode toward Katrine. She unwound the black braid that crowned her head, letting her hair fall loose over her back. Then she removed the gold circlet from her head and handed it to the saint.

Azalea approached Sol cautiously and peered into the basket.

"You have a new sister, Azalea," Sol said.

Kelan sighed. They hadn't just adopted one daughter, now they'd adopted two.

Sol looked up and laughed when she saw his face. "What?"

He shook his head and sprawled on the sand beside her. "I'm just happy to finally have somewhere we'll be safe."

"No more running," she whispered and took his hand.

A sudden gust of wind whipped across the beach and blew through the trees. Sol sat up and her eyes went wide as the wind whistled in their ears.

He sat up and could hear the name the wind whispered: *Sol. Sol. Sol.*

"It's the mountains." She shook her head and wrapped her arms tight around Kelan. "No. I'm not going back. I don't know why the mountains call to me, but I won't leave you."

Kelan stared at the trees as the wind yanked at the boughs. They stopped sighing her name, and now were singing a different lament. "The winds howl with the cries of men. The mountain has stolen their hearts," he murmured.

She put a hand on his chest. "I don't need to go back to the

Ulves. I thought my heart would stay there in the mountains, but it's here, Kelan. It's wherever you are."

He kissed the tip of her nose. "Maybe you still have your heart, but mine was plucked out long ago."

She laughed as she slid her hand beneath the collar of his shirt and pulled gently on his pyra. His worry and his hope and his love bled into her. As she drew his fire into her, his pyra dampened until his blood ran clean of its taint.

Kelan blinked. He looked down at her hand pressed against his skin and then grinned. "Sol. I think I know why I'm not possessed anymore."

"You do?"

"Are you going to board?" Ingrid called. She was up to her waist in water, holding the rowboat in place and waving for them to get on.

Kelan picked up the baby's basket, and Sol took Azalea's hand.

He kissed Sol softly on the cheek as they turned their backs on the trees and faced the sea.

EPILOGUE

SOL

The island was a barren landscape of dry, dead grass and crooked, wind-blown pines. There was more rock and sand than soil. It was a dry and desolate place that reeked with the decay of kelp stranded on the beach.

The ship was anchored offshore, and Sol and Kelan had come ashore with Ingrid and Silas to inspect their new home.

Sol wandered the island alongside Kelan, looking under rocks and walking up and down the beach. The island wasn't large, and its only feature was the small hill in the center. Sol took Kelan's hand, and they raced to the top of the hill. From there, amid the dry grass, the whole island came into view, but there wasn't much to see. Only desiccated pines and empty beaches.

They were supposed to farm here and create a new life here? Sol tried and failed to imagine how they could turn this place into something livable.

"Well," Kelan said, "at least we have the boat to live on for a while. Just think how fun it will be to be crammed in with the children all winter."

She knew he was trying to get a smile out of her, but Sol could do nothing more than sigh. She had left behind her beautiful mountains for this wasteland?

But at least Kelan was beside her. She squeezed his hand and leaned against him.

There was a warmth in her pocket that swelled and grew and made her body tingle. She reached into her pocket and pulled out the glowing acorn the Ulves had given to her. It whispered and called to her. It wanted to be planted.

Sol bent down and scooped aside a handful of packed gravel to plant the seed at the top of the hill.

"What do you think it will grow?" Kelan asked.

"Something to help me remember where I came from."

The ground below them buckled, and a green sapling shot out of the earth. Kelan yanked Sol backward, and they scrambled away as a tree grew and swelled and spread its massive canopy over their heads. An enormous trunk erupted through the hard soil, pushing packed earth out in clods and chunks as the tree expanded.

The ground shook beneath their feet. Sol clung to Kelan as mountains pierced the sea like spears, rising up to greet the sky and ring their tiny island. Green blankets of grass spilled down the sides of the mountains and across the desolate earth. Wildflowers sprung up around their feet. A waterfall poured from one of the peaks and a river tumbled down the mountainside and poured into the sea.

The ship, which had once been offshore, was now ringed by mountains and swayed in a lagoon at the center of the new island. Cliffs had risen up behind the ship, and a narrow channel cut through the mountains toward the ocean.

As abruptly as it had shifted, the earth fell still once more. Sol stood and spun in a slow circle, gazing at the peaks of the mountains around her. They were different from the ones at home, and yet familiar.

She placed her hand on the trunk of the great oak that had sprung out of the hillside. Energy and life buzzed beneath the tree's bark.

She looked up at Kelan and smiled. "Now, I'm home."

ACKNOWLEDGMENTS

I'd like to first thank my husband for being my cheerleader, my first reader, and for encouraging me to pursue my dreams. I couldn't do this without you! I also wouldn't stay sane for very long either.

And of course I have to thank my wonderful editor, Theodora Bryant who made this novel twice as good (literally) and answered my thousands of questions.

Thank you to Amanda for the adorable headings and Pauliina for the amazing illustrations. Your art captured the beauty of the world I was trying to create.

And thank you to my amazing Kickstarter backers who made this project a reality. And a special thanks to David and JoLynn Anderson, Tracie Brown, Tucker and Ashley Longley, Pam McMahon, Marlin, Stephen Ballentine, Tony Salva, Bruce "Hoss" Collins, S Busby, Travis Kelly Wilson, Omar Mazin, Chand Svare Ghei, and Doc Bowman. You are all wonderful!

And thank you to the readers for sticking with me until the end. I wouldn't be here without you!

ABOUT THE AUTHOR

Camille Longley is the author of the Flameskin Chronicles and the Talons and Teeth series. She grew up in Arizona, graduated from Brigham Young University, and now lives in the Bay Area with her husband and daughter. She can be found at camillelongley.com.

instagram.com/camillelongley

CPSIA information can be obtained
at www.ICGtesting.com
Printed in the USA
FSHW020343200820
73126FS